Matthew and his friend Cory are thrilled to attend one of the most prestigious universities in the UK. On their pre-entry visit, they met Morgan Bentley and his stuck-up friends. Matthew takes an instant dislike to the arrogant, conceited, self-obsessed, beautiful, intelligent, and charismatic boy. Throughout the next year, Matthew harbours his dislike, never missing the opportunity to complain to his best friend, Cory, what a bastard Morgan is.

Then, an unexpected turn of events catapults Matthew, Morgan, and Cory into a nightmare, and all the things Cory had said about Matthew's true feelings about Morgan come crashing down on his head, and he realises that what he thought was hatred and anger was, in fact, growing attraction and begrudging admiration. But when the deadly nature of the elusive Project X is revealed, it seems their budding romance is doomed before it begins, as one of them is unlikely to survive.

Project X
Copyright © 2019 Cheryl Headford
ISBN: 978-1-4874-2167-0
Cover art by Angela Waters

Published by eXtasy Books Inc or
Devine Destinies, an imprint of eXtasy Books Inc

Look for us online at:
www.eXtasybooks.com or www.devinedestinies.com

PROJECT X

BY

CHERYL HEADFORD

DEDICATION

To Andrew Gordon, the first person to highlight this book for publication. Without him, it would be languishing on Gay Authors with many more of my works which will never see the light of day. To Lily Velden, who gave me my first chance. To everyone at eXtasy who worked so hard to make this book the best it could be.

CHAPTER ONE

Morgan Bentley was a bastard. An utter, complete, A-one, cut-glass bastard. He was arrogant, selfish, cold, stand-offish, cruel, and completely heartless. His history was peppered with broken hearts and broken people attesting to the fact. There was no doubt about it — he was a bastard.

Morgan didn't have any friends. What he had was an entourage — people who cared less for the person he was than for the prestige his company brought. At the moment, he had a girlfriend, the undoubted Alpha Female of the university, a bitch called Charlotte Lethbridge, whose father owned half of Mayfair. The relationship wouldn't last, though. They never did. And next week it could just as easily be a boyfriend.

No one ever said no to Morgan. No one outside his circle of *friends* ever said anything at all unless he invited them to, which he rarely ever did.

Cory often said Morgan was sad — he had to be. He had to be lonely and sad because he had no real friends, no lasting relationships, no one to share with. Not like us. Sometimes I had to stop myself laughing when he said that. *Morgan Bentley sad?* Not bloody likely. He had everything. I mean *everything*.

His father was a research chemist, heading a huge multi-national corporation. They manufactured drugs and engaged in research projects, sometimes for the government. I think that's why Cory was so fascinated with Morgan. He was getting a degree in biochemistry and wanted to be a researcher himself. Cory was awesome . . . but he had flaws, and his fascination with Morgan was one of them. Personally, I wouldn't

1

care if I never saw his smug face ever again. Hell, I'd have been so much happier if I hadn't.

Because of his father's job—he had to work long hours and take frequent business trips—Morgan was often home alone, and what a home it was. Fortunately, he lived quite close to the university—not that he would have stayed in the student accommodations, even if he'd lived a hundred miles away—in a house almost as big as the university itself. The estate comprised a good few acres of grounds, enclosed by a wall topped with electrified barbed wire. I've never been lucky enough to be invited inside. *Hah!*

I say it was fortunate he lived at home, because he rarely spent any time at the university when he wasn't actually in class or working in the library, so I didn't have to put up with him after hours, so to speak.

Unfortunately, Morgan was taking the same degree I was. He was even in my tutorial group. I hated him even more because he was brilliant in every way. He had a natural aptitude for the subject, speaking with passion about justice and honour, holding a debate with fluency, and having an uncanny memory for detail. In addition, when he wanted to, he could turn on the charm and had personality in bucketfuls. He outshone us all, although I was almost able to hold my own . . . sometimes.

It was truly unfair how Morgan had it all and didn't seem to care about any of it. Did I mention he was gorgeous? Of course he was. How could he possibly not be? I swear the entourage would still have licked his arse if he was ugly, but perhaps we wouldn't have had to put up with the adoring looks and mooning fans. I saw them everywhere. They would light up as soon as he came into the room. Their eyes would go round, and they would babble incoherently with soppy smiles on their faces. I hated them . . . and I hated him.

I was thinking all of that as I sat in a tutorial and listened to him talking about the assignment we'd been given. The topic was all about arguing a case involving easements and rights of way. My interest didn't lie with property law, and although I'd researched and prepared, I hadn't been able to drum up much passion about it. Morgan, however, did everything with passion — except live.

Morgan had this dark-and-dangerous image thing going on. He always dressed in black, wore silver jewellery, and sometimes black fingerless gloves. He painted his nails black, too, and of course, his hair was long and black with a blue streak. I don't think he dyed it. Someone had once called him a Goth, but that was so the wrong word for him. There was no right word for him. He only wore designer . . . anything. He listened to classical music, and I'd heard, he played the piano like a pro. He drove an *Audi* convertible, or sometimes a monster silver bike. He defied description. He was unique.

That day, as usual, he was sitting in front of the window. I swear he did it for effect. The late autumn sun made his heavy hair shine with the sheen of silk. It was easy to get lost in the shine and the way the thick, vivid blue streak at the front stood out, jewel-bright in the sunshine.

Not that I cared. I barely noticed. I was too busy being infuriated by how effortlessly he tossed about arguments based on fine and obscure points of law. I'd never even heard of them, let alone considered them when preparing my arguments for today. *How the hell was I supposed to counter that?*

My mind worked furiously, casting about for a way I could get around the arguments he was raising. I barely understood what he was saying, although the lecturer clearly did and was, just as clearly, impressed. She was probably half in love with him, too. It was sickening the way everyone got sucked into the phenomenon that was Morgan Bentley.

And didn't he know it? He lounged in his seat, soaking up the admiration, the half-circle of adoring faces turned up to him. His arm was stretched across the back of the chair next to him. If it hadn't been too high, I swear he'd have had his feet up on the table. He was a study in crafted, conscious boredom.

Our gazes met, and I was momentarily stunned by the power of those startling green orbs—slanted like a cat, sparkling but curiously empty. I snarled at him, and Morgan smiled.

When it was my turn to present my response, I stumbled and stammered for a while before I found my stride. Then I began to do pretty well. But for every argument I raised, he had a response. For every point I made, he had three to the contrary. Halfway through the presentation, we started to spar. I deliberately goaded him, and he responded. Although we were icily polite and kept to the topic of discussion, we fought like fencers, the words our épées.

By the time it was over, I was exhausted, and I had no idea who'd *won*. From the dazed expressions of those around us, including the lecturer, I guessed neither did anyone else. It was almost embarrassing.

I gathered my books and began to store them in my backpack. A shadow fell across me, and I looked up. Of course it was Morgan. I'd known it would be, even before I raised my eyes.

"Good job."

I glared at him. What? Did he expect me to thank him for his praise, this meagre scrap from the table of his greatness?

"Yeah. You, too."

Morgan smiled. It wasn't his usual smirk. Neither was it the ironic twist of the lips he sometimes gave. This was a real smile, small and brief, but natural. I'd never seen a smile like that on his face before, and I found myself returning it before I realised what I was doing and stopped. For an instant, the briefest of instants, an expression flashed through Morgan's eyes I would have sworn was . . . disappointment. Then he turned and walked away.

When I was telling Cory about it afterwards, he laughed at me, but then he wouldn't tell me why, which made me even more irritated.

"And you can wipe that I-know-something-you-don't-know expression off your face. You're starting to look like Morgan."

"I should be so lucky."

"Yeah, right." I glanced at my friend, surprised by the wistfulness in his voice. He was smiling, but there was something in his eyes. "You don't, do you? I mean, you're not jealous of him?"

"No-oo, not exactly." He wouldn't meet my eyes, and I knew I wasn't going to like what he was thinking.

"Oh, for gods' sake, Cory, you're twice the man he'll ever be. There's absolutely nothing about Morgan Bentley you should be envious of."

"Huh! Nothing? Not even his looks, his wealth, his unnatural sexiness, the women who hang on his every word, the house he lives in, the —"

"All right, all right." I held up my hands, laughing. "So what? He's got all that, but he's a git. He's an utter bastard."

Cory laughed, making his blue eyes sparkle behind the thick glasses he wore. He ran his hand through his short, sandy hair and grinned at me. "Granted. I just happen to think he's a gorgeous, rich bastard, and I wouldn't mind a tad of his gorgeousness and wealth myself."

I frowned, peering intently at my best friend, and his smile slipped a little. True, he wasn't much to look at — a bit skinny, a bit geeky, a bit . . . well, ordinary, except for those amazing eyes, but he was Cory. I mean, I never really thought about what Cory looked like. We were way too close for that. I didn't see what was there on the outside, only what was on the inside. I'd never thought Cory might have seen things differently.

Thinking about it, Cory had never seemed interested in his appearance at all. He dressed neutrally, mostly in jeans and t-shirts, which were usually slightly grubby and bore geeky type logos and slogans I sometimes didn't come close to understanding. Today his shirt read *I am a computer geek* on the front and *No, I will not fix your computer* on the back.

His hair was usually kept short—and even then, it was always messy—and his face was often unshaven, as if he just forgot. He almost always wore a puzzled expression, and if it weren't for the startling blueness of his eyes, his face would have been completely unremarkable. He was the kind of person who never stood out in a crowd.

His brain, though—now that was really something remarkable. He was a computer geek of the highest order and could write as fluently in computer code as English. Sometimes, I thought, even more so. Surprisingly, he was also a biochemistry genius, and I often quipped that one day he'd combine his specialties and make a cyborg. Come to think of it—his interests really weren't that diverse. He liked to break things down to their smallest component, then build them back up again, improved.

Cory and I had been friends since we were five, and we complemented each other's strengths and weaknesses. I dragged him out from behind the screen to go fishing or hiking. I taught him to skateboard—never well—and made him go to parties. I even introduced him to his first girlfriend—first and last. On the other hand, he'd taught me all I know about computers, opened up a whole new world in nature I never knew existed, and fascinated me with his world view . . . which was microscopic.

It never occurred to me that Cory cared about anything

much outside his own world, and it certainly never occurred to me he might have been harbouring insecurities about his appearance. Cory was certain about everything.

"You're not serious, are you? I mean you're not really jealous of him? Of Morgan?"

Cory smiled, but it was somehow strange. "No, not jealous, I wouldn't want to be him, for all the wealth and privilege he has. It's just . . . just that sometimes . . ."

"What's on your mind?"

He shook his head. "Nothing. Nothing much. Don't worry about it. Are you coming round tonight to try out that new game I've finally downloaded?"

"Oh, no. You don't get out of it that easily. There's something on your mind, and I'm not moving from here until you tell me what it is."

"It's nothing, Matthew, honestly. It's just . . ."

"Just what?"

"It's just . . . it's all right for you. You're cute, you're popular, you fit in. Sometimes . . ."

I couldn't believe what was coming out of his mouth, or the sadness in his eyes. "But you're popular. You have friends . . . and you're cute, too . . . in your own way."

"You are gravely deluded, my friend. Blinded by your own awesomeness. I'm popular, in a way, because I'm your friend. I have friends . . . because they're your friends. I'm accepted . . . because of you. If it wasn't for you, no one would give me the time of day. They wouldn't even notice me."

"That's ridiculous."

"Is it? You can be so blind, Matthew."

"But . . . but . . ."

Cory sighed. "Never mind. I still love you. Now, can we please go get something to eat before I completely waste away?"

He walked off, and I was left staring after him in shock.

Was he right? Was I blind? Was I, in my own way, as blink-ered as the likes of Morgan Bentley? I deliberately hung back, and although Cory glanced over his shoulder now and again, he didn't wait, and I basically stalked him, noticing the way people reacted to him.

Mostly people ignored him, simply didn't register his pass-ing. Now and again, Cory smiled and said hello to someone, who usually appeared slightly uncomfortable when they gave him a brief nod of acknowledgement, then went straight back to what they were doing. Those same people, who hadn't noticed Cory, all noticed me — all called welcome. And those same people who had barely acknowledged Cory not only acknowledged me but tried to draw me into their activi-ties.

I reached the refectory in a daze. Gods, Cory was right. I *had* been blind. I stood in the door and watched Cory negoti-ate the tables. There was a strict hierarchy, and he went straight past the ones occupied by the likes of Morgan Bent-ley, Charlotte Lethbridge, and their cronies and made for an empty bench on one of the larger tables by the window. There was already a half dozen people sitting at the table, and not one of them did more than glance in his direction when he sat down.

I watched him turn away from them, almost uncon-sciously, and stare morosely out of the window. Frowning, I began to weave through the crowd. My focus was entirely on Cory. And so, of course, I wasn't looking where I was going, and of course, I bumped into someone, and of course, it had to be the last person in the whole fucking room I wanted to bump into.

I gazed in horror at the tray of food that had crashed to the floor, then up at Morgan. He grinned at me. It seemed as if everyone in the entire room was staring at us, and I was even more embarrassed. My face was slowly turning beetroot red, as red as the streaks that set fire to my otherwise dull brown hair.

"Oops," Morgan said and smirked. Morgan was always smirking, but this time was different because this time he was smirking at me. I glared at him.

"Are you going to get that?"

"What?" I snapped.

"You knocked my tray right out of my hand, Matthew, isn't it? Well . . . Matthew, do you really expect me to pick it up myself?"

I was blindingly angry. Not so much that he expected me to pick up his food—after all, that was only fair, considering I'd knocked it down in the first place—but more with the tone of his voice. I was furious with the infuriatingly smarmy tone, and even more that he'd pretended to be unsure of my name. He fucking well knew my name. We were in the same goddamn tutorial twice a week. I was even more furious with myself for being embarrassed. I don't do embarrassed well.

Childishly, I kicked his tray, muttered, "Clean up your own fucking mess, Morgan." Then I stalked off to the sound of laughter. Surprisingly, though, not his laughter. By the time I sat down, someone else was clearing the mess.

I deliberately chose to sit opposite Cory, facing back into the room. I was surprised Morgan was still standing where I'd left him, staring after me. The instant our gazes met, he turned away, but there was something in that look, in the moment. Was it anger? Confusion? Frustration? Or something else? Whatever it was made me feel good. I'd got to him. *Great!*

"What are you grinning about?"

"I just knocked Morgan Bentley's food tray on the floor."

"That wasn't very nice of you."

"I didn't do it on purpose, you idiot. I was distracted. Too busy wondering why my best friend's acting like he has the weight of the world on his shoulders to pay attention to where

I was going."

Cory grinned. "So what did the great man say when you deposited his dinner on the floor?"

I growled, angry again. "He told me to pick it up and pretended not to remember my name."

Cory frowned. "Yeah, don't you just hate that?" he asked wistfully. I barely noticed as I was in mid-rant.

"I mean, can you believe it? He's in my tutorial group. We have lessons together twice a week. He *knows* my fucking name. Can you believe anyone would . . . what's the matter?"

Cory was staring at me, his eyes narrowed. He shook his head. "Sometimes you can be a complete asshole, Matthew."

"What? What do you mean?"

"You know what? You complain about Morgan all the time. You're always ranting on about what a bastard he is, how he takes everything for granted, how he doesn't appreciate what he has, doesn't even notice it. Well, you and he have a lot in common, and you can't even see it."

"What? What are you on about? I have nothing in common with Morgan Bentley. Nothing."

"Are you sure about that?" he asked quietly. "Are you really sure?"

"Cory, you're acting really weird today. What's wrong? What's going on?"

He regarded me for a moment, then shook his head. "Why even bother? Come on, let's get some food."

He half rose, and I grabbed his arm and pulled him back. "Wait a minute." At first, he resisted, trying to pull away. "Please, Cory."

Cory glanced around, noticing the enquiring glances we were attracting from the others at our table, and from wider afield. His shoulders sagged.

"All right, but not here. Let's get something we can take out, and we can talk by the tree."

The tree was our special place. Just outside the refectory was a path leading into the woods backing the university buildings. It was wide and well worn, cutting straight through the trees to one of the accommodation blocks. About halfway along was another, less well-trodden path slanting off into the woods. It headed toward the river and eventually found its way there. Before it reached the water, it opened out into a small clearing where an ancient oak tree had fallen a long time ago.

The fallen trunk was covered with lichen and grass and appeared more like a grassy bank than a tree. However, if you knew where to look, you could find a cave-like entrance covered with hanging branches, and if you thrust them aside, you could crawl inside. It was warm and dry and smelled of wood and mushrooms. It was secluded, safe, and private. It was the place we came to think, or to brood, or just to be alone.

There was barely enough room for the two of us, and we were shoulder to shoulder, trying to unwrap our sandwiches on bent knees.

"So? What's going on?"

Cory put down his sandwich and stared at the wall for a while. Then he gave a huge sigh and turned his face toward me. "You don't get it, do you? You don't get it at all. It's all so easy for you."

"What is? What are you talking about?"

"You're oblivious, Matthew. You always have been. You're . . . comfortable with yourself and with everyone else. You like people, and they like you. They're drawn to you because you're easy to be with. You make people laugh. You always know what to say. You're cute, a great guy. Haven't you noticed how you get noticed? People look up when you walk in a room. All right, they don't worship you like they do Morgan, but they notice you."

"I don't know what you mean."

Cory looked sad. "I know you don't. You don't notice. Why would you? For you, it's natural, normal. What's more natural than people acknowledging you when you walk in? Except it isn't like that for everyone or for most people. In a place like this, most people are pretty much anonymous. Most people don't *want* to be noticed."

"Okay, I buy that. I appreciate a lot of people like to stay under the radar, and I've never been that kind of person. I get that people notice me and . . . yeah, I like it. I like that people say hi to me. I like that they're pleased when I sit with them, that they include me in things—but I didn't realise it was a big deal. I thought that's why they did it, because I like it because I don't try to make myself invisible. I get caught by the radar because I don't try to sail under it, not because I'm anything special."

"But see . . . that's where you're wrong." He spoke very quietly, and I stared at him hard. He looked so damn sad.

"I don't understand."

"No. No, you don't."

"Does this have something to do with Morgan?"

He looked genuinely surprised. "Morgan? Why would it have something to do with him?"

"I don't know. It's just that we were talking about him when things got freaky."

"No, it has nothing to do with him, at least . . ." He sighed deeply. "At least not directly."

I sighed just as deeply. Trying to get Cory to talk about what was bothering him was like trying to eat soup with a fork. I munched on my sandwich for a while, noticing Cory made no attempt to touch his.

"So? What's really wrong? You can't tell me you're upset because I'm popular. What's really bugging you?"

Cory shrugged. "I don't know. Maybe . . . maybe it's just

that . . . *I'm not.*" He practically whispered the last words and hung his head. I stared at him.

"Since when do you care?"

"I've always cared, Matthew. I've always . . . cared."

There was something behind his words that I couldn't figure out, but when I pressed him on it, he wouldn't open up any further. I hated being shut out and felt I was somehow letting him down by not understanding what he was going through. I surmised he was feeling lonely, that he was upset because people were shutting him out and not being as friendly as they could have been.

Actually, I thought it was mainly his own fault. He didn't make any effort to get to know people. If he was deep in thought about something, which happened often, he tended to shut out the rest of the world and would ignore even me, even when I was directly talking to him. Fortunately, I'm sensitive enough never to say it.

We danced around the issue for a while, until Cory changed the subject and started to talk about a new project he was getting involved with for his dissertation. He was doing something that involved a comparison between the way computers work and how living organisms work, all on a molecular scale. He wasn't talking very long before he completely lost me.

I was jolted back to attention when he mentioned ITM— Information Technology and Medicine. It was a company involved with research relating to the use of computer technology in medicine. It was a huge multinational company handling research contracts from all over the world. It was also the company Morgan's father practically ran.

"What did you say about ITM?"

Cory sighed. "I knew you weren't listening. And I knew that would get your attention." He sounded utterly despondent and made me feel disproportionately guilty.

"Sorry, Cory. Go on. I promise I'll listen this time."

"I'm sure you will," he said sarcastically, which shocked me because Cory was usually too straightforward for sarcasm. I smiled in what I hoped was an encouraging way and motioned for him to continue. "ITM offers internships. A kind of part-time scholarship, cum research post, for students in the final year of either a technology or biomedical degree course. I put in a tender with my dissertation project synopsis, and they accepted me."

"Oh, wow, Cory!" I said excitedly, then tentatively hazarded a question, hoping he'd not already answered it in the part of the conversation I hadn't been listening to. "What exactly does that mean?"

"It means that one day a week, and part of each weekend, I'll be working with the researchers at ITM on a specific project designed around my dissertation. I'll get to use their equipment and their expertise, and I'll be involved in real research projects. And I can use the data in my thesis. No ITM intern has ever got less than a first class honours."

"But that's awesome. When did you find out? Why didn't you tell me you were applying?"

"Yesterday. Because I never thought in a million years, I'd get it."

"Are you kidding? You're a genius. What research team in their right minds wouldn't want you onboard?"

"This is different, Matthew. This isn't University. This is the real world. I'm playing with the big boys, and it's scaring the hell out of me."

"Scared? Why on earth would you be scared?"

He gave me a dark look, then hung his head. "You don't understand. I've been crazy about *this science stuff,* as you put it, forever. I'm passionate about it, as passionate as you are about law and . . ." He paused and bit his lip, then shook his head. "And I want to make it my life. I've spent every day studying, not because I have to but because I want to. I've read everything I could get my hands on and spoken to everyone I could get to speak to me. I've lived it, breathed it . . . but these guys . . .

"The opportunity to use the equipment alone . . . they have stuff in there no one else in the world has. Some of the projects they're working on are so futuristic they'd make your hair curl. And I'm going to be a part of it. It's like . . . I don't know . . . it's like you getting to represent one of the Royal Family at the *Old Vic* or something."

I couldn't help but smile. "It's the *Old Bailey*, Cory. The *Old Vic* is a theatre."

"Whatever . . . you get the picture."

"Yeah . . . I get it. I get this is an awesome opportunity, and it's been given to you because you're the best there is. You said they only offer it to people who are gifted in either biomedicine or technology. I bet they've never had one who's a genius in both before."

I glanced at him sideways and was rewarded with a bright grin. "Thanks, Matthew."

"Cory, I have faith in you. You don't need to be jealous that people pay more attention to me now. University is an unreal world. It's a blink of an eye. When it comes down to what really matters — the real world, real life . . . you're the one that's going to make a difference. You're the one who's going to take the world by the balls and squeeze. You're going to be a fucking legend, man."

Cory leaned slightly toward me and rested his head on my shoulder. He sighed, and I wondered for a moment whether he was crying. I felt awkward and didn't know what to do. But when he spoke, his voice was completely level.

"I feel this is the start of something big for me, I really do. I don't know what it is. It's just . . ." He shrugged. "I don't know. Saying I can feel destiny breathing on my neck is very overly dramatic, but that's how it feels. As if something huge is going to be set in motion as soon as I walk through those doors."

"Too fucking right, it will. I told you . . . you're awesome, and you're going to knock them all dead. I wouldn't be surprised if you got a job offer before the end of the project."

He sat up, his eyes glowing. "Do you think so? Really?"

"I told you . . . I have faith in you, buddy."

He smiled, then turned introspective, and suddenly he seemed really sad.

"What's wrong? That's what you want, isn't it?"

"Of course . . . yes . . . kind of. It's just . . ." He glanced down at his hands, picking at the edges of a tear in his jeans. "I . . . it's just . . . I know when uni is over, we're bound to drift apart. We'll get jobs, separate lives . . . probably won't see much of each other, but I was putting it out of my mind. There's over a year before we have to think about it, so I wasn't. We've been friends forever. You've always been there for me, and I . . . I'm not good on my own. Usually, the project starts over the summer, before the final year begins. You go in for a couple of weeks for orientation and to get to know them and the projects so you and they can work out what's best to fit in with them and the course you're studying.

"But this time they want me to start at Christmas, to spend part of the week before and part of the week after with them, then get into the programme when we start back next term and work intensely with them over the summer. It means that after the next couple of weeks I won't be seeing much of you at all, and the summer we planned is . . ."

"Is still going to happen, Cory. You're a student. You aren't a full-time worker, so they can't expect you to spend every minute there. Okay, we won't have as much time as we thought, but we'll still have some . . . enough. And as for after . . . we're best friends. We'll always be best friends.

Wherever we end up, we'll never lose touch, never stop being friends. Every summer, we'll go on holiday for a couple of weeks . . . ditch our wives and families and spend time, just the two of us."

"Do you promise?"

"Of course I do. Did you think once I got a job and a family, I wouldn't want to know you anymore? You're my best friend. You've been part of my life forever. I can't just forget that, wipe you out of my life because I don't see you every day. I love you, man . . . and I always will."

Cory stared at me. For a moment, it seemed as if he was either going to say something or burst into tears. In the end, he grinned and hugged me, then started stuffing down his sandwich as if he was starving.

CHAPTER TWO

I don't know why, but after the day in the canteen, I kept running into Morgan . . . literally. It felt like everywhere I went he was there, and I kept bumping into him, opening or closing doors in his face, even spilling my drink down the front of his trousers. He, of course, always took it with grace, that damned supercilious smile, and a sarcastic comment or two.

It got so bad I was checking everywhere before I did anything, and the Morgan lovers on campus would glare at me every time they saw me. That, at least, made me smile. What? Did they think I was doing it deliberately, that I was waging some kind of campaign of terror against their hero? As if.

However, I do admit there were occasions I found the whole thing hilarious. And even when I was getting more and more irritated by his smarmy smile and sarcastic tongue, I allowed myself a secret smile. He wouldn't forget my name again in a hurry.

About a week after the incident in the refectory, I walked into our tutorial. As usual, I sat as far away from Morgan as possible. He was, as per his usual, sitting in front of the window soaking up both the sun and the adoration, emanating this time from two girls who were fluttering about him, praising his performance in the previous day's mooting competition. He was part of the university's law department moot team, and he'd literally slaughtered the competition, reducing the poor girl almost to tears.

Mooting was a big thing at our university and was taken

very seriously. In essence, a moot is a mock court hearing. There are two teams, sometimes of one person, sometimes of two, representing the prosecution and defence in the case. The moot judge takes the place of the trial judge. In large competitions, there's sometimes a jury, too. The case papers are sent to each team before the competition, and they prepare the case as if for a real trial.

Of course, Morgan excelled and was the star of our team. I'd been asked to join but declined — mainly, I have to say because of Morgan. Not only would I have had to spend more time in his presence, but I would also have worked myself into the ground trying to best him. I would never have succeeded, so why cause myself grief?

Morgan led the team to win after win and was set to steal the show at the national championships just before Christmas. It was the first time in years our university had a prospect of winning, and it was sickening how the lecturers toadied around Morgan because of it.

The whole thing set my teeth on edge. It was just so unfair. He had everything! Why did he have to have this, too? If it hadn't been for him, it would have been me. I knew I was good enough, at least I could have been if I'd let myself. Ah, fuck it . . . I didn't need the attention.

Morgan raised an eyebrow. I realised I'd been staring. I frowned as the familiar hot feeling began to rise from beneath the neck of my t-shirt. I beat it down frantically. That was the last thing I needed — Morgan Bentley seeing me blush — again. Gods, he might misunderstand why. He might not realise how much I hated him and actually think that . . . that . . . I liked him. I shuddered at the thought and turned away.

When the lecturer entered, she smiled at us in a way that made me think *uh oh*. If only I had known, I think I might have crawled under the table and stayed there, curled into a ball, for the next few months.

"In light of our recent successes in the National Moot," she gushed, with a flutter of her eyelashes toward Morgan, "I thought it might be fun for you all to get some practice in mooting. Therefore, your assignment between now and next week will be to prepare a case, and we'll hold our own moots the week before the Nationals." She continued as she was met with groans from various people, "Now, don't panic, we won't be doing this in public. It will be just between ourselves, here in class.

"I'll be dividing you into fours, and then into pairs, and each pair will work on one side of the case. As there are eighteen of you, there will be four groups, with two over. All tutorials over the next two weeks will be suspended, and you can use the time for preparation of your case. On the third week, we'll hear two cases during each tutorial period, so you'll each have fifteen minutes to present your cases, with five minutes for the leaders to sum up and five minutes for judgement at the end.

"The moots will be part of the end-of-year exams and will count as part of your degree credit. You'll be marked on preparation, content, and presentation, so this is no easy ride."

I groaned inwardly and zoned out as the lecturer read off the pairs and handed out the case notes. It really didn't register she hadn't called my name, or handed me any papers, until the end.

"Now, I'm sure you've noticed that four into eighteen doesn't go, and two of you have not been paired or given an assignment." I perked up at that, wondering what was coming next. I was sure I hadn't somehow been let off for good behaviour. "I wasn't quite honest when I said none of your moots would be held in public. In order to inspire you, and to give you some pointers for your own presentations, Professor Blackmore and I have decided to take part in the first moot ourselves. It will take place on the Monday of the week in which the rest of the moots will be heard and will be held in the main lecture theatre.

"Attendance by yourselves and by Professor Blackmore's tutorial group, who are engaging in the same task, will be compulsory, but otherwise attendance is strictly voluntary and open to everyone.

"Professor Blackmore and I will be participating as the prosecuting team, and Dr Martin, the Head of School, will be honouring us by sitting as the judge. As you know, Dr Martin practised as a barrister for many years and is well versed in the art of advocacy. He will be putting the participants through their paces with no mercy for student or staff."

While she spoke, my heart sank lower and lower as a sick certainty settled in my stomach. *Fuck.* I glanced at Morgan, who seemed perfectly relaxed and well within his comfort zone as he listened intently to the lecturer's words. He didn't even flick a glance in my direction.

"Professor Blackmore and I were consulted in the choice of the two students to take part in this somewhat unusual moot, and I'm sure it comes as no surprise they are both from this class. Morgan Bentley and Matthew Hopkins." *Ah shit.*

Everyone stared at me, and the blush broke through my control and overwhelmed my face. I glowered resolutely at the desk. I heard the murmur around me but deliberately phased out the words, so all I was aware of was an angry buzz.

I didn't raise my eyes, even when a sheaf of papers was thrust under my nose. I had no chance of reading it. I was in hell. Not only was I going to have to stand up in front of what — given Morgan was involved — was likely to be pretty much the whole school and present a case in front of the Head of School, I was also going to have to spend time with Morgan preparing the case. If that wasn't bad enough, which it was, it meant I'd get to spend even less time with Cory before he headed off on his internship.

When I looked up, Morgan was grinning at me. I'd never wanted to hit him so much.

"Right. Well, if you'd like to divide up into your pairs and carefully read through the cases? If there are any questions, please feel free to ask, but then you're free to begin preparing. Good luck to you all."

Good luck indeed. She sounded so cheery, so excited. I'll bet. It meant she got free time from cancelling of the tutorials *and* she got to show off in front of the Head. I mean, she'd been a solicitor for like a hundred years and was well used to appearing before a court. Professor Blackmore was just as bad. He hadn't been a practising lawyer as such, but he'd given lectures all over the world on the finer points of consti- tutional law and had been part of a committee which advised the European Court of Human Rights in Brussels. Even with Morgan on the team, they were going to cream us.

I groaned and let my head fall forward onto my arms. Great . . . just fucking great! Could life get any worse?

Ignoring the scraping of chairs and general movement of bodies, I struggled to get a grip on my morose thoughts, which wasn't helped when someone slid into the seat next to me and slapped me on the back. I groaned again as a mocking voice, smooth as chocolate laced with poison, purred, "Hey, superstar, try not to get too carried away with enthusiasm, eh?"

I lifted my head and glared into the mocking green eyes.

"Fuck off, Morgan."

"Well, I could, but if you think I'm going to carry you, you're sadly mistaken. We're supposed to be a team, remem- ber? So you can bloody well take your share of the work."

"Who said I wasn't going to?"

"Just making sure we get things straight from the start. I've glanced at the case, and it covers the same areas of law I have to research for the Nationals, so I won't have to split my time, but that doesn't mean you can piggyback off me."

"Fuck you." I was absolutely livid. How dare he? How dare he think I wouldn't carry my own weight? Just because he was some fucking mooting superstar didn't mean I was going to let him take all the glory.

"You wish."

My eyes went wide. Had he just said what I thought he'd said?

"Not in your wildest wet dreams. You're not my type."

He arched a perfect brow. How did he do that? I couldn't do it. "Really?"

"Yeah, really. Not everyone is a member of your fan club, and if you think I'm going to spend the next two weeks drooling and fawning over you like everyone else in your sad little world, you can fucking well think again. If I have to work with you, I will, and it's going to be you working your fucking arse off to keep up with me and not the other way around, but don't think for one minute I'm going to like it, or that I'm going to be pussying around you."

He gaped at me, and I think he was genuinely shocked. It spurred me on to continue. "In fact, while we're at it, maybe it would be wise to set a few ground rules. We've got to work together, so there's no point in moaning about it, but that doesn't mean I have to like it, or that I have to like you. I'll work with you and work hard, but I don't want any of your shit-faced attitude and smarmy remarks. Don't expect me to kiss your arse. And if you so much as think of coming on to me, I'll fucking kill you."

"After the way you've been beating me up these last few days, I'm going to have to take that threat seriously."

He was mocking me, his eyes sparkling and his lips twisted in that bloody infuriating smile of his. I growled and started leafing through the papers. Fuck!

"Fuck."

The words on the paper caught and held my attention, and I couldn't stop reading. Morgan remained silent until I got to the end. I glanced up at him, and he simply nodded.

"Good, isn't it?"

"But why?"

He tilted his head to one side and watched me with cool eyes. "What do you mean why?"

"Why would they give us something like this? It's too . . . too . . . big."

"Nah, nothing's too big for you and me, kid. Between us, we're the dog's bollocks."

"Morgan, be serious. Did you say this is the same case you're going to be arguing at the Nationals?"

"Same areas of law. Different application."

I glanced down at the papers, then back at him. "You're going to love this, aren't you?"

"Fuck yeah."

I groaned again and shook my head. "All right. So, where do we start?"

"How about you come out to my place and take a look at the notes I've already made for the Nationals? It's a good base, although we're going to have to take it in a different direction."

I glanced sharply at him. Venturing into the lion's den was not what I had in mind at all. However, he seemed sincere, and it did sound like a good idea.

"I'm meeting Cory for lunch," I supplied lamely.

"Cory?"

"My friend."

"Oh, the little geeky guy? The one who's got the internship at my father's place?"

"Cory is *not* a *little geeky guy*. He's my best friend, and if you want me to co-operate with this crazy fucking situation, then you can lay off him—and lay off me, too."

Morgan shrugged and spread his hands. "Okay, okay. Bring Cory, too. We'll get lunch at mine."

"What about this afternoon's lectures?"

Morgan shrugged again. "What about them?"

I shook my head and gave an exaggerated sigh. "I'll ask Cory."

"Is he your boyfriend?"

What the fuck! "Since when would that be any of your business?"

He gave the same little non-committal lift of the shoulders. "It isn't. Just asking so I don't make a faux pas."

"Not that it *is* any of your business, but no, Cory is definitely not my boyfriend. I don't *have* a boyfriend, and I don't *want* a boyfriend. I am not inclined that way."

Morgan tilted his head again and gave me a long, appraising look from his cool green eyes. Finally, he smiled a slow smile. "That surprises me. I would have bet money you were . . . inclined that way."

I got to my feet and bent close to him so the lecturer, who was wandering among the intensely chatting students, wouldn't hear.

"Fuck you, Morgan Bentley, fuck you to hell. How dare you make assumptions about me? How dare you pry into my private life? How dare you presume you know me? How dare you suggest I—that I'm—fuck you!"

Livid with anger, for no real reason other than I hated him—and his smug smile, and his condescending attitude, and his stupid assumptions—I scrunched up the papers and threw them in his lap.

Leaning even closer, I hissed, "Stuff the fucking case right up your tight, smug, arrogant arse. Stuff your notes, stuff your lunch, and stuff yourself. You're already so far up your own arse you can scratch your balls with your toothbrush, so if you think you can handle it, do it. Just don't expect me to be your whipping boy.

"If you let me know which parts you want me to research, I'll do the work in my own place in my own time."

It felt so good to see the stunned expression in his eyes, and I was grinning on the inside when I strode out of the room. I could feel those emerald eyes boring into my back as I did so, and I was on top of the world.

At a bit of a loose end, I wandered up to the refectory and sat, staring out of the window. It started to rain, and the trees of the woods became blurred and indistinct, somewhat like my thoughts. Gods, I hated Morgan Bentley.

I was still lost in thought when Cory, collapsing on the seat opposite, startled the hell out of me.

"I'm completely fucked."

"As in *up shit creek without a paddle*, or *in need of a padded cell and a nice cosy straightjacket*?"

"Neither . . . as in *I'm so fucking tired I'm not even sure what day of the week it is*."

"Tuesday. What's up?"

Cory smiled. He took off his glasses and massaged his temples. "Oh, nothing. I've just had a package through from ITM with a load of things they want me to cover before I start. A lot of it I've already done, but there's more than a little extra work in there and not a lot of time to get it sorted."

"Are you really sure this is a good idea?"

"What? The internship? Fuck yeah. You can't buy experience like this, and it's not unknown for them to take on their interns permanently at the end of the year. If I could get my foot in the door at ITM, I'm made for life."

"Well . . . if you're sure."

"As sure as I can be. It's going to be great, Matthew, but gods it's hard work."

"Just make sure you don't overdo it. I know what you're like. You don't know the meaning of the word moderation."

"Yes, I do. I just choose not to use it very often."

"You'll never guess what happened to me today?"

"You're right, I won't, not in this befuddled state. You're just going to have to tell me."

I quickly outlined the events of the morning, while Cory's eyes grew wider and wider.

"You're kidding me?"

"Nope, not a word."

"He said that? Morgan said he'd bet money on you being gay?"

"What? Oh, trust you to pick up on that particular point. Yeah, he said that."

"But why? Why would he say that?" Cory stared at me, sounding intensely annoyed and defensive. It wasn't entirely unexpected, but the antagonism was overdoing it a bit, I thought.

"Because he's an absolute arse, that's why. I keep telling you . . . Morgan Bentley is an A-one bastard."

"Yeah, I know but—"

"Look, just drop it, okay? It was embarrassing enough at the time without you bringing it up again."

Cory looked outraged. "I didn't bring it up, you did."

"Yeah, yeah . . . whatever."

"So when are we going?"

"Going where?" I was confused. Cory was a master at changing the subject. He had the kind of mind that thinks about five different things at the same time and swaps between them without letting the person he's talking to catch up. He could have been referring to anything.

"To Morgan's place, of course."

I was even more confused as I gazed into his excited blue eyes and wondered if he'd lost his mind.

"Why the hell would we go there?"

"He invited us, didn't he?"

"Well, yeah, just before I told him to fuck himself and walked out. I doubt if the invitation still stands."

Cory looked crushed, and I swear he pouted. "Aw."

"Why would you want to go there, anyway?"

"Are you insane? Have you seen the place?"

"Yeah, all right, it's a nice house, but . . . it's got Morgan in it."

The way I said Morgan's name—as if it referred to some kind of disgusting, gross insect—made him chuckle, and that lightened my mood. The lightness didn't last long, though, because shortly afterwards I noticed Morgan making a bee-line for us through the usual lunchtime crowds.

"Oh, great."

Cory glanced up, saw the expression on my face, and turned just as Morgan sashayed through the last of the crowd and slid into the seat next to Cory. He pushed some papers across the table to me.

"You forgot these."

"I didn't *forget* anything. What do you want?"

"I was just wondering if you needed a lift out to the house. I wasn't sure if you knew how to get there."

"What makes you think I have any intention of going any-where near your house?"

"I thought that's what we agreed."

I could tell from the twinkle in his eyes he knew perfectly well I had no intention of going to his house.

"That was before I told you to stuff the papers up your arse and go fuck yourself."

"Oh, yes, so it was." He shrugged and grinned. "I didn't think you meant it."

"Point of information . . . yeah, I meant it."

"Oh." His attention wandered over my shoulder to the

rain-spattered window. I noticed his eyes weren't completely green. They had a dark blue ring around the edges.

"So, are you coming or not?"

I opened my mouth to tell him no, but Cory beat me to it. "Sure. We'd love to come."

Morgan whipped his head around and glared at Cory, and a blush crept out from under Cory's collar. It made me angry. How dare Morgan look at him like that? How dare he make him feel uncomfortable? How dare he make him blush?

Morgan gave a full-on hundred-watt Morgan Bentley smile, and Cory melted.

"Hi. You must be Cory. I'm Morgan."

Taking the proffered hand weakly, Cory nodded. "I know who you are."

"Oh? Has Matthew been talking about me?"

"No. I mean yes. I mean, he doesn't have to. Everyone knows who you are."

"Everyone? Surely not?"

Was there the tiniest hint of discomfort? Surely the great Morgan Bentley couldn't actually be the slightest bit embarrassed by all that attention . . . could he?

Cory smiled coyly, and Morgan turned his attention back to me. "So. Do you want a lift, or are you going to make your own way?"

"We'll make our own way."

As if I was going to travel in a car with that arsehole. As if I was going to let myself be at his mercy with regard to getting back. *As if.* Morgan smiled. Was I imagining it, or was it slightly rueful?

"Okay. Here's directions with the code to punch in at the gate. Text me when you get to the gate, and I'll meet you at the door. Don't worry about lunch. We can eat while we work."

I shrugged, Cory babbled, and Morgan left.

"What the fuck, Cory? Why did you have to go and do that?"

"Do what?" He had a dazed and slightly stupid smile on his face.

"Commit us to going to Morgan's house?"

"Didn't you want to go?"

"Of course I didn't want to go. Why the fuck would I want to go to Morgan's house? I hate the guy, remember? I was just telling you how pissed I am at having to work with him and how I *didn't* want to go to his house."

"Oh . . . right." He was still grinning but seemed a little confused now. "Sorry."

"What's up with you? Anyone would think you were happy to be going into the lion's den."

Cory grinned and shrugged. I glared at him with narrowed eyes. He was glowing.

"Fuck, Cory. You're not falling for him, are you?"

Cory's eyes widened, and he shook his head, blushing. "No, I . . . it's just . . . well I—"

I groaned. "Oh no, not you, too. It's like a bloody zombie virus."

"No, it isn't that, Matthew. It isn't what you think. It's just . . . well . . . the stuff I got from ITM is awesome. Some of the things they're working on are unbelievable. I really wish I could tell you about it, but I had to sign this confidentiality agreement. The research projects I've been reading about are so far out there I can hardly believe it's not a wind-up, and Morgan's father is awesome."

I groaned again. "Even greater. You haven't got the hots for Morgan . . . it's for his father. That's sick."

"I haven't got the hots for him . . . only for his mind."

"So what's so great about him?"

"I wish I could tell you. There are three projects he's directly involved in. Two of them are pretty mainstream, albeit at the brilliant end. But there's one of them . . . I don't know much about it to be fair and . . . erm . . . I don't think I'm exactly supposed to know even that. I . . . er . . . never mind." He continued rapidly, "Anyway, it's awesome, almost science fiction. If the things I saw are real and not some kind of wind-up, it's the biggest thing I've ever heard of, let alone been involved in."

"O-kay. Well, anyway, let's get moving. If we have to go, let's go. I'm hungry. We'll take your car."

"My car? Why my car?"

"Because it's nicer than mine. I'd be utterly ashamed parking my pile of crap on the drive next to the *Audi*." Cory groaned. "What?"

"Last time we took my car you threw up in it. It took me hours to get the smell out."

"I'm not going to be sick this time, idiot. How far is it to this place? Five minutes?"

Cory scanned the directions. "Hmm, about twenty. You keep the window open the whole way, right?"

"Whatever."

CHAPTER THREE

Morgan's house was amazing. I have to admit I was nervous when we pulled up to the huge, ornate, cast-iron gates. They loomed over us in an otherwise blank expanse of wall, topped with twisted, sharp metal.

I punched the numbers Morgan had given me into the keypad at the side of the gate, and they swung open, slowly and silently. It was like something from a horror movie. I couldn't get back into the car fast enough. I glanced over my shoulder as we drove, shivering when the gates closed behind us.

The house seemed a very long way away, along a drive that zigzagged through neat lawns and over a small stream. It was grand and imposing, built of dark grey rock, bleak and intimidating. The thought made me angry. No way in hell was I ever going to get intimidated by anything that was Morgan's. It wasn't all that, after all. It was just a house.

The drive split into two and circled the house in either direction. The *Audi* was parked beside a set of stone steps that led up to the main doors. Cory pulled up next to Morgan's car, and we got out, looking around in total shock at the sheer size and awesomeness of our surroundings. It was like visiting a museum or something. It was hard to believe someone actually lived here.

"So, what now?" Cory asked, sounding nervous.

"Try the front door?"

"The front door scares me."

"Scaredy cat." Cory shadowed me as I strode up the steps, still determined not to allow myself to be intimidated by this place. I put out my hand, but before I touched the knocker, the door swung open. Morgan grinned.

"I thought you were going to text me when you got to the gate."

I shrugged, cringing inside. Why did we have to forget? Why did we have to start this whole thing on the back foot? "So shoot me."

"How did you know we were here?" I groaned at Cory's awed voice. The last thing I wanted was for Morgan to get the idea we were impressed.

"When the gate opens, it triggers an alarm in the security office. I asked them to let me know when they got it. I figured you'd forget the text."

Figuratively gnashing my teeth, I glared at him. "So, are you going to invite us in, then? Or are you going to leave us standing on the doorstep all afternoon?"

"Of course not. Do come in."

Morgan stood aside, and we walked past him into the biggest entrance hall I'd ever seen outside of a public building. The ceiling was so far overhead we could hardly see it—there was just an impression of darkness high above from which hung a chandelier. And what a chandelier—the bloody thing was as big as a car. The floor was dark wood, inset with parquetry designs reminiscent of a giant compass, lozenges of lighter coloured wood radiating out from a rose in the centre.

Corridors radiated off the lower floor, while a graceful staircase swept upward in wings on either side to two tiers of balconies. The quality of the light in the hall was strange. I turned toward the door to find two enormous stained-glass windows arching upward toward the ceiling on either side of it. I was surprised I hadn't noticed them from the outside. Between the windows was an equally enormous framed painting, but I couldn't make out any details from here.

I was staring. I knew I was staring. I hated myself for doing it, but I just couldn't help myself.

"It's pretty awesome, isn't it?"

I was surprised. Morgan wasn't gloating. He wasn't showing off. If anything, there was a note of — what, resignation —
in his voice. I glanced at him sharply. He was staring upward,
his face blank.

"Yeah, it's impressive." Gods, it was hard for me to say
that. Morgan grinned at me as if he knew, and for some reason, I regretted it.

"What do you want to do first? Read through the notes or
have lunch?"

"Read the notes," I said.

"Have lunch," Cory said.

Morgan smiled. "I'll have lunch served in the study."

Following Morgan across the echoing hall, I couldn't help
but look around. It was grand, for sure, but it wasn't homey.

Morgan paused before a door and opened it. "Go on in. I'll
make arrangements for lunch. I won't be long. This is my personal study so . . . well . . . you know."

When Morgan had gone, we explored. Fucking hell, the
place was huge. There was a grand piano in one corner, and
a full-sized snooker table in the other. In between were
shelves and shelves of books, some of which appeared old
and valuable. An open fire roared in a solid oak fireplace, on
which rested a number of animal skulls. Over the fireplace
hung a pair of crossed swords, and there were more around
the room.

In the middle of the floor was a work station. It was a huge
oak desk with a computer, printer, scanner, various other
electronics, and sheaves of paper, all in neat piles. We both
wandered over to the desk. Cory was immediately absorbed
with the computer, while I couldn't help but rifle through the
papers.

We both jumped when the door opened, and the pile of

papers I was leafing through reacted to the jerk of my hand by flying off the desk and scattering all over the floor. With a sigh, I bent down and started gathering them together as fast as I could. When I looked up, Morgan was standing in the doorway, watching me with an expression of disappointment on his face. Like I cared.

"Food's on its way."

He stooped and took the papers out of my hand, shuffling them into the right order. For a moment, our gazes met, and the expression in them startled me. It was the most open expression I'd ever seen on his face, almost as if he was reaching out. For an instant, I almost . . . but . . .

I got to my feet abruptly. "So, where are these notes? Let's get to work so I can leave."

For a moment, Morgan remained where he was, his gaze on the papers in his hand. Then he stood, and his face was set in his usual sardonic, infuriating expression. He turned to the desk and handed me a different pile of papers. I sat in a chair by the open fire and flicked through them. After a few pages, I was hooked.

"Where did you find this stuff? It's awesome."

"I have my sources." Morgan sounded bored. I glanced up. He was lounging against the fireplace, watching Cory drool over his computer. "Feel free to power it up if you want to. Anything I don't want you to see is password protected. Just don't give me any viruses."

I snorted. "As if. Cory's a bloody genius with IT."

"So I hear."

Cory looked up, surprised. "You do?"

"My father was excited by your application." He smiled ironically. "Well, as close to excited as my father ever is about anything."

"He was?"

"I think I just said so. I'm not in the habit of lying to make people feel good."

"Fucking right."

Morgan turned his head to face me. His eyes seemed to glow in the firelight, chips of emerald in a face as pale and flawless as the marble bust on the stand behind him. For a moment, I thought he was going to say something, but he changed his mind. "Let me know when you're finished, and maybe we can have a *civilized* discussion."

The retort was on the tip of my tongue, but I never made it. Instead, I went back to reading the notes. They were mostly typed, but there were annotations in the margins in a small neat hand that was so *Morgan* it almost made me laugh. My own writing was somewhat chaotic. It was as if the jumbled confusion of my mind demanded to be set down so desperately my hand couldn't keep up. Morgan's was everything mine wasn't—neat, legible, and coherent—just like Morgan, really, except his writing didn't reveal what an utter bastard he was.

Before I finished reading, there was a tap on the door, and it opened to admit a young woman in a neat uniform of a black skirt and white blouse. She was pushing a trolley from which delicious smells snaked out to tease my nose and tantalise my palette. I held back, waiting for an invitation, but Cory was on the trolley before the wheels had stopped turning.

"Help yourself," Morgan said unnecessarily, as Cory began to heap his plate.

I would never have admitted it, not to myself and certainly not to Morgan, but the food was amazing. I had no need to express appreciation because Cory was exuberantly enthusing enough for both of us.

I ate in silence and watched Morgan surreptitiously. He seemed nervous, and he wasn't eating. He just took a little food and stared at it, then pushed it around on his plate a bit.

After a while, he put the plate back on the trolley and wandered around the room, touching things without any real interest, finishing up at the window, staring out. It had started to rain.

I made sure I finished every bite, prolonging the silence, the tension stretching between us. Morgan's obvious discomfort made me smile, as did Cory, who was very much at home, clearly torn between his two loves—food and computers—compelled to linger over the one, while at the same time being drawn back to the other. Eventually, he put his plate on the severely depleted trolley and sat back down before the computer.

Morgan turned at the sound of the plate being replaced and seemed disappointed that it had been Cory and not me. I grinned and stretched out the silence for another ten minutes before I rose and replaced my empty plate.

"At last. Can we please get down to work now?"

"Have I been stopping you?"

Morgan sighed and ran a hand through his hair. He looked tired, and the gesture no longer appeared to be an affected pose. He had a habit of doing it all the time, as well as flicking one side over his shoulder. I later learned it was a sign of tiredness or discomfort. At that point, I think he was both.

"All right, where do you want to start?"

We sat together, side by side at the desk, and spread out the papers. The fire crackled in the fireplace, Cory tapped away at the keys on the computer, and we worked together as if we'd been doing it all our lives. It surprised me how well we fit. Morgan was brilliant, inspired, and—when not competing with me—generous with his talents.

Morgan didn't steal the thunder, as I'd expected him to. He didn't try to show off or thrust his genius in my face. He made suggestions, listened to mine, and together we made far more progress that afternoon than I would have in a week on my own.

We were discussing a fine point of law on which we disagreed when Cory interrupted us. I felt a guilty lurch, in that I'd all but forgotten he was there. I was also irritated because we were in full flow and I was enjoying myself immensely, not least because I was actually keeping up with Morgan.

"Morgan, could you explain this to me, please. I saw mention of it in the stuff I had from ITM. It didn't make sense then, and it doesn't now."

At the name of his father's company, Morgan's head shot up, and his face went cold. When he saw the screen, the colour drained out of him, and he grasped the edge of the desk with white knuckles before getting to his feet and striding over to the computer. He took the mouse out of Cory's hand and shut it down.

"Is this the way you repay my hospitality? By hacking into my computer?"

"No. No, you don't understand. That project . . . I found something about it in the stuff from ITM and then I saw it here . . . I couldn't help it. It's fascinating. Is it real? Are they really doing that stuff? I mean genetics are fascinating, but this . . ."

"The only way you could have found anything about that particular project was if you went beyond what you were given. Do you make a habit of hacking computers, Cory?"

His voice was cold and angry and his face a mask, set and hard. Cory blinked at him. "I . . . I didn't think . . . I didn't mean."

"ITM . . ." Morgan hesitated, still simmering with anger. "They're not safe, Cory. You fuck with them, and they will fuck you up."

I was stunned. How dare he speak to my friend like that? Cory was staring at him with wide eyes that glistened with shocked tears.

"I'm sorry. I'm really sorry, Morgan. I didn't mean . . . I . . ."

"Do you realise if I told my father what you've done, not only would they withdraw the internship, but your career would be over before it had begun? Shit, if they told the police . . . you do appreciate what you've done is a crime?"

Cory cringed, tears spilling, and that's when I got really angry. "Who the fuck do you think you are, talking to him like that? He didn't mean any harm. He was curious, that's all. If you had this fucked up stuff on your computer, maybe you shouldn't have let him use it in the first place."

Morgan turned to me. His eyes were chips of green ice in a face that was paper white, apart from two hot spots of angry colour on his cheeks.

"If I'd thought he was going to hack my computer, I wouldn't have. That file was password protected, and most people would have realised that if it's protected, it means it's private. Silly me, I thought that as a guest in my house, and a friend of . . . the person I'm working with, I could actually trust him. Don't worry, that won't happen again."

"What's the big deal anyway? It isn't as if Cory's going to use the information for industrial espionage or anything like that. Fuck, he's going to be working at ITM in a couple of weeks, and he'll probably be told all about it anyway."

"The big deal, Matthew . . ." Morgan spoke slowly, his face set and his eyes flashing, "is that your *friend* betrayed my trust. He hacked into my computer, opened files I've shown to no one else — no one — and threw my hospitality back in my face. What he does with the information is irrelevant."

"I-I'm sorry, Morgan. I swear I didn't mean to do it. I just . . . I didn't think."

"I suggest you learn to think before you start working at ITM. Because if you even consider doing something like this when you're there, you're going to be in more trouble than you can begin to imagine."

"Are you threatening my friend?" Without even realising it, I was on my feet, facing him down, my own anger rising to meet his.

"It's not a threat, Matthew," he said quietly. "It's a warning, and one he'd better heed. These people are not to be messed with."

"*These people* are your own father. Are you telling me he's a crook? Doing some dodgy dealings he doesn't want the world to find out about?"

Morgan went even paler, if that was possible. "Hacking into the computer of a multinational company that deals with contracts from the government is not a smart thing to do, Matthew. I'd have thought even you would have realised that. And it has nothing to do with what they have to hide, or why."

"Oh, for fuck sake, get over yourself. Get down off your high horse, why don't you, and try mixing with real people once in a while?"

"Real people?" Morgan closed his eyes and shook his head. When he opened them again, they had a dangerous glint. "You don't get it, do you? Why is it that your friend has been playing a very dangerous game, hacking into computers, betraying the trust placed in him . . . by the company, by me . . . and yet somehow, I'm the bad guy here?"

"This isn't a game. It isn't downloading free music from the Internet, or copying CD's, or engaging in a little plagiarism in an essay. This is serious stuff, and if he's caught, there will be serious consequences. You don't mess with these people. They are not nice."

"If your father's anything like you, I can believe it."

Morgan winced as if I'd slapped him, and it gave me cruel satisfaction. He went still for a minute. Then he murmured, so quietly I barely heard, "My father is *nothing* like me." He turned his back and walked to the window. "I think you'd better go. Take the notes and work on them yourself. We can combine notes on Thursday. I'll meet you in the library."

I stared at him for a while, but he didn't turn around. Grabbing Cory by the shoulder, I steered him out of the room, out of the house and out of the situation. Gods, I hated Morgan Bentley.

Cory sat in silence on the journey back to the university. He was in such a state, I drove. I kept sneaking looks over at him. He was staring out of the window, crying softly. I didn't know what to say to him.

"I didn't mean to do something bad, Matthew. Honestly, I didn't. I just . . . you know what I'm like. I get carried away. I never know where to draw the line. It's so tempting and so easy. I know I shouldn't have hacked the computers, either of them, but I was so interested in that particular project. It was like something from my wildest dreams come true, and I had to look. I just had to find more. And then when I saw the reference on Morgan's computer . . . I'm sorry, Matthew."

"Sorry? You don't have to say sorry to me. I'm only sorry Morgan was such a prick."

"No," he said quietly, "Morgan was right. I'm sorry I got between the two of you when you were starting to be friends."

"Friends?" I almost laughed in his face but decided at the last minute he was too fragile. "Morgan and I are never going to be friends. How many times do I have to tell you? I hate him."

"Maybe." He gave me the strangest look. I couldn't hold it, or I would have crashed the car, but something about it bothered me.

I didn't have a chance to ask about it, though, because as soon as I stopped the car, he was out of there, and I had to hurry to keep up with him as he powered back to our apartment block.

"Wait, Cory . . . please." I grabbed his arm and swung him around. "Look, don't let this bother you. Morgan Bentley is a first-class tosser. He made a mountain out of a molehill. I have to work with him on this stupid project, but I can assure you I won't be going to his house again. So don't let him get to you, okay?"

"I can't avoid him, Matthew, and neither can you. It just wouldn't work."

"What do you mean?"

"You have to work with him, and I'm going to be working with his father. One way or another, he's in our lives, and it feels like . . ."

"Feels like what?" He was freaking me out now because there were tears in his eyes again and he was gazing at his shoes as if he wished the ground would open and swallow him.

"I don't know. I get the feeling something bad's going to happen. It's been that way for a while, a long time. I don't know what it is, can't put my finger on it at all, but I know something bad is going to happen, and it involves Morgan."

"What are you talking about?"

"I told you, Matthew, I don't know. I've been feeling uneasy for ages, ever since you started with the hate thing."

"What do you mean *the hate thing*?"

"Morgan. You've been doing it all year. Going on and on about how much you hate him. You're always talking about him, always watching him. It makes me uneasy."

"I so do not."

"Yes, you do." He looked as if he was on the verge of bursting into tears, and for some reason, this made me angry.

"What are you trying to say?"

"Nothing. I'm not trying to say anything. I'm just pointing

out you've had a bee in your bonnet about Morgan all year. There's never a day goes by when you don't talk about him, almost every conversation. Whenever he's around, you're jumpy, and you watch him all the time, to the point of zoning out sometimes."

I was completely shocked, more that he seemed so devastated by it than anything else. I was about to argue, to tell him he was insane, or a complete idiot, but something stopped me.

"Am I really that bad?"

"Worse."

"Shit. I really let the arsehole get under my skin, eh?"

Cory nodded.

"I'm just so damned competitive. Too competitive. I could forgive him a lot—hell, I probably wouldn't even have noticed him if he was on another course—but the fact he's so fucking effortlessly brilliant, when I've worked so hard . . . I guess I'm jealous."

"Jealous? Is that it?"

"I guess." I shrugged. "What else would it be?"

Cory grinned sheepishly. "Nothing. Come on, let's get inside. It's cold out here."

I didn't let go of his arm. A worm of suspicion was forming and writhing its way through my brain. "Hang on a goddamned minute there, partner. You thought I fancied him, didn't you? You thought I was falling for him." I could tell by the look on his face, I'd hit the nail on the head, and I couldn't help but laugh aloud. "Oh, come on . . . please, Cory, give me some credit for taste. As if."

I threw my arm around his shoulders, and we walked in the direction of the entrance.

"Didn't I tell you that if I ever start feeling like that for someone, you'll be the first to know? I promise, mate, if I ever decide I want to try a taste of life on the gay side, yours will be the first pants I seek entry to."

"What makes you think you'll get in?"

"Because you're my bitch. You're all mine, honey buns, always have been and always will be. Any man that wants you is going to have to come through me."

"What, literally? Are you going to test drive all my boyfriends?"

Relieved to hear the lightness back in his voice, I thumped him on the shoulder and laughed. "Hell yes. Any man who seeks to plough the virgin furrow that is my best friend is going to have to get my seal of approval, and then some."

"Now you're just being greedy."

"What's wrong with that?" Something occurred to me. I stopped and turned him around again. "Hey, this isn't about? I mean, you're not . . ." Cory's eyes went wide, and I could feel him tremble. I groaned inwardly. "You're not in love with Morgan, are you?"

For a moment, he stared at me. Then he began to laugh. There was a hysterical edge to it, and in the end, he had to bend over, clutching himself. I watched him with a smile on my face. I had no choice—his laughter was infectious, but I didn't understand what was going on at all.

Eventually, he straightened, wiping tears of laughter from his eyes, and composed himself with a struggle.

"No, Matthew. I can honestly say, hand on heart, I'm not, never have been, and never will be in love with Morgan Bentley. He's a bastard."

Laughing for real now, I hugged him again, and we hurried into the warmth of the university accommodation complex where we had rooms in the same block.

CHAPTER FOUR

For the next few days, I found myself, by and large, alone. Cory was completely wrapped up in the work from ITM. He spent hours on the computer. And when he wasn't staring at a screen, he was reading a book, even while eating. Or working in the lab with his professor, who was as nutty and focused as he was.

Morgan was avoiding me whenever he could, and when he couldn't, he was an absolute pig. At every opportunity, he made a snide comment, a joke at my expense, a derogatory remark — anything and everything he could to put me down, make people laugh at me, or just plain get in my way or on my nerves. I hated him more than ever.

I knew why he was doing it, and it was ridiculously childish. Okay, we'd had a row, and I'd walked out of his house. Cory had hacked his computer, and he was mad at him. So what? How did that make it all right for him to treat me like I was a piece of shit on his shoe? Not that I'd have worried if he hadn't done it so publicly.

I simmered but said nothing. Let's face it, with the university one huge Morgan Bentley fan club, what could I have done? If I'd said one word out of place, made any attempt to retaliate against the great Mr Bentley, I would have had half the university on my back, and I'd seen what something like that could do to people. I wasn't kidding when I said Morgan left broken people in his wake.

To be fair, I'm not sure Morgan was even aware of all the people he broke. Half the time . . . well, most of the time, when he was not trying to be a bastard, he just wandered around in a world of his own, a world peopled with syco-phants, who smoothed over the harsh edges and handed things down to other lackeys, who dealt with the nitty-gritty. If someone upset Morgan, they got taken care of, and most of the time, it seemed as though Morgan never even knew.

The meeting on Thursday was a nightmare. We sparred the whole time, dancing round the issue of Cory and never actu-ally mentioning it. We did get a lot of work done, though. I couldn't escape the fact Morgan was a genius, and he dragged up my own game to almost as high a level.

We started off in the library. But when our arguments got heated not even Morgan could charm the librarian into letting us stay. So we tried the refectory, but there were too many adoring Morgan fans. For once, they irritated him and got in the way, and so somehow, we ended up back at my dorm.

The basic dorm unit was the same on every floor. On either side of the landing were two corridors, holding eight rooms. At the end of the corridor was a shared kitchen cum sitting room, and between each pair of rooms was a shared bath-room, which was the size of a matchbox. Cory and I had ad-joining rooms and a connecting bathroom. Cory, of course, wasn't around, being out somewhere doing his research, and I didn't know whether to be glad or sorry. One of our block-mates was getting ready to go out and disappeared hastily in the middle of one of our more heated *discussions*. The others were either in classes or in their rooms, so we were all alone as we sat at the kitchen table and tossed ideas back and forth.

After we'd pretty much exhausted ourselves, I got Morgan a cold beer from the fridge. He stared at it with surprise when I offered it to him.

"What's this for?"

"It's beer. It's for drinking."

"I know that, arsehole. I was just wondering why you're offering it to me when we've spent the whole afternoon locked in conflict."

"The conflict was interesting and stimulating, and we got a lot done. I didn't take a moment of it personally. Why? Did you?"

Morgan opened his mouth to say something, but changed his mind and took the beer instead. I surreptitiously watched him over the top of my can, and the expression of sheer joy on his face, when he took a long drink, would have been heart-warming if I'd liked him.

It felt a bit rude just to throw him out, so I offered him another drink. For a short while, I actually began to enjoy his company as we chatted about things related to the course and the university in general.

That all ended when Cory got home. As soon as he walked through the door, Morgan gave him a look that would have frozen lava, and Cory shrank into himself instantly. He grabbed a beer and hurried into his room.

"Has your little hacker friend been breaking any laws recently?" Morgan asked in a tone that dripped scorn. It was like a red rag to a bull.

"That's my best friend you're talking about, arsehole," I growled, and Morgan blinked at me with surprise. The easy manner that had begun to make an appearance fell away, and instantly he was his usual arrogant, sarcastic self.

"Oh great . . . here we go again. You hook up with a sociopath who can't keep his sticky fingers off other people's property, and somehow it turns out to be my fault. I never did get my head round that one. Perhaps you'd care to explain."

"No, I fucking won't explain. What's the point? You're an arrogant, self-absorbed, selfish bastard, Morgan, and anything that doesn't accord with your own world view isn't worth knowing. The fact there is a world full of people out there who aren't like you, who you could never understand if you tried for a million years, but who are just as good as you if not better, has completely passed you by. If you haven't realised it by now, nothing I have to say would make any difference at all.

"Cory isn't like you. He's sweet, and kind, and gentle, and oblivious to most of the bad things that go on in the world. He's very focused on making it a better place, and if his methods are a little unconventional, I'm not going to be the one criticising him for it."

"Unconventional is one thing," Morgan said, getting to his feet, "but criminal is another. I warned your boyfriend because—whatever you might think—I'm not a complete bastard, and I know he's a nice kid. The people at ITM are not nice people. They are abject professionals, and they don't cut any slack, not for anyone. If he carries on, he's going to get hurt—a lot."

"He's not my boyfriend," I countered lamely. Morgan shook his head sadly.

"Look, if you want my advice, tell your friend to stay away from ITM. Say *thank you very much, but I have a better offer* and just walk away. They're very focused and all that, but they're focused on getting results, not how they get them, not who they hurt to get them. If they find out what he knows, they will hurt him. Maybe not physically, but certainly professionally. They're just not worth it."

Putting the half-finished can of beer down on the table, he grabbed his coat off the back of the chair. Then he strode out, slamming the door behind him.

A few minutes later, Cory crept out of his room. I was still staring at the door Morgan had slammed.

"I'm sorry, Matthew. I didn't mean to spoil your afternoon."

"Don't mention it. You did me a favour."

"I did?"

"Yes, you did. I was almost starting to see Morgan as a human being. Thank you for reminding me what he really is."

"An arrogant, scheming, self-satisfied bastard?"

I grinned at him. "Nail on the head, mate. Do you want another beer?"

"As long as I don't have to finish the one Morgan was drinking."

On Friday, I met Cory for lunch in the refectory. As I was walking back to my seat with my tray in my hand, who should I bump into but Morgan? Fortunately, this time we didn't knock anything onto the floor. We just glared at each other.

I have to say, Morgan looked rough. It was the most *uncool* I'd ever seen him. His smooth-as-silk hair was messed up, and his eyes were red and dull. If I hadn't known better, I'd have said he'd been crying. But that was impossible. Morgan Bentley never showed any emotion at all, let alone cried.

"Watch where you're going, arsehole. What's the matter with you? Up all night fucking that scrawny girlfriend of yours?"

Morgan narrowed his eyes, a spark of life kindling the smoky green. Then he sighed and shook his head, turning to walk away. As if something had occurred to him last minute, he turned back again.

"My father's home. He wants to meet the prodigy. Dinner party. Saturday night." As an afterthought, he added, "I suppose you'd better come, too. Dress smart. Be there at eight."

Then he was gone, leaving me feeling slightly stunned. I stared after him for ages. There was something wrong with his voice, too. It was scratchy, as if he had a sore throat or . . . or as if he'd been crying. Surely not? Surely the great man would not have fallen so far as to let some emotion or other touch him enough to bring tears to his eyes.

Maybe Charlotte had ditched him? But no, she seemed as attentive as ever, leaning close into him, her long fingers toying with his hair, twirling it round and round. Well, if she thought she was going to wind him around her finger, she had another think coming. He was made of sterner stuff. Morgan Bentley bent for no one.

The direction of my thoughts startled me. I was falling into the trap of thinking of Morgan as a rounded, three-dimensional human being with feelings. I would have to be careful because that wasn't what he was at all. He was a cold, emotionless, unfeeling bastard.

Cory knew something was going on as soon as I sat down. "What's up?"

"Morgan."

Cory groaned and rolled his eyes. "Oh, no. Now what?"

"His father wants to meet you. We're both invited to a dinner party on Saturday night."

Cory went pale and stared at me, his fork hovering halfway to his mouth.

"You don't think . . . you don't . . ."

"No, I don't," I said firmly. "They're not going to invite you to a dinner party just to tell you, you're sacked. It's not their style. They wouldn't waste the energy."

"You're right." He smiled and continued eating, although I was uneasy. What if they did?

When I finished my food, I excused myself from Cory, who was already engrossed in the book he'd brought, and went in search of Morgan. I needed to know. I needed to make sure I wasn't leading my best friend into hell on Saturday.

I searched everywhere—the library, the lecture theatre, the bookshop, empty classrooms. His car was still in the car park, so he couldn't have gone far, but he was nowhere to be found.

Plenty of people had seen him, just not recently.

In the end, I gave up. I went back to the refectory, looking for Cory, but he'd gone. I was restless, reluctant to go back to my room. It was a beautiful day, cold and clear, so I decided to take a walk up to the tree. When I got there, I sat on top for a while, listening to the sounds of the woods around me. It calmed me like it always did, but today I was too restless to sit still for long.

I got to my feet and continued my walk, deeper into the wood, heading toward the river. The sound of running water told me I was near, and I followed it until I broke out of the trees at the edge of the water. It had been raining a lot the previous week, and the river was swollen and angry.

I wandered along the bank for a while, letting the churning water calm my restlessness. At some point, as I walked, I became aware of another sound. At first, I couldn't make out what it was, as it was in some ways similar to the murmuring and bubbling of the river. I stood still and listened carefully. Then with a jolt, I realised it was someone crying, great wracking sobs, the kind that tear at your soul just to hear.

I should have turned back. I knew it. This was an extremely private moment, and I was intruding, but the sobs sounded so sad and lonely. I pressed through the bushes obscuring the path and came out into a bright space. The river bent sharply, holding a small meadow in its crook. Fertile with river silt, it was lush with flowers and grasses.

At the edge of the river was a large flat stone, and someone was sitting on it, probably not more than twenty feet away from me. They had their knees drawn up, hugging them, forehead resting on them. The whole body was shaking with the violence of the sobs, and the hands, locked together around the legs, were white-knuckled, as if the person were literally trying to hold themselves together.

I almost turned to leave. Almost. I would have left, and he

would have been none the wiser, if I hadn't stepped on the twig as I inched back into the brush.

The sound was like a gunshot. I froze, but it was too late. He'd heard. His head came up sharply, and he regarded me surprisingly calmly from bright, deep green eyes. Emotions churned behind the screen that had suddenly fallen, mirrored by the swirling water behind. I could see the effort he was making to control himself. The struggle was epic. His chest was heaving with it.

I had no idea what to do. Morgan wasn't moving, wasn't saying anything. What could I say? Or do? Well, I couldn't just stand there staring. So I walked calmly across the clearing and sat down next to him. Picking up a handful of stones, I began flicking them into the water, and he watched as if hypnotised.

I waited until the sound of his breathing grew calmer, then said, "Do you want to talk?"

He didn't reply, and in fact, started sniffing again, so I didn't say anything more. Neither did he.

After a time, he leaned against me and rested his head on my shoulder. I was surprised but didn't do or say anything. I didn't know what to do or say. Although the greatest temptation was to pull away, how could I do that after what I'd just seen? All right, Morgan was a bastard, but whatever I sometimes thought, he was a human being, and human beings reach out to each other and don't slap each other in the face when they're really low, as he obviously was.

And so I sat, stiff-backed and immobile, while he rested his head on my shoulder and we watched the river. At least he wasn't crying now.

Morgan Bentley was so . . . perfect. He always looked perfect. He always behaved impeccably, and he always kept his cool. It rocked the foundations of my world to see him falling apart in front of me.

"My father," Morgan whispered after a very long time. I almost groaned aloud. Whoop de fucking doo. So the golden boy was having trouble with Daddy. Big fucking deal. I wasn't exactly on the best terms with my own right then.

"Welcome to the real world."

"No," he said and started to cry again. Great. Just fucking great.

Awkwardly, I put my arm around to pat him on the back, but suddenly he turned and clung to me, sobbing again. I rolled my eyes. I didn't know what to do. What could I do? I did the only thing possible—I put my arms around him and held him until he calmed.

Holding Morgan in my arms was strange. It was awkward and uncomfortable, and yet . . . I glared at the top of his head, until I gave in and rested my cheek on his hair. It smelled good. Like incense. Smoky. It felt good, too, having someone in my arms . . . anyone. Even Morgan Bentley.

He was strong, and his embrace was desperate, crushing me. I wanted to ask him to ease up a little, but he was too lost in misery to have heard me even if I had, and I didn't want to risk hurting him by prising myself out of his embrace.

I began to wonder about Morgan. What it was that had made him crack so badly. He wasn't going to be pleased about this when he got over it. He was definitely not going to be pleased that out of all the people in the university, in the bloody world, who could have walked in on him in that moment of absolute vulnerability, it had to be me. Hell, I wasn't too happy about it myself.

Nope. Tomorrow Morgan was going to be pissed with me big time. He was probably going to take it out on me something wicked. Tomorrow we were going to glare at each other again and grind our teeth at every word the other said. Tomorrow we were going to torment one another and try our very best to tear the other down at every possibility.

Tomorrow we would hate each other again, but today . . . today was something different. Today I was holding him in my arms. Today I was resting my cheek on his hair. Today I was feeling his heart beat next to mine. Today I was . . . I was . . .

It took a long time for Morgan to calm down. I was getting cold, and he was shivering uncontrollably. Unconsciously, I started to stroke his hair, and it seemed to get through to him, because he calmed, and for a while, he was still in my arms. I don't know why, but I kept on stroking his hair.

It was the sigh that did it. It was deep and shaky, but strangely content, and it was accompanied by a little movement of his head, as if he was snuggling into me. That's when it hit me. Fuck. I was sitting on a rock in the middle of the woods, hugging a boy. And even worse, that boy was Morgan Bentley. What the hell was I doing? What was I thinking?

I immediately went stiff and stopped stroking his hair. I pushed him away, none too gently. Startled, he gazed at me, his eyes shocked. It was almost as if he'd had the same realisation at the same moment.

He looked awful. Not even the great Morgan Bentley was immune to the ravages of intense sobbing. His eyes were swollen and red, his cheeks puffy, and his face covered with tears and snot. The bastard was fucking gorgeous. Those emerald eyes, over-bright and more intense than ever, seemed to peer right into my soul. *Why was I even noticing that?* It's not as if I was . . . and even if I were, I wouldn't be . . . not with him.

"You're all right now?" I asked awkwardly. He shook his head. "Oh."

After staring at each other for a while, he mumbled, "You'd better go."

"I'm cold. So are you." The awkwardness was growing, and he ducked his head, shrugging.

"Are you coming back?"

He glanced up sharply and gave me that strange searching look again, then crumbled. He nodded stiffly. I got to my feet and extended numb fingers to him. He used them to haul himself up, then let go as if they burned him.

We walked back in silence. At one point, Morgan stopped and knelt by the river, splashing water on his face. It must have been freezing.

When we got to campus, we paused, embarrassed, not looking at each other.

"Thanks," he said, gazing at the floor.

"No problem."

"See you tomorrow, then."

"Tomorrow?"

"The dinner party."

"Oh. Yes."

"Do you still have the gate code?"

"Probably . . . somewhere."

"Do you want my number, my private one, just in case you can't find it?" he added in a rush.

"Sure." I fished a piece of paper out of my backpack, and he wrote down a number. I don't know why, but I tore the paper in half, scribbled my number, and handed it back to him. He looked at the paper, then up at me, then back down again. His hands were trembling.

"I . . . thanks." Thrusting the slip of paper into his pocket, he turned and strode away. I watched him until he was gone.

I surprised myself by the way I told Cory about the incident . . . in that I didn't, not really. I mean I told him I'd stumbled on the great Morgan Bentley sobbing his heart out by the river, but for some reason, I just couldn't talk to him about the way he'd clung to me, the way I'd comforted him. I was embarrassed by it now. It felt . . . wrong.

Cory wasn't really listening anyway. He seemed strangely

distracted, staring out of the window most of the time I was talking.

"Are you even listening to me?"

"Sorry. I was just thinking. What if they're going to . . . I'm afraid they're going to say something, do something. I . . . he scared me, Matthew. Morgan scared me. I know what I did was wrong, but I didn't think. I never think. I see a computer, and I have to touch it, try it, stretch it. And that project . . .

"I'm intrigued by that damned project. I saw a trail of it in the things they sent me, a hint in what wasn't there. I had to know what should have been filling the blanks. I kept searching, and I kept finding things, and it made me want more. I just kept getting deeper and deeper.

"I couldn't find it in the computers at ITM, and then when I saw the symbol on Morgan's computer, I had to look. I couldn't help it. I just had to. But what I saw didn't add up. It didn't fit with what I'd seen on the main computers. I wanted to ask him about it, that's all. I just wanted to ask him why it didn't fit. What it meant. I didn't expect him to freak out quite so much."

He chewed on his pen, and before I could say anything, he continued. "I really do know what I did was wrong. I'm not completely blind. I can't really blame him for being cross. I suppose I shouldn't have said anything, but I just couldn't help it. I was surprised."

"Cory." I sighed. As much as he said he knew what he'd done and that he was aware he'd been wrong—he wasn't, not really. He'd seen a puzzle he wanted to solve, and I knew what that did to Cory. He had to do it. He couldn't rest until he had an answer. He didn't have a clue, not really. There was a part of him that recognised perhaps he shouldn't have told Morgan what he was doing, what he'd found, because of the reaction he'd received, but he didn't understand why Morgan was so upset. He didn't understand why he shouldn't have done it, what was wrong with hacking into someone else's personal files. He really didn't have a clue.

"Cory, you really shouldn't have been hacking into his personal files. There's obviously something in there he doesn't want you to see."

"Why?"

"Who knows?"

"But it was about the project. It was about Project X. That wasn't personal. It was about the company, an über secret project. Why would it be on Morgan's computer anyway?"

"He *is* the boss' son, Cory, and he does have a brilliant mind. Maybe his father wanted him to help with something."

"I doubt it. Morgan's brilliant, but he's a law student, not biomedicine. How would he know anything about this?"

"I repeat, he's the boss' son. Do you think Daddy doesn't discuss shop over the dinner table?"

"Maybe."

"Besides, Morgan isn't happy with his dad right now. He's had some big fight or something. Maybe he was doing his own snooping, and that's why he got so defensive."

Cory's eyes widened. "Do you think . . ."

"I think I wouldn't put anything past Morgan Bentley. I wouldn't be surprised if he was up to something, not surprised at all."

"Do you think they're going to do anything? I mean, why do they want me to go back to that house? What are they going to say? What are they going to do?" His voice was rising, edged with panic, and I felt out of my depth. Could I really reassure him? Hadn't I suspected the same thing myself? Why hadn't I asked Morgan when I had the chance when he was open enough to maybe have told me?

"How the hell should I know? They're not going to chain you to the wall in the dungeon, Cory, so stop worrying."

"How do you know? How do you know they haven't got a

dungeon?"

I laughed, and he joined me . . . finally.

CHAPTER FIVE

Cory and I were like two teenage girls getting ready for their first high school party. We threw just about every piece of clothing we owned on the bed, dressed, changed, changed again and then, bit by bit, changed what each other was wearing, until we were wearing what we had right at the start.

It was hilarious. We laughed ourselves silly, but there was a somewhat hysterical edge to it. Truth be told, neither of us was looking forward to the dinner party, although I wasn't in the state of anxiety Cory was. He was convinced Morgan had discussed him with his father, and the whole dinner party was a set-up.

Previously, I might have shared his fears, but somehow, ever since the incident at the river, I'd seen Morgan in a different light. He'd shown me a different side—a far more human, vulnerable side—and it changed the way I felt about him a little. Granted, he hadn't chosen to show me that vulnerability. He neither expected nor wanted my intrusion, and he probably bitterly regretted it. Nevertheless, I'd seen behind his carefully erected screens to the emotional mess lying beneath.

I'd never have believed it, but there it was—Morgan Bentley was a human being, with flaws, fears and faults, who felt pain just like the rest of us. Who would have thought it?

By the time we finally pulled up outside the gate, Cory was in such a state I had to stop to give him a pep talk. He was all over the place, acting so jumpy and guilty that even if I hadn't known anything about what happened, I'd have suspected him of something.

"Cory, you've got to chill out. If you don't, they're going to tear you apart in there. The way you're acting's practically telling them you've done something wrong. Just relax."

"I know. I know that, but . . ."

"But nothing. Morgan's an arse, but he was right in what he said. You were playing with fire, but he pulled you out of it in time. Just chill, relax, and stop acting so bloody guilty."

"I-I'll try, but I am guilty."

"No, you're not . . . just misguided and a bit blinkered. Don't worry about it. Just chill, okay?"

"Okay. I'll try."

I slid out of the car and punched the code into the keypad. As I got back into my seat, the gate began its slow, sinister swing. Cory seemed better, but not much.

When we got to the front door, it was opened by a middle-aged man with immaculate black hair, greying at the temples, dressed in a black suit. For a moment, I thought it was Morgan's father, but then he bowed politely. "Good evening, gentlemen. Please come this way. Mister Bentley and Master Morgan are awaiting your arrival in the study." I almost giggled. I'd thought the butler was Morgan's father.

The study was not the same one we'd worked in last time. This one was larger, grander—and minus the skulls.

There's no way I'd ever mistake Morgan's father for a butler. He oozed confidence and poise. Where Morgan was arrogant, he was self-assured. Where Morgan was over-confident, he was effortlessly debonair. Where Morgan was a bastard, he was a complete bastard.

As we entered, he zeroed in on Cory with a smile that would have put a crocodile to shame.

I ceased to notice what the father was doing as soon as I set eyes on the son. I literally couldn't stop staring. Morgan was gorgeous. I knew that. I'd always known that, and to be honest, I'd pretty much hated him for it from the first moment I'd laid my rather stunned eyes on him.

But tonight . . . tonight, Morgan wasn't gorgeous, Morgan was . . . he was . . . there was no word to describe what he was. He was leaning against the fireplace with a glass of brandy in his hand, wearing the tightest pair of leather trousers I'd ever seen. Not only were they tight, but they were split up the sides and laced, showing off a good two inches of skin on either side.

If that wasn't enough to make me shiver, his top half was encased in a close-fitting, soft leather waistcoat over a white linen shirt. The crisp whiteness set off the inky blackness of his hair, which was loose around his shoulders. He'd even outlined his eyes in black eyeliner. It made the green more vivid than ever. Shit, he was every girl's wet dream. He even had me feeling hot and uncomfortable under that vibrant, electric stare.

"Hello, Matthew," he said in this soft, husky voice that made me suddenly want to leave the room.

For a moment, a kind of electric attraction shot through me, a longing so intense I could almost taste it, almost feel his hands on my body, his lips on . . . abruptly, the attraction turned to anger. What the fuck did he think he was doing? Did he really think if he pulled out all the stops to seduce me, I'd fall into his arms like the rest of the sheep he dragged around in his royal train? Fuck that. Fuck him.

Well, two could play at that game.

I crossed the room on soft feet, keeping my eyes locked with his, and when I was a heartbeat away, I took the brandy glass from his hand, making sure my fingers brushed his. Morgan's eyes widened slightly, and he licked his lips, watching intently as I drained the glass. Still keeping my eyes locked with his, I leaned in close to reach past him and set the glass on the mantle. My resolve almost wavered when I inhaled the sweet, earthy smell of him, which reminded me of the time by the river, but hell . . . this *was* Morgan Bentley, after all.

He was biting his lip when I straightened, and that small show of uncertainty was so cute. I grinned inwardly.

"Well, well, Morgan," I said softly, "you've really outdone yourself tonight." He gave a smile that on someone else I might have thought coy, but on him could only have been contrived. "If I'd known it was fancy dress, I'd have made more effort. Tell me . . . doesn't dressing like a whore embarrass you in front of your father?"

Emotions danced across his features. He wasn't sure how to take what I'd said, and confusion turned to hurt, then to anger. I didn't stay to watch it all, turning my back to him and wandering over to where Mr Bentley Snr was chatting animatedly with Cory. I was relieved to find he was a lot more relaxed than he'd been on arrival.

This, of course, set the tone for the evening. Morgan was cold as iced fire. He attacked, I parried and ended up almost enjoying myself. It seemed to amuse his father, too, because I often caught a certain twinkle in his eyes when he watched our exchanges.

Dinner was an elaborate affair, and if this was the *lesser* dining room, I'd have loved to see the *greater* one. Mr Bentley told us the bigger room could comfortably accommodate up to a hundred guests. I couldn't even imagine a dinner party with that many people.

The table around which we sat would probably have fit thirty people. We only used one end of it, with Mr Bentley taking the place of honour at the head and Cory and I facing Morgan, who initially made a point of talking mainly to Cory, until Cory became more and more drawn into conversation with the senior Mr Bentley.

We were served by waiters, supervised by the butler I'd first mistaken for Morgan's father. Course after course appeared and disappeared, and I thanked my lucky stars my mother had drummed table manners into me, including the correct usage of multiple sets of cutlery. Morgan watched me like a hawk, and I was sure he'd have made an issue of it if I inadvertently used the wrong fork.

"So, Cory, you seem to have been studying the material we provided very thoroughly. I'm impressed. Is there anything in what you've seen so far that's particularly caught your eye?"

Cory almost choked on his trifle. Taking a large gulp of wine, he steadied himself and answered, with tears streaming down his face, which he swiped away in frustration.

"Um . . . no. No, sir. That is . . . everything I've seen so far has caught my eye."

"A very wise answer. Wait until you've had a chance to see the laboratories, equipment, and practices we use before committing yourself. Keeping your options open is very commendable."

"But surely, Cory," Morgan said, in a voice as smooth-as-silk and deadly as a razor blade, "weren't you talking to me the other day about one project that had you particularly hot under the collar?"

Cory flushed and lost the power of speech. I could practically feel his heart beating ten to the dozen. The bastard. The absolute bastard. Surely, he wouldn't. He wouldn't use Cory to get back at me for rejecting his advances? He wouldn't ruin a man's career just because he couldn't get what he wanted? But this was Morgan Bentley. Of course he would — he was a bastard after all.

"I think you're mistaken, Morgan. As I recall, Cory was saying he was fired up about working on the projects at ITM — all of them, not one in particular."

I glared at him, and he smiled, flicking his gaze toward Cory, who'd gone deathly pale and was practically peeing his pants.

"No. I distinctly remember, when he was sitting at the computer terminal in the study, that he mentioned there was one particular project that fascinated him, and he was desperate to find out more about it."

I was practically grinding my teeth, but if he thought I was going to give up that easily, he had another think coming. "I think where you're mistaken is that he did say the one *project* he was most looking forward to was getting the chance to work on the legendary computer system at ITM. Computers are Cory's first love, after all."

"No," Morgan countered smoothly, "I don't think that was it. He was definitely looking at something he'd called up on my terminal. Now, what project was it?" He leaned his chin on his hand, tapping his lips with one finger.

"Morgan, sometimes you can be such a — "

"Boys, boys. I'm sure you find this little . . . game amusing, but for those of us" — he caught Cory's gaze inclusively — "who are not privy to the joke, it's becoming a little tedious. It's hardly fair to spend an entire evening *playing* with each other to the exclusion of everyone else.

"Morgan, while I am pleased your new *friend* clearly has a lot more about him than the previous vapid parasites you've trailed through here, this kind of foreplay is really not appropriate for the dinner table, especially when you have another guest and family to entertain."

I thought Morgan was going to explode. The expression in his eyes was deadly, and the look that passed between Father and son was so full of venom it almost made me gasp aloud.

There was hardly less heat in the glare he shot at me. "For your information, *Father*, as you are woefully incapable of making any judgements on the matter for yourself, Matthew and I are not *friends*. In fact, I believe Matthew's stated opinion of me is — an arrogant, self-absorbed bastard. My opinion of Matthew is best left out of the equation. I tolerate him as he is the only person in my tutorial group who presents any challenge at all, and we've been forced to work together for a presentation at school. He's here as moral support for his friend and nothing more. Oh . . ." He shifted his burning gaze from me — and boy, was I glad about that, because then he couldn't see my slack jaw and shocked expression — to his father, and again the venom was unmistakable in his expression and his voice. "And given the circumstances, I'm sure you'll appreciate why I'm not up to *entertaining* tonight."

Morgan got to his feet, but his father was having none of it. "Sit down, Morgan. You will leave when I say you can leave and not a moment before. I tolerate a lot from you, including turning up for dinner dressed like a whore, but I will not tolerate rudeness in front of guests. Sit down and behave yourself."

Morgan expression was mutinous, and for a moment, I thought he was going to defy his father and walk out. His father must have had the same thought, because he murmured, "Remember, Morgan, you need me now, more than ever. Don't make me regret my recent decisions and leave you to your fate."

Morgan was trembling with rage, his eyes practically producing sparks. "*You* regret . . . *you* . . ." Grinding his teeth, he sank back into his seat and reached for the wine bottle. It was next to me, and I held it out to him. Snatching it from my hand, he tilted it, spilling red wine over the white tablecloth. It spread like a blood stain over the pristine surface.

"How careless of you, Morgan," Mr Bentley purred mildly. Morgan ignored him and proceeded to drink directly from the bottle until it was empty. He then signalled a waiter to bring him another, which he treated with more decorum, drinking from his glass. All the same, he was really throwing them back.

After dinner, we retired to the study for coffee and brandies. I have to admit I was feeling fairly mellow. Mr Bentley was an entertaining host, although I was angry with him for the way he'd treated Morgan. All right, Morgan wasn't my friend, and he was a bastard, and the things he'd said to me at the dinner table hurt, but still . . .

His father had humiliated him, and that wasn't fair. Morgan hadn't spoken a word to me since the incident. Although I kept stealing glances at him, he resolutely kept his focus on the table and didn't speak unless he absolutely had to. I could tell he was simmering and hoped it wasn't me who would take the brunt of the explosion when he blew.

Despite the fact Morgan had been drinking heavily all through dinner, he didn't seem drunk when we entered the study. He went straight to the drinks cabinet and poured himself a generous shot of whisky. Ever the rebel.

As before, Mr Bentley and Cory were instantly absorbed in conversation, and when Cory was led over to the computer and sat in front of the screen, I knew I'd lost him for the rest of the evening. I glanced at Morgan, who was staring morosely into the fire, sipping his drink, and sighed.

Wandering around the room, I came to a cabinet filled with certificates and trophies. I wandered over to take a look. It was fascinating. Apparently, the Bentley family had been geniuses for generations, in every area from music, to art, to sport. There were trophies for cross country running, boxing, swimming, certificates for art, prizes and music scholarships, to name but a few, stretching back centuries.

I noted with interest that Paul Bentley, Morgan's father, had represented his university team at a semi-professional level in polo. A suitable sport, I thought, for such an obviously aristocratic yet restrainedly violent person.

As my gaze roved across the rows of memorabilia, I caught sight of a rather unpretentious but classy little certificate. It drew my attention because it bore the name Morgan Archibald Nathaniel Bentley, and I couldn't help a little chuckle. Peering closer, I could see it was an award certificate for *The Most Promising Young Pianist of the Year 2010*. I remembered I'd heard somewhere Morgan played piano, and there was one in his own private study. Interesting.

"I didn't know you played piano."

"What?" Morgan glanced up, and for a moment, I could see how drunk he was, but he recovered quickly. He really was a master of control.

"I was looking at your award. I didn't know you're such a genius on the piano."

"Morgan could have been accepted as a scholarship student at the *Royal College of Music*. However, his interests lie elsewhere."

Paul Bentley's voice was absolutely neutral. There was no hint of either pride or disappointment. Morgan glared at me. Of course, that spurred me on. I knew he wouldn't be able to play the piano in his drunken state.

"I've never heard you play."

"And you're never likely to."

I was impressed. His words weren't even slurred, and the whisky glass was empty.

"Why not?" Mr Bentley asked. Was there an edge of vindictiveness in his voice?

"What?" Morgan turned to look at his father suspiciously.

"I've always said you don't appreciate your talent enough, Morgan. You should play whenever the opportunity arises. Shall we adjourn to the music room? You can show your friends what you can do."

"No way. Not a chance."

"Come, come now, Morgan. Modesty is a virtue, but letting

a talent like yours atrophy and die through lack of use is a sin. I'm sure your friends would love to hear you play."

"It would be great. Really, Morgan, I'd love it." And I would. This was a win-win situation. If Morgan refused, he'd look like an idiot. If he agreed, he'd play like one. Payback time.

Morgan glared at me and snarled. Then he threw his glass theatrically into the fireplace and stalked toward the door.

"Oh, what's the point in fighting it? Come on, then, if you really must."

To give him his due, he was steady and purposeful as he strode through the hall to a door almost directly opposite. Yet again, I was struck by the sheer size of the house, especially the hall with its enormous stained-glass windows, and the awesome beauty of the rooms. The music room was filled with instruments of all kinds, along with shelves and shelves of records, CD's, books, and piles of music. It smelled like the music room at school, mixed with lavender polish and flowers.

Without pausing, Morgan walked straight to the enormous white grand piano and sat, lifting the lid from the keys. He glanced up at me and cocked his head.

"What kind of music do you like?"

I wondered what he was expecting. All sorts of ideas flew through my head, but in the end, I decided on the truth.

"Jazz. I like jazz."

"Ah," Mr Bentley said, throwing himself into a cream-colored leather armchair. "An excellent choice."

Morgan said nothing, but he closed his eyes and began to play. I'd expected him to make a complete mess of it, to be too drunk to squeeze a tune out. But I was dead wrong.

The piece was most certainly jazz, and not watered down, either. It must have been technically difficult, but it was perfectly executed in every way. Every phrase, every note, every cadence, every riff—as far as I was aware, it was perfect. It was angry, vicious, attacked with passion, and absolutely perfect.

When he finished, he played a classical piece, one I vaguely recognised. It was also aggressive, dark and violent, and equally perfectly executed. Then he moved on to something gentler, almost pensive. All the while, he kept his eyes closed and got lost in the music pouring from his fingers.

As Morgan began to relax, the music changed. Whereas previously it had been technically perfect but somehow cold, now it was far more . . . inspired, passionate. The notes tumbled and rolled, and Morgan swayed as he played.

I watched him. I couldn't help it. I was enraptured by the music and the spectacle of Morgan playing it. He was so caught up in the emotions, the experience, finally relaxed and in his element. His face glowed, his hair flew, and his fingers worked magic. He was a phenomenon . . . simply awesome. I couldn't take my attention off him.

Eventually, the passion died. The music fell silent, and Morgan opened his eyes, seeming a little stunned. Our gazes met. I was grinning like an idiot, and slowly he smiled, lowering his head to gaze up at me coyly, suddenly shy.

"That was awesome, amazing. You're really talented."

"Thank you, I . . ."

"He's off form tonight. The jazz was out of synch, your phraseology was off in *Nocturne,* and the whole thing was peppered with wrong notes and hesitations. You really shouldn't play when you're drunk, Morgan. You don't have the self-control."

Morgan stared at him—his face incredulous. Slowly, his colour drained, and his eyes became feverishly bright. He was controlling himself, but only barely.

"I think perhaps it's time I went to bed."

"Show your friends out on your way, Morgan. I think I'll

stay here and listen to some music for a while." He got to his feet. Taking it as a signal, Cory and I did the same. Mr Bentley took Cory's hand and shook it warmly.

"It's been a pleasure, Cory, a real pleasure. It's rare I find someone with your enthusiasm and natural talent. I'm truly looking forward to working with you. In fact, I'll have my team send over some more papers at the beginning of the week. I think you might find them most stimulating, and they'll help you better prepare to step straight into full productivity when you arrive."

"Thank you, sir," Cory said warmly. I was happy to see him so relaxed and happy, very different to the way he'd been at the beginning of the night. Morgan, on the other hand, was also very different from how he'd been, but in the opposite direction. His hair was mussed, his face slack and his eyes dull. He almost looked ill, and all the triumph I'd felt when I thought to force him to make a fool of himself by playing drunk, evaporated. Suddenly, I felt very sorry for him.

"I thought you played very well."

"Oh, yes. You were awesome." Cory joined in with his eyes wide.

"Father was right. I made way too many mistakes."

"They weren't obvious to me."

"Me either."

"They were to me, and clearly they were to my father also. Can I help if you have no musical discernment?"

"I was trying to be nice, Morgan. There's no need to get snippy with me."

"Isn't there?" He turned his eyes on me, and they made me shiver. "Are you going to tell me you didn't goad me into playing so I'd make a fool of myself because you thought I was drunk?"

"The thought never crossed my mind."

Morgan glared at me. Then despite himself, he had to

smile. "Yeah, right."

"You did better than I expected, considering the amount you had to drink. If it had been me, I'd be completely sloshed."

Morgan chuckled. "I am."

"You still managed to play really well."

"I love to play." He spoke softly and with obvious passion. "The music takes me over. It's almost as if it isn't me playing at all, but something else playing through me." He paused, then shook his head. "Now you'll think I'm completely mad. Just put it down to the alcohol."

"No, I don't think you're mad. I've heard talented musicians and artists say that before, that the creativity takes hold and just carries them. It's the muse."

Morgan laughed. "Yeah . . . the muse. She's a bitch."

"Nice tits, though."

He gave me an uncertain smile. At the door, he paused, one hand on the frame, barring our exit.

"Will you come round tomorrow?" I hesitated, and he rushed on, "To work on the moot. We only have a week."

"Okay, but you had better not dress like that. It's too . . . distracting."

Morgan grinned. "All right. Just plain jeans."

"And a shirt."

"Of course, a shirt. I'll drive you after classes."

"How will I get back?"

"You won't. I'm going to drug you and chain you in the dungeon for my perverted pleasure."

"You have a dungeon?"

He laughed again and moved so we could pass. As he did so, he swayed dangerously, almost falling. I grabbed him and pulled him up against me to steady him. He froze, making no move to pull away, until Cory, apparently also trying to help, albeit clumsily, jerked his arm and sent him crashing back into the door.

"Woah there. Damn, you're strong. I guess I'm more pissed than I thought."

He was grinning, and I wondered. I didn't think he was—not really.

Cory was silent on the trip back, until we were almost home.

"Morgan looked good tonight."

"It was pretty spectacular, wasn't it? I suspect it was all for the benefit of his father."

"I wonder." He spoke softly, his head down, his voice strangely subdued.

"I'm sure of it. You saw how they were. I mean for gods' sake, his father said he was dressed like a whore."

"I wouldn't have gone that far. He was certainly dressed to impress."

"Impress? More likely to shock, I'd say."

"Whatever. It was very impressive. He was very impressive."

I thought back to my first sight of him, standing against the fireplace with the glass of brandy in his hand. It made me unconsciously shiver. Then I thought about the way he played, the way he'd fallen against me at the door . . . the way he smelled, the way he spoke, the way he looked.

"Yes. Yes, he is. I mean was. He *was* very impressive." I was surprised to find myself smiling, and my voice sounded strange, even to my ears.

"Be careful, Matthew. Please, be careful. Morgan Bentley is more than a bastard—he's a dangerous bastard, just like his father. I'd hate for you to get hurt by someone like him."

"Hurt? By Morgan? No way. I'd never let him close enough to hurt me."

"Wouldn't you? Haven't you?"

"What are you trying to say, Cory?" He seemed so sad, so

heartbroken, and it tugged at me. I couldn't understand what was wrong with him. He'd been buoyant and happy. Now suddenly he'd completely crashed.

"I saw the way you were looking at him . . . and the way he was looking at you."

"The way I was . . . what are you talking about? What way was I looking at him?"

"Like you were starving, and he was a feast. He was looking at you the same way. All that dressing up and stuff . . . he did it for you. You know that, right?"

"I think you must have bumped your head somewhere, Cory. You're delusional. That never happened, any of it. He dressed like that to piss off his father, and the only way he was looking at me was as if he wanted to kill me. We've been through this before. There's no way Morgan's interested in me, not in that way. And I'm certainly not interested in him. I don't even like him."

"Promise me you're not falling in love with him."

"What? You're insane, Cory, truly insane. Do you know that? I'd never fall in love with Morgan Bentley. For one thing, he's a man, and I am not gay, and for another . . . well . . . he's Morgan Bentley, and Morgan Bentley . . . is a bastard," we both chorused and dissolved into laughter, although I was still aware of Cory giving me veiled glances for the rest of the journey home.

I smiled to myself. He must be mad. It was ludicrous, ridiculous. Falling in love with Morgan? He may as well ask me if I'd been dancing on the moon. It was impossible, stupid. He should know better. That was just . . . the smile faded as I saw again, in my mind's eye, the flickering fire reflected in the golden brandy, the brooding presence, the expression in Morgan's awesome green eyes. By the time we got home, I was frowning.

CHAPTER SIX

I was surprisingly nervous the next day, as I waited for Morgan at the university gate. Not only was he late, but when he appeared, he was surrounded by his usual entourage. He waved when he saw me, ignoring the fact everyone else scowled.

"You don't mind if we hang around with some friends for a bit before we get down to business, do you?" he asked, his arm around his drippy girlfriend.

"Hell no, especially if there's more of that excellent brandy we were drinking last night." I wanted to scream at him, to ask him what the hell he was playing at. The last thing I wanted—the very *last* thing I wanted—was to have to hang around with those losers. They all hated me, and I hated them. What was he doing? Of course it wasn't okay. But what could I say?

We piled into two cars, and I found myself sitting between rich but stupid dude number one and beautiful but stupid girl number two. Beautiful but stupid girl number one, aka Charlotte, was sitting in the front next to Morgan. She turned as we drove and made an attempt to smile at me.

"You must be very excited to be working with Morgan on this project thingie."

Project thingie? What was this girl doing at university? I'd have been surprised if she met the entry qualifications. Ah no, wait, of course, she had the highest qualifications of all— money and connections. I nodded.

"Absolutely ecstatic."

Glancing up, I caught Morgan's eye in the mirror. He wasn't smiling and mouthed, "Sorry." I grinned.

I have to admit that, despite my original reservations, I actually had fun that afternoon. Morgan's friends weren't as bad as I'd thought. Morgan had a games room, and we hung around playing computer games and pool, with refreshments provided from his seemingly inexhaustible and ever-accessible kitchen and bar.

The only blots on the landscape were the drugs and the constant reminders I wasn't from their world. To be fair, they were never deliberate or malicious—they were just matters of natural conversation, which flowed between the others and stalled with me. For example . . .

"Have you thought about what you're going to wear to the Riverside Ball? It's a bummer that it's a masquerade. We have to wear silly face masks, and all black and white."

"Who are you taking, Roger?"

"Of course, Charlotte will be going with Morgan."

"What about you, Matthew? Oh. Of course. I'm so sorry, I didn't think."

Then a bit later someone asked, "Is anyone else going to Aspen for Christmas?"

"No, I'm spending it on Daddy's estate. My fourth stepmother wants to do the family thing."

"Do you ski at Christmas, Matthew? Oh. Of course. Silly me."

"Did you hear Angel and Marcus got together? Who'd ever have thought?"

"Well, I always knew Angel was a bit . . . well, you know . . . but Marcus!"

"That whole affair was awful, wasn't it?"

"I know. Imagine someone actually trying to hurt Angel. He's such a sweetheart. It just goes to show you never can tell with people. What do you think, Matthew?"

What was I supposed to say to that? I just shrugged, and the girl giggled and hugged me before weaving off somewhere, saying, "Oh, sorry, Matthew. I keep forgetting. You don't know them, do you? You're not like us."

None of it was malicious. At least I didn't think it was. Of course, it could have been. They could all have constantly been laughing at me behind their hands, and I wouldn't have known because it was all very much an *in* joke and I was most certainly not *in*.

Apart from that, everyone was charming, open and friendly. Even Charlotte turned out to be not as empty-headed as I thought. I did notice, though, there seemed to be something of an atmosphere between Charlotte and Morgan, and halfway through the afternoon, they vanished.

By this time, I was half-drunk and having fun, so I barely noticed them leave. It was also about this time the drugs came out in earnest. Almost as soon as we arrived, someone lit a joint, and I shared in the commonality of passing it around. I'd smoked spliffs before, and it helped me relax and begin to let my hair down.

However, when they laid out the paraphernalia for snorting coke and began cutting lines, I bailed and wandered out into the garden. It was a miserable day, dark and cloudy but not actually raining. It wasn't long, though, before I wished I hadn't left my coat inside.

Hearing voices, I headed toward the sound, only to be almost knocked off my feet by Charlotte, all but running around the corner of the house. She steadied herself against me and brushed me down. She'd been crying, but not much.

"I'm so terribly sorry, Matthew. I wasn't looking where I was going. I'm leaving now. It was terribly nice to meet you. We shall have to do it again soon."

I had no chance to ask her *do what* because she gave me a brief kiss on the cheek, barely a brush of her lips, then turned away. However, as I was about to do the same, she turned back and grabbed my arm.

"Do be careful. I think you're a nice boy, and Morgan isn't himself right now. I don't know what it is, but . . . you're not part of this world, Matthew, and I wouldn't want to see you hurt by the games we play. I like you, so just . . . be careful."

I was completely stunned, caught off-balance, and I shook my head, bewildered. "Be careful of what?"

"Of Morgan, Matthew. Be careful of Morgan." She released my arm and was gone.

I stood where I was for a moment, considering whether or not I should go back. However, I thought about what was going on in the games room and really didn't want to be part of that, so I continued around the corner. Morgan was leaning against the wall, smoking a cigarette, one foot up. He was staring into the distance with a strange expression on his face.

"Did you have a fight with Barbie?"

Morgan turned his head slowly. He seemed slightly unfocused. "Who?"

I laughed. "Oh sorry, that's what Cory and I call Charlotte. Naughty, I know."

His lips twitched. "So, am I Ken?"

"Gods no. You're far too dark and dangerous to be Ken."

His smile was a little more expansive this time.

"So, did you have a fight?"

"What's it to you?"

"Nothing. It's just she ran into me and almost knocked me off my feet. She seemed upset."

"Do you care?"

I shrugged. "Not really. Just making conversation."

He turned and leaned back against the wall. "We broke up."

"Oh, sorry."

He shrugged. "It wasn't going anywhere. We've both known for a while."

"It doesn't surprise me. You never stay with anyone for

very long. She was the longest so far."

He glanced at me sharply. "So now you're an expert on my love life?" There wasn't any malice in his voice. He just sounded tired . . . defeated, almost.

"Not really. I just notice things."

We were silent for a while before he asked, "What are you doing out here anyway?"

"Your friends are turning the house into a drug den. It's just not my style."

Morgan sighed and flicked away his cigarette. "Mine either. I did try to ask them not to, but no one ever listens." He sounded tired again. "Do you want to do some work?"

"What about your friends?"

"Give them half an hour, and they'll forget all about me. They'll wander off eventually."

"Isn't that . . . I don't know . . . rude?"

"So is taking drugs in my house as soon as I turn my back, even though they know I don't like it."

"True."

He smiled at me then, a proper smile, and led me back to the study where we spent an enjoyable couple of hours sparring and got a lot of work done.

"Are you nervous about Monday?"

"Nervous? Why would I be?"

"We're doing it in front of everyone, arguing against two of the keenest legal minds in the school, maybe the country."

Morgan laughed. "The better the competition, the bigger the challenge and the greater the opportunity to shine."

"Or to be left looking like a complete fool."

"We won't be left looking like fools, Matthew. You know that."

It must have been nice to have so much confidence. Right now, it was impossible to believe he was ever uncertain about anything. "Hmm . . ."

"Are you hungry?"

"A little."

"How'd you like to get out of here? We could grab a *McDonalds*, or I could take you somewhere nicer."

"Um." There was something about the way he said it that made me feel somehow uncomfortable, and I shook my head. "Nah, *McDonald's* is cool. We can get a drive-through. It's getting late, and I need to get back. I have work to do for tomorrow."

"Oh. Okay." He looked disappointed, and I felt a bit mean, given he'd just broken up with his girlfriend and all, but . . . to be truthful, that's what made me most uncomfortable, especially after my conversation with Cory. Could it be . . . I shook myself impatiently and stopped feeling guilty about disappointing Morgan.

"What about your friends? Are you sure they'll be okay if you just abandon them?"

"I'd be surprised if they're still here. Even if they are, they'll be unconscious. They'll just wander off when they wake up."

Just as he'd suspected, the little red sports car I'd noticed parked on the drive had gone.

We drove back to town in silence, save for discussing our order at *McDonald's*. We ate in the car and stared out of the windows at life passing us by. It was raining, so Morgan had the hood up. With the darkness of the cloud-stuffed sky outside, it made the car a warm, dry cave. Morgan turned off the windscreen wipers, and I watched the rain running down the window.

"Rain makes me sad."

I almost jumped at the sound of his voice.

"It does? Why?"

"It makes me think of tears and —" He stopped, as if afraid he was going to say too much.

"And?"

"Nothing. Never mind. I just don't like rain, especially when I'm in a car."

"I do. It makes me feel calm and peaceful. I love that I'm warm and dry when everything outside the bubble isn't. It makes me feel safe. Somehow everything is cosy."

Morgan laughed. "You're insane . . . but in a nice way."

I grinned, stuffing fries into my mouth. Morgan ate delicately. I could never imagine him stuffing anything into that finely shaped mouth. He nibbled. He didn't consume. Today, he didn't even touch his burger, only half the chips and a few onion rings. I watched him screw up the bag with the remains of the meal and wondered if he was upset, if breaking up with Charlotte had hit him harder than I'd thought.

"Do you want to talk about it?"

He jumped half out of his skin and turned burning eyes on me. I almost wanted to shrink away from him, but I forced myself not to. No way was I going to show a moment's weakness to Morgan Bentley.

"What do you know? I mean . . . what do you mean? Talk about what?"

"Charlotte. There's no reason to get mad with me. I just thought you might be upset and want to talk about it."

He immediately relaxed. "Sorry. I'm kind of touchy at the moment. No thanks, I'm fine about that. As I said, it's been coming for a while, and to be honest, it was a relief. She's a nice girl, but she's not the most stimulating company, and she's really possessive. Besides, I . . ." Again, he caught himself in the process of being about to say too much and bit his lip, letting his head fall forward, so his hair curtained off his face.

"I like your hair."

"What?" His head shot up, and his eyes were wide. I froze with my hand half raised to touch it. What the hell was I thinking? What was I doing?

"I . . . er . . . I mean . . . you know . . . the blue and stuff. It's freaky, but I like it."

Morgan jerked his face away, clearly embarrassed, and stared out of the window. "Thanks."

"Why do you do it? I mean the whole thing? It gets a little over the top sometimes, and I don't suppose it goes down too well with . . . people."

"My father, you mean?" His face had gone dark, and his mouth was a compressed line. I thought he was angry with me and it started me thinking. *What a jerk. He shouldn't do it if he doesn't want comments on it.* Then he spoke again, quietly.

"I don't know. I suppose it started because I wanted to be noticed. I didn't care how I was noticed, as long as I was. It didn't work. At least, not how I wanted it to, but, well, it felt comfortable after a while. Sometimes . . . sometimes I feel . . . dark on the inside, so why not reflect that on the outside." He turned and grinned at me, his eyes sparkling. "Besides, I like to shock."

"Oh, you do that. You certainly do that."

We shared a moment of comfortable companionship. Then I had to go and spoil it. Me and my big mouth.

"You know, sometimes you can be all right, Morgan. Why is it that most of the time you're a complete bastard?"

"What? Is that what you think of me? That I'm a complete bastard? Why? What have I ever done to you to make you think that?"

Uh oh. I should have shut up right then, but of course, I didn't. "It's not what you do to me, although you're a jerk to me sometimes. Like Saturday night for example, with all the shit about Cory with your dad . . . but usually it's just the way you are with everyone. It's like you have to have everything, then show how little you value it — things, people, the way you look, your intelligence. You use everything you have, everything you've been blessed with, to put other people down."

"I don't understand what you mean."

"Well, take all the Morgan fans, for example. The school is full of them, boys and girls. They follow you around with goofy expressions on their faces. They vie with each other for your attention, and you soak it all up. You bask in it and show off to it. You play to the crowd, then just walk away. You use people to stroke your ego, then just walk away. And you don't care if you walk all over them to do it."

"Is that what you think I do?"

"It *is* what you do, Morgan. I've watched you do it over and over and over. You don't care about anyone, but yourself and you use people for what they can give you, then drop them."

"I . . ." He seemed stunned. Again, I really should have stopped.

"You're the same with relationships. Do you have any idea how many hearts you've broken . . . and not just broken . . . trashed? Nothing ever lasts for you. You don't value anything you have."

"That's enough, Matthew. I get the idea. You should have told me you felt this way about me and I wouldn't have . . . I . . ." He leaned forward and started the car. His voice sounded choked, and I suddenly realised what I'd done.

"I didn't mean it like it sounded. I'm sorry I was so harsh."

"No, you're right," he said as he pulled out of the parking space. "That's the thing. You're absolutely right. I do treat people like shit. It's the way I am. When I try to reach out to people, it always blows up in my face, so I really don't know why I bother anymore. I'm not a people person, and I suppose . . . I suppose I'm not a very nice person, certainly not an easy . . . I'm not a good . . . never mind."

I didn't know what to say to him. He sounded as if he was

on the verge of tears, but his face was hard and set, his eyes like chips of glass, fixed on the road. I felt as if I'd crossed a line and it had turned into a barrier between us, a barrier I couldn't hope to cross, so what was the point in trying?

We pulled up outside the complex, and I struggled to find something to say. I didn't just want to get out of the car and leave everything up in the air.

"I'm sorry, Morgan. I didn't—"

"Don't worry about it. I think we have enough material to work separately on this for a while. Perhaps we should get together on the weekend, just to draw in loose ends and practice our presentation."

"Okay."

The barrier was impenetrable now, a huge rift, a chasm between us. I turned to get out of the car. I had nothing else to say. Morgan was silent, but as I turned to say my last goodbye, he leaned across the seat.

"You might not want to, as you hate me so much, but I'm having a party on Saturday night. It was supposed to have been a birthday party for Charlotte." He shrugged. "It's too late to call it off, and I don't really want to so . . . it would be cool if you and Cory could come."

"I-I . . . um . . . I suppose that would be okay. Sure we'll come."

"Cool. Be there about seven-thirty, then?"

"Okay. See you Saturday."

I stared after the car as it drove off. What the hell was that all about? I'd just insulted him and clearly hurt him deeply . . . and he invited me to a party? What kind of shit was that?

Cory narrowed his eyes at me when I told him, and I sighed. "Yeah, yeah, I know what you're thinking . . . and you're wrong."

"Am I?"

"Absolutely. For gods' sake, I'd just told him exactly what I thought of him. I told him he's a bastard."

"And he invited you to a party?"

"Well, yeah. I thought that was a bit odd. I mean, why would he ask someone who just insulted him to a party? Unless he's intending to get his own back on me? Hmm, I didn't think of that. Maybe I won't go."

"I think you're wrong. I think he asked you so he could prove you wrong." Cory looked tragically sad, and I had to stop myself laughing. That would have been cruel, so I forced my face and voice to remain level.

"I know what you think. You think he's got the hots for me, and that's just silly."

"Is it? Are you sure?"

"Absolutely. There was nothing like that. Nothing at all. Besides, it won't do him any good even if he does. I don't know how many times I have to tell you, Cory, I'm not gay. And if I was, then it would be with you. I mean, look how cute you are." I ruffled his hair, making him blush, and hurriedly smoothed it down again. "And I wouldn't even have to take you out on a date and waste time and money courting you, because we already live together."

Cory was clearly uncomfortable, and I almost said something. He was too introspective lately. All this nonsense with ITM had not been good for him.

"Hey, it's cool, buddy. There is not, will not, and cannot be anything between Morgan and me. Okay?"

"Just be careful, that's all."

"I'm always careful."

"So, are we going to the party?"

"We? I don't remember mentioning you're invited."

"Oh." He looked crushed, and I had to laugh.

"Of course you were invited . . . specifically. Hey! Maybe it's you Morgan has his sights on."

Cory blushed even more deeply. "Yeah, right!"

I pushed him, and he pushed me back, and before we knew it, we were tickling the hell out of each other and laughing like idiots.

Morgan basically ignored me for the rest of the week, except when he was forced into my company. When that happened, he only acknowledged by mocking me or making sarcastic comments. There were times when I wished the floor would open up and swallow me, and other times when I wished it would open up and swallow him.

He was acting strangely, far more withdrawn and isolated than usual, except when he was taunting me. I put it down to the fact he'd split up with Charlotte, who was very much giving him the cold shoulder. Or maybe I'd bruised his ego, not that I thought it would have affected him much.

Nevertheless, I caught him on a number of occasions staring off into the distance with a frown on his face, or sitting alone somewhere with his head in his hands, as if he had the weight of the world on his shoulders. He looked as though he hadn't been sleeping too well, either. I wondered if the pressure of the moot was getting to him more than he'd admit. I never asked him. I knew he wouldn't have told me anyway.

I don't know how many times I decided I wasn't going to the party. I was absolutely not going. Definitely. Certainly. Positively *not*. So how come at seven-thirty on Saturday, Cory and I were punching digits into the gate box again?

This time there were lots of cars parked outside. I counted seven, and that didn't include Morgan's, which was probably in a garage somewhere. The sound of laughter drifted to us from somewhere, and we hesitated on the doorstep.

I'd almost decided to turn around and go home when the door opened, and Morgan stood there, apparently somewhat tipsy, and of course, drop-dead gorgeous. His usually smooth, silky hair was artfully messed up, and although he was more conservatively dressed than he had been on the previous occasion, black leather and white linen were prominent, as was heavy eye makeup.

He didn't say anything when he opened the door. He simply stood there, staring at us with a strange smouldering expression. He was holding a cigarette in one hand and a full glass of something deeply spiritual in the other. Taking a long drag on his cigarette, he moved out of the way, motioning us to pass, without saying a word.

We both hesitated for a moment, then shuffled into the hall. Morgan closed the door and stood with his back to it, still not saying anything. I wondered if he'd been taking drugs. He looked ill, but that could have been the eye makeup.

Finally, he waved a hand toward the back of the house. "Make yourselves at home. The food's that way." Then he turned and disappeared along one of the corridors off the hall. We didn't like to follow him after he'd specifically directed us elsewhere, so we headed off, searching for the food.

For the rest of the evening, we only saw Morgan very briefly, now and again. He was always draped over someone, either kissing or sharing a joint or doing something intimate. He seemed intent on working his way around everyone—boys, girls, he didn't care, and neither did they.

I didn't fit in. Even Cory was having a better time than I was. As before, Morgan's friends weren't unfriendly, but they were so . . . different. They knew the same people, moved in the same circles, and we were very much on the outside. That bothered me, but Cory was oblivious. He soaked up the attention, and he got plenty of it, in the way of bored people with an interesting new curio. I lost him after an hour and drifted aimlessly . . . alone.

CHAPTER SEVEN

I was sick and tired of this. This wasn't a party. This was some kind of fucked-up wake. Where was the life? Where was the energy? Where were the people enjoying themselves, letting their hair down?

Most of them had already passed out, and those who hadn't were either having sex, trying to have sex, lying around on the verge of passing out after having sex, or taking drugs in various ways, possibly as a substitute for sex.

I couldn't find Cory, so I wandered out into the garden, with every intention of leaving as soon as I found him. I hadn't seen Morgan for ages, and he hadn't spoken to me all night. I was thoroughly pissed off at him and couldn't wait to get the hell out of there.

It was a fine night, but cold. The sky was absolutely clear, and stars twinkled overhead, mirrored by fairy lights woven into the trees surrounding the patio. The chill was lessened somewhat by patio heaters, but their warmth dissipated as soon as you left their circle of radiance.

A few people were lounging around, engaging in illegal activities, and I couldn't be bothered with them. The whole thing bored me. Grumbling to myself, and cursing Cory, I wandered out of the warmth of the patio and onto a path leading around the side of the house.

The air began to grow fragrant with smells I recognised — lilac, lavender, sage, thyme. I must have been heading toward the herb garden, which would be near the kitchen. I smiled. If there were no accessible computers around, Cory would gravitate toward his second love—food.

I followed the path through some bushes, and as I stepped out into the moonlight among the sage bushes, a figure loomed to my left, scaring the crap out of me.

"Fuck!"

"I didn't have you down for the nervous type, Matthew," a voice purred from the darkness.

I groaned inwardly. I'd have known that soft, supercilious voice anywhere. Bloody typical.

"Fuck off, Morgan."

"That was a bit rude, considering you're a guest in my home."

"Yeah, well, get over it."

"You really don't like me, do you?" The voice was absolutely emotionless.

I turned toward him and looked at him for the first time. He was lounging against the trunk of a tree, smoking a cigarette, his hair loose around his shoulders. If it had been someone else, anyone else, I'd have thought him devastatingly handsome. No, not handsome—beautiful. He blended with the shadows, and even moonlight couldn't leech all the colour from his eyes. But I didn't think that. I definitely didn't think that, not even for a moment. What I thought was—what a poser!

"Genius points to the man in black."

Morgan pushed himself off from the tree and flicked away his cigarette. At that point, I so wanted to turn and leave, but he was, after all, the host, and I was brought up not to be a complete tosser, not like Morgan.

When he was a few steps away, he stopped and just stood, staring at me silently.

"What?" I was getting irritated with the whole act, and I just wanted to find Cory and go home.

"Why don't you like me?"

"Because you're an utter bastard and you treat everyone like shit. You think you're better than everyone else and give them all the brush off, even those poor sods who worship the ground you walk on. Everywhere you go, you leave behind a trail of emotional destruction, and you don't even see it. You have everything and care about nothing. You're a waste of space, Morgan, and I've no idea why you even invited me here. You've been avoiding me all night, and while that's just fine with me, it's boring me now, so I just want to find my friend and go home."

As I spoke, Morgan's eyes widened and his lips compressed into a tight line, slashing across the pale oval of his face. When I finished, he was silent for a moment.

"Say it as it is, why don't you?" His voice was slightly unsteady, but I barely noticed.

"Yeah, well, it's about time someone did. You walk over everyone, Morgan. You're like a vampire, squeezing what you can out of people, then casting them aside. Well, I'm through being squeezed. I'm out of here while I at least have a shred of self-respect left." I was about to turn and walk away when I had another thought. I may as well get it all out there, while I was at it.

"You have everything, Morgan, everything—money, looks, a fucking incredible home, a brain that's so sharp it isn't even funny—but it's not enough for you. None of it is. You have to have everyone adoring you, fawning at your feet, bowing and scraping, and even that's not enough. You're desperate for attention, but when you get it, you throw it back in our faces. You're so up yourself."

"Is that what you think? Is that really what you think of me?"

I'd expected him to be angry, but he wasn't. In fact, from the sound of his voice, if I hadn't known better, I'd have thought he was on the verge of tears.

"What else am I supposed to think?"

Morgan bit his lip, then turned his face away. Suddenly, he wasn't the perfectly poised, self-assured, answer-for-everything bastard I'd known. His shoulders slumped, his head drooped, and he looked like a lost boy.

"Morgan?"

He started at the sound of my voice. When he raised his gaze to me, his eyes seemed to be burning with fury. There, at last, was the anger I'd been expecting, but it was different now because, just for a moment, I'd seen something else, something vulnerable under the hard shell.

"You think I have everything? Really? Yeah . . . I have money, a nice home, flashy cars, designer clothes. I have a good brain, and I play the piano. I do a lot of other things, too, but I don't share them. That's the rub, you see. I don't share anything, with anyone." He made a sweeping gesture with his hand. "All these things, bricks and mortar, twisted metal, pieces of paper. You can't have a conversation with them. They can't hold you when you're scared or unhappy. They can't . . . they can't kiss you."

His voice faded as he spoke, and I was left staring at him with my mouth open.

"Are you seriously trying to tell me you're lonely? Fuck that. You have people around you all the time. You were going out with the hottest girl in the school, for the love of the gods. You always go out with the hottest people in school. You could have your pick of any of them. So don't give me that bull about not having anyone to speak to, to hold, to kiss." I mocked him.

He winced as if I'd hit him and shook his head.

"How the fuck could I ever have thought you'd understand? You've always hated me. You've always treated me as if I was . . . as if . . . do you really think I have friends? Do you think any of those people are friends? They hang around with me because it gives them something — status, position, drugs, whatever. It certainly isn't because they're interested in me, not me as a person. They don't care about me. Sometimes I don't think they even see me. No one does. They just see what they think ought to be here."

"But . . . but Charlotte . . ."

"Charlotte is an empty-headed bimbo. She didn't even care about my money. All she cared about was that I'm pretty, and I made her look good."

"You don't have any friends? Real friends? None at all?" He shook his head. "Sucks."

"Yeah. It sure does."

"What about your family?"

"What family? My mother died when I was thirteen. My father's hardly ever home. I was brought up by nannies, but I'm too old for that now, so I'm pretty much completely on my own."

"Double sucks."

Morgan didn't seem to hear what I said. He wasn't talking to me anymore. He was just talking. "When my father's here, we don't talk. We have dinner together, at opposite ends of the table, and never speak beyond *pass the peas*. Although lately . . ." He shrugged, thinking better of what he was about to say. He seemed to come out of his trance and notice me.

"Look, this is very sad and all, but you should have thought about it before you turned into a complete bastard. Loosen up a bit sometimes. Try treating people like people now and again, and you might actually find someone who likes you."

"If I did that . . . would you like me?"

"Probably not."

"Why not?"

I shrugged. I was bored with the conversation now, bored with the situation, bored with him. I wasn't the slightest bit interested in the way the moonlight was making his hair so shiny, or the way the breeze was lifting the ends of it and fanning it out around his shoulders, or how green his eyes were, or . . .

I shook myself mentally. What the hell was I thinking? "We're just too different, Morgan. I'm a real person, and you're—"

"I'm what?"

"Nothing. It doesn't matter."

"I'm not a real person? Then what am I?"

"I don't know. What are you? Do you know?"

He stared at me for a moment, then shook his head. "I guess not."

After staring at me for another long moment, Morgan shook his head again and turned away. Before he could take more than a step, he swayed and sank to his knees. I groaned inwardly. Great. Just what I needed. If Morgan passed out, I couldn't just leave him here in the garden. He'd probably freeze to death.

With a sigh, I crouched next to him and put a hand on his shoulder. His head was bowed, his hair shutting him away from me, from everything.

"Are you all right?"

"No."

"Have you had too much to drink?"

"No. I haven't had enough. I'm still conscious."

I smiled at that one. "Okay, let me put it another way. Are you pissed?"

Morgan raised his head. "If I'm not, then I wasted a hell of a lot of money on that load of crap I've been tipping down my neck all night."

This time I groaned aloud. "Great. Just great. Get up, you arse. You can't stay out here."

"Why not?"

"You'll freeze to death."

"I thought you hated me."

"I do, but I still don't want you to freeze to death."

Morgan stared at me, the light from the house falling on his face, making his eyes dazzlingly green.

"Do you care?"

"Only about having to explain your body to the police. Come on, get up."

He wasn't making any effort to get up, so I slung his arm over my shoulder, put mine around his waist, and heaved. After a brief struggle, I got Morgan to his feet, but he was so unsteady he almost pulled me back down with him.

"Hey, steady on. Be careful. If you fall again, I'm leaving you here."

"Would you?"

Our gazes met, and his were so . . . different. I found myself shaking my head. "No. No, I wouldn't leave you here." He just stared at me. I wanted to turn away, but there was something there. Was it vulnerability? Was it fear? Or was it something else?

"Ah, shit." Morgan broke the connection, turning abruptly away from me and pulling out of my arms. I felt cold where he'd been pressed against me.

Morgan was on the ground again. By the sound of it, he was being sick, horribly sick. I hated sickness, so I stayed the hell away until he was finished.

"You okay down there?"

He was kneeling on the ground, bent over, hugging himself. He groaned.

"No."

"Serves you right. You shouldn't have got so pissed."

"Thanks for the tip." Now there was the sarcastic git I knew so well.

"Get the hell up and go to bed."

"No."

"Oh, for fuck's sake, just get up, Morgan."

"No."

I was getting really angry now. It was bloody freezing, away from the patio heaters and the warmth of the house. I was shivering, and all I wanted to do was find Cory and go home.

"Get the fuck up, Morgan. Just do it. I'm cold, and I want to go inside and get warm."

"Then go." His voice was soft and slurred. It made me furious.

"I told you, I am *not* going to leave you here to freeze to death, even though you deserve it. Now, will you please get up?"

"No."

"Why not?" I snapped, getting even more irritated.

"Because I can't."

"What do you mean you can't?"

"Don't feel so good." He was decidedly slurred now, and his words were almost a moan.

"Well yeah, tell me something I don't know. But you still can't stay here all night."

"Like you care."

"Oh, for fuck's sake. You're really sorry for yourself tonight, aren't you? Well, whoop de do. You're right, I don't care. But if I leave you here, I'll feel guilty when I see them carting you off in a body bag on the news tomorrow. So you're going to get your drunken arse up off the floor and let me get you into the house, or I'm going to kick you until you do."

"Yes, sir." Morgan chuckled and tried to get to his feet, but he was right, he couldn't, and the effort made him throw up again. I sighed and sat down with my back to a tree, watching him until he'd finished being sick. He slumped sideways, dragging himself around to half sit, half lie on the ground, facing me.

"I feel like shit."

"You look like shit. You have sick all over your shirt."

He shrugged. "I have other shirts." Then he groaned and lay down on the ground. I groaned, too, inwardly.

"Oh no, you don't. No going to sleep in the dirt or I'm never going to get you inside. I swear I meant it when I said I'd kick you."

With some difficulty, I managed to get him back on his feet. Despite the smell, I found it felt good to have my arms full of Morgan. No, not a good thing to be thinking. *Just remember how much you hate him, Matthew. Just remember what a bastard he is, what a first-class —*

"Matthew?" he whispered indistinctly.

"Yeah?"

"Thanks."

"Er . . . no problem. Let's just get in the house, yeah?"

"I'm cold."

"Of course you're cold. You've been lying on the ground with nothing on but a thin silk shirt."

Step by step, we managed to get to the kitchen. The heat hit me in a wave of welcome warmth as I opened the door.

Everyone looked up as I hauled Morgan over the threshold. It was a big kitchen, a very big kitchen. A familiar face appeared from around a set of shelves.

"Cory. I've been searching everywhere for you."

"Seems like you found someone else."

"He's pissed. He almost passed out in the garden. Gods, it's freezing out there. He would have frozen to death."

"Yeah, right." Cory gave me what he liked to call his *knowing look,* and I made a face at him.

"Jokes later. Right now, we need to get Morgan to bed . . . and no jokes about that."

By now, Morgan was completely out of it, barely able to keep on his feet. I was angry with him again.

A middle-aged woman came bustling down the kitchen, fussing.

"What on earth's been going on here? Oh no, not again."

Cory and I exchanged glances . . . again?

The woman pushed back Morgan's hair and lifted his face. He mumbled something at her, but it wasn't coherent enough for anyone to understand.

"What have you gone and done to yourself now? Why do you do this?" There was such sorrow and tenderness in her voice that I was completely taken aback and totally unprepared for what happened next. The woman turned to me, waving a wooden spoon in my face.

"Just what the hell do you think you were doing, letting him get in this state? You're supposed to be his friends. Friends? Hah! Friends do not let this happen to each other. Friends take care of each other."

For a moment, I was speechless, gawping at the angry woman and the waving spoon.

"Er . . . I'm not . . . not . . ."

"Oh, I'm sure you have plenty of excuses. You always do. I'm sick of the lot of you. Just because you have money, you think people don't count. Well here, in my kitchen, they do. So thank you very much for seeing Morgan back where he belongs. Now, help him sit down in the chair, then get the hell out of here. Go back to whatever you were doing. I'm sure it's so much more fun than helping a *friend*."

"Hang on a minute. I-I'm not —"

"It's all right, Mrs Wight, Matthew's with me."

The formidable Mrs Wight froze and peered at me. She glanced at Cory, then back to me, blinking. "You? You're Matthew?" she asked incredulously.

Suddenly, I was unaccountably uncomfortable. "I don't know what Cory's been telling you —"

"Not a thing, bro," he said, sounding as confused as I was.

"Then who . . ." She must have seen my eyes widen because she became all brisk efficiency.

"All right, you boys, take Morgan up to his room and make sure he's comfortable. I'll check on him later." It was on the tip of my tongue to say no, but Cory was already ducking under Morgan's arm, so I really didn't have much choice but to do the same. I was about to say I didn't know the way when Mrs Wight motioned to one of the kitchen staff. "Ben, show them to Morgan's room, please. Take them the back way, away from those gormless louts. I'll get Forbes to clean up the mess."

The young man, Ben, nodded and stood by, waiting while we hauled Morgan to his feet. He roused a little and managed to stand and walk, although he appeared dazed.

Ben led us along corridors and up two flights of steps, all of which were more like a hotel or a hospital than a home. Then he opened a door, and we emerged onto a landing that made my jaw drop in shock.

To one side, an ornate marble banister was all that stood between us and the cavernous hall beneath. Just overhead, the enormous chandelier glittered on a slightly convex, dark blue ceiling. It hadn't been quite so impressive from below. On the wall opposite, the two enormous arched windows twinkled, their stained-glass dulled by the artificial light. Between the windows was the oil painting I'd noticed before. I could now see clearly it was of a very severe-looking man, with grey hair and cold green eyes. There was something about the expression in the eyes that made me shiver.

Ben paused in front of one of the doors lining the wall, and when we caught up, he bowed to me. Yeah, he actually bowed. Then he disappeared back the way he'd come. I hesitated, but Cory reached for the handle and opened the door. Darkness spilled out and wrapped itself around us.

"Can you manage him on your own for a minute?"

"Sure."

We leaned Morgan against the wall, and Cory slipped out from under his arm, disappearing inside. Moments later, the room flooded with light. Shit. It was enormous, bigger than the entire ground floor of my house.

For a moment, Morgan was forgotten as I stared in awe at his room. It was obviously a man's room. Everything was black, grey, and white, and the furniture was heavy oak and old. The bed was massive, a carved oak four-poster with black velvet curtains pulled back and tied to the posts.

In the middle of one of the walls was a huge marble fireplace with an unlit fire set out in the grate, surmounted by a framed oil painting of stormy seas and lightning-streaked clouds. Other pieces of art dotted around the room had similar themes—brooding skies and storms. It wasn't the most cheerful room I'd been in, but it was far and away the most opulent.

There were few signs this room was occupied by a young person. There were no clothes on the floor, draped over the back of chairs, or lying on top of cupboards. There were no discarded CD cases on the floor or any of the other usual debris. The only place in the whole room not as neat as a new pin was a desk in the corner, which housed a state-of-the-art computer and was strewn with papers.

Cory, of course, immediately drifted toward the computer, but I wasn't going to let him get drawn in, or I wouldn't be able to regain his attention for hours.

"Cory, a little help here?"

"Oh, sorry. It's just . . . never mind."

Casting longing glances toward the computer, he turned and headed back toward me. Taking up his previous station, he helped me haul Morgan across the room and deposit him on the bed. The room was warm, and so we didn't bother with the covers. We were about to leave when Morgan reached out with surprising speed and accuracy and grabbed my wrist.

"Get off, Morgan. Just go to sleep and try not to choke to death." I was snapping and fractious. At that point, I didn't mean to be, but it had been a really, really long night.

"Matthew?"

His voice was very soft, and his eyes unfocused. I groaned inwardly. *Now what?* Cory was no help. He was already wandering off in the direction of the computer again, already running his hands lovingly over the strangely shaped keyboard, murmuring to himself.

"Matthew?"

"What! Just let go, Morgan, and fucking pass out or something. I'm leaving."

"Please . . ."

With a sigh, I gave in and allowed him to pull me closer. The bed was so high, I hardly had to bend at all to bring myself level with his face. He blinked and tried to focus. Then he smiled. It was such a genuine one it took me by surprise. As unfocused as they were, the expression in the startling green eyes was strangely intense.

"Can I trust you, Matthew?"

Oh shit, here we go. Drunken revelations he'd more than regret in the morning. This is why I didn't get drunk, at least not unless I was surrounded by people I knew I could trust.

"No. Don't trust me, Morgan. You'll only regret it in the morning."

"You're my friend, Matthew, my only friend."

"No, I'm not. I'm not your friend, Morgan. I hate you, remember?"

"Please help me, Matthew. Please be my friend." He sounded desperate. He was begging, tears in his eyes, the whole thing.

Inside, I was screaming *no* over and over. I didn't want Morgan to pour out his heart to me. I didn't want Morgan to open up to me. I hated Morgan, and I didn't want the stress of knowing secrets about him. I didn't want there to be a link between us, and I didn't want the hassle I knew was coming tomorrow when he woke up with a terrible hangover and a gut full of regret that he'd ever been in this situation with me. Yet, I didn't pull away.

"Don't do this, Morgan," I said softly and as kindly as I could in the circumstances. "You're going to regret this hugely in the morning. Don't tell me secrets. Don't pretend you like me. Don't open your heart to me, because I will stamp on it. I don't like you. I'm not your friend."

"But I-I like you."

"Great. Good for you. I still hate you. Just let me go and go to sleep. Forget about tonight, and so will I."

He looked confused. "I . . . can't . . . forget. I want . . . I wanted . . . I need . . ."

"Yeah, yeah. You want. You need. Tell me something new. It's always about what you want and need. Don't worry about it. You've been the centre of attention, the focus of adoration, for so long you just can't deal with someone who isn't sucked into it. You'll get over it. Now let me go."

"Please, Matthew. I need you. I need help."

"Yeah, yeah. You need help. I get it. Go see a shrink. Find someone who cares. Why not talk to Daddy once in a while?"

Morgan's eyes went wide, and he shook his head. "No. You don't understand. My father hates me. He's going to kill me, Matthew. Please help me."

"Ri-ight." Great. Not only was he pissed, but he was also delusional. He was so way out there it wasn't real. "No problem, Morgan. Your father wants to kill you. Sure. Of course I'll help you. Now go to sleep, and we'll talk in the morning."

"Do you promise?"

"Why not? We'll speak in the morning, and I'll help you. Now for fuck's sake, go to sleep."

Morgan stared up at me for a while, his gaze distant but struggling. I couldn't pull away. I couldn't stop staring at his eyes. They really were fucking amazing. As I watched, they flickered, and although he tried to force them open, something, presumably the alcohol, was too strong for him, and with a sigh, he closed them. His fingers released my wrist and fell with a thud onto the bed.

I should have walked away right then, but something held me. I don't know what it was, because I still hated him. He was still an arrogant bastard who walked over everyone to get what he wanted. He was still the person who used and abused people with careless disregard. And yet . . . and yet, suddenly he was something else, too. He was a human being, with flaws and weaknesses. He was lonely and desperate, confused and hurt—just like the rest of us. Suddenly, I saw not my arch-nemesis but a real person.

The feeling confused me. It was easier when I hated him. Growling to myself, I turned to undertake the task of convincing Cory he really shouldn't be poking around in Morgan's computer, not after what happened the last time. But this time Cory was strangely intent and strangely resistant. It was almost twenty minutes before I finally managed to drag him away, and when I did, he was frowning.

CHAPTER EIGHT

On Sunday, I should have telephoned Morgan. I knew we needed to work on our presentation for the moot on Monday. But I was angry with him for the way the party had gone the night before, so I was determined not to telephone him — and he didn't telephone me.

On Monday morning, I was incredibly nervous. The moot was set for two o'clock, and from what I'd heard round and about, half the university's student body was going to be there. I couldn't eat breakfast, and I must have organised and rearranged my notes a dozen times. I waited and waited for Morgan to call me, to arrange somewhere to meet to go over things, but when I'd heard nothing by eleven, I caved and called him.

The first time, he didn't answer, so I kept ringing, and at the fourth attempt, he picked up.

"Hello?" He sounded as if he'd just woken up.

"Where the hell are you?"

"What?" His voice was slurred and unfocused, and it infuriated me.

"Where are you? You were supposed to be going over the presentation with me before this afternoon."

"This afternoon?"

"The moot? You do remember the moot, don't you, Morgan? Us against the staff? Witnessed by half the world?"

There was silence for a while. Then Morgan all but whispered, "I don't think... I don't think I can come." He sounded spaced out, and I wondered if he'd just been deeply asleep, or maybe he'd continued the party from Saturday.

"Are you pissed?"

"No."

"Stoned?"

"No."

"High?"

"Fuck off, Matthew. I'm not anything, just tired." His voice rallied for that.

"Join the fucking club. I didn't sleep a wink last night, especially as we were supposed to be meeting up to go over this . . . and you just didn't bother."

"Sorry."

"Yeah, you sound it." He didn't. He just sounded tired. I sighed and tried, unsuccessfully, to keep my intense annoyance out of my voice. "Look, I don't know what's going on with you, but it was your arrogance that got us into this in the first place, and I'm not going to make a fool of myself in front of the whole school by trying to do this on my own. So you'd better get your arse down here, right now, or I'm coming up there to get you."

"Sorry, Matthew." The phone went dead.

"What the fuck?" I rang him again, and again, and again, but he didn't answer. My previous nerves were blasted out of the way by red-hot anger. I just couldn't believe Morgan was doing this to me.

On the spur of the moment, I got into my car and drove out to Morgan's. I rang him from the front doorstep. This time he answered.

"Matthew, I—"

"I'm outside," I snapped.

"Outside where?"

"Outside your front door. Open it."

"I . . ." It was just a breath, but it conveyed a world of

indecision and confusion, which only made me angrier.

"Morgan, get your arse down here and do it now."

There was silence for such a long time that I thought he'd put down the phone. "All right," he said finally. "Wait there."

"Yeah, don't worry, I'm not going anywhere."

After what seemed like a very long time, the door opened, and a very different Morgan stood in the doorway. He was dressed in jeans and a long-sleeved black shirt. Both were rumpled, as if he'd just thrown them on. His hair was a mess, and he looked as if he hadn't slept since I last saw him.

"Shit. What have you been up to?"

"Had a rough weekend."

His voice was scratchy, as if he'd been smoking too much or coughing a lot.

"Well, never mind that now. Get in the car."

"I'm not going, Matthew," he repeated stubbornly.

"The hell you're not. I'm *not* going to do this on my own, and it counts to the end-of-year exams, so I'm not going to walk away either. I don't know what the hell you've been up to, and frankly, I don't care. You're my partner in this thing, for better or worse—and you'd *better* get in the car, or it will be the *worse* for you."

"I can't." He seemed so dejected I almost felt sorry for him for a moment, but only for a moment.

"Sure you can. Get in the car. Now. We can practice on the way."

"Matthew, I can't. I don't . . . I don't feel . . ."

"I know you don't feel good. I can see that, and I don't give a shit. You knew we had this presentation, and if you decided to get fucked up, then good for you, but you're not getting away from it, no way. If I have to hit you over the head and kidnap you, then so be it, but you are *going* to the fucking moot, even if I have to drag you there kicking and screaming."

"I . . ."

"Morgan, it isn't fair. I've worked hard on this, and it's my grades on the line as well as yours. Some of us don't have the advantages you do and need to get good degrees to have a chance in life."

I could see he was wavering, literally. He had one hand on the door frame, and I was sure if he hadn't been holding on to it, he'd have fallen. It was strange, but as rough as he was, as dishevelled and un-Morgan like, he'd never been more human, more . . .

Gah! I had to stop thinking like that.

Morgan stared at me, his eyes wide and mouth open. *Shit! Was I that obvious? Had he seen it on my face? Fuck! Now, what was I going to do?*

"Don't worry. It's okay. I won't—" He shut his mouth with a snap, and I started to panic. What had he seen? What did he think? What was I thinking?

"I don't know what . . ." I started.

"It's okay. I'm just . . ." he said, at the same time.

We both shut up and stared at each other for a moment. Then Morgan sagged wearily against the door frame and sighed.

"Give me ten minutes."

"I'm timing you."

He smiled thinly and disappeared.

I paced back and forth for twenty minutes and was about to hammer on the door when Morgan appeared with his backpack over his shoulder. He'd simply thrown on a jacket over the clothes he'd been wearing and possibly dragged a comb half-heartedly through his hair.

"Where have you been?"

"I needed to get my stuff together."

He climbed into the passenger seat of my car and slouched down as low as he could, turning his face away from me and closing his eyes. I got in and headed out of the gate.

"So, are we going to practice?"

"No."

"Oh, great."

"I'm not up to it, Matthew. Don't hassle me. I'm here, isn't that enough?"

"Erm . . . no. We're about to go up against two lecturers in front of the whole school. This counts to our final grade. This is a big deal. Just being here is really not enough."

"Tough."

"Morgan. What the hell has got *into* you? Why are you being such a shit about this?"

Morgan growled and slid lower in his seat.

I simmered and slammed the car into gear.

"Don't." He sighed.

"Don't what?"

"Don't be so mad at me."

"Mad? Fuck, Morgan, you're a piece of work, do you know that?"

"Yeah, I know that." He sounded tired and fed up and defeated. He sounded completely unlike himself.

"What's the matter? Why are you so . . . like this?"

"I'm just not feeling well."

"Have you got a hangover or something?"

"Or something."

I sighed. He sounded so miserable I couldn't stay angry with him. The anger just leaked out and left me strangely empty. Suddenly, I wasn't nervous anymore, wasn't angry, wasn't frustrated . . . wasn't anything. Morgan sighed.

"You okay?" I asked mildly.

"No."

"What's wrong?"

"I told you . . . just don't feel good."

"Are you ill?"

"Kind of."

"And?"

Morgan turned his head toward me. His eyes were dull and heavy. He did look ill. I was beginning to regret my reaction.

"And I feel really shitty." He tried to smile, but it came out as more of a grimace. "I'll do my best, though."

"Thanks."

"Wouldn't want you to get a bad grade because of me, would I?" The sarcasm was creeping back into his voice. He just couldn't help it. I groaned.

"Just shut up, Morgan." But it came out in a friendly way and made him smile a proper smile.

When we got to the university, it was gone half-past twelve. Only an hour and a half left. I parked the car, and we headed for the refectory. As soon as we walked through the door, we were mobbed. Everyone was talking at once, and they were all excited. For once, I wasn't elbowed out of the way to allow them to get to Morgan. This time they were there for both of us.

In the ten minutes we endured, I got a taste of what it was like to be Morgan, and it wasn't fun. He just stood there the whole time in a daze, and in the end, I hauled on his arm and hightailed it out of there, dragging him behind me.

Everywhere we went there was someone who wanted a piece of us. Morgan was completely out of it, and the more people around us, the more spaced out he was, which didn't bode well for the moot.

We ended up in the library, which was a little better because people weren't allowed to talk to us. Morgan collapsed in a chair and leaned his elbows on the table, cradling his head.

"Shit. You really are fucked up today, aren't you?"

Morgan groaned but said nothing. I noticed his hands were trembling.

"Do you really think . . . are you really not up to doing

this?"

He lifted his head and focused on me. I could tell he was finding it difficult. "I-I'll try."

I frowned. He meant it, that he'd try, but . . . shit, the boy was shaking. He looked like hell.

"Are you really sick? Not stoned, or hungover, or anything like that?"

"Nothing like that."

I sighed. What could I do? I was torturing him, and much as I'd fantasised about doing just that, now it came down to it . . . it wasn't fun at all. "Okay, wait here."

I left him with his head on his arms, half asleep, and went in search of the lecturers. I found them in the lecture theatre, setting up the moot.

"There you are, Matthew. We were getting concerned we hadn't seen either you or Morgan this morning. I hope you're well prepared."

"I am, but Morgan isn't well. I left him in the library, and he's really not up to this."

She frowned. "Are you sure it isn't just nerves?"

I stared at her blankly. "This is Morgan."

"Yes, of course. Okay, let's go and see what the trouble is."

I took her back to the library where Morgan was asleep in the same position I'd left him. He jumped violently when the lecturer put a hand on his shoulder.

"Are you all right, Morgan?" she asked gently.

Morgan blinked up at her, then squinted. "I'm . . ."

Becoming almost motherly, our lecturer put her hand on his forehead. "Hmm, you don't have a fever, but Matthew's right. You don't look well. Are you up to this moot?"

"I-I said I'd try." He sounded breathless, and the lecturer frowned at him, although not in an angry way.

"Okay," she said brusquely, "stand up."

Obediently, Morgan tried to stand, but he was unsteady on

his feet and sat down again suddenly, with a surprised expression on his face.

"Right. There's only one place you're going, young man." She turned to me, still frowning. "Matthew, could you take Morgan home, please?"

"But what about the moot?"

"I assume you've taken notes?"

"Yes, of course."

"Very well. Prepare the notes as you would an argument and hand them in before the end of the week. Your marks will be allocated according to those. When Morgan's feeling better, we can re-schedule the moot. In the meantime, the professor and I will handle the demonstration today."

"Thank you."

"Morgan, if you're not feeling better by the middle of the week, you'd better let someone know so they can substitute for you in the Nationals." Morgan glanced up sharply. She was still frowning, and I couldn't work out whether she was concerned for him or for the school losing its chance in the National Moot.

With a smile and a pat on Morgan's back, the lecturer walked away, and suddenly I felt . . . awkward.

"I'm sorry."

"Sorry?"

"I was so focused on the moot, the mark, I didn't realise you were really ill. I suppose I didn't care. All I cared about was getting through the moot and getting a good mark. I was selfish. I'm sorry."

Morgan shrugged. "I know."

"Come on. Let's get you home, where you should have stayed."

It said a lot for the way he was feeling that Morgan didn't say a word as he got shakily to his feet and followed me meekly out to the car.

On the drive back, we were both silent. I was embarrassed and sad about the way I'd treated Morgan. I really hadn't cared about how he was feeling when it had been obvious from the start that he wasn't well. I'd been quick to assume it was self-inflicted, far too quick. And even when I realised there was something really wrong, I'd still pushed him. What a jerk I was. How like Morgan.

"You okay?"

"I'm surviving."

"I'm sorry I was so hard on you. I didn't realise —"

"I know."

"You gonna be okay?"

"Yeah, fine." He sounded somehow uncertain, as if something was lurking under the surface, something he knew and I didn't.

"What is it?"

"Nothing. It's nothing. I'll be okay."

We fell silent again, and Morgan dozed. He didn't wake up when I got out to open the gate — I knew the number by heart now — or when we stopped outside the front door. I sat for a while, watching him sleep. His hair was all over his face, and I just had to tuck it behind his shoulder. He did stir then but didn't wake.

"Morgan," I said softly at last when I just couldn't bear it any longer. He woke with a start and sat bolt upright. Turning to me, he stared with wide eyes and shook his head.

"What's wrong?"

With an obvious effort, he pulled himself together and forced himself to relax.

"Nothing. It's okay. I was asleep, that's all. You startled me."

"Are you okay now? Do you want me to come in with you?"

He stared at me for a long, hot moment, then shook his

head. "Thanks, Matthew," he said, with more sincerity than anything he'd ever said to me.

"No problem." I smiled at him, but he didn't return it.

Morgan got out of the car and walked toward the door. At the last minute, he turned and stared back toward the car. I waited for him to turn, to move, but he didn't. He just stood and stared at me. I wanted to . . . I felt like . . . I jammed the car into reverse and skidded away.

Morgan wasn't in classes for the rest of the week. There was a lot of conversation about it, conjecture, and even the lecturers were restless, worrying about the Nationals. It made me angry. None of them worried about Morgan. That made me angry, too. Hang on, what the hell did I care if they were concerned about Morgan or not? Morgan was nothing to me, not even my friend.

Speaking of friends, Cory seemed to have deserted me, too. He was never around. And when he was, he was sullen, distracted, and tired. I was beginning to get fed up of the whole thing.

So many times, my hand reached for the phone. Sometimes I even got as far as to dial Morgan's number, but I never connected. I don't know why, but for some reason, alarm bells went off in my head whenever I seriously thought about speaking to him.

I was lonely. I'd never been lonely before, and I didn't like it.

Toward the end of the week, Cory stopped coming home at all. When I called, he didn't answer at first, and when he did, he was distracted and annoyed, I'd interrupted him. He was strangely secretive about where he was and what he was doing, but that wasn't really anything new. He was often like that. I wasn't worried, just annoyed. I needed him, and he wasn't there. Yeah, yeah, I know . . . childish and selfish . . .

but hey.

The National Mooting Competition was due to take place on Monday morning. I kept watching the boards for notices of a change in participants, especially when Morgan didn't show for classes at the end of the week.

I finally bit the bullet on Friday and asked the lecturer, to be told Morgan had confirmed he'd be attending the competition, and he'd been given special dispensation from the lectures that week to prepare. I ground my teeth with frustration and anger. I couldn't believe I'd actually been worried for the bastard and all he was doing was skiving, to supposedly prepare for the competition when I knew full well that he'd already done that.

I spent a miserable weekend completely alone and working hard on projects that had been shelved while I was wasting energy worrying about Morgan and Cory.

I did some Christmas shopping, wrote some Christmas cards, and considered decorating. Some of the other guys had put up a Christmas tree and made a half-hearted attempt to decorate it. I knew it would offend Cory's OCD tendencies and I thought about tidying it up, adding some of our stuff, but to hell with that. He could do it himself when he deigned to return.

By Sunday, I was exhausted. I was actually asleep when the phone rang at about six o'clock. I didn't even look to see who it was before I answered blearily.

"Hello?"

"Matthew?"

In the instant it took for the voice to hit my ear and my mind to make the connection—Morgan—I sat bolt upright, my heart pounding. In the next instant, I cursed myself for my reaction. He sounded tired.

"Yeah, what's up?"

"Are you coming tomorrow?"

"Coming where?"

"To the Nationals, idiot."

"Oh that. I wasn't planning to. Why?"

"Oh. Nothing. I just thought . . . never mind." He sounded deeply disappointed, and I should have left it there. I really should have said *okay, goodbye*, but I didn't.

"What's on your mind?"

"Nothing. I just thought, if you were going anyway, you might want to drive up with me rather than take the bus. You know . . . to practice and stuff."

"Oh." I had no idea what to say to that. The school was putting on a coach to take a load of supporters, and I really was intending to go. Now I had to choose—not go, go on the bus and offend Morgan . . . or go with Morgan. Two hours in the car with him felt like too much.

"It's okay. If you don't want to, that's fine. I just thought—"

"No, it's okay. I'll come with you. It's got to be better than the bus, eh?" Oh, fuck! Now why the hell had I said that? I could have bitten out my tongue. I was so angry with myself.

"Yeah."

"You up to this?"

"Up to it?" He sounded defensive.

"I mean, you were pretty sick on Monday, and you haven't been in all week."

"Were you worried about me?"

"Of course not. I hate you, remember?" I was teasing.

"Of course. You never let me forget it, do you?" He wasn't.

"Certainly not."

"So, shall I pick you up? It starts at eleven, and I have to be there at least half an hour before, so it'll have to be about eight-thirty. Is that okay?"

"Sure. You remember where I live?"

"I'll meet you outside the main gate. That's not too far, is

113

it?"

"Nope, that's fine."

"Cool." He sounded happy. I felt . . . nervous.

"Morgan."

"Yeah."

"You are okay, aren't you? I mean, I hate you, but . . . well, I was a bit . . . you know?"

There was silence for a while, and I thought I'd pushed things too far, made it awkward again, somehow crossed a line. I felt as if I had, but I didn't know what the line was or what crossing it meant.

"Yeah, I'm okay. Thanks, Matthew."

Before I could say anything else, the line went dead. I was glad but somehow bereft at the same time, although I was smiling when I set my phone down on the table and whistling when I went to take a shower and check out my wardrobe for the right outfit for the next day.

CHAPTER NINE

I was sitting on the large flat rock outside the entrance to the university at eight o'clock Monday morning. At precisely eight-thirty, the sleek, silver *Audi* purred to a halt next to me. My heart skipped when I saw it, and my hand trembled as I opened the door. How stupid was that?

Cory hadn't been home, and I was annoyed I hadn't been able to talk this over with him. For the millionth time that weekend, I found myself wondering where he was. I was particularly annoyed because it was just over a week to Christmas and we'd done none of the pre-Christmas things we'd always had such great fun doing together. It just didn't feel right on my own, so there was no Christmas tree, no decorations, and I was pretty sure Cory hadn't got any presents bought.

"Where's your friend?" Morgan asked as I got in. "I meant to say it would be okay for him to come, too."

"I've no idea. He's bailed on me. I haven't seen him for days."

Morgan frowned as he eased the car out into the road. "Is he okay?"

"Yeah. He does this sometimes. He gets absorbed in stuff and forgets about everything else until he gets through the part he's working on."

"What's he working on now?"

"No idea."

"I hope it's nothing that's going to get him into trouble."

That annoyed me. That really annoyed me. What right did

Morgan have to make judgements about Cory? He didn't even know him.

"He's not in the habit of getting into trouble, you know."

"I must bring out the worst in people."

His voice was light, and he was clearly trying to make a joke of it, but that just annoyed me even more. I sat and simmered as Morgan concentrated on the road.

After a while, I started sneaking looks at him. He looked good. He was wearing black slacks and a white shirt, and I'd noticed one of our university jerseys slung carelessly in the back. Fortunately, it was black, or I had the feeling he'd be rebelling about wearing it.

For now, at least, his hair was loose and blew around his shoulders, because he had his window slightly open. It was certainly not the weather to have the top down. For some inexplicable and highly uncomfortable reason, I found myself wanting to touch his hair. Ridiculous, I know, but I kept remembering how it felt when I was stroking it down by the river, so soft and silky. It was like that now, even blowing in the breeze.

Blinking, I realised I'd been staring at him, and another glance at his smug smile told me he'd noticed. I turned my face away and stared out of the window.

Morgan turned on the radio. As he did so, his hand brushed my knee and sent shivers through me. I groaned inwardly and moved my leg away, shifting slightly in my seat, so there was no chance of any part of him touching me accidentally. He noticed that, too, but his smile never faltered. That, of course, made me angry. He was making huge assumptions, and the fact that *A* I was doing the same thing in assuming he was making them and *B* they were very likely correct did nothing to make me feel more comfortable or lighten my mood, which was suddenly vile.

The radio was playing something classical that sounded

vaguely familiar. After a while, I remembered where I'd heard it — it was one of the pieces Morgan played the night of the dinner party. I closed my eyes and listened to the music, not as it was playing now, but as I'd heard it that night. My mind added the image of Morgan, his hair loose around his shoulders, his eyes closed and his face rapt, his hands flying over the keys.

Abruptly, I opened my eyes as I found myself reacting to the memory in an entirely unexpected and undesirable way. I stared out of the window, seeing a pale ghost of myself staring back. *Shit! Was Cory right after all? No way! Not about this. This was not happening.* I made a vow to myself there and then, that no matter what he did, no matter how hard he tried, there was no way Morgan Bentley was going to seduce me. That was one road I was not going down because I knew what was waiting at the end of it — embarrassment, frustration, and heartbreak.

Besides, I wasn't really attracted to him at all. I hated him. It was just those bloody eyes and that smile. *Shit! Shit! Stop thinking about that smile.* The evidence was going to be too hard to hide in a minute. No. I wasn't attracted to him. I was attracted to his smile, but that wasn't enough, not nearly enough, not for what I wanted.

I was waiting for the right person. I'd know her when I found her — or when she found me. I'd kissed a few frogs, but none of them had turned into the prince of my dreams. The princess. The princess of my dreams. I wanted a family — something I'd never had, not really — and it was important to me. I wanted to settle down with a nice girl, have children, and live happily ever after.

I'd wanted that since I was old enough to know what I wanted. It was a dream that had kept me going all those times I'd lain in my room, with my head under the pillow, listening to my parents' row. All the times I'd sat at the dinner table and watched one or the other storming out, knowing the one who was left would take out their anger on me. All the times I'd stood between them when one or the other had a fist raised — or a knife in their hand.

It was a dream I wasn't going to let go of easily, and it was a dream I was certainly not going to realise with Morgan. If he wanted a brief fling and a casual goodbye at graduation, he could find someone else. That wasn't my style, not my style at all, and I knew only too well it was his. Besides, I'd promised Cory.

I had kind of an idea Cory might be at least half in love with me. It had never become an issue between us because he knew I was straight, and I knew he wasn't. We were totally cool with each other. I'd joked with him, since he came out to me when we were eleven years old, that if I ever felt the urge to experiment with a man, it would be him. I never had — until now. Even now, it wasn't so much an urge to experiment with a man. It was more . . . more a . . . well, if we're being honest, what it was, what I really didn't want to admit, was that it was an abject and complete infatuation with Morgan Bentley.

It had crept up on me so slowly I hadn't seen it coming, but now that it was here there was no denying it. I'd known for a while, but it was only at that moment, in the car, I actually admitted it to myself. The realisation hit me with all the force of an emotional brick, and I think I actually gasped aloud.

"Are you okay?"

"Fine," I snapped, really not wanting to speak to him at that moment of shocking epiphany.

"You're not going to be sick or anything, are you?"

"If I am, you'll be the first to know."

"Good, because I'd kill you if you were sick in my car."

"God forbid."

"Well, something's wrong. You haven't spoken a word to me in over half an hour. You're not mad about what I said about Cory, are you? I was only joking."

"Maybe a little. Maybe I was wondering what the hell gives you the right to judge someone you don't even know?"

"That's harsh."

"Maybe."

"I didn't mean to be judgemental. I was only trying to help. I know what my father's like, and I don't want Cory to be hurt."

"Cory can look after himself. He's like a cat. He always lands on his feet. And he's a bloody genius. No one can catch him out on a computer. No one."

"And that's exactly the kind of attitude that would get him into serious trouble. There is always someone better than you are. No matter who you are, what you do, or how good you are at what you do, there's always someone better."

"If you say so."

Morgan sighed and shook his head, then lapsed back into silence, concentrating on his driving.

"Why did you agree to come with me?" he said softly.

"Huh?" The question came out of left field after almost an hour of silence, apart from the radio.

"Why did you come with me? You clearly don't like me, and you aren't comfortable in my presence, so why did you agree to be cooped up in a car with me for two hours — four if you count the trip back?"

"I might be getting the bus back."

"Whatever. You didn't answer my question."

I gazed at him and thought about it. Why had I agreed to come? Could I tell him it was because I'd been so relieved to hear his voice, to know he was all right, after a week of worrying myself sick? Could I tell him that although I hated him with a passion and felt acutely uncomfortable every moment I was in his presence, I lived for the excitement of that first glimpse, the flash of his eyes, the quirk of his smile? Could I admit that he utterly fascinated me and that as hard as it was to be with him, when I wasn't, he was all I could think about?

"It was better than the bus." I shrugged. He turned his head sharply, and our gazes met. It was only for an instant, because he had to turn back to the road, but it was such an intense moment I felt he had to know . . . he had to.

I don't know what would have happened if we hadn't arrived. The bland voice of the satnav informed us we should turn left and then we would arrive at our destination. The left turn was through a set of large ornate gates into a courtyard in front of a very impressive building. A myriad of signs directed us around the side of the building to a car park, which was already full. There were people everywhere.

When we parked, Morgan remained immobile, staring out of the window. I was acutely uncomfortable, wondering what he was thinking.

"Can I talk to you, Matthew?" he said in a tight voice throbbing with tension and . . . something. "Can I trust you? Can I tell you something?"

"I suppose," I said in a carefully non-committal way.

"Seriously, Matthew, I need . . . I need to tell . . . someone."

"Why me? It's not as if we're friends or anything."

Morgan turned to me, and his eyes were fathomless. After a while, he pursed his lips and gave the parody of a smile. "No," he said and bit his lip, lowering his eyes and making me notice how ridiculously long and thick his eyelashes were. "No, we're not. Never mind."

Almost as soon as he got out of the car, Morgan was gone, walking fast, swallowed into the crowd. I was frustrated and annoyed with him. What the hell did he expect?

The hall was packed when I got inside. It was filled with students, not only from the two competing universities but also from those who'd been knocked out in previous rounds.

I couldn't find anyone I knew, so I just sat where I could. The action was taking place on a circular platform in the middle of the tiered seats. It was set up like a mock courtroom. My eyes ached as I stared at the front rows, seeking out Morgan's face, but he wasn't there.

It was almost half an hour later, when I was as bored as I have ever been, the lights finally dimmed and a spotlight came on, focusing on the stage. A hush fell over the crowd, and a man stepped out.

He welcomed everyone and explained the rules and programme for the day. Opening speeches would take place first, followed by the questioning of the witnesses. There would then be a break for lunch, which would be available to everyone in the refectory, then closing speeches and a break while the judges chose the winner.

Then came the moment I'd been both waiting for and dreading. The contestants were introduced. First, a smarmy boy whose short hair and arrogant manner made him look like a lawyer, then Morgan. He was relaxed, polite, easy and . . . simply . . . awesome. My stomach flipped at the sight of him, and I pushed the feeling away impatiently. I was going to have to speak to Cory later.

The other team opened, and I listened carefully as the boy put forward a compelling argument. He was good, very good. I don't know why that surprised me. If he hadn't been, he wouldn't have been in the final. I found myself drawn into what he was saying, unconsciously searching for the flaws in his argument. I found them but got a little nervous as there were a few that were too obvious, too blatant. As he was drawing to a close, I realised he'd very skilfully set a trap. I could see what he was doing as clear as day, but would Morgan? Of course he would. He was better than me, and if I could see it . . .

If the opponent had been good, Morgan was astounding,

121

astonishing, amazing. He sparkled, he glittered darkly, and he captivated. Everyone was on the edge of their seats. Morgan's argument was fluid and sensible, but he skirted the areas his opponent had opened up for him, skimming over the thin ice. I couldn't tell if he'd seen the traps and my heart began to pound.

Why was I getting so nervous? I didn't know. I wiped my sweaty palms on my jeans and, taking a deep breath, sat back. This was just ridiculous. It wasn't as if I cared—about the competition, the school, or even Morgan. Then why was I here?

The questioning of witnesses went very well, and it was exciting to see how the two boys used their skills in very different ways to draw out the things they wanted the actors to say. To my relief, Morgan dealt with three of the traps, sweeping them out of the way by charming revelations out of the opponent's witnesses, where the opponent had failed to bully anything out of Morgan's.

But that still left two huge problems with his case he had to get over, and which his opponent had carefully and skilfully laid out so as to present a real danger to Morgan, in the form of a thinly concealed trap hiding a far more subtle and dangerous one beneath. If Morgan fell for it and sprang the first trap, unaware of the second, he'd lose.

The only reason I saw through the charade was because this was something I'd studied when researching and practising for the moot I was supposed to do with Morgan. Because of the circumstances, we'd worked separately and never managed to get together to combine our notes. Had he found the same things? Had he seen this? Was he going to fall into the trap and lose the moot? Why did I care?

The first half of the moot passed without Morgan getting himself into any trouble. When we broke for lunch, I made up my mind to find him and warn him. I fought my way through the crowds until I found a group of students from my own school.

"Where's Morgan?"

"Oh hi, Matthew, we didn't know you're here."

"Where's Morgan? I need to talk to him."

"The competitors are having lunch in their own dining room. They're not allowed to talk to anyone now the moot's started, in case they get an unfair advantage by getting advice from someone."

"Oh, great."

"What's the problem?"

"Nothing, it's just—nothing." And it was, wasn't it? I didn't care, did I? Morgan would win anyway, wouldn't he? And if he didn't, it wouldn't matter, would it?

I joined the rest of my group for lunch, feeling uncomfortable and on edge about the whole thing. It was just a competition, and Morgan was brilliant. Of course he'd have seen the trap. Of course he'd be able to deal with it. He was better than me, after all. He was . . . he was . . . Morgan.

Just before the competition was about to start, my mobile rang. It startled me, mainly because I'd forgotten it was switched on. We were supposed to turn all mobiles off before entering the auditorium. I glanced at the display, intending to simply switch it off. It was Cory.

Sighing, I took the phone outside. It was quiet there.

"Hey, Cory. Where you been, dude? I've been missing you."

"Matthew. I can't talk long. I've kind of . . . I've got myself into a bit of trouble. It's nothing to worry about, at least not for now, but . . . I-I've found some scary stuff, some things about ITM."

"Have you been hacking them again? For gods' sake, Cory! You're going to get into so much trouble." I was angry with him, and it showed in my voice.

For a moment, there was silence. "I already am. I-I think I went too far . . . they know."

"What? Where are you?" I was suddenly afraid, remembering what Morgan had said about them being dangerous. I had visions of Cory being hauled off to jail—or worse. "Are you okay?"

"I'm fine. I . . . look, I can't really talk over the phone. Can we meet?"

"Not now. I'm at the moot competition."

"Did you go with Morgan?" His voice was so cold it could have frozen fire. I had no idea what to say, so I settled on the truth—or at least a version of it.

"Yeah, he called to see if I wanted a lift, and I didn't have the heart to tell him I wasn't going."

"Be careful, Matthew. His father's bound to tell him what happened. Don't go anywhere on your own with him. He might . . . they might . . . hurt you, to get at me."

I almost laughed out loud. "For goodness sake, Cory, you're losing it. This is not Chicago, you know. ITM are not the mafia and Morgan is definitely not—"

"Matthew, I'm being serious. I-I've found some things that are . . . they're bad, not legal. They know and . . . I was lucky, the person who found me, at least the first one . . . he was mad about what they were doing, too. He was kind of working undercover for another group. He's helping me, but I need to see you, Matthew, as soon as possible. I need you to know. Please. Please don't trust Morgan."

"You know I've never trusted Morgan, but this . . . Cory, I think you're taking this way too far. If they are doing something illegal, they're not going to go to the police about you, are they? Just go back and say you're sorry. Okay, maybe they'll sack you, but—"

"You don't understand. It's gone way beyond that. It's so much more. It's bad, Matthew, really bad. I think if they find me, they'd . . . they'd hurt me, hurt me badly . . . and maybe you, too. Be careful of Morgan, please."

"I . . . all right. Of course I will. I'll be careful. Where do you want to meet and when?"

"Tomorrow. I'll call you and let you know where and when."

"Okay." I suddenly found myself caught up in the drama, and even though I still thought he was overreacting, I found myself saying, "Be careful."

"I'm okay, Matthew. I'm safe here. You're not. Remember that."

The phone went dead, and I walked back into the auditorium feeling . . . strange. I sat down numbly in the nearest seat, my mind churning. What the hell had Cory got himself into now? What had he got us into?

I barely listened to the first closing speech. I was too distracted. It wasn't until I heard Morgan's voice I was brought back to the present forcefully. Shit! I'd missed what the little bugger said, but by the sneer on his face, he'd done it well.

I stared at Morgan, willing him to see the chasm opening beneath his feet. But he didn't. He walked straight into it, and I groaned along with a number of other people who'd seen what I saw.

The opponent was grinning all over his face. Clearly, he was already celebrating his victory. Morgan paused and smiled to himself, then delivered a speech that had us all gasping. He picked up, spun around, and demolished the opponent's argument, turning the trap on him and snapping the jaws shut. When he finished speaking, there was a standing ovation, and although the judges still retired to make their decision, there really was no doubt about what it would be.

The two competitors sat in their seats on the stage while the judges were conferring, and I saw Morgan intently scanning the crowd. I wondered what he was searching for. Then his gaze met mine, and I knew. His face lit up. His gaze was so bright it made me burn, bringing the hot blood racing to scald my cheeks. I lowered my gaze, blushing furiously, and when I looked up again, he was grinning at me, a knowing expression on his face.

He couldn't have seen me blush, at this distance, with the lights off. He couldn't have. The blush intensified, and so did the grin. Suddenly I was angry with myself for allowing him to affect me like this. I frowned, hating him. I fucking hated Morgan Bentley.

I got up and walked out of the auditorium. I was cross, and worried, and nervous, and confused. As well as being worried about Cory, I was unsettled by the way I was feeling about Morgan. I hated him. I'd always hated him, and yet . . . suddenly something was hanging between us, something that was making me lose my perspective entirely.

I wandered the halls, listening to the echo of my footsteps, until I was swept up by a tide of bodies. They saw my school jersey, and I was surrounded, my shoulders being slapped and congratulations ringing in my ears. It wasn't a surprise.

I got away from them as soon as I could. It was too much. I couldn't handle it. My head was spinning, and I didn't know what to do about it. I was helpless in the grip of it—helpless to help Cory—helpless to help myself. I found myself outside and made my way to where Morgan had parked the car. Part of me wanted to go back on the bus, dreaded the thought of two hours trapped in a car with him, but I didn't know where the bus was and . . . besides . . .

"I wondered where you got to."

I spun round. Morgan was carrying a trophy half as big as he was.

"I tried to get them to take it on the bus, but they insisted I take it home and show my family." He laughed. "As if he's going to care. Ah, well." Opening the boot, he flung the trophy inside. It was almost too big. Stripping off his jersey, he threw it in after the trophy and slammed the boot shut.

Getting into the car, I felt strangely nervous and didn't really know why. There were people everywhere, and for a while, Morgan had to concentrate closely to negotiate the car safely out onto the road. When we were free and clear, he heaved a sigh.

"That was wild."

"You were awesome."

"Awesome? How American," he sneered.

"Oh, stop being a jerk. You were amazing, incredible, fantastic. I was scared stiff. I thought you were going to fall into the trap the little weasel laid for you."

"Please, Matthew, we'd covered that ground in the research for our own moot."

"I did. I've no idea what ground you covered. If you remember, we never got the opportunity to put it together."

Morgan winced. "Yeah, I'm sorry about that."

I shrugged. "It's past." Suddenly shy, I smiled. "You really were great."

"I know."

"Oh, listen to Mr Modesty."

"What's the point?"

"The point?"

"What's the point of being modest? I know I was good. I was great. I did a fantastic job . . . demolished him, ripped him apart. I'm the toast of the school, for a while. Then they'll forget me and move on to someone else, so I may as well bask in the glory while I can."

"Fat chance anyone's going to forget you. You won't let that happen."

"Maybe."

After a time of uncomfortable silence, I cast around for something to say, and what I said was typically lame, for me.

"You're going to make a great lawyer."

"Who said I was going to be a lawyer?"

"Well, duh, you're at law school."

"Yeah well, putting a duck in a chicken coop doesn't make it a hen."

I thought for a moment. "That doesn't make any sense."

"When has making sense ever had anything to do with anything? Half the things lawyers say in court don't make sense."

"True. So you're not going to be a lawyer, then?"

"Probably not."

"Then what?"

"Huh?"

"If you're not going to be a lawyer, what are you going to do with your life?"

"My life?" He snorted. "What makes you think I have a life?"

"Now you're really not making sense."

"No, I don't suppose I am. Look, Matthew, you think you know me, but you don't. You think you know about my life, but you haven't got a clue. You might think I have everything, but . . ." He turned for a moment, his eyes bleak. "Things are not as simple as they seem. My father . . ." He stopped and bit his lip, but I had a good idea where the conversation was leading.

"He wants you to go into the business, huh? To be involved with ITM?"

For a moment, Morgan squeezed his eyes shut. Then he nodded and smiled a strange, twisted smile. "Something like that."

"But you don't have the right qualifications, do you? I mean you've done nothing with biomedicine or IT."

"You'd be surprised. Actually, right now, I have *all* the right qualifications. You've no idea how involved I already am."

There was something in his voice, an undertone, as if he was trying to tell me something he couldn't put into words. I immediately thought of Cory. "Do you know anything about what's going on with Cory?"

"Cory? No. He hasn't started yet, has he?"

"I . . . no, not exactly."

"Oh gods, Matthew. He hasn't been poking around in the system again, has he? You've got to stop him doing that. He has no idea what a ridiculously stupid thing he's doing."

"Why? If they have nothing to hide, then they should have nothing to worry about." I was really mad. I remembered how frightened Cory had sounded, how freaked out it had made me. I was angry with ITM for doing that to him, and by extension, with Morgan.

"Who on earth ever said they had nothing to hide? They're a research company . . . of course they have something to hide. Some of the projects are being worked on by half a dozen companies. Whoever gets the results first gets the pay-off. All the rest have wasted years of time and billions of pounds on something they have to throw in the rubbish. Industrial espionage is a big deal. If they ever find Cory snooping, they'll come down on him like a ton of bricks."

"Well," I said uncomfortably, "if a lowly student can get so close it gets them all hot and bothered, they should get better security, shouldn't they?"

"Half their budget goes to security. It's the best there is."

"Oh."

"Seriously, Matthew, if you want my advice, tell Cory to just walk away."

"If I wanted your advice, I'd have asked for it."

Morgan shrugged and lapsed into silence again. In fact, we barely spoke for the rest of the journey. It was a great relief when we arrived back at the flat, and Morgan pulled up outside.

"Thanks for the lift, Morgan."

"No problem. Any time. Will you be in class tomorrow?"

"Of course I will."

"Oh. Okay. I-I suppose I'll see you there, then."

"I suppose so."

As I turned to get out of the car, he put his hand on my arm, and I turned back. Something in his eyes sent shivers up and down my spine.

"Matthew . . ." He fell silent, still with his hand on my arm. The touch burned me.

"What?"

My word broke him out of his dream, and he shook his head, snatching back his hand.

"Nothing. It doesn't matter."

I stood and watched the car until it was out of sight. My mind was burning with all the things I should have said, picking through all the things I had said, and thought, and done. Then into the swirling mix came all the things Morgan had said, and all the things he hadn't said. The blush crept up on me and made my face burn. Even though there was no one there, I turned up my collar, lowered my head, and made a run for the safety of my room.

CHAPTER TEN

"Matthew?" Blearily, I registered Cory's voice on the other end of the line.

"Cory?"

"Matthew, you have to do something for me. You have to do it and not ask any questions. Just do it, okay?"

"Cory, what are you talking about? What time is it?" I peered at my clock and swore. "Fuck, Cory, it's five AM What the hell? Surely you don't want me to meet you now?"

"Just promise me. Promise you'll do exactly what I ask you, and no questions."

"Where are you?" I was still half asleep and what he said was making no sense, but the intensity in his voice, the half-restrained panic, started getting through to me.

"For the love of God, Matthew, just promise."

"All right, all right, I promise. Now, what's going on?"

"I can't tell you, not yet. You have to do something, and you have to do it now."

"Is this something to do with ITM?"

"Yes. I've found out what they've been doing, what Project X is really all about. It's big, Matthew, fucking huge, but . . . but . . . it's wrong. It's horrible. I have to . . . I have to *do* something. I don't know what, but I have to do something. And before I can do anything, you have to do something for me."

"You know I'd do anything for you."

"Not quite anything, Matthew." The tone of his voice changed, for a moment turned introspective and almost wistful.

"What do you mean?"

"Nothing. Never mind, it's nothing. But you have to promise to do this and not ask any questions."

"How can I promise anything when you haven't told me what you want me to do?"

"All right, but you can't discuss this with anyone, and you can't ask questions about it. You have to promise, Matthew, or . . . or . . . I don't know what will happen."

"All right, okay, I promise I'll do whatever you ask me, and I won't tell anyone or ask any questions. Now, what the hell is this thing you want me to do?"

"I've e-mailed an address to your phone. I've sent sat-nav coordinates. Don't worry, it's scrambled. No one can intercept it. You do remember how to unscramble stuff I send you, don't you?"

"Yes, of course, I just—"

"Hush, Matthew, don't say it aloud over the phone."

"All right, double-oh-seven. You want me to meet you at this place, wherever it is? That I can do. And see? No questions."

"That's not all."

Now, why did that not surprise me? Cory was like this all the time, making drama where there was none, getting into scrapes and out of them again. This was typical Cory, and nothing ever came of anything, so why would this time be any different? Cory would flutter his eyelashes in the right direction, impress someone, and it would all be sorted. That's what always happened.

However, his next words made me sit up and take notice. "I need you to get someone and bring him with you. I need you to get Morgan."

"Morgan?"

"No questions, Matthew. Just go get Morgan—right now—and bring him with you."

"What if he doesn't want to come?"

"Then you're going to have to persuade him."

"Persuade him? But I-I can't turn up at his house at five in the morning, wake him up and say . . . you have to come with me right now. I don't know where I'm going, and I don't know why you have to come, but we have to go now. Sure, he's going to come."

"Listen to me. I can't go into details, but Morgan's in danger, terrible danger. You have got to get him out of there, and you have to do it now, or it'll be too late."

"Why should I care if he's in danger?" I retorted, remembering our fight from the day before.

"Because you care for him."

"Care for him? Hah! Who are you kidding? Don't I keep telling you I hate him?"

"Yes, you do." The tone of his voice spoke volumes.

"You don't think I do . . . hate him?"

"Matthew, this isn't the time. Whatever you think of Morgan, he's a human being, and you're the closest thing to a friend he has. Trust me, he really needs friends now. Please, please go get Morgan and bring him to the safe house."

"Safe house? What game are you playing now, Cory?"

"It's not a game. I wish it were a game, but it isn't. Please."

"All right, all right, I surrender. I'll go to the house and talk to Morgan, try to convince him, but I'm not making a fool of myself in front of him again. If he won't listen, I'm leaving."

"Matthew." Cory's voice was soft and for some reason, it sent shivers down my spine. "If you don't ever listen to anything I ever say again, listen to this now. You have *got* to get Morgan out of that house, right now, today. If you don't, if you leave him there, he's going to die. Do you understand?"

"What? If this is some kind of game . . ."

"It's no game, believe me. You have to do this. I wasn't joking. Morgan's life depends on you."

"Oh great, just fucking great."

"You'll do it?"

"Of course I'll do it. When have I ever let you down?"

For a moment, there was silence. Then Cory said softly, "Never. Not deliberately."

"Not deliberately? Cory, what . . ."

"Never mind, just do it. Get here as quickly as you can. Call me when you're on your way. And don't forget . . . no matter what it takes, you *have* to bring Morgan with you. No matter what."

"Yeah, yeah, I get it, no matter what. But what if—" I was left dangling as the phone went dead.

I got out of bed with a sigh and dragged on some clothes. It was bitterly cold, and I was shivering as I climbed into my car. Of course, with Cory not around, I had to take my own pile of shit, which had the crappiest heater in automotive history. I had to open the window to warm up and could barely see through the misted windscreen.

I was shivering so hard when I got to the gate it was a relief to get out to punch in the numbers. It occurred to me if this was as serious as Cory said, it might not have been the best of ideas to announce my arrival to security. But I didn't know any other way in, so there really wasn't a choice.

I parked the car next to the steps and wondered what to do next. I was sure I'd be making no friends if I rang the front doorbell, and I'd be announcing my presence even more loudly. In the end, I decided to try for the kitchen. Maybe I could persuade that nice cook woman to help me. She seemed to like Morgan.

Although it was still only six AM, there was plenty of activity in the kitchen. I hovered around near the door until Mrs Wight noticed me.

"Matthew? What are you doing here at this time of the morning?"

"You tell me," I muttered. "I need to see Morgan. We . . . ugh . . . we have to do some work."

Mrs Wight gave me a long, hard look, then put her hands on my shoulders.

"You seem like a good man to me, Matthew. Morgan needs someone like you. He needs a friend. Not like those parasites who usually hang on his coattail, but a true friend. He's a good man, too, if you give him a chance, but he's lost. He needs a life raft, Matthew. Can you be that for him?"

To say I was stunned would be a huge understatement. Was everyone insane today?

"Um . . . I . . . er . . . I'll try."

She smiled and released me. "Do you remember the way?"

I thought about it and shook my head, so she despatched Ben to direct me.

Morgan's room was in darkness—the curtains pulled across the window. I snapped on the light, but the figure in the bed didn't stir. I crossed the room and stood at the side of the bed. I had to laugh. Even his pyjamas were black.

He was so peaceful when he slept, so calm and . . . beautiful. His eyes were always a distraction and today, with them out of the way, I could focus on the rest of his face, which was worth focusing on. Strange how I noticed things, little things. Like the tiny scar at the edge of his eyebrow, or how long his eyelashes were, coal-black against pale skin, or the curve of his cheek, or the trembling of his lips as he breathed.

Suddenly aware I'd been standing there for ages, just staring, and annoyed at myself for getting lost in him like that, I reached out my hand, and it paused, trembling slightly, aching to touch his face. Instead, I shook him roughly by the shoulder.

He didn't come awake suddenly, as I'd expected, but simply sighed, his eyelashes fluttering.

"Morgan. Morgan, wake up."

I shook him again, and he stirred, sighing again. Gods, he was a heavy sleeper.

"Morgan, for goodness—oh." As I shook him again, his eyes flew open, startling me as always with the sheer intensity of the colour.

"Matthew?"

"No, it's the bloody tooth fairy. You have to get up."

Morgan smiled, in an unfocused sort of way, and yawned, showing his perfectly even, perfectly white teeth. Was everything about this man perfect? It was beginning to set my teeth on edge.

"For fuck's sake, get it together, Morgan. You need to get up—now."

"Why?"

"Do you have to question everything? You're so bloody frustrating."

Morgan frowned. "Now I know you're not a dream. You never speak to me like that in my dreams."

"You dream about me?" My eyes went wide with shock, and I wondered if I'd heard right.

"Um . . . yeah . . . sometimes." He stared at me, with an expression in his eyes that made me feel distinctly uncomfortable. The look stretched, and I felt I should break it, but somehow, I couldn't. Somewhere deep inside, I didn't want to. My fingers twitched. He raised a trembling hand. It hovered in the air for a moment, then fell back to the covers, where it clenched into a fist as he turned his face away.

"Why are you here?" His voice was tight, and I laughed nervously.

"Funny you should ask. I don't really know."

Morgan turned his head again, a question in his eyes.

"The truth is, I don't know why I'm here, and you're probably going to think I'm completely insane, but . . ." Now it came down to it, I could hardly bring myself to speak. It was so crazy.

"Yes?"

"It's Cory. He's got this wild idea you're in danger. He says I have to get you out of here right now or you'll die." I laughed again. "Crazy, eh?"

Morgan didn't laugh in my face as I'd expected him to. He just kept staring at me, his eyes blank.

"Morgan? Say something. I mean . . . I know it's crazy, but do you think you could . . . you know . . . humour him?"

"You came here in the middle of the night because your friend said I was in danger?" He sounded incredulous, and now I heard it coming out of his mouth, it sounded even more ridiculous.

"Well, it isn't exactly the middle of the night, it's six AM, but . . . well, yeah . . . I guess."

"And you don't even believe him?"

"No."

"So, why?"

"I don't know. Because he might be right."

We were staring at each other again, and the intensity gripped me so hard it made me feel nauseous.

"He found it, then," Morgan said quietly at last.

"Found what?"

"What he was looking for. You should tell him to drop it, erase his tracks, and get the hell out of there. It's not a threat, Matthew. He honestly doesn't know what he's getting into. They're dangerous. If they find out, they'll hurt him."

I laughed derisively, but there was something . . . he was so serious, his eyes so sad. "You're not joking, are you?"

He shook his head. "No."

"And you? Would they hurt you?" He gave me a strange, sardonic smile and nodded again.

"So Cory wasn't fooling? He was right?" A cold hand gripped my stomach and clenched. I almost doubled over, and my heart started to pound so hard it hurt.

"To a point."

"You're in danger?"

"More than you can imagine." His smile wavered, and tears sprang to his eyes. It was this, more than anything, that really panicked me.

"Then what are you doing just lying there? Come on, get up. Cory told me to take you to a safe house. We'll fix it. Come on."

Morgan didn't move. "You care? You care I'm in danger?"

"Of course I care, you idiot. I'd be more of a bastard than you are if I didn't. You're . . . you're my . . . just get up, will you?" I finished in frustration.

Morgan looked crushed. "Can't you even bring yourself to say it? Is the mere thought so repugnant to you?"

"What are you talking about? Please, Morgan, hurry. I'm scared."

"You're scared? You're not in danger, Matthew, not yet. If you're smart, you'll just walk away and forget me. Tell your friend to do the same, and you'll both be safe."

"Don't be ridiculous. I'm not going anywhere. How can you ask me to forget you?"

"Why not? Shouldn't be too hard. You hate me, remember? You can't even bring yourself to call me a friend."

"A friend? Is that what you think we are . . . friends?"

He closed his eyes and swallowed hard. Jewel-bright droplets of moisture rolled down his cheek. I followed the trail until it got lost in his hair. When I flicked my eyes back, his were waiting.

"I hope so. I'd like . . . I mean, I think of you . . ." He faltered to a stop, and there was something in his eyes that made me shiver.

"You should know you don't make it obvious. You really could have fooled me into thinking being my friend was the last thing you wanted. There were moments when I thought maybe, just maybe we could be friends, but every time, you ended up going psycho on my arse again and made me think you hated me as much as I . . . as I hate . . . hated you. You treated me like shit. Friends don't do that."

Morgan turned away. "I know. I'm sorry."

"So why? If you wanted to be my friend so much, why did you work so hard to drive me away?"

"I don't know. Because I was scared. Because I didn't think . . ." He sighed, a tight expression on his face. "Because I'm an idiot?"

"Good, glad you're finally starting to see it. We have it sorted. We're friends, okay . . . friends. And I don't turn my back on my friends. So get your arse out of bed, get dressed, and let's go!"

He shook his head again and said something too low for me to hear.

"For gods' sake, Morgan, get up! What? What did you say?"

"It's too late."

The bleakness in his words hit me like a fist, and I froze. "What the hell do you mean, it's too late?"

"You can't save me."

"This is crazy. It's all crazy, and you're really freaking me out now. Cory rings me, practically in the middle of the night, and spins some story about getting caught and taking you to a safe house because your life's in danger, and I thought you'd laugh in my face. But you didn't, and now . . . if this is real, then what the fuck are we still doing here?"

Morgan sat up and scooted up the bed, so his back was against the headboard. He pulled the duvet up around him and motioned for me to sit. I was reluctant to do so because I just wanted to go. I wanted to run and take him with me, far away from this place. However, there was something in his face that made me comply without question.

"I don't know if I should tell you this. Trust me, I'm not doing you any favours, but I . . . I need . . . I need a friend. I need someone to know." Tears rolled down his face again, and I was suddenly cold. I don't know why—maybe it was because Morgan, for the very first time ever, looked lonely and scared—but I took his hand, squeezing it tightly.

Morgan stared at our linked hands. His fingers trembled in mine. He was very cold.

"I don't care, Morgan. I don't care if what you have to tell me puts me in danger. I can tell it's eating you away inside, and if I can help, I want to."

"You can't help, not really, but . . . but maybe . . . maybe if I tell you, it will make it easier . . . if someone knows . . ." Morgan glanced up, and his eyes were terrifying. He didn't pull back his hand, though.

"My . . . my father has been working on a secret project. It's called Project X, and it's what Cory found on the computer, on my computer, that day. At one time, the whole company was involved. It started as an attempt to develop a drug to increase psychic awareness." He must have seen my blank expression because he sighed and leaned back, letting his fingers slide out of mine.

"You know mammals only use part of their brain. There are whole chunks of it no one really knows about . . . no one has been able to access. My father hit on the idea that if he modified the genetic code of an organism, it could unlock the potential of those closed-off parts. There's some evidence these areas are the places where we've locked away our innate abilities of a psychic nature—telepathy, teleportation, telekinesis—you know the kind of thing."

"You're trying to tell me your father was working on a drug that makes people psychic?" Wordlessly, Morgan nodded. There was an uneasy feeling deep inside me that overrode my natural scepticism, so I spoke carefully, keeping my initial reaction of scorn out of my voice. "Okay. So . . ." I motioned for him to continue.

"There was a time when it seemed very promising. They developed a serum that changed the genetic code of the cells infected by it, so they mutated to generate more energy. The cells are located deep in the brain, and because it's a genetic mutation the serum doesn't, or shouldn't, affect anything other than the specific cells it attaches to.

"When the cells start to generate extra energy, they create new synapses in the brain that stimulate the dormant sections, waking them up if you like. It's supposed to promote enhanced awareness, deep meditational states, and theoretically, psychism."

"It worked?" This time my scepticism crept through, and for a moment, he paused. When he continued, it was with a degree of defensiveness.

"At one time, the government was interested in the project, as were military authorities in a number of countries. I don't suppose I need to spell out what it might mean if he was successful. The military applications alone are astounding . . . espionage, interrogation, even mind control."

"It all sounds pretty farfetched to me. Very sci-fi."

"Maybe it does, maybe it is, but there were some very high-level negotiations going on for a while."

"So, I take it that it didn't go as smoothly as they would have liked."

Morgan shook his head. "No. Unfortunately, the animal subjects only reacted well up to a point. They became more aware, for sure, more focused, more influenced by their environment, maybe they even became more psychic. Unfortunately, the mutation was unstable, and it invariably degraded, and eventually, the subjects died, all of them.

"My father and his team theorised this was because of the

different physiology, the fact that animals naturally accept and use their psychism, or quite simply have different brains with less potential. He was certain it would be different with humans. He tried to get the drug licensed for human experimentation, but the General Medical Council wouldn't give it to him. It was just too dangerous. He couldn't prove humans would be any more stable, or any safer, than the animals.

"The GMC wanted some evidence human tests would be safe. They're not going to license a drug with the potential to kill every human subject who tested with it."

"I can understand that." That gnawing cold feeling inside me grew. I studied Morgan's face, but it was inscrutable. His eyes were distant, as if he was far away, almost as if he was distancing himself from the words so they wouldn't have any power over him. He wasn't succeeding, though, because I could practically see the fear emanating from him. I wanted to take him into my arms like I had at the river, but something stopped me. Not only was I pretty sure he'd push me away, but something inside was telling me it would be a really, really bad thing to do at that point. As much as the temptation grew, the more Morgan looked vulnerable and afraid, the more I resisted the urge to touch him at all.

"When the license was refused, the interest waned, and even ITM wanted to shelve the project. Suddenly no one was taking my father seriously anymore, and he hated it. He got more and more withdrawn and angry. It was hell living with him, not that he was ever here. At first, he spent all his time at the lab, driving his team on, harder and harder, demanding more than ever before.

"To be honest, I don't know why they didn't just up and quit on him. I know what he's like when he's in that sort of mood, and I stay away from him as much as I can, but they can't. They have to work with him every day. In fact, one of them did quit, one of the senior scientists, and it hit Father hard. After that, he became even more driven." He sighed and ran his hands through his hair.

"I've never been very close to my father. Before ... when my mother was alive ... we were a proper family, and he loved me, at least I thought he did." He paused, and another tear ran down his face. One thing I'd grown to like about Morgan—gods, it was hard, even then, to admit even to myself there was anything I liked about him—was he was so unashamed to cry. It didn't seem to embarrass him at all.

"We did things together like normal people, ate dinner, went on outings. When I was little, he even read me bedtime stories and tucked me in at night. But when she died, everything changed. It was as if a light went out of him, and he withdrew from me, putting all his energy into his work. He was hardly ever here, and when he was, he was cold and distant.

"I was only thirteen when she died. I didn't understand. It was as if I'd lost both parents and I blamed myself. I-I believed it was my fault my mother died, and he was punishing me for it."

"How did she die?"

Morgan started, as if he'd forgotten I was here. He tried to smile, an apologetic smile that turned into a grimace.

"I'm sorry, Matthew. I didn't mean to turn this into some kind of ... feel sorry for me session."

"No, that's all right. I-I'm interested. Please."

"It started with a virus. She got a virus in the brain stem, and she was really ill for a while. She took them all by surprise and fought it off. She was getting over the virus, but it left her exhausted and with all sorts of weird neurological symptoms. I think that was when Father started to get interested in the workings of the brain. Eventually, she stopped getting better and started going down again. She was having seizures, and they got worse and worse.

"I was thirteen, an obnoxious teenager, and I didn't under-stand. To be fair, they kept a lot of it away from me, and I had no idea she was so ill. I pushed and pushed, and one day I really wanted to go to a party. It was raining a storm, and there was no one available to take me. Father was supposed to do it, but something came up with work, and he told me no. He took the chauffeur because he was going to some busi-ness meeting and there was going to be alcohol.

"When he told me, there was a huge fight. There'd been a lot of tension building for a while, and it all came out. We both said some pretty harsh things, but he was worse." Morgan closed his eyes. "He told me I was a self-absorbed, selfish, ar-rogant, worthless piece of shit. I wasn't, not then. I-I was just a kid." He opened his eyes, a self-deprecating smile twisting his lips. I didn't return it. I was getting a whole new picture of Morgan, and it was so far out of whack with the one I'd been carrying around with me for the past two years, it made the whole thing blurred and indistinct.

"The row ended horribly. I told him I hated him, and he hit me. Not hard, not really, but it shocked the hell out of me. He told me I'd better grow up and stop behaving like a child, and walked out." Morgan shuddered at the memory. "I was a quivering heap on the floor, and my mother couldn't bear it. She told me to go and get ready for the party, and everything would be all right.

"I was numb. I wasn't thinking. I just wanted to get out of there, to have some fun. So I got ready for the party, and I got in the car with her. We were halfway there when she had a seizure behind the wheel and crashed the car. She was killed instantly. I was barely scratched."

I was awash with horror. I could almost feel the terrible emotions Morgan was holding tightly inside. Now, more than ever, I wanted to hold him, but as I moved forward, he drew away and shook his head.

"I think from that moment, Father hated me. He grew cold and distant, and when I did see him, he barely exchanged two words with me. He spent more and more time at the lab until . . . until . . ."

Again, he paused, and I could see he was expending an enormous amount of energy to control himself. I wished he wouldn't. I wished he would let himself go, let himself fall apart, so I'd have an excuse to take him in my arms, to hold him as I had before, to comfort and console him. I wanted it so bad it hurt, and this time I didn't question it, not at all.

"A couple of months ago, my father started to be at home more and more. By that, I mean for a few hours a couple of times a week, not every couple of weeks like before. We started eating dinner together again, and he talked to me, telling me about what was happening at the company. I . . . I didn't respond well. I couldn't go back to the way it was, the way he wanted it to be. Here he was, at last, doing the very thing I'd longed for, reaching out to me, wanting to be my friend, and I couldn't respond. It was awkward. It was uncomfortable . . . and then it got strange.

"He got mad and shouted at me. We'd argue, and he would storm off. It fell into a pattern very quickly, and I-I started to get tired. I mean really tired, almost too tired to get out of bed for days after his visits. Then the headaches started, and I didn't even want to be around him. I tried to get out of seeing him when he came, even hid in my room.

"One day . . . the day before that time by the river . . . I was hiding from him. I knew he was in the house. He summoned me to dinner, and I wouldn't go, so he came to my room. He asked me why I was avoiding him, and I told him I thought the stress of our arguments was making me ill. He laughed at me. He actually laughed at me and told me it wasn't that at all. He knew what it was and it certainly wasn't stress . . . and then he told me."

I didn't want to know. I so didn't want to know, but I couldn't stop myself. I had to ask. I had to know.

"What did he tell you?"

Morgan gazed at me for a while, his face completely blank, then slowly drew back his sleeve and held out his arm. It was puffy, red and inflamed with a number of strange circular bruises. I glanced at it, then up at him. I didn't know what he was showing me, what he was trying to say. Maybe I didn't want to know.

"I don't understand. What does it mean?"

Morgan dropped his sleeve and hugged himself. "It means my father didn't abandon Project X. He just went ahead with it without telling anyone, even me. It means you're too late to save me. It means I'm doomed. It means . . . it means . . ." His voice cracked, and he crumbled. "It means I'm Project X, and I'm going to die."

CHAPTER ELEVEN

This time I didn't have to think. He was shaking violently, clearly scared and upset. I could barely believe what I'd been told, and if I was shocked and upset, how must he be feeling? I practically threw myself at him, and he clung to me, very much as he had at the river. His hands clawed at my back, convulsively grabbing fistfuls of my clothes.

I've no idea how long we clung together—Morgan sobbing and me too shocked even to think. I started stroking his hair again, then his back, trying anything I could think of to calm him, while my battered brain struggled to understand what he'd told me, what the implications were.

I just couldn't get my head around the idea that any man would deliberately use his own son as a guinea pig, and these drugs had killed everything they'd been given to. The GMC had refused to give them a license with good reason. What kind of man would not only break the law but calmly and cold-bloodedly put his son's life on the line . . . without even telling him?

I think I was in shock, completely and utterly. My mind shut down, my thoughts blanked, and all I could think of was comforting Morgan. He was the only real thing in my world right then.

We clung to each other, and slowly Morgan's sobs died, and he grew still in my arms. He still held me, though, tightly, the same way I held him. Then he pulled back so he could look up into my face.

For the second time, I couldn't help but wonder how, even

with a face swollen by crying, soaked with tears and snot, Morgan could still be so beautiful. Maybe it was all about the eyes, those amazing green eyes, filled with such sorrow and such. I shivered and tried to turn my head away, but this time it was impossible.

Morgan shifted slightly, leaning back against the headboard, and pulled me with him. I overbalanced, and before I knew it, my body had slammed against his, and . . . and . . . his eyes were so damned bright, so damned beautiful, and so damned close. His face was barely more than an inch away, and we were both frozen, that same strange intensity sending shivers through us. I could feel them in him, and it stopped my breath.

"Matthew," he whispered, and I've no idea how it happened, who moved, who initiated it, but suddenly we were kissing, and it was . . . it was . . . desperate. We were both desperate, for different reasons I think, and it was the most passionate, most intimate, most exciting kiss I've ever had. In the middle of it, Morgan twisted my body, so I fell backward onto the bed, and he, still locked with me, fell over me. The weight of his body on mine, the smell of his hair in my face, the feel of his skin under my hand where it slid under his pyjama jacket and up along the smooth muscles of his back of its own accord . . . it was all driving me crazy.

Morgan broke our kiss and raised his head. For the first time, I was truly able to let myself see him, unburdened by my attempts to control my feelings, to label them with a different name. Gods, he was beautiful. The vivid green of his eyes was being swallowed by pupils wide with desire, but still, they were startling, drawing me in with the intensity of their gaze.

With trembling fingers, I reached up to push the long, silky strands of hair away from his cheek so I could see him better, and the softness of it distracted me. I let out a little sigh. I hadn't realised it, but I'd been waiting a long time for this.

"I'm sorry, Matthew," Morgan whispered.

"Sorry?"

"I know you didn't want this."

"Oh gods, Morgan, I want it. I've wanted it for so long."

"I know. I've watched you struggle with it. I can't deny, I've been . . ." He was trembling, and he closed his eyes, struggling with his feelings, overwhelmed with emotion.

"I know you have. There have been times . . ."

He smiled. "I know, but . . ."

"Are you regretting it?"

"No," he said quickly. "No, I'm not regretting anything, nothing about you. Never. It's just . . ."

"What?"

"I know you don't want this. I know you want something different. A family."

"What? How? I mean . . ."

"I see it, Matthew," he whispered. "Even now, I see the struggle in you. Your dreams are so close, so important to you. You don't want to let go of them. I'm everything you've fought against for so long. But —"

"What? Wait." I stopped him, my eyes widening as realisation dawned. "You can read my mind, can't you? Those drugs . . ."

Morgan frowned, thoughtfully. "Not exactly. It's not exactly what you'd think. I can . . . for a while. A few days after . . . I can see . . . shapes. The shape of your thoughts, your dreams. That's how I knew —"

"You knew how I was feeling? All the times I struggled and tried to stop it?"

"Not all the time."

Shock coursed through me, memories of the thoughts and feelings I'd suppressed, the way I'd felt every time I was near him — and all the time he knew. No wonder he'd had that

149

smug look on his face. I wasn't sure how I felt about it, that someone could see the innermost workings of my mind, the hidden secrets.

"Please, Matthew. I don't—I don't . . . pry. I don't deliberately search for secrets. I can't help it. I can't control it. It just . . . happens."

He seemed so lost, so sad. Another shocking realisation hit me—he could see how I was feeling. Right now. The anger, the shame, the bitterness—he could see it all. What should I do? Try to hide it? Try to suppress it? Force myself to think of other things?

"That doesn't work."

"What?"

"Trying to hide your feelings just makes them . . . darker. It hurts when you do that."

"Hurts?"

"It makes me feel like you're hiding from me. That you're . . . I don't know. It's hard enough being a freak without knowing your friends are scared of you, embarrassed by you, wary of you."

"I'm none of those things."

"I know." He said it flatly, but suddenly I started laughing. It was so funny.

Morgan's eyes widened with shock. The laughter had come from nowhere, and it surprised both of us. Slowly a smile spread over his face and soon we were both helpless.

After a while, Morgan collapsed at my side, wiping tears of laughter from his eyes. He turned on his side and stared into my eyes, brushing strands of hair out of my face. My hair was a lot shorter than his, but still long enough to get into my eyes. He ran the back of his fingers over the side of my face, and I shivered to my core. I couldn't take my attention off his face, which was suddenly serious and intense again.

"Matthew."

I didn't need to be able to read his mind to know what he was thinking. I opened myself completely, so he'd have no trouble seeing what I was thinking. Essentially, I was screaming *yes* on all levels. Morgan's eyes widened.

"Are you sure?"

"What do you think? You're the mind reader."

"It's not . . . it's fading." Suddenly the intensity disappeared from his face, to be replaced with something else. Sadness?

I ran my fingers through his hair, stroking his face at the same time. "Don't. Not now. This isn't the time for sadness. Later. We'll talk later, okay?"

He smiled thinly and nodded. Oh gods, he was so beautiful. I had to touch him. I had to . . . I had to . . .

Pushing him backward, I slid forward until I was lying half on top of him, and took possession of those sweet, sweet lips. For a moment, he was taken aback, but only for a moment. This time I wasn't just reacting, I was making the play. Gods, I was actually . . . I was . . . oh fuck. Oh fuck.

Somehow, my hands had found their way under his pyjama jacket, and all the buttons had popped, leaving his chest bare. While I was covering one side of it with my body, the other was open to me — so soft, so muscular, so . . .

Morgan moaned as my fingers roamed over his skin and found his nipple. A deep shudder went through him, and I pinched harder. He raised himself off the bed, arching his back, and actually lifted my whole body. Gods, he was strong.

Rolling over, so he was on top of me again, Morgan broke the kiss, and for a moment I actually panicked, until I realised he was frantically scrabbling to remove his jacket altogether. I froze, and so did he. He was kneeling over me now, bare to the waist, his hair like a cloak of shadow over his shoulders, his eyes glittering like chips of emerald. I was awestruck. I couldn't move. I could barely breathe.

Smiling in a slow, sexy way, Morgan reached down and tugged my shirt out of my jeans. I shivered as he pulled it upward, shifting my position slightly so he could get it over my head. Then it was gone, and Morgan was running his hands over my bare skin. I closed my eyes, overcome with sensation.

Slowly, so slowly, he repositioned himself, so he was kneeling between my legs. Then he lowered himself, so he was lying fully on top of me. We were roughly the same height, so our hips fitted closely together. Surprisingly, that was the first time it hit home we were both sporting monster erections because suddenly they were getting up close and friendly with each other, and it scared the shit out of me.

Shit! I'm making out with a man! Shit! We're on his bed and both half-naked! Shit! He was moving his hips in a way that suggested not only did he know exactly what he was doing, but he'd done it before . . . a lot! Shit! It was Morgan. It was Morgan Bentley. Out of all the men I could possibly have imagined I'd have my first gay experience with. Out of all the men in the world. Out of all the people in the world. I would never . . . I would never . . . I . . . never . . . I . . .

"Oh, fuck."

Morgan stopped grinding his hips into me. Instead, he slid down and started kissing my chest, making a little trail down over my collarbone. When his lips closed around my nipple, I sucked in my breath and buried my hands in his hair. Part of me wanted to pull his head away, and part of me wanted to push. They paralysed each other. Playfully, he nipped me, and I jumped, rising off the bed to fall back as he moved on, following his trail downward.

Morgan was good. By the time he slid my jeans over my hips, I was practically delirious and trembling so badly I couldn't have stopped him if I'd wanted to, which I didn't. My dream was fading fast, and an entirely new one was taking its place.

I had my eyes closed and was entirely unprepared when

his lips closed around my cock. I cried out and bucked my hips so hard I almost knocked him off the bed, but he kept his lips firmly sealed around my shaft, and what he was doing with his tongue was dangerous. I couldn't believe it. It was utterly beyond any experience I'd ever had before, mostly because it was Morgan who was giving it to me.

I groaned aloud, and it had more to do with what was happening inside my head than what was happening down below. It was a simple thing really, a very simple thing. It happened every day, to people all over the world. It was just a small click, a slight shift, a sudden realisation. All those hours I'd spent telling Cory how much I hated Morgan. All those glares and snipes and posturing. All the times I thought I hated him — it was all a show, an act, a pretence. I was working so hard to fool myself. Had I ever fooled anyone else? The truth was . . . the simple, perfect, absolute truth was . . . I was in love with him. I was in love with Morgan Bentley, and I think I always had been.

I could remember the very first time I saw him. Cory and I were visiting the university on an open day. We pulled up in our battered old shed and got out of it in immediate awe at the glory and wonder of our surroundings. We were staring at the beautiful architecture of the old buildings when a car came screeching around the corner and skidded to a halt next to us, showering us both with dirt. It wasn't the *Audi*, but something sleek, black, and vicious. The windows were all tinted black, and we watched curiously until the doors opened and people began to spill out.

They weren't in awe. They didn't look as if they'd ever be in awe of anything. There were four of them — two boys and two girls. They were beautiful, all of them. Cory and I exchanged glances because we'd never seen such beautiful people close up. They were laughing and joking and not paying any attention to us at all . . . to anything. Then one of the boys took off the dark shades he was wearing and glanced over at us.

I will never forget the expression on his face in that moment. It was . . . curious, but at the time, I'd thought he was being arrogant, deigning to throw a crumb of his awesome presence at the feet of the plebs. I suddenly realised it was more than that. The look had been hungry. Not sexual, not then. He was hungry for something else — the closeness Cory and I so obviously had. How I wish I'd known then. Almost two years wasted. Two years of hating him, of avoiding him while craving for every moment in his presence. And now . . .

I gasped as Morgan began to massage my hole, quite firmly. I was shocked, and for a moment, I wondered if that had been the intention. He could, after all, read my mind and I supposed he didn't want me drifting off in the middle of . . .

The tip of his finger slipped inside, and I lost the ability to remember, to think about anything other than the incredible things this boy — this man — was doing to my body.

I lay writhing in a fever of sensation as Morgan licked, sucked, squeezed, nipped, and penetrated me, bringing me almost to the point of orgasm, then pulling me back, until I was just about ready to burst. Then he stopped.

Shocked more by his withdrawal than anything he'd previously done, I stared up into his face as he knelt over me, panting.

"Don't stop. Please," I gasped.

"How far do you want to go?"

"How far? I-I don't . . ."

Morgan's eyes were fever bright, and he was shaking as much as I was. He tweaked my nipple, and I almost came. Morgan smiled, almost shyly.

"I want to fuck you, Matthew. Do you . . . can you . . . how far do you want to go? Because we can stop. Or I can—"

I grabbed him and pulled him down onto me. His mouth

tasted of me, and it sent me half crazy.

"All the way. I want to go all the way."

I could barely believe what I was saying. I'd never had sex with anyone before — not all the way — with a man or a woman. I was scared half out of my mind, but . . . but . . .

Morgan slipped his tongue into my mouth, and the buts disappeared. I was barely aware of his hands, which were all over me, until he rolled me over on my side, and his finger slipped inside me. I stiffened. I couldn't help it. It wasn't that I didn't want it, but it was unexpected, and it hurt a little. Morgan relinquished my lips and breathed into my ear. The sensation drove me so crazy that I barely heard the words.

"Any time you want to stop, I'll stop. This is all about you."

"Mpfh," was my only response, the only sound I was able to make. I felt Morgan smile against my neck. Then he bit me, distracting me as his finger completed its entry. I gasped and unconsciously clenched on him, which made him moan with desire. Feverishly, he kissed and bit my neck and shoulder as his finger moved in and out, driving me into a frenzy. My hands clawed at his back, and whimpers bubbled from my lips. There was no question of any kind of conscious thought, and my body went completely into instinct mode, reacting to every move of his without any control.

When Morgan stopped what he was doing and moved himself from me, a sense of loss and a pain shot through me. I rolled onto my back and clutched at him. "No, don't go. Don't stop."

"Wait." He was as breathless as I was, and after a few moments, he was back.

"What?"

"Shhh."

He did something with his hand, and something cold touched me, making me jump.

"Shhh, just relax."

155

This time the finger slid in easily, and the sensation was far beyond anything I'd ever felt before—but it didn't end there. After a moment, he withdrew, and the next time, there were two. Again, I stiffened and clenched, and he paused until I relaxed. After the initial sharp pain, it started to feel good again. As he penetrated deeper, I started to tremble uncontrollably, and I moaned, over and over.

I barely noticed when the third finger went in. I was way too far gone, riding a roller coaster of sensation that threatened to carry me over the edge far, far too soon.

As if realising it, Morgan withdrew and sat up again, kneeling between my legs. I lay panting and shaking, staring up at this unreal creature crouching over me. The shadows were black and white, the world around me dim and insubstantial. The only things of colour were the glowing green orbs, dominating my vision and possessing my soul. I reached for him, but he shook his head and leaned backward.

I realised he was stroking himself, and his eyes were half-closed as his erection grew in his hand. Hungrily I reached for him, replacing his hand with mine. He moaned and leaned back even farther. Feeling the hot, soft skin under my hands, the swelling evidence of his excitement, my own cock jumped against my belly, and I began to shake again.

After a remarkably short time, Morgan groaned and batted my hands out of the way.

"Stop. Stop or I'll . . . stop!"

I raised my head and watched as, with trembling fingers, which were almost too clumsy for the job, he tore apart a silver wrapper and unrolled a condom over his throbbing erection. When he was done, he squeezed something from a tube onto his hands and liberally coated the condom with it. I didn't know what he was doing, but I was prepared to go with it. He clearly knew what he was doing, and I placed myself entirely in his hands.

I let my head fall back and closed my eyes as long, slippery fingers stroked me and brought my softening penis back to life. I moaned and was barely aware when Morgan raised my hips and inched forward until they were supported on his knees. Strong thigh muscles flexed and raised me higher. Then he slipped a finger inside me. It was easy this time, aided by the added lubrication, and I shuddered with sheer pleasure.

He stroked himself with his other hand as he penetrated me with two, then three fingers. Although it wasn't easy, it wasn't painful either, and I moved my hips back to meet him eagerly. He chuckled deep in his throat, then shuddered and sighed, and I felt something bigger than a finger pushing at my entrance.

For a moment, I was afraid. It felt so big. I tensed automatically, and Morgan stopped.

"It's all right, Matthew. I told you I won't . . . I won't go any further than you're comfortable with. If you want me to stop, I will."

The sound of his voice, and his fingers which had begun to stroke me again, stole my voice and my inhibitions. My answer was a thrust of my hips against him and a low moan. Morgan didn't say anything else, but the pressure on my hole increased, and suddenly there was a strange feeling, like something popping, and a searing pain that made me gasp.

Morgan froze, and we just lay there, both of us panting, until the fiery pain dulled to an ache.

"Go . . . go on."

"Are you sure?"

"Do it."

I couldn't say anything else. I was pretty much beyond speech, but my whole being was possessed by him, and I wanted — no, needed — more . . . more . . . more.

He eased himself into me, inch by inch, pausing after each

one while my body acclimatised itself to fit him. Then he was all the way in, and both of his hands were massaging my abdomen and my cock, so I was entirely distracted from the pain in my ass, which really wasn't that bad.

The whole bottom half of my body was trembling so much I barely had any control over it, and when Morgan started to slowly rock his hips back and forth, causing his cock to slide in and out of me, just a little, just . . . just . . . just.

I made a weird wailing noise, and my body raised itself clear off the bed, incoherent sounds coming from my mouth. I clutched convulsively at the bedclothes. Morgan leaned forward, and it didn't even occur to me until later how flexible he was. His lips met mine, and his tongue probed me as he began to move in and out with more purpose. Every time he thrust into me, he hit something deep inside that made me shudder and grunt. The feeling was almost too intense to bear.

Morgan's movements rubbed his belly against my cock, massaging it on the outside as his own cock massaged my insides. I was shaking so badly, I was incapable of conscious movement, and I couldn't return his kiss, only squirm, greedy to claim the incredible sensations, both inside and out, until they built so high that I thought I was going to either explode or pass out. Morgan's breathing was ragged and fast, and he moved faster, his thrusts getting more urgent and more penetrating. I whimpered as it all began to overwhelm me, with wave after wave of a strange deep tingling, each more intense than the last, radiating out from whatever he was touching inside.

I tried to speak, to tell him I was close, but all that came out were whimpers. He was gasping and trembling, and he made grunting sounds and thrust violently into me as I felt his cock spasm and twitch. He howled. Morgan's orgasm was all I needed to send me over the edge into my own, and I convulsed, shuddering and thrusting upward as my cock erupted over and over, until blackness crawled over my senses and I pretty much collapsed, struggling to remain conscious.

Morgan fell across me, knocking the breath out of me so that, for a moment, I think I did pass out, but only for a moment. Then I was opening my eyes and staring in wonder at the dark head lying on my shoulder. I just had to stroke that glorious hair, and from there, my hands wandered down over the muscular shoulders and a smooth back, slick with sweat.

Slowly, Morgan rolled off me. He took care of the condom, then lay on his side, with one leg still hooked over mine. I half-turned to face him and pushed the heavy, damp hair out of the way so I could see his face. He was smiling, his emerald eyes dreamy, his lips swollen from kissing.

I felt my lips twitch, but my brain wasn't yet connected enough to initiate speech.

Reaching out with a hand that still shook slightly, Morgan stroked my cheek and brushed my lips with a finger that tasted like strawberry. I licked my lips, puzzled, and Morgan smiled.

"Flavoured condoms and lube." He shrugged at my wide-eyed surprise. "I know, but . . ." He shrugged again. "It tastes a whole lot better than latex, especially when you're sucking."

I blushed at that, and Morgan laughed. "You're awesome, Matthew. After what we just did, you can blush at the mere thought of oral . . . just awesome."

My blush deepened, and I lowered my eyes, but I was grinning like a fool.

Morgan sighed deeply, and I raised my eyes again. There was a wistful expression in his eyes.

"What's wrong?"

"Nothing. I just wish we could stay here, like this, forever. That . . . that things weren't so complicated."

"Are they complicated? It all seems very simple to me. I've never felt, never experienced — fuck, I'd kill to do that again. I love you, Morgan. I think I always have."

The wistful smile turned even more introverted. "I know. It's not you. It's not us." He sighed again, and his lips trembled. "It's me. My situation."

For a brief moment of blessed numbness, I had no idea what he was talking about — then it all came crashing back. How could I have forgotten, even for a moment? Tears sprang to my eyes, and I blinked them back impatiently.

"How long?" I whispered.

"I don't know. He's never really talked about it. In the beginning, when I first found out, I fought against him. Sometimes he shouted at me and sometimes tried to reassure me. He told me he was sure the modifications he'd made rendered the drug stable and safe for humans. When it became obvious it wasn't, he told me the lab was working round the clock to fix things. He said he was sorry. He'd never have done this if he'd known . . . but I don't know if I believe that."

Lifting his gaze over my shoulder, as if he couldn't bear to look at me when he spoke, he murmured, "Recently he's been . . . harsher. Whenever I've asked him . . . sometimes begged him . . . to tell me what's happening, what's going to happen, he just shuts me out. I've done my own research, as best I can, not really knowing what's in the injections he gives me, and it doesn't look good. The one thing he will tell me is that if I don't get the injections regularly, I'll die. If he misses a couple of days, I get really ill."

"So, as long as he keeps giving you the injections, you'll be all right?" Hope flared, but it died when his eyes caught mine again.

"No. The drug is changing me genetically, changing my body chemistry, but it isn't stable, which means it's degrading, slowly but surely, and at some point, my own body's defences will realise it's being attacked and fight back. Once that happens, I'll go down fast."

"No. I won't let that happen. I won't. I'll find a way somehow. I-I don't exactly know how, but there must be a way. Cory. Cory said he was . . . well, he seemed to suggest he was . . . and Cory is . . . he . . ."

I stuttered to a halt as all hope was swallowed by the hopelessness in his eyes. "I've kind of come to terms with it, I suppose. I can feel it . . . the changes happening. And I can feel when . . . when it all starts breaking down. Most of the time I'm strong, but if my father's a day late with the injection . . . it used to be once a week, then twice, and now it's every day. If he misses a day, I get ill very quickly, and I don't think I could last more than two days without one. With the time gap getting shorter and shorter, I figure I don't have much time left. Maybe a couple of weeks, a bit more—if I get the injections when I need them."

I was speechless. What could I say? What could anyone say? I just looked into his eyes and tried to will him to know how deeply I felt, how much I loved him and wanted him to be well and strong. He stroked my cheek again.

"I know."

CHAPTER TWELVE

We must have fallen asleep because I was suddenly jerked awake. For a moment, I had no idea where I was, or what had woken me. Then I saw Morgan, fast asleep, his head on the pillow next to me. I automatically reached out to touch him. He sighed and snuggled into the pillow but didn't wake.

Then I realised what had woken me was my mobile. It was ringing in the pocket of my jeans, which were . . . somewhere.

Morgan and I were still tangled together, and separating wasn't as easy as might be expected because we were literally stuck to each other. Morgan muttered and stirred, and eventually rolled away from me, still not waking. I took the time to pull up the covers and tuck them around his naked body before I slipped out of bed. The action was not entirely altruistic as I would never be able to have a coherent conversation with anyone while gazing on perfection.

The ringing stopped as I was fishing the phone out of my pocket — typical. I groaned when I saw the call was from Cory. Shit! I was supposed to have been there by now, wherever *there* was. I quickly called back and wandered over to the window while the phone rang the other end.

"Where the fuck are you?" Cory hissed without preamble.

"At Morgan's."

"Why are you still there? I've been frantic. You should have been here ages ago."

"Yeah, well . . . um . . . things are a bit more complicated than we thought."

"What do you mean?"

"It's too late, Cory. Morgan's father's been giving him the drugs for weeks. He can't leave. He needs the injections every day, or he'll die."

Cory swore, using words and phrases I'd never heard pass his lips before. "Hang on," he said shortly at the end, and I was left staring out of the window, holding a silent phone to my ear for at least five minutes.

"Bring him here, quickly."

"Cory, didn't you hear what I told you? He can't. He needs—"

"Just bring him here, Matthew. We can handle it. You have to get him out of there before his father arrives today. He'll know by now what we've done, and he'll kill Morgan if he thinks there's any chance we can get to him. I'll explain everything when you get here, only please, Matthew, please get out of there . . . *right now.*"

"All right, all right, calm down." I forgot to lower my voice and heard Morgan stir behind me. "Cory, just calm down, and I'll see what I can do."

"*No*! Don't *see what you can do*. Get out of there now. If he finds you there, he'll kill you, too. He won't let you leave because he knows you're my friend. Please, Matthew. *Please.* Just get out of there. If Morgan won't go so be it, but just leave. Leave right now."

"All right already, I get the message."

"Matthew?" Morgan's sleepy voice spun me around. I smiled and waved to him, indicating I wouldn't be long.

"No, you don't. I'm not joking, Matthew, really. You're in danger. You're both in danger. He'll be on his way there by now. You don't have much time. Please!"

"All right, Cory, don't worry. We're leaving. We're leaving now. Are you sure Morgan will be—"

"I told you, I've got it covered. Don't you trust me?"

"Of course I trust you. It's just—"

"Since when have you been so concerned about Morgan anyway?" There was something strange in his voice, and I didn't have time to work out what it was.

"Since . . . since . . . it doesn't matter since when. The fact is I do, so—"

"Trust me." Cory's voice was soft and held a note of—what—sadness?

"I trust you. I've always trusted you."

"You still have the directions?"

"Of course I do."

"Hurry."

"I will."

When I hung up, I was feeling decidedly shaken and uncertain. I wasn't sure what to do. I'd turned back to the window, and I found for a moment I couldn't move. Fear and indecision gripped me and held me, until a pair of warm, strong arms slid around my waist from behind. I jumped, startled, then relaxed and leaned back into the embrace.

"Cory?"

"Yeah."

"Is he giving you hassle?"

"Kind of. He says we have to get out of here because your father knows what he's been doing and is on his way here. He . . . he says he's going to kill you to stop anyone else getting hold of you and—"

"I can believe that." Morgan's soft voice in my ear was flat and hopeless. Suddenly, anger fired in me, and I turned in his arms, breaking his hold. I put my hands on his shoulders and made him meet my eyes.

"Cory says they can help you. They can at least keep you alive until—"

"Who's *they*?"

"I don't know. He's working with some group or something. I don't really know what he's up to. He said he'll explain when we get there."

"We?"

"Of course, *we*. I'm not going anywhere without you."

Morgan looked sad, sadder than I've ever seen him. "He's right about you. You have to go. If he knows what Cory's done, he can't find you here."

"I'm not going anywhere without you," I repeated flatly.

"I can't leave. You know that."

"No. You have to come with me. If you stay here, your father will kill you."

"Maybe."

"Cory says he can help you, and I believe him. I trust him. If you stay here, you *know* you're going to die. If you come with me, maybe . . ."

For a moment, something flared in his eyes, something that could have been hope, but it didn't last long. I watched it die. He shook his head.

"I can't, Matthew. You don't know what it's like, what it feels like, this thing inside me. It hurts, and I-I don't want to hurt anymore."

I knew what he was really saying and it terrified me. "Please, Morgan. Please don't do this."

"I . . . at least here I'm in my home, with my family."

"The family who cared so much about you, he was prepared to throw your life away for a dream. If you stay here, you know you're going to die. I can't—"

Morgan put a finger on my lips. "Yes, you can. You can do anything, Matthew, anything."

"There's one thing I can't do, Morgan."

He tilted his head to one side quizzically. "What's that?"

"I can't leave you here to die. If you stay, I stay."

Again, something flared in his eyes, but this time it was less definable. "I can't let you do that!"

"It isn't a matter of *let*. How do you think you could stop me? Throw me out of the window?"

He shook his head, then gazed deeply into my eyes. I projected everything I was feeling as hard as I could. The absolute certainty I'd rather stay here and die with him than leave him to die alone. The burning love I felt, that permeated every cell of my being. My trust in Cory. The hope. The fear. Slowly, I watched something change—something fall—something die and something spring into life.

At last, he nodded purposefully. "All right. You win. I want to be with you, Matthew, for as long as I can. I don't care if I die sooner. It's worth it. And if you have that much faith in Cory . . . okay, I'll come."

I hugged him tightly and didn't want to let go. I could tell he didn't either. We were both shaking.

"Get dressed," I ordered more harshly than I meant. I released him and scrabbled on the floor for my discarded clothes.

In only a few minutes, we were both dressed. Hastily, Morgan threw things into a backpack. The last thing he did was fire up his computer, press some buttons, and pocket a memory stick. I waited in a frenzy of impatience, staring out of the window, expecting at any time to hear footsteps in the hall.

Finally, he was ready.

"Come on."

Cautiously, we opened the door and made sure there was no one on the landing before we crept out. Now he'd made his decision, Morgan was purposeful and didn't seem nervous or even in any particular hurry.

Rather than leading me toward the main stairs as I'd expected, he drew me along the landing, and I realised we were making for the back stairs, the ones I'd been led up by Ben, the kitchen hand, only a few hours ago.

The kitchen was warm and in full swing. Mrs Wight came

scuttling up to us and gave Morgan a hug.

"It's lovely to see you, Morgan. I've been worried."

"I'm all right, Mrs Wight. I'm going to stay with Matthew for a while, but I'd prefer if my father didn't know."

Mrs Wight gave him a hard look, and with a strangely motherly gesture, brushed his hair back behind his shoulders.

"You take care of yourself. Like I said, I've been worried about you. You haven't been yourself lately. Don't worry about your father. He won't hear a word from me or anyone here." She glared at everyone who'd been watching the little scene with interest. They hurriedly went back to work.

Leaning closer to Morgan, she spoke low and conspiratorially. "Your father's on his way. He rang through about half an hour ago to ask if you'd eaten yet. If you want to miss him, you'd better get going. He'll be here in ten, fifteen minutes."

Morgan looked startled. "Thank you, Mrs Wight. If he asks, can you tell him . . . tell him . . . tell him I've gone to the university, to pick up some papers or something. Tell him anything so he won't come after me."

"Of course. Morgan, is everything all right?"

Morgan tried to smile, but it just didn't work. This woman clearly knew him too well.

"No, not just now. I'm hoping . . . I hope that . . . that we can . . . but . . ." Horrifyingly, tears started to leak from his eyes. He dashed them away ineffectively as they flowed down his cheeks. I suppose it suddenly hit him this might be the last time he stood here, in this warm, familiar place with these warm, familiar arms around him. It was unbearable, and it made the whole situation suddenly more pressing, more real.

Mrs Wight hugged him tightly. Her eyes spoke volumes. I shrugged. What could I say?

Pulling back a little, but still holding Morgan firmly by the shoulders, she peered into his face, but he wouldn't meet her eyes.

"What's going on? Does this have something to do with your father?"

Dumbly, he nodded. Mrs Wight opened her mouth to say something but then shook her head. "If that's the case, you'd better be gone before he gets here. You can tell me about it another time."

Morgan's head snapped up, and I thought he was going to say something, but he seemed to change his mind at the last moment, and all he said was, "Yeah, another time." It was all there in his voice, and Mrs Wight gave him another hard stare.

"Go. Keep safe." She glared at me, a piercing look that stripped me bare to the soul. "You take care of him."

"I swear I will. At least, I'll do everything I can."

Mrs Wight narrowed her eyes, then smiled and nodded. "It finally happened, then."

I was shocked rigid. What did she mean? Did she know? Had Morgan been talking to her about me? My mind was flooded with questions, but she merely shooed me out the door.

Morgan led me around the side of the house to a large garage, where several cars gleamed dully in the dim light. One of them was the black car I'd first seen him drive. He ignored that, though, and headed for his silver convertible.

"Morgan, my car's parked outside the front door. If your father sees it . . ."

Morgan stared at me for a moment, then nodded. "Wait in the car." Tossing me the keys and his backpack, he disappeared. For a long moment, I stared after him, my heart racing, before I opened the door. Throwing the pack into the back, I slid into the passenger seat.

Morgan wasn't gone long. He smiled when he got into the driving seat. "All taken care of."

The car purred to life, and Morgan slid it expertly out of the garage through a space I'd never have tried to drive through, especially not in a car like this. I supposed he must have been used to it.

I gripped tightly to the door handle as the tires spun on the gravel, and the car shot down the drive as if the hounds of hell were after us. As we approached, the gates swung open and I panicked, thinking it was because Morgan's father had opened them from the other side, but there was no sign of any car as we shot through.

"How did the gates open?"

"There's a built-in sensor in the car. They open automatically when they pick it up."

"Wow."

Morgan shrugged.

We'd been driving for at least fifteen minutes, with Morgan peering in the mirror every few seconds, before he glanced at me and asked, "Where are we going?"

It made me laugh. I don't know why, but the thought we'd been driving for all this time without him even thinking to ask where we were going struck me as hilarious. For a moment, Morgan seemed shocked. Then he smiled, too.

"So . . . where?"

"I don't know. Hang on, and I'll find out."

I took my phone out of my pocket and found Cory's message. It took a moment to unscramble it and switch on the sat-nav.

"Can you program that into the car? It would be easier for me."

"I can try, but Cory's the technical genius, not me."

After five minutes of pressing buttons and almost deleting the message, I gave up. Morgan pulled over and programmed the coordinates I gave him into the car. We discovered we'd been heading in the wrong direction and turned around.

After about ten minutes, my phone rang. It was Cory.

"Are you on your way?"

"Yes."

"Is Morgan with you?"

"Yes."

"Oh, thank God. I've been so worried. Are you sure you're not being followed?"

"As sure as I can be. We left before Morgan's father got there."

"But he might have had the gates watched."

"Cory, Morgan's been looking over his shoulder every five seconds. No one's following us."

"And you unscrambled the directions okay?"

"Yes. We started off driving in the wrong direction, but we're on track now."

"Where are you?"

"According to the sat-nav, about half an hour away."

"Good. I'll ring you again in ten minutes to make sure you're still okay."

"Cory, I'm in a car, driving with Morgan. What could possibly happen to me in ten minutes?"

"I'll ring to make sure," he insisted stubbornly.

"All right. Whatever."

Morgan was silent for a while after I hung up. I sneaked glances at him, and he seemed to be deep in thought. The thoughts were clearly not pleasant ones. That didn't surprise me.

"Are you okay?"

"For now."

"What are you thinking about, if it's not a stupid question?"

Again, he was silent for a while. His hands on the wheel were white-knuckled.

"You and Cory are close, aren't you?" he said finally.

"Yes. We've been friends forever."

"I wish I had a friend like that."

"You've got lots of friends."

"I have a lot of people who hang around with me. That's not the same as friends."

"No, I suppose not. Well, you have friends now. You have me, and by default that also means Cory, whether you want him or not."

Morgan laughed shortly. "I doubt Cory's going to want to be my friend. Now less than ever."

That really shocked me. "Why? He won't hold what your father's doing against you."

"No, not that. But there is something he *will* hold against me."

"Don't be silly. What on earth would Cory have to hold against you? He barely knows you."

Morgan licked his lips slowly and flashed me a look, his eyes dark. Then he said softly, "You."

"Me? What do you mean?"

"Don't you know?"

"Know what? You're not making sense." My words came out more harshly than I'd intended because they called to something that had been niggling in the back of my mind for some time, something I didn't want to acknowledge. I hadn't meant to snap at him, and I hated that he winced at the annoyance in my tone, but he shook it off.

"I'm sorry. A lot of things in my life make no sense at the moment." He closed his eyes briefly, but thankfully opened them again pretty quickly, given that he was driving.

"So," I tried again, more calmly, "what are you trying to say?"

"I'm not trying to say anything. I'm merely pointing out that when Cory finds out about us, he isn't going to be very pleased and certainly not in any rush to be my best friend."

"Why not? Do you think he'll be jealous? That's silly. Cory wouldn't be that shallow. It's not as if . . . as if . . ." I stumbled to a halt, a horrible little kernel of suspicion gnawing at the back of my mind. I stared at Morgan, who was keeping his eyes firmly fixed on the road. "Don't tell me. Just *don't* tell me. I don't . . . you . . . you shouldn't! *No!*"

"I'm sorry. I thought you knew."

"No. I-I've never. Well, of course, I kind of did. I mean, I always . . . but . . . but we never and . . . and you shouldn't have," I finished lamely.

"I couldn't help it. I didn't need mind-reading skills to see that. It was written all over him, which is why I thought you knew."

"You've made a mistake. You must have. It's never been like that between us, never. We're friends, that's all." But what about all those times we'd fooled around, and I'd jokingly promised if I ever thought I might be gay, I'd come to him first? What about all the times he'd jokingly told me if I hadn't been straight, he wouldn't be able to keep his hands off me? I was joking, and I thought he was, too, but hadn't I always known . . . hadn't I?

"No. It just can't be," I said firmly, not because I didn't think it was, but because I didn't want it to be.

We drove the rest of the way in silence, with me brooding and Morgan thinking gods knew what. There was a barrier between us that hadn't been there before.

In the end, we were driving along country roads and eventually turned into what appeared to be a farm, with a farmhouse nestled into the crook of a hill, a scattering of outbuildings surrounding it and a large barn just across what I suppose would have been termed the farmyard. The only thing that suggested maybe it wasn't a farm was that there were no animals in sight.

As we bumped along the road toward the farmyard,

Morgan turned his head toward me, just for a moment, and I got a flash of green through the curtain of hair that practically hid his face.

"I'm sorry."

"Sorry? Why are you sorry?"

"For everything. I should never have . . . all this time I was . . . and I never . . . at least when I knew how you felt, what you were hiding, I should have said something. I should have . . . and now everything's screwed, and I don't want to come between you and Cory. I don't want to spoil what you have when . . . when I . . . when maybe we won't be . . . it won't be long."

I didn't know what to say but saying nothing wasn't an option. "Well," I said carefully. "I think if you'd said anything sooner, I wouldn't have accepted it. It wasn't just a case of you being interested in me and me being interested in you. Okay, I felt an attraction right from the start, but for a long time I was convinced what I felt was contempt because it couldn't be anything else, because I'm straight . . . right?

"If you'd done anything to show you're attracted to me, I'd have run a mile, so there really wasn't anything you could have done, other than what you did. And as for things being screwed . . . I can't disagree with you there, but it isn't your fault. None of it's your fault. As for me and Cory . . . well, we've been friends for a long time, a very long time. I know him better than anyone, or at least I thought I did. This is not going to come between us. Never.

"And . . . and . . . well, the rest of it's going to have to come as it will, but I'm not going to let you go without a fight. If Cory can't help you, I'm going to find someone who can. I don't care who and I don't care how. I will."

We were pulling into the farmyard at this point, and as Morgan slowed to a stop, he turned to me. There were tears in his eyes.

"I love you, Matthew. Whatever happens after this, always remember that. I love you. I've loved you for a long time, and I will love you until my last breath and beyond. Don't ever forget that."

"I won't forget it, because I'm going to make you say it to me every day for the rest of our lives."

He smiled wryly, and I knew what he was thinking, but he didn't say anything, and neither did I. By the time the moment passed, there wasn't time or opportunity to say anything because a whirlwind hit us . . . a whirlwind called Cory.

He came running around the side of the house with another man close on his heels. Skidding to a stop, he yanked open my door and practically dragged me from the car. The other man was doing the same with Morgan, who resisted quite a bit more than I did.

"Get out of the car, Morgan," Cory snapped irritably. "We have to get it undercover, out of sight. Are you sure you weren't followed?"

"Yeah, we're sure. We haven't seen a soul for the last couple of miles."

"Good. Come on."

"Where are we going? Where is this place? Cory, we're in the middle of nowhere. I hope you know what you're doing. Morgan . . ."

"Yeah, yeah, I know. Come *on*, will you?"

He dragged at my arm and shot a glance at Morgan, who shrugged, then whipped around as his car practically did a wheelie and raced off in the opposite direction, over a field.

"Is my car going to be all right?"

"I think that's the least of your worries," Cory said, so coldly it shocked me.

"Cory? What's going on?"

"Let's get out of sight, and I'll tell you. No, I'll show you." Changing direction, he towed me toward the barn. With nothing else to do, Morgan followed us.

The doors of the barn were enormous, but there was a smaller entry cut into the bottom of one. Cory rapped on it in a complicated tattoo that resulted in the door swinging open and an anxious-looking young man peering out. His eyes widened when he saw Morgan, but he stepped back and let the three of us duck inside.

I'd been expecting a gloomy, cavernous space — it was anything but. A large sheet of thick plastic hung from ceiling to floor — stretched over a frame to make a kind of temporary wall — separating the main body of the barn from a kind of reception area of about ten feet by thirty — the width of the barn. Against the outside wall were a number of battered lockers, and there were a few hard, wooden chairs scattered about. The young man who'd let us in was dressed head to foot in white — a white jumpsuit with a hood, to be exact, and white pumps. He had a mask around his neck, as if he'd just pulled it down.

"Wait here."

Cory seemed a lot more relaxed, now we were safely inside, and he sank into one of the chairs. Morgan and I both remained standing.

"What the hell is this all about, Cory?"

"I'm not really sure."

"Oh great, now you tell me. Do you have any idea what Morgan's risking coming here? You said you could help him. I only brought him because you promised you'd be able to—"

"And I will."

"How can you be so sure?"

"Because. Look, to cut a long story short, I hacked into the main ITM computer and downloaded all the files relating to Project X. I saved them on my computer and started going through them. When I got to the part where the GMC refused the license, and the government backing was withdrawn, I thought that would be it. It was the end of the files I had, but there was something odd. It wasn't . . . final enough.

"So I went back and had another look. It took me a long time to get in there, and in the meantime, I found someone I thought could help me. I sounded him out, felt I could trust him, and we worked together to find the key."

"So that's why you haven't been around."

"I've been here most of the time—over the last couple of days—since I found it. They have some awesome equipment here. It wasn't set up to work on Project X, but there have been some pretty similar experiments going on. It was all done in secret, because they were worried about what Morgan's father would do if he found out he had competitors who were, well, using his work as a sounding board."

"Stealing his research, you mean?" Morgan asked dryly. Cory glared at him, and goodness knows what would have happened if I hadn't intervened.

"Not now. If you really have to, you can go through this later. For now, can you please get to the point? How you, or whoever, plan to help Morgan."

Cory gave Morgan a final glare. "Okay, but let me get one thing straight. My friends were not, and are not, trying to steal your father's research. At first, they absolutely forbade me from looking for more matter from ITM, but you know what I'm like. I couldn't let it lie, and in the end, they helped me. When I eventually got in, I was delighted—until I read the files. I only managed to get them completely decrypted last night. They're not up to date. I thought they were, but they only got so far as talking about . . . about what he intended to do, and it was pretty cryptic about who the subject was, but it was pretty obvious to me, so I called you straightaway."

"So why all the cloak and dagger?"

"Because when I downloaded the files, I triggered some

kind of device. ITM know they've been hacked, and pretty soon they'll know by whom. Fortunately, I used my own server, so they can only trace it back to me, not to this place, but . . . well . . . it pretty much means I can't go back to our place . . . and neither can you."

"Why can't I?"

"Because they know you're my friend and they'd use you to get to me."

This was all getting a little too much *James Bond* for me, and I didn't know whether to laugh, walk out, or break down. It was only the fact Morgan was standing beside me, his head bowed and his body trembling, that kept me focused.

"So these people you've been working with. You're sure you can trust them?"

"Oh, yes." Cory beamed. "They know all about ITM. They worked with Morgan's father at one point but parted ways when he started talking about going behind the GMC's refusal to grant a license. They know all about Project X, and they've been working on similar projects but in far more ethical ways."

"And you really think they can help Morgan?"

"I—"

"Let me answer that, if I can. I'm afraid I can make no guarantees, no more than Professor Bentley can, or ever could, but I believe you have more chance with me than you do with him, Morgan."

Morgan's head snapped up at the sound of the voice, and his eyes went wide.

"Professor Burridge!"

CHAPTER THIRTEEN

"Hello, Morgan," the professor said quietly. "I'm so sorry it's come to this."

"Not as sorry as I am."

"You know him?" I was shocked, I have to admit, although I wasn't entirely sure why. This was all happening so fast and was all so strange that if I thought about it . . . of *course* Morgan would have known the other protagonist. How many people do things like this? It made sense they all knew each other.

"Professor Burridge used to work with my father. He left when ITM lost the license and government contract."

The professor peered at him over his glasses. "Not precisely *left*, Morgan. Your father and I had . . . let's say a difference of opinion regarding ethics and methods. I was given an ultimatum—compromise my morals or leave. I had no choice but to be true to myself."

"Where were your morals when you stole my father's research? I presume that's what's going on here."

"You surprise me, Morgan. Still defending your father after everything he's done to you?"

"No, I'm not defending him. I just hate hypocrisy."

"So do I, and I can assure you that, until Cory here came to me, there was nothing in my research I stole from your father. All I brought here was my own work and knowledge. If it were not that Cory unearthed such disturbing information about your father's intentions, I would not have entertained looking at his files."

For a long moment, Morgan locked gazes with the professor. Then he nodded and sighed, bowing his head. He seemed exhausted, and I moved closer to him, protectively. He turned his head and smiled at me, draping an arm around my shoulders casually. No one but me realised how heavily he was leaning on me.

"As it happens, you are fortunate I've continued with my own work, Morgan. Your father and I disagreed about some of the most basic premises of the research. He was looking for end results, and I was more interested in consolidating what we have before we reach for more. That's why his formulae were always unstable, while mine, although less advanced, are far more stable."

"And you think you can help me?"

"I can try. How long has your father been giving you the serum?"

"I'm not sure. I didn't know about it to begin with. I've only known about it for a couple of weeks."

"And how is it affecting you?"

"The effects work, for a while, in a way. Then they fade, and I go down with them. In the beginning, when I didn't know what he was doing, I found that every couple of weeks I'd get really tired and drained of energy. Then my father would visit, and I'd suddenly be on top of the world—hyperaware, all my senses firing on hyperdrive, and I'd have this . . . this . . . ability to see the shape of people's thoughts.

"As time went on, the gaps between feeling good and feeling like shit got shorter and shorter. I think that's why he told me, in the end. Now I have to have the serum every day."

"How long has it taken to go from once a week to every day?"

"Three or four weeks. It's speeding up every day."

"That's worrying, but I'm fairly certain I can at least slow it down, buy time. I need to do some tests before I can say any more."

Morgan's head was up now, his eyes burning. His fingers gripped my shoulder so hard it hurt, really hurt, but he wasn't doing it consciously, and he needed it, so I didn't say a word.

"Do you mean . . . do you think . . . do you think there . . . there's a chance you might be able to . . . to stop . . . to . . ."

Professor Burridge smiled kindly and shook his head. "I don't know, Morgan. My own research is showing very promising results. It's not killing the subjects like your father's did, but whether I can modify it to reverse the effects of his, I just don't know. I need to find out what's going on inside you before I can even begin to consider whether I can do anything about it."

Morgan nodded gravely, relaxing his grip on my shoulder. "I appreciate that."

"I'd like to have the opportunity of talking this through with you, Morgan. Of showing you my research and discussing the options, but I really don't think we have the time."

Morgan swallowed and shook his head. "You don't."

The professor put a hand on Morgan's shoulder and squeezed affectionately. "I've known you since you were a little boy when your father would bring you to work with him. I remember showing you how to use a microscope when you were too small to reach the eyepiece. I've watched you grow up, and I'm damned if I'm going to watch you die."

Morgan hesitated, looking so . . . lost. I found myself putting my arm around his waist and pulling him close. For a moment, he rested his head on my shoulder, then straightened, dropped his arm, squared his shoulders, and nodded. "Whatever it takes."

I glanced up, aware of eyes on me, to find Cory staring at me with the strangest expression on his face. It was a complex mixture of anger, sadness, loss, and fear. I was suddenly uncomfortable, and for the first time since we'd known each other, I couldn't look at him.

"Before you go inside, you're going to have to change. It's a sterile environment. You'll have to wear protective suits."

Cory was already opening a locker and pulling out one of the white coveralls the other boy was wearing. I followed, and Morgan moved to copy, but the professor stopped him.

"Not you, Morgan. I'll fix you up with something else in a bit . . . when we know where we're going."

Morgan's eyes widened a little, but he didn't say a word. Strangely, I could see the turmoil going on behind his eyes, even though he was wearing his usual unruffled and slightly sardonic exterior. It came as a shock to realise that all this time it had only ever been a façade.

When we were done, and I was feeling like a freak in the stiff white overalls and soft-soled plimsolls, we followed the professor through the plastic screen and stopped, awed. Inside, the barn had been converted into a sterile laboratory. The bare stone walls had been covered with sheets of plastic which stretched across the beams, high above.

All along one side were benches heaped with equipment — some electronic and some laboratory. Four people, dressed in the same white coveralls, so it was impossible to tell if they were male or female, were working at the benches and didn't even glance up when we entered. The other side of the barn was screened off into cubicles, which seemed about ten feet square. It was just possible to see the shape of someone moving about in the nearest one.

Overhead, in what I supposed had once been the hayloft, the sound of animal occupation floated down like chaff. Craning my neck, I could see the metallic gleam of cages. Shit . . . this was the real deal.

The professor led us down the length of the barn and sat at a desk set at right angles to the working tables across the back wall of the barn . . . laboratory. The desk was strewn with papers, gadgets, and equipment. He scooped up the papers into an untidy pile and pulled forward a strange piece of equipment resembling a camera on a poseable arm, mounted on a black box, with a piece of glass set into it. The lens of the camera pointed downward, toward the box. The box itself was connected to the computer.

"I need to run a few tests, Morgan, to see if my serum will help or hurt you even more. Is that all right?"

Morgan nodded. He looked even more tired and sort of defeated. I put my arm around his waist, and he gave me a tight smile before resting his head on my shoulder with a sigh.

"Okay, sit down." Professor Burridge motioned to a chair at the end of the desk. Morgan sank into it.

"Are you all right?"

Glancing up at me, Morgan smiled thinly. "No, not really. It's well past time, and I need . . ." He shuddered. "I need my shot. I'm starting to feel . . . not good."

The professor patted his hand, which rested on the corner of the desk. "Don't worry, Morgan. It may not be of particular comfort, but at this stage, the worse you feel, the better. The results of our tests will be much clearer if they're not obscured by the serum in your blood."

"Great."

"This won't take long. I'll be as quick as I can."

He didn't hurry as he thoroughly examined Morgan. He listened to his heart, squeezed various parts of his body, peered for ages into his eyes, using various items of equipment, and finally drew blood and stared at it for what seemed like hours, through the camera type thingie that turned out to be an electronic microscope.

Through it all, Morgan remained silent, and for most of the time, his gaze was locked with mine. Many expressions, from fear to hope, chased through the deep emeralds. I was lost in them. If I hadn't been hopelessly, completely, and totally in love with him before, I was now. There was something about his vulnerability — that he was reaching out to me for comfort — that was deeply attractive.

While the professor was still examining his blood through the microscope, Morgan wilted. It didn't happen suddenly, but it was quick nevertheless. At first, he just looked more and more tired. He massaged his temple, as if he had a bad headache. I stood next to the chair and put my arm around his shoulder. He rested his head against me, but not for long.

After only a few minutes, he pulled away, folded his arms on the desk, and lowered his head. I watched him for a while as the tension in his shoulders increased.

"Professor?"

The professor actually jumped. He raised his head from the microscope, glaring at me with a mixture of annoyance and surprise.

"What?" he said irritably. "Can't you see I'm busy? This is fascinating, fascinating." He smiled happily and moved to turn back to the microscope.

"I'm sure it is, but are you going to be long? I don't think Morgan's doing too well."

At the sound of his name, Morgan tried to raise his head but only made it a couple of inches. He glanced at the professor with eyes that looked drugged, before his head fell again. I thought he'd passed out, but when the professor spoke to him, he answered groggily, in short syllables.

"Oh, dear. Do forgive me. I got carried away. Morgan, are you able to hold on for a little while longer?"

"Yes."

"Have you been like this before?"

"Yes."

"This bad?"

"Yes."

"Worse?"

"Yes."

The professor seemed shocked. "Did your father deliberately let you go down as far as possible so he could observe the results?"

"Yes."

"Every time?"

"No. Sometimes he was in a hurry."

The professor let his hand rest on Morgan's head for a moment, in an affectionate gesture.

"I won't do that to you, Morgan. I won't treat you as an interesting experiment . . ." He appeared slightly uncomfortable and ashamed. "Not anymore."

More brusque and business-like, he turned back to the microscope, inputting something with the keyboard as he did so. After only a few minutes, he laid it aside and sat for a moment, tapping his teeth.

"My serum is very different from your father's. I think from the residue in your blood, his degenerates at a far more rapid rate. Even in the time I've been observing it, it has broken down. And it has a tendency to invade local cells, so it's no wonder it makes you feel so ill.

"Part of the problem is that when it's injected into your blood, it's carried around your body before it gets to the cells it was designed to bond with. As it travels, it tries to bond with other cells and in the process destroys them. The good news is that it takes a lot of mutated cells to attack a single healthy cell, and the attacked cells are destroyed, not mutated. The mutated cells die with the healthy ones, so they don't multiply. The bad news is that it's having a lasting effect on your blood. The red cell count is extremely low, and that's making you ill, as well as the effects of the serum.

"Have you been feeling tired, Morgan? Dizzy? Even just after being given the serum?"

"Yes. More . . . and . . . more." Morgan was breathing fast

and having trouble speaking. I put my hand on his shoulder and noticed he was trembling. I had the feeling he wouldn't be able to raise his head at all now.

"Has your father never checked your blood count, Morgan?"

"No." This time, Morgan had to consciously take a breath before he could reply, and it came out on the wings of a sigh. I watched the professor anxiously, but if he noticed how fast Morgan was failing, he didn't show any signs of being concerned about it. Unhurried, he pinched his lip thoughtfully.

"All things considered, I don't think this is a bad thing. So many of the mutant cells are being soaked up in the blood before they reach their destination . . . not many can be getting through. This is good, very good, because it means the core mutation is not as advanced as it might otherwise have been. I believe there's a good chance we might be able to, if not reverse it, then at least stabilise it. It will only require fairly minor modifications to our research and development."

Despite my growing concern for Morgan's present condition, that piqued my interest.

"What do you mean? Do you mean you can cure him?"

"Not cure, not as such. This isn't a disease or an infection. It's a mutation of the basic genetic makeup of certain clusters of cells in the brain and —"

"Please, I don't understand any of this stuff. Just tell me simply. Does this mean you can help him, that Morgan won't die?"

"We all die, dear boy. Some sooner, some later. But we all go down that road in the end. What it means is that I may . . . and that's a big *may* . . . be able to stabilise the mutation and prevent it degrading further and affecting any more of his unmutated cells. What that means, I can't be sure in the long term. But at least in the short, and possibly the medium term, it appears promising for a —"

"I asked for simple."

"Simply? Maybe, at least for a while. Our serum is very new, even more so than Morgan's father's. The results are excellent so far, but we don't know what will happen in months . . . or years. All I can say is, if my suspicions are confirmed, and if we can deliver the serum to the right place at the right time, we may well be able to help him for now. I don't know what will happen later."

"That's good, yes? You do a couple more tests, give him the serum, and he's good for at least a couple of months, and possibly for years, or forever."

"It's not quite as simple as that. The tests themselves are—" The professor cut himself short as if realising for the first time he was talking to me. "I think this is something I should be discussing with Morgan himself. It's going to take time to set up the tests and procedures I'll need—" He stopped, seeming a little irritated, as he searched for words. Presumably to dumb it down. "There's a difference between animals and a human being, even in the way the equipment is set up. That's going to take some time. I'll give Morgan a shot of the serum, which will buy us time to do that. Unfortunately, there's a distinct likelihood my serum will attack his blood and nervous system, just as his father's did. It's not an ideal method of administering the drug, and it's never going to be anything less than destructive and dangerous."

The professor stared into the distance and pinched his lip harder. "Perhaps I can arrange a transfusion to boost the red cell count . . ."

"Professor, perhaps you can consider that later. For now, I think you need to concentrate on stabilising Morgan."

I was surprised to hear Cory speak, and I felt a jolt of guilt I'd actually forgotten he was there.

"Oh, dear. Of course. Morgan, are you still with us?"

There was no response whatsoever, and I quickly moved

my hand down his back until I could feel his heart beat and his chest rise. Even then, the panic didn't leave me completely.

"Oh, dear." Getting up abruptly, the professor hurried off and spoke briefly with one of the people working at the tables. Not that any of them were working. No, they were all watching what was going on, with what I considered to be somewhat indecent curiosity.

"Don't worry," Cory said. "The professor's brilliant. We've done so much these last few days."

"*We*? How long have you been leading this twisted double life?"

I tried to keep my voice light, but Cory winced at the note of accusation I really couldn't keep out of it.

"Just a few days. Well . . . I've been in touch with the professor for a few weeks, but only peripherally. I found his name in the Project X files and did some research. I tracked down his email and asked him about the project. He freaked out and came to see me. We talked, and he brought me back here.

"I am, of course, sworn to secrecy." He sighed deeply. "And any possibility of an internship disappeared from that moment."

"So you haven't been working on ITM stuff as you told me?"

"Not for ages."

"But why didn't you tell me?"

"Because I didn't want you to get involved. What we're doing isn't strictly legal. Not only that but if the good people at ITM find us, they won't worry about legalities."

"Shit, Cory, what have you got us mixed up in?"

"It's not only me, Matthew. You've got pretty mixed up yourself." Now it was his turn to use an accusatory tone.

"What are you on about?" He flicked his gaze to Morgan,

and I understood. "Fuck, Cory, it was you who sent me there."

"I sent you there to get him out of danger, not to . . . not to . . ."

"To what?"

Cory dropped his head, but not before I saw bitterness flare in his eyes.

"Why don't you try telling me the truth, for once?" I said quietly. "Just say what you're thinking, what you mean, what you want?"

Cory raised his head and opened his mouth, but before he could speak, the professor was back.

"Can you help me, please, Matthew? Just sit him back in the chair."

Morgan stirred and moaned when I took him by the shoulders and eased him back. He opened his eyes and gazed up at me. Unbelievably, he smiled and reached for my hand. I glanced at Cory. His face had hardened, his eyes chips of blue ice. I couldn't think about that, not then, not when Morgan moaned again and began to shiver, deep shudders running through him.

"Take it easy, son," the professor said. For once, he worked fast, and by the time I tore my glance away from Cory, he was already sliding the needle out of Morgan's arm. "It'll take effect very shortly, and you'll feel much more yourself. I think you'll find my serum is kinder than your father's." Morgan's only response was a groan.

I hovered anxiously as Morgan's face twisted with pain and he moaned. For a while, I was very afraid the serum hadn't worked. But he gradually relaxed, then sighed, taking deep, steadying breaths. Eventually, he squeezed my hand, and a few moments later, opened his eyes and sat up straighter in the chair.

"Feeling better?" The professor had been watching him as

anxiously as I had, but his voice was cheerful and confident, and he smiled reassuringly as Morgan nodded, then raised a hand to massage his head.

"The headache's no better." His voice was weak but clear. Although he still looked very tired, life was returning to his eyes.

The professor shook his head sadly. "I'm afraid it's going to get worse before it gets better."

Morgan glanced at him sharply, and the professor's expression became rueful. "I believe I can help you, Morgan. I can't promise I can undo what your father has done to you. I can't promise to give your life back, not completely. But I think I can give you time. I don't know how long . . . months, years . . . time enough, I hope, for my research to progress to a stage where I can give you more."

Morgan smiled and was about to say something, but the professor shook his head. "Let me finish. I only *think* I can do this. My research is still in its infancy, and I've never used my serum for this purpose, or on a human being. I can't give you any promises at all, and the process itself is not without dangers. Before I can be sure my serum can help you, I have to test the mutated cells. I have to see what effect the serum has, and is having. How far the mutation has progressed, what modifications, if any, I need to make to my formula. Do you understand?"

Morgan's eyes had widened, and his grip on my hand increased. He nodded nervously, swallowing hard.

"I don't. What are you talking about?"

The professor seemed irritated again and sighed. "The serum causes cells to mutate. I have examples from Morgan's blood of those mutated cells, but they're the wrong cells. That's the problem. The serum is designed specifically to act on cells in a certain part of the brain. Those cells will have mutated in a very different way. The right way, so to speak.

The cells in the blood will disappear. The real genetic changes are happening inside the brain. I need a sample of those cells, to see exactly what the serum is doing and what, if any, modifications I need to make to mine to stabilise it."

"Okay . . . and . . ."

"The location of the host cells is somewhat difficult to access, at least safely."

"I-I don't . . ."

"They're in my brain, Matthew," Morgan said bleakly. "He has to get the cells from deep in my brain."

"Oh shit." I didn't know what else to say. To say I was stunned was an understatement. I was lurching from one shock to another and beginning to show the strain. "But I mean, you've done it before, haven't you? You won't hurt him, will you?"

"Yes, I've done it before . . . with rats, guinea pigs, even monkeys, but never with a human. My subjects survived, but who knows what effects they may have experienced that weren't apparent."

"I . . ."

"He means the rats could have had brain damage, but they couldn't tell because they were rats."

"Oh." Having Morgan to translate was . . . interesting, but the flat, emotionless way he conveyed the information was almost as terrifying as what he was saying.

"When I have tested the cells, if they are compatible, if I'm able to modify my formula, then I have to administer it. The dosage required to make a significant difference would be potentially enormous, and to have that travelling through your blood would be too dangerous. No, it would be inevitably fatal. It would have to be delivered in very small, concentrated doses over a period of time, direct to the host cells."

Morgan closed his eyes and shuddered. I couldn't close mine — they were too wide.

"Oh shit."

Morgan squeezed my hand, and when I glanced up at him, he was smiling at me. "You have a way with words, you know."

I had to smile. Otherwise, I'd have burst into tears, and that wouldn't have been *very* reassuring, not to mention incredibly embarrassing.

"So?"

Morgan blinked at him, confused. "So what?"

"Do you want to proceed?"

"Want to? No. I don't want to. Of course I don't want to. The mere thought terrifies the hell out of me. But I don't have a choice. I don't want to . . . I have to. If I don't, I know I'm going to die. Not in weeks, or months. I'll be lucky if I have days. I don't—" He paused and frowned. "I don't want to die. I'll do whatever it takes."

The professor nodded kindly. "Perhaps it would be better if you went over to the house. You'll be more comfortable there while I set up. I'll come over and fetch you when I'm ready. I assume you want to get this over with as soon as possible."

"Yes. Yes, I do."

"What do you want me to do, Professor?"

The professor regarded Cory thoughtfully. "I would be grateful for your assistance and input in the testing and formulaic process. You're young and inexperienced but very creative. However, I won't require you for setting up. I'm going to need to modify equipment and facilities. I think Brian will be more suited to that. Besides . . ." He smiled sadly at Morgan. "I think your friends need you more than I do right now."

"Friends?" There was wistfulness in his voice, and a hardness in his eyes that turned my stomach, but he nodded. "Whatever you want." His voice was tight, and he turned without another word and stalked out. The professor watched him curiously.

"My, my, what on earth has got into him? I can assure you he's not usually like this, so rude." He grinned at me suddenly. "But of course you don't need me to tell you that. He's your friend."

Dismissing us from his attention, the professor turned to peer intently into the microscope again, leaving me to help Morgan to his feet. He was much better now, only slightly shaky, and quite steady on his feet. He grinned at me, and we walked across the barn, hand in hand. When we glanced back from the door, the professor was issuing orders, and people were scurrying about all over the place.

Morgan sighed as he let the plastic fall, and I changed quickly out of the white suit before following him outside.

CHAPTER FOURTEEN

When I left the barn, I was surprised by how cold it was outside. The sun was falling, and there was a hint of frost. Morgan leaned against the wall, with his head thrown back, breathing in the clear, afternoon air.

"Are you okay?"

Morgan turned to me, still leaning against the wall, and smiled. I thought about the way he used to smile, the way it used to annoy me, enrage me even. Now it lit up my world. What a difference a day makes.

"Why are you staring at me like that?"

"I was just thinking what a beautiful smile you have."

The smile widened, and suddenly he pushed off from the wall, and I was in his arms. After everything that had gone on in the last couple of hours, all the tension and fear that had built inside me, just feeling his arms around me, his strength enveloping me, made me feel weak. I started to cry and hugged him hard, more because I was afraid my legs were going to give way than because I was feeling particularly amorous at that point.

"Hey. Hey, it's going to be all right. I know it's going to be all right. Don't crumble on me now, Matthew. I need you."

The raw vulnerability in his voice made me hug him even tighter, but he prised me free and pushed me slightly away so he could look into my face.

"Don't be afraid, Matthew. It's going to be all right. I thought . . . I really thought I was going to die. I mean, that it was for sure, and I . . . well, to be honest, I didn't care, not really, not until . . . not until you came, until we —

"I know it seems I have it all, but it never meant anything. I was never happy, never had anything to value. It was all so easy, especially after my mother died. My father threw money at me, and things, anything to avoid actually having to spend time with me, to look me in the eyes . . . to admit how much he hates me." Morgan hung his head, and I raked my hands through his hair, but he wasn't finished, and he raised his head, finally speaking with passion in his voice.

"Today, for the first time, I feel . . . I feel as if I have a reason to live. I want to live, and for the first time since my father — since this happened, I feel there might be a chance. I want there to be, because of you."

Morgan's eyes dazzled me. He held my upper arms lightly, and his touch made my skin burn. I was stunned. I didn't know what to say. Bizarrely, the only thing that went through my mind was . . . *Cory was right.*

"Right about what?"

"Shit, did I say that out loud? I didn't mean to actually say it."

Morgan shook his head. I shivered as I understood. "So what was he right about?"

"He always said that having everything didn't mean you were happy."

Morgan snorted. "Yeah, he's right about a lot of things." His smile faded. "In fact, I think I owe him an apology."

"An apology?"

"If he hadn't hacked the computer . . . and I gave him a hard time about it. I need to apologise."

"He's cool."

"Yeah, well, I need to, for me."

Something twinged deep in my breast and my own frown faded. "I don't think that's the thing he's feeling bad about at the moment."

"Oh?"

"No. You said once, at least I seem to remember you did, about Cory . . . the way . . . the way he feels about me . . ."

"Ah. Is that why he was looking at me as if he really wanted to stab me in the eye with a scalpel?"

"He was not."

"All right, then, as if he wanted to hit me over the head with a microscope."

I had to smile at that. "It's his way. He goes up in the air, then calms down, and he's fine. I think . . . I think he knew." As soon as I said it, I realised that of course, he knew. I remembered all the odd things he'd said, sentences that had ended in silence. Then there were the odd glances, the worry I was getting too friendly with Morgan. When I asked Cory if he was falling for Morgan, I was dead wrong. He'd been worried I was.

"Ah, shit. This is getting complicated."

"What do you mean?"

"Morgan, I think Cory's jealous of us."

Morgan stared at me for a moment, then burst out laughing. "You're such a . . . I don't need to be a mind reader to know that. He always has been."

"Bugger. Does everyone know everything about me before I know it myself?"

Leaning forward, he kissed me lightly on the forehead. "Only the ones who love you."

It was getting quite dark now, and the stars were coming out behind him. His eyes were brighter than any of them and far, far more beautiful.

"We should go inside. It's getting cold," Morgan said, rubbing my arms.

"We should talk to Cory."

Morgan made a face. "Yeah. I wouldn't want there to be bad feelings between us, especially between you two. You're going to need him if . . . if . . ."

"No. Don't even think about it. Nothing's going to happen to you, Morgan. Not now, not when — not when we — "

"When I finally have something good in my life, something that actually means something to me."

I couldn't stop the big stupid grin breaking over my face, and I couldn't stop myself burying my hands deeper in his outrageously gorgeous hair and kissing him.

When we got into the house, Cory was in the kitchen, slamming cups in a pretence of making coffee. His face was black as thunder.

"What's the matter?"

"Nothing. There is *nothing* the matter with me."

Glancing behind me, I noticed a large window over the sink, a window that was directly across the yard from the barn. *Uh oh.*

"I think we need to talk."

"There's nothing to talk about."

"I think there is."

Cory slammed a cup of coffee down on the table next to me, sloshing the liquid all over the cloth.

"Steady on." I dabbed ineffectually at the spilled coffee.

"What do *you* want?"

"Sorry?" Morgan seemed startled at the tone of his voice, which dripped poison and said quite clearly without actually saying it — *I hate you.*

"To drink."

"Um. I don't mind, whatever."

Cory poured a coffee and practically threw it at him, sloshing the burning liquid on his hand, causing him to jump back and cry out.

"Cory! What the fuck do you think you're doing?"

"Making coffee." He picked up his cup and stormed out of

the room. I stared after him, stunned.

"I'm sorry, Morgan. He's not usually like this. I don't know what's got into him."

"I do," he said softly, rubbing absently at his hand where the coffee had burned him.

"Is your hand okay?"

"Huh?" He looked up at me, distracted.

"Your hand? Did that coffee burn you?"

He glanced down, then back up and me and smiled briefly. "Just a bit. It's the least of my worries. We should go and talk to him."

"He doesn't deserve it."

"He doesn't deserve his best friend . . . the person he's loved for a very long time . . . the one who he always hoped would eventually return that love . . . turning his back on him and walking straight into the arms of someone else, someone he's been afraid for so long would make him do just that."

I stared at him, dumbstruck. "Since when have you been so . . . perceptive?"

Morgan smiled thinly. "Since I could look at someone and see their pain as clearly as their face."

"Shit. I keep forgetting."

"I wish I could."

I risked a quick hug, then picked up my coffee and reluctantly dragged my aching heart into the living room. Morgan followed close behind.

Cory was sitting in front of the television, staring at some bland soap. I knew he wasn't watching because he hated that kind of thing.

I sat down on the coffee table, facing him. He deliberately avoided looking at me.

"Do you want to talk about this?"

He glanced up briefly, and his gaze flicked to Morgan. "Nothing to talk about."

He fixed his eyes firmly on the television again, with a closed-down look I was familiar with. It gave me a sinking feeling in the pit of my stomach.

"I have an apology to make to you, Cory," Morgan said softly.

Shocked and angry, Cory glared at Morgan, with an expression in his eyes that made me shiver. I considered saying something, but before I could, Morgan pressed on. I noticed he didn't exhibit any of his usual cockiness and was actually very . . . subdued.

"In fact, I have two. You've no idea how sorry I am I was so harsh with you about the computer thing. I'm so grateful you did that now. It's just . . ." He glanced away, biting his lip, then back again, more resolved. "I was never mad at you for hacking the computer. I was worried about you, really, I was. I don't know if you believe me, but . . . my father's not a good man. I think you've realised that by now. I was afraid that if you got too deeply involved, if he found out, he'd hurt you, really hurt you, and I didn't want that to happen. I like you." Swallowing hard, he continued, "And then there was . . . I didn't want you to find out . . . about me . . . about what he was doing to me." He gave me a shaky smile. "Of course, the way it turned out I'm really glad you did."

Cory seemed stunned. There was a war going on behind those cool blue eyes. Now, more than ever, he wanted to hate Morgan, and now, more than ever, Morgan was making it very hard for him to do that. Not only because of the words he was saying, but by the way he was saying them, betraying that sweet vulnerability Cory had never seen before.

"That's not all. I have something else to apologise for, too." He stopped and lowered his head, as if the curtain of hair that fell between them would protect him from the hurt in Cory's eyes. "I knew. I've pretty much always known. I didn't need to be a mind reader to see the way you look at him. I've been watching, you see, because . . . because I was looking, too." His voice faded to little more than a whisper on the last phrase.

"If I'd seen anything to make me think he felt the same way about you, I'd never have . . . it's just . . ."

Morgan didn't see the expressions chasing themselves over Cory's face, but I was. I was on the verge of begging him to stop, when he looked up, tears running down his face.

"I kept my distance for so long because I didn't want to come between you. It's been so hard. I've . . . I think I've been in love with him for —" He closed his eyes. I don't know whether it was because of the emotional pain he was feeling or to cut off the look of shock and anger in Cory's eyes. "For a long time. I was scared of what you have between you. What I've never had. I was scared that if I tried to . . ."

Taking a deep breath, Morgan opened his eyes again and met Cory's square on. "I've never had a proper relationship, not with someone who loves me, someone who was in it just for us and not what it could buy them. I've never had a friendship like yours. Someone who's there for me no matter what, who'd watch my back and not care if I was rich or poor, good looking or ugly. Someone who cared just about me, the real me, the one buried so deep I didn't even know who he was anymore.

"I wanted it so much, but I was scared. I was scared of taking off the mask, of exposing myself. I didn't know who the person under there was any more and I didn't know if I'd like him . . . me. I was scared stiff that if-if I let you, either of you, see what's really there, you wouldn't . . . that I'd be left alone . . . again." Morgan's face was dead white, the only colour in his eyes, which held an expression of desperation. They were pleading. I dared not glance at Cory to see the reception.

"It's not as if I didn't try. There were times, lots of them when I tried to, but it always went wrong, and I was so scared it would happen again. I didn't mean to hurt you. I didn't mean to hurt anyone, I never have, but it always happens. Whenever I try to be open and honest and, well, myself, it always goes wrong. I got to the stage where I started to believe I wasn't . . . I didn't deserve love. God knows my father drummed that message into me often enough. Fuck!"

Abruptly, he turned and walked away, back to the kitchen. I could see him standing at the window, staring out. I knew he was crying, and I so wanted to go to him, to hold him, to comfort him, but I couldn't because Cory . . . because Cory was . . . and he would . . .

Surprisingly, it was Cory who got up, putting his mug carefully on the table next to me. Morgan jumped when he felt the touch on his shoulder and turned round, his eyes wide, shocked. I wondered why he might be so shocked for a moment . . . until I remembered he could see what Cory was thinking, then I wondered even more.

"I need to know." Cory's voice was soft, but deadly, and I was suddenly afraid. What was he going to say? What was he going to do?

Morgan shook his head convulsively. "No. No, it isn't that. I swear it isn't that."

I couldn't see Cory's face, because he had his back to me, but I saw him start and take a half step backward. Morgan flinched.

"I'm sorry. I can't help it. I can't help what I am, what he made me. I don't try to do it. It's just . . . there."

For a moment, there was silence as the two men stood still, staring at each other. It killed me that I couldn't see Cory's face. I felt as though I should say something, that I should do something, but I didn't know what I could say or do that wouldn't make it worse. However, I felt, whatever I wanted, this was something they had to resolve between them. They had to work this out for themselves.

"If you can see what I'm thinking, then answer me."

"I thought I had."

Now both of them were speaking softly and coldly, dancing around each other like fencers, their épées drawn. Circling, testing, waiting for an opening. I was scared of what would happen when one of them found one.

"All you've given me so far is a good show. I know you, Morgan, I know your kind. Words come easy to you, and manipulation is second nature. I've watched you, too. I've seen the way you've played us, both of us. I accept you may have been concerned about my safety with the hacking, and anyway you had every right to be angry with me, but as for the rest . . .

"I've seen the way you work. I've watched how you treat those around you. I've seen you hunt. You fix on someone, focus on them, bestow your favours on them . . . until you have them. Then you cast them off like yesterday's dirty underwear.

"I've watched you watch Matthew. I've seen the way you've goaded him, tested him. But he's never been interested in you. He's never taken the bait, has he? And it's stuck in your craw. You pulled out all the stops with him, and it never worked. He was immune to you. And it killed you.

"You've done everything you could to seduce him, and now you've succeeded. What happens now? Now you have him, how long before you get bored with him, like all the others? Let me see . . . I think a month is your absolute limit. It's usually more like a week, or even a few days."

Morgan's face had grown pale, even paler than it was already. His hand ran through his hair again and again, in the nervous gesture I'd become so familiar with.

"I . . ."

"Let me make it easy for you, Morgan. Matthew is everything to me, everything. Do you understand? You're right,

I've loved him for . . . forever, and I hoped . . . I hoped one day . . ." He paused, and I felt my stomach was going to either drop to my feet or rise through my mouth. I was shocked to my core. It was his voice—the rawness, the pain, the . . . love.

"But deep inside, I knew it would never be. When I saw the way he looked at you, I knew I didn't have a chance. He talked about you all the time, trying to convince himself he hated you, but I knew. I've always known. I dreaded this day. I knew it was coming. The worst thing is, I knew I could never compete with you. We're friends, yes, best friends, and I hope we always will be, but he's never looked at me the way he looks at you, and I have no weapons to fight that.

"You have everything . . . the looks, the money, the brain . . . everything he wants, he needs. You're worthy of him, and . . . and I'm not."

My stomach lurched again as I remembered the conversation Cory and I had that day in the refectory, the day I found Morgan at the river. Now I knew what it had all been about. Cory was right. I was blind, and I'd been a fool.

Cory leaned forward, almost as if he was going to kiss Morgan, stopping inches away from his face. Morgan was too stunned to move and just stared at him, his green eyes wide and his mouth half-open as if he'd been about to speak. "If you hurt him, in any way, I'll . . . I don't know what I'll do, but it won't be good, and I'll keep on doing it for the rest of your life."

Cory leaned back, leaving Morgan practically cowering over the worktop. I wondered what it was like for him, hearing the words, seeing the expression in the snapping blue eyes, and at the same time seeing . . . or feeling, the emotion, the truth behind it. I'd rarely been on the receiving end of real anger from Cory—I made efforts to avoid it because it scared me too much.

For a moment, Morgan held Cory's gaze. Then he lowered

his head, turning away, saying softly, "I'd never hurt him, Cory, never. I-I know how it seems. I know what it must look like from the outside, but it wasn't like that. It was never like that. I didn't get bored, not with any of them. I was searching for something-something I never found. Mostly, it was them who left me, when they realised I couldn't, or wouldn't, give them what they wanted.

"I-I'm damaged goods. I told you . . . I can't do relationships. In the beginning, it's always good. I think I've finally found someone who likes me for myself. I try to give them that, but it's never what they wanted. They wanted the image of me they'd built up in their head, and maybe I've fed into that, made the mask too real. But when I wanted to be me, when I wanted to show them what's behind it . . ." He shrugged helplessly. "I don't know, maybe it scared them, or repulsed them, or . . . they didn't want the scared little boy. They didn't want the hurt, the pain. They wanted the image, not the person who's wrapped in it.

"I didn't cast anyone away, but maybe I did push them. Maybe I got scared when they got too close. Maybe I wasn't ready or able to expose the vulnerability I feel every moment of every day.

"I . . . I did . . . I was . . . I did try to . . ." He ran both hands through his hair and groaned. "I'm making a mess of this, just like I always do. How can I make you understand? After my mother died and my father made it clear he hates me, blames me for her death, I was alone. I died inside when she did, and I had no one to comfort me, no one to turn to. Everyone I turned to moved away from me in the end, and I was terrified of opening myself to anyone.

"The first moment I saw you, the two of you, standing outside the university, I could tell straight-away how close you were, and I envied that. There was something about you and . . . and . . ." His gaze flicked up to me over Cory's shoulder. There was something there that was almost pleading with me, and I smiled at him, trying to put everything I felt for him in that one look. But he didn't smile.

"When I saw him—Matthew, for the very first time there was—there was a certain strength about him, a confidence I knew wasn't a façade." His face and voice softened for a moment, and he smiled wistfully. "And he was so beautiful. It was natural, not styled and forced, not . . . created. He wasn't false. The more I got to know him, the more I realised so much of that beauty was on the inside. I wanted to get to know him, to be his friend . . . to be more. But I was scared. And when I get scared, I get defensive. So, every day, I goaded him and teased him and did everything I could to push him away and make him hate me because . . ."

"Because it was easier to drive him away than to pull him close and then have him leave you?"

Cory's voice had softened, and there was something indefinable in its tone. Wordlessly, Morgan nodded.

Cory shook his head and turned away with a sigh. "You know, you're making it practically impossible for me to hate you."

"Practically?"

Cory turned and grinned at him. "Don't push it."

Morgan sagged, his relief almost palpable. I know how he felt. My legs were jelly. Cory turned sad eyes on me.

"Cory, I . . ."

"Don't. It's all right. You can't help who you love, and I never gave you a chance to love me."

"But I do love you. I do. I always have, and I always will. Just not . . ."

"Not enough."

"No, not that. You're my best friend, Cory. I love you more than I love myself. It's just . . . just in a different way."

After a long, tense moment, Cory nodded and folded into

a chair, burying his face in his hands. As if I'd been released from a spell, I threw myself to the floor next to him and took him in my arms. He clung to me as Morgan had done only a few hours before. It felt good. I couldn't deny that. It felt right, but . . . just not the same.

I glanced up at Morgan over Cory's head, and he gave me a shaky smile. Thrusting his hand into the pocket of his jeans, he pulled out a packet of cigarettes and lit one, drawing deeply as he turned to gaze out the window again. Cory sat up, rubbing at tears and snot with his sleeve. He certainly did not look good after crying, not like . . .

"You okay?"

"I will be. I'll get over it. Just tell me you're happy, that this is what you want."

"Happy? Hell no. I won't be happy until this is . . . until he's . . . but yes, this is what I want. *He* is what I want."

He nodded, and with an effort pulled himself together. "Then we'd better make sure we get this thing sorted, hadn't we?"

"I have faith in you, Cory . . . always have, always will."

He grinned, and it was so good to see the old Cory back. He glanced over at Morgan. "You should stop that, you know. It's a terrible habit. It'll kill you."

Morgan turned and smiled, shrugging. "Something's got to."

After a moment of shocked silence, we all began to laugh, and the tension melted away.

"So, what do we do now?"

"Just wait, I suppose. The professor knows what he's doing . . . at least as much as anyone does."

"He's a good guy. I thought there was more to his leaving than my father told me. They were friends before my mother died. I've known him since I was, well, since I can remember. He used to come round to dinner all the time. He was the one who got me interested in science. Not as much as law, of course, but . . . he was the one who sat me on his knee and held a microscope to my eye, who let me play with the equipment at the lab. He even set me up with my own little work station. My father was never interested, even before . . ." He stopped and took another pull at the cigarette, almost choking because he'd been too hard, too desperate.

"It hit you hard, didn't it? When your mother died? Both of you?"

"That's the understatement of the year. It knocked us both for six, but we dealt with it in different ways. Well, apart from one thing." He sighed. "We both blamed me."

"You're not still doing it, are you? I mean, there's no way it was your fault. You were just a kid . . . not responsible." Morgan shrugged. "Morgan, she was the responsible adult. She was the one who put you both at risk, driving when she knew it wasn't safe. She did a really stupid thing that could have killed you both."

Morgan's eyes widened, and for a moment, I thought he was going to snap at me for daring to speak that way about his mother, but he didn't. He just shook his head and slumped with a sigh.

"You're right. Completely right, of course. I suppose I've always known it. I just didn't feel it. My father didn't help."

"Sounds like your father hasn't helped you with anything all your life."

Morgan smiled. "I think you're right about that." He looked thoughtful, then wistful. "I never thought he'd end it, though."

"He hasn't."

"Not yet."

That was too much for me. I couldn't stay away from him. Not when there was so much fear and raw vulnerability in his voice. The Morgan Bentley we'd known was a man of ice who never showed true emotion, and certainly not weakness . . . but he was gone now, and the man who stood before me was nothing like him. He was very real. His pain, his fear, his uncertainty — none of those things were flaws to me. They were blessings, gifts bestowed on me, glimpses of a soul that burned, even now, with a flame of passion that enthralled me.

I put my arms around him, and he rested his head on my shoulder. He didn't put his arms around me, and I knew it was because of Cory. So did he. Fortunately, Cory is a sensitive soul, and he recognised true need when he saw it. I also think he found the sight of Morgan in my arms unbearable.

"I'll just go and check on how they're doing in the barn. If you need anything, just shout."

As soon as the door closed, Morgan wrapped his arms around me and pulled back his head so he could look into my eyes.

"I don't think I could do this if it weren't for you, Matthew. In fact, I wouldn't be doing it. I'd still be at home, dying slowly." He raised a hand and tenderly stroked my face with the backs of his fingers. "You give me the strength I didn't know I had. I think without you here, I'd be . . . I don't know . . . paralysed with fear. Or maybe not."

He lowered his eyes, then raised them again. "I think without you, I wouldn't care. I'd still be afraid, but I'd just let it take me. I'd pretty much given up hope, decided there was nothing to fight for, so I may as well give up. I wasn't fighting. Maybe that's why I was going downhill so fast."

"You're fighting now, though, right?"

"I will. To be honest, I feel better than I have for ages. This isn't like it was before. I don't know how to explain. I feel . . . lighter. The effects are different, more muted, controllable. I don't feel so heightened." He sighed. "I don't know how to explain, because I don't know how to describe it, this feeling. With my father's drugs, it was like being high for a while, then feeling like I was looking in on my life, on everyone's life from the outside, totally disconnected. This time it's more real, more grounded and in tune. I don't know. I have a feeling I'm not going to crash so hard or so far this time. I feel . . . strong, powerful in a way."

"That's good."

"I don't know if it is."

"What do you mean?"

"I'm scared, Matthew, really scared. I know what they're going to do to me, and . . . and when I was really ill, I didn't care. I wanted them to. I just wanted it over. But now . . . now I feel strong and well. I . . . I don't want . . ."

I didn't know what to say to him, so I did the only thing I could think of—I kissed him.

For a moment, he seemed stunned. Then he responded. His arms tightened around me, his lips crushed mine, and I melted. For a moment, all the fear, the sadness and the stress melted away. There was just us—me and Morgan. *Fuck!* Me and Morgan Bentley, and it was heaven.

CHAPTER FIFTEEN

The kiss deepened, and I couldn't help my body responding. I knew it was probably, no definitely, neither the time nor the place, but I had no control. I pressed myself shamelessly against him and felt him respond in the same way. Not breaking the kiss, he moaned softly and ran his hands up and down my back, causing my own hands to bunch in the material of his shirt.

Breathing hard, I ground my hips into him, and his arms convulsed around me, driving my breath from my body and pressing me even closer. It was the most intensely intimate experience I'd ever had, and I never wanted it to end.

When he broke the kiss and drew back a little, I felt like crying — except those incredible eyes were gazing at me with an expression that drove all thought out of my head, and his hand, sinking into my hair, made me shiver and moan with the sheer pleasure of the sensation.

"I want you, Matthew. I need you so badly. Will you . . ."

"Should we?"

"Who's to say we shouldn't?"

"But what if . . ."

"Who cares?"

"What if someone comes?"

"What if they do?"

His voice was husky and so sexy I couldn't resist it. I couldn't resist him, and I didn't want to. Too breathless to speak, I nodded, and he took me by the hand, leading me through the house toward the stairs.

I had a moment of doubt when we entered the first bed-room we came to, which was clearly occupied by someone, but it melted away when he started to tug my t-shirt free of my jeans. Feverishly, I did the same, and in moments both garments were on the floor.

Lifting me off my feet, Morgan practically threw me onto the bed and himself on top of me. Once again, the breath was knocked from my body, but I didn't care because he was kissing me again, and I gave myself over to the wonder of it.

The friction of his bare skin on mine was almost too much to bear, and when he ran his hand down my arm, I moaned and arched my back, lifting us both off the bed. I felt him smile. Then he shifted a little, twisting his body to the side so he could caress my chest. I started to shiver, and when he pinched my nipple between his thumb and finger, I jumped and moaned even more loudly.

Lifting his head, Morgan let his gaze run appreciatively over my face and body. Just that, just the look, did strange things to my insides, and I swear I almost came just from the sight of him. I had to close my eyes and take deep breaths, trying to think of non-sexy things. Morgan laughed softly and rested his hand over my heart, giving me space.

When my heart began to calm down, he ran his hand down over my stomach and started to undo my jeans. I had no strength or will to do anything but lie there and let him. It seemed to take forever, and by the time he'd tugged the zip all the way down, I was feverish with anticipation, as he'd been very careful not to touch me any more than he absolutely had to.

He didn't have to pull my jeans off, because as soon as I was able, I did it myself, practically tearing the material in my desperation. Morgan didn't need any encouragement to do the same. As soon as we were naked, we pressed our bodies together chest to toe, both lying on our sides facing each other, and for a while we just lay like that, savouring the feel of it, allowing ourselves to calm down a little.

Eventually, Morgan began to softly stroke my back, slowly moving lower until he was caressing my buttocks. I did the same for him and felt him twitch between us. Until now, Morgan had been doing all the running, and I decided it was time I did some of my own. Pressing the palm of one hand against his chest, I pushed him over onto his back. He complied willingly, with a deep smile in his eyes.

Closing my eyes, I lowered my head and began to kiss him, just brushing my lips over his, while at the same time running my hand over his stomach, which tensed under it and began to tremble. He was so beautiful. Even with my eyes closed, I could feel how beautiful he was. There was not an ounce of fat anywhere on him, no spare flesh, only gently toned muscle and smooth, velvety skin.

I tugged gently at the soft fur between his legs, and he jumped a little. When I touched the base of his cock, he threw his arms around me and pulled me down hard to deepen the kiss as I slowly ran the tips of my fingers up and down the hard velvet shaft. He shuddered and moaned. It was such a beautiful sound.

I lifted my head. "What do you want to do? I'm all yours."

"Fuck . . . that's not something I've ever heard before."

"Then get used to it. I am going to say it to you every day for the rest of our lives, along with I love you."

"You do?"

"Fuck yeah. I've loved you for ages. I just misunderstood. I thought I hated you."

"I thought you hated me, too . . . sometimes."

"We were both wrong."

Morgan smiled that slow sexy smile that melted me, and my hand closed around him of its own accord. Throwing back his head, he gasped and shuddered, his eyelids fluttering. I began to massage him slowly, tightening and relaxing my grip, causing him to moan and the muscles of his buttocks, abdomen, and legs to twitch convulsively.

I continued for a while, until Morgan was quivering and feverish. Then I slid down and licked the swollen head, savouring the sweet, salty taste of him.

Morgan moaned and thrust his hips, taking me by surprise and mashing his cock into my face.

"Be careful, you could put my eye out with that thing."

Morgan's laugh was more of a grunt, which turned to a half-sob as I took him fully into my mouth. It was the first time I'd ever had a cock in my mouth, and at first, it made me gag. Morgan stopped thrusting and let me get accustomed to the feeling, making my own moves in my own time, slowly withdrawing, then taking it in, deeper and deeper with each stroke.

It was an incredible, powerful feeling, to have someone like Morgan, someone as wonderful as Morgan, writhing and moaning under me, responding to everything I did, every movement, every breath. I'd never felt so close to someone. He abandoned everything to me—his body, his soul—and now, when he was at his most vulnerable, his most open, I was in total awe of him.

I knew before he did when he reached the edge. I could feel it in the way his body trembled and tightened. I let him slide out of my mouth, intending to finish the job with my hand so I could see his face at the moment of release. However, Morgan had other ideas. He caught my hand with his and pulled it away from him. I looked up in surprise.

He raised his head from the rumpled pillow, his eyes dark with desire. He was panting heavily and could barely speak.

"Fuck me. Please . . . please."

"But I-I don't have . . . I don't know . . . how."

"Just, do it. Please, Matthew, please. I swear I'm safe."

"Safe?"

"I-I've never done . . . never . . . without a condom . . . I'm not . . . I don't . . ."

Realising what he was saying, I almost laughed out loud. As if I cared. At that moment, I wouldn't have cared if he was infected with the plague. My need, my desire, was too great. My concerns lay elsewhere.

I took his face between my hands. It was hot and slick with sweat. I stared deeply into his eyes, and in that moment of incredible connection, I would have given him my soul if he'd asked for it.

"I'm afraid I'll hurt you."

With his breathing calming, he found his voice and whispered, "There's no way you could hurt me, Matthew, not unless you leave me."

"I'll never do that, never. I love you, Morgan. Oh gods, I love you." I started speaking but ended moaning, and I had to kiss him. While we were kissing, Morgan reached down and began to stroke me, at first with feather-light strokes on my stomach, but gradually moving lower and getting firmer until he grasped my already half-erect penis and ran his thumb over the head.

I jerked and moaned, making Morgan smile. Then I sighed as he fell into a slow, easy stroke. He turned over on his side and took my hand, guiding it downward, continuing his stroking, although his hand and my cock were now sandwiched between us. For a moment, I was completely passive, lost in the sensations he was arousing in me. Then he raised his leg, hooking it over mine and parting his buttocks.

I finally got the message. "We need something, don't we? Lube or something."

"Look in the drawers." Morgan gasped, releasing me. "Be quick."

It felt wrong, searching through someone's personal stuff.

My face burned when it crossed my mind it might be Cory's, but it wasn't. I know Cory's stuff, and this wasn't it.

I didn't find any lube, but I did find a tin of lip balm. "Will this do?"

"I don't care," Morgan moaned. "Just do it. Do it *now*."

I hurried back to take my previous position. Not really knowing what I was doing, I scooped some out and smeared it on my fingers, then reached behind him and slid a finger inside him. Unlike me, he didn't clench around me, and the finger went in easily. Morgan shuddered and groaned as my finger slid in and out. That excited me to increase my speed and push deeper. I've never felt anything like it, and the thought it would soon be my cock almost flung me over the edge. I pressed my belly against his, and he stopped moving his hand, understanding.

"Two," he whispered, still kissing me.

Again, it took a while for the message to sink in. Then I withdrew my finger and added another. This time it was more difficult and took a little time to work the two of them into him. If it hurt, he never gave the slightest indication of anything but extreme pleasure, and it soon got easier.

"Three," he moaned.

"Are you sure?"

"Yes."

"Won't it hurt you?"

"Matthew . . ."

"Okay."

With a degree of trepidation, I began to work three fingers into him, and this time his moans had an edge to them. I stopped, but he begged desperately.

"No . . . no, don't . . . don't stop." So I didn't. Although I was sure I was hurting him, I worked my fingers in as far as I could, as Morgan started to pump my cock again. I went wild with passion and stopped worrying about hurting Morgan.

His body bucked against me, and he clenched around my fingers. Again, the thought this could be my penis flashed through my mind.

Suddenly, Morgan wriggled his hips so I'd withdraw, then he turned over to lie face down on the bed.

"Now," he commanded. I moved to kneel between his legs. He raised his hips, and I was lost for a moment in the sheer wonder of his form — the lithe curve of his back, the shock of raven-black hair spilling over his shoulders, the sheer beauty of his flawless buttocks and the inflaming promise of what lay between.

With a groan, I tried to enter him, but a cock is a very different piece of equipment to a finger, and it just wouldn't go in. I was almost in tears, feeling I was letting him down. It was so important to me to give this to him when . . . when it might be . . . when he might . . .

"No . . ." I moaned, as the sharp pain of possible loss, combined with the sense of frustration I couldn't perform as I wanted, caused my cock to deflate faster than a discarded birthday balloon.

"Hold it," Morgan instructed. "Hold it at the base and . . . and . . . try a different angle."

Stroking myself, I regained the hardness and grasped my penis firmly at its base. I shuffled forward a little and rubbed the head of my cock up and down over his hole for a while, until he was whimpering. I thought it was the cutest thing I'd ever heard. He was thrusting his hips back toward me, and my hand was trembling so much I could hardly direct my cock at all.

I pressed my cock-head against his entrance, and it finally began to open to accommodate me. There was resistance for a time, and I was about to withdraw, admitting defeat, when there was a strange sensation, like a pop, and I was in. Morgan clenched and groaned, and I froze, my hand unconsciously massaging his buttock.

"Are you all right? Did I hurt you?"

"Yes. No. No, I . . . give me a minute."

Still stroking the part of me that was outside him, I waited until Morgan whispered, "Just a little more."

I pushed in and waited again. The sensation was amazing, and it was nothing I could even begin to describe. The muscles clenched and relaxed around me, and it almost brought me over the edge again. I had to think frantically of an ice-cold waterfall to stop myself coming there and then.

"Okay . . . you're good."

I barely heard him. I was too lost in my own mind, and when I didn't make any move, Morgan thrust his hips back, and suddenly I was buried in him to the hilt. The shock pulled me away from the edge, and I was able to focus a little more on slowly moving in and out. The sensations were so intense that for a while, they overwhelmed me.

Reaching around, I took Morgan's cock in my hand and tried to synchronise my strokes with my thrusts. As we both got more and more excited, the synchronicity went to hell, and my thrusts grew more and more desperate.

At one point, my legs were trembling so much I thought they were going to collapse under me, and I had to lock my hips and practically fall against him. I thrust so deep inside him that his body convulsed. He moaned in such pleasure, and I did it again . . . and again.

Morgan was jerking under me now, and the motion excited me so much it catapulted me over the edge so fast it would have been impossible to pull back. I thrust deep inside him and ejaculated, caught in the grip of the most powerful orgasm I'd ever had. Almost immediately, Morgan came, and his spasms wrung another spurt from me. It was so intense it was painful.

When we were done, Morgan collapsed, and I fell on top

of him. We were both shivering and panting, and I was utterly spent. With an extreme effort, I rolled off Morgan and lay staring at his perfect body. I stroked his back gently, and he turned his head toward me. His face was nearly covered by his hair, but I could see his eyes glowing.

"Fuck, man."

"Yeah," he breathed. "Thank you, Matthew."

"Thank me? Thank you. I've never experienced anything like that before. It was amazing."

Morgan smiled. "The first time always is."

"First time, last time, every time — with you."

Morgan reached out and laid his hand gently on the side of my face, drawing it down to kiss me. Laughing, I pushed his hair out of the way first, and the kiss was the sweetest I'd ever had.

When I raised my head, Morgan was staring at me with sleepy eyes.

"You look tired." I stroked his hair, and he practically purred.

"I am."

"You should try and get some sleep."

"Will you stay with me?"

"Fucking right. Try to tear me away."

With a body heavy with weariness, Morgan rolled over, laughing when he stuck to the bedclothes.

"I should take a shower."

"I don't know if there is one."

"Ah, well."

Slipping under the covers, he curled up with one hand under his cheek. He seemed so young and vulnerable, and I was swept with a surge of protectiveness that surprised me.

I scrambled under the duvet and shifted closer to him, so I could stroke his shoulder and his arm. He looked utterly spent.

"Are you okay?"

"Just tired."

"Are you sure?"

He gazed at me for a moment, then shook his head slightly. "Don't feel so good."

"Was it me?"

He laughed. "Of course not. Silly boy."

Morgan pulled me into an embrace and kissed me, then pushed me over onto my back and laid his head on my chest, hooking one leg over mine. I stroked his back until his breathing told me he was asleep. I didn't go to sleep. I lay staring at the ceiling.

At first, I was lost in the memory of the incredible experience I'd just shared with the most incredible person in the whole world.

But then my thoughts turned darker, and I started to think of what was about to happen. I was gripped by horrendous, gut-clenching fear. What if this was the last time I made love with Morgan? If this was the last time I lay holding him as he slept, the last time I stroked his silky skin? What if he died? What if he left me now when I was completely, utterly, and gloriously in love with him?

I couldn't bear the thoughts going through my mind, and I tried to shut them out, closing my eyes and willing my body to relax. Usually, it worked, no matter how frenetic my thoughts were, but this time there was nothing I could do. I had to lie there, my body tense, grappling with my fears.

Chapter Sixteen

It was lucky I didn't fall asleep, because I heard the footsteps on the stairs and the voice calling, "Matthew? Morgan? Where the hell are you?" just in time to fling myself out of bed and put my back against the door before the handle turned.

"We're in here, Cory. Um . . . just give us a minute."

I was so glad I couldn't see his face when he said, "Oh."

"Morgan was tired." It was lame, and it came out half as a whine.

"Oh. Oh, right. Yes. Well, they're ready. Don't be long."

"Okay. Won't be a minute."

"See you downstairs, then."

I listened to his steps retreating down the stairs and almost melted with relief. When I turned back to the bed, Morgan was sitting up, rubbing his eyes. His hair was all over the place, and he looked younger than ever.

"What's going on?"

"We were almost caught by Cory."

For a moment, there was a wickedly evil gleam in his eyes, but it was quickly replaced with remorse. "Hell, that would have been . . . difficult."

"Morgan, it would have destroyed him."

"I know. I-I know. I'm really glad you stopped him. Really."

I couldn't help but smile. He was pouting, and so cute I wanted to climb straight back into bed. I sighed.

"We need to go."

Morgan's eyes widened, and he froze for a moment. Then

he sighed and nodded.

"Are you okay?"

"No, not really."

"What's wrong?"

He sighed. "I don't know. It doesn't feel the same as before. I just feel drained, exhausted."

"Perhaps it's just that you are. You've been pushing yourself hard lately, and you've been wound up about this. Perhaps you're just genuinely tired."

He gazed at me, and I could see the truth written all over his face, but he smiled wearily and nodded. "Perhaps."

I had to help Morgan get dressed, because as soon as he stood, he swayed and faded, almost passing out. When we were done, I put my arm around his waist and had to support him down the stairs. We almost fell a couple of times, but we made it to the bottom. Cory had been staring out of the window. When we entered the room, he glanced up, his face tight and his eyes cold.

"I'm glad you two were enjoying . . ." He stopped, and his eyes widened when he saw Morgan. "What's wrong with him?"

"I don't know. He was fine. He just faded out. Help me."

Morgan raised his head when Cory slipped under his arm. He looked drunk or drugged, and almost immediately, his head fell forward. He managed to walk all right, and the cold air outside revived him a little. I didn't bother to change into one of the white suits as I was anxious to get Morgan to the professor.

There was no sign of him when we entered the laboratory, but someone saw us and ducked into one of the cubicles, emerging a few moments later with the professor. Initially, he was smiling, but that changed to a frown very quickly.

"Morgan, what happened?"

Morgan glanced up, still looking half-doped but more

coherent. "I don't know. I was . . . I felt . . . tired."

The professor took Morgan's chin in his hand and tilted his head up, peering into his eyes. "Hmm, I was afraid of this."

"Afraid of what?"

The professor smiled at me. "Don't worry, Matthew. It'll be all right. If this works, it will fix everything."

"And if it doesn't?"

The professor frowned at me for a moment, then nodded and gave me a tight smile. "Then it won't matter." I shuddered deeply and stared after him as he pulled aside the plastic covering from the front of one of the cubicles, motioning us inside.

I turned to Morgan, and he was already staring at me. We nodded and smiled uneasily at each other, then headed after the professor.

Inside, the cubicle had been modified to make it bigger, but it was still crowded and stuffed full of equipment. In the middle of it all, was a shabby treatment couch, the kind that could be raised at the head. The professor had sent someone to the house for a pillow and had wrapped it in a stiff, white cloth. It didn't look very comfortable, but it was better than one of the tables in the lab.

Together, we helped Morgan up, and he lay back with a sigh.

"You okay?"

He stared up at me. I'd never seen him so lost and scared, but he reached for my hand and squeezed it, managing a small smile.

"I'm going to be fine."

The professor laid a hand on his shoulder. "I'm going to take good care of you, Morgan. If there's any way to get you through this, I'll find it, I promise."

Morgan tore his eyes away from mine and turned his head to the professor, his smile fading.

"It's not very likely, is it?"

"Don't think like that, Morgan. Stay positive. This is not impossible."

"It feels like it is."

"I'm sure it does, but you're not in the best position to see the whole picture right now. Try to keep perspective, take a step at a time."

For a moment, they just stared at each other. Then Morgan sighed and closed his eyes. The professor squeezed his shoulder.

"Are you ready?"

"No," Morgan said without opening his eyes. "But that doesn't matter, does it?"

"I'm afraid not. It's now or never. I'm sure you realise my serum is not doing as well as your father's did in boosting you. It's very different and . . ." He paused, as if carefully considering what, or how much, he was going to say. "You're fading, and if we don't do this now, it will be too late."

"I know."

"Try not to worry."

Morgan laughed shortly. "Yeah, like that's going to happen."

The professor turned away. When he turned back, he held a needle in his hand.

"Morgan, I'm going to put this needle in the back of your hand so I can give you medication when I need to. You know the score. Are you okay with that?"

"As okay as I am with any of this."

The professor patted him and got on with it. I couldn't watch him do it, so I watched Morgan's face instead. He didn't even flinch. I brushed the hair away from his face and used my fingers to fan it over the pillow. He opened his eyes at my touch and smiled at me.

"Will you stay with me?"

"Of course I'll stay with you. Where would I go? You're the best thing that ever happened to me, and I'm not going to walk away now."

His smile broadened, and something shone out of his eyes that made me shiver. He squeezed my hand and lifted it to his lips. The kiss was nothing more than a gentle brush of his lips, but it made my heart miss a beat.

"Does that feel okay, Morgan?"

Without taking his eyes off me, he whispered, "It feels great."

"I'm going to give you an injection now, which will send you to sleep. When you wake up, the first stage will be over, and we'll be working on the most important part. Okay?"

Morgan turned his head to stare at the professor, and his grip on my hand tightened. "I might . . . it's possible I might not wake up, isn't it?"

The professor regarded him thoughtfully for a moment, then nodded gravely. "I won't lie to you. The equipment we have is crude, especially for use on a human. Everything is modified and adapted, and the procedure is risky. It's a possibility, yes."

Morgan swallowed. He bit his lip, and it was left to me to explode. "What? But if it's that risky, can't you . . . isn't there . . . do you have to do this?"

The professor smiled at me kindly. "I'm doing what I have to do, Matthew. Nothing more, nothing less. If there was another way, I'd take it."

"What are you going to do?"

The professor glanced at Morgan. He nodded slightly, his eyes burning. The professor pulled over a strange piece of equipment. It was white and looked like an overhead projector, but with an eyepiece on the side.

"This is a thermal imaging scanner. The cells inside Morgan's head, which are mutating, are giving off a faint radioactive trace. This will pick it up, and they'll be a different colour to the other cells around them. If I'm correct in my estimation, the cells will be clustered in a tight bundle in one specific part of the brain. When we've isolated them, we can draw some off with a needle and examine them.

"If it goes as expected, once I'm able to closely study the cells, I'll be able to modify my serum to neutralise them . . . to stop, if not reverse, the mutation."

"But won't it be pretty much completed by now? The mutation, I mean?" Morgan said hoarsely, demonstrating the major difference between us, in that all I'd heard from the whole conversation was the fact they were going to stick a needle into Morgan's brain.

"Maybe not. I can't be sure, but I have a strong suspicion your father was, himself, trying to undo the damage he's done. I've closely examined the blood we took, and the mutated cells it contained were . . . not right."

"Not right?"

"Not right for what I thought they were trying to achieve. I think, at least in later days, he's been trying to undo what he did. That's what the regular injections were for, and why you felt ill when they wore off. The initial mutation is what's killing you, Morgan, and as soon as your father realised that, he tried to reverse it, but the most he could manage was to slow it down, to protect you from its effects for a while. And the serum got less and less effective as time went on and the mutation took hold."

"He was trying to save me?"

"I think so."

Morgan looked completely confused. "But . . . but why? Why was he trying to save me when he hates me . . . when he wants me to die?"

"You don't know that, Morgan. It's a very harsh judgement on him."

"He's hated me ever since my mother died. He blamed me, and he wished it was me and not her. He pretty much told me as much. That's why he decided to test the formula on me. He didn't care if it killed me. He wanted it to."

"Is that what you really believe, Morgan?"

Morgan bit his lip and nodded.

"I think you're very wrong. When this is over, you should talk to him."

Morgan snorted. "*If* I can speak when this is over, he's the last person I want to speak to."

"We'll see. Are you ready?"

"Yes." Morgan's eyes were dark when he turned them back to me, and he was clearly struggling with something.

"Don't worry about that now. You can deal with your father when you're better and when you're strong again."

"I don't think I'll ever be strong enough for that."

"You will. I'll be there with you all the way."

"All the way?"

"Fucking right. It's been a long journey, and a bumpy road, but now I'm here, with you, there's nowhere else I want to be."

"Even if I have to walk away from everything — the house, the money — "

"Especially if you walk away from it. You're going to be an awesome lawyer. We'll make our own money, get our own house."

"You're jumping ahead a little, aren't you? You've got us practically married, and we've only just got together."

I blushed and lowered my head, but when I raised it, he was smiling. "I know a good thing when I see it, and I'm not about to let it slip through my fingers."

"Matthew, I . . ." He paused. The smile faded from his face. He blinked as if trying to clear his vision. "Shit, I-I didn't ex . . . pect . . ." His voice faded out as his eyes flickered closed, and his hand slipped from mine. I was startled and scared. It had been so fast.

I looked up at the professor. "Is he okay? Was it meant to knock him out that fast?"

The professor continued to smile and nodded. "He's perfectly all right. I think it would be better if you waited outside while we do this."

"No. No, I promised. I promised to stay with him."

"I appreciate that, Matthew, and I'll make sure you're back with him before he wakes up. But this is a very small working space, and I'm going to need my assistants in here. There really won't be room. Besides, I think it would be best for you, if you didn't . . . if you weren't here."

"I'm not scared." It was a lie, of course. I was scared to death. But the thought of leaving him, of not being with him if the worst happened, was even more frightening than staying with him and watching what they were going to do to him.

"I'm sure you're not, but still . . . I'm going to have to insist, Matthew. I'm afraid you'll only get in the way, and we have a lot of work to do. There's still quite a lot of setting up, and I want this done as quickly as possible." He regarded at me with a serious expression. "We don't have much time, Matthew. Once we have the cells, it's going to take some time to find the correct formula to deal with them . . . time we don't have. You know what's going on inside Morgan's head is killing him. It's killing him right now. Not in a few weeks, or even a few days, but right now. I have no idea how long it will be before he goes critical, but I know it can be counted in hours, a day or so at the most. I don't have time . . . and neither does he."

I stared at him, wide-eyed. I'd known, of course I had, but I'd never expected it to be this . . . present. And I'd never had it spelled out so clearly. I nodded, shock paralysing me.

"Go and wait in the house with Cory. I'll call you the minute we're done."

"How long?"

"Only about half an hour."

I nodded. "All right."

Someone touched my hand, and I turned to see Cory's earnest face. He was so familiar, so dear to me, that I lost it and started to cry.

"Come on. I'll take care of you, Matthew."

I turned back to Morgan and kissed him gently, not caring Cory was there, not caring about anything but the fact I was terrified that when I came back, he would be . . . if only I'd known we had so little time. Stroking his face, I whispered through a throat constricted with tears, "I won't be long, my love. You hang in there until I get back. You hear me? You better just . . . you better not . . . don't you dare leave me . . . do you hear? Don't you dare."

Of course, he didn't respond, not at all. He was so still and quiet—I couldn't bear it. In the end, it was almost a relief to follow Cory out of the cubicle. The professor called to two of his assistants, who scurried to his side as we left.

I was in a daze as I crossed the courtyard, shaking uncontrollably, tears streaming down my face. As soon as we were inside, Cory turned to me and hugged me. It wasn't the same as it was with Morgan. There was nothing sexual in it. It was just Cory.

I let go, let myself fall apart. Cory held me tight, gave me his strength and put me back together again without ever saying a word.

Finally, I pushed myself away from him and gazed into those familiar blue eyes.

"I'm sorry, Cory, so sorry. I've hurt you really badly, haven't I?"

He turned away from me, suddenly embarrassed. "It's

okay, Matthew. I know you didn't mean to."

"No. I didn't mean to, but I did, and that hurts. You were right. I was blind. I never saw this coming, never thought for one moment . . ."

"And if you had?"

He sniffed, his eyes swimming with tears, and it was my turn to turn away.

"I don't know. I really don't know. I'd like to say that if you'd told me how you feel, I'd at least have given it a chance, but I really don't know. You've always been my best friend, closer than a brother. I-I'm not sure I could ever see you in the way you want me to." I turned back. "I'm sorry."

"I told you, there's no need to be sorry. None of us can help the way we feel. Not you, not me, not anyone."

"So what happens now?"

He looked surprised. "What do you mean?"

"Are we still cool?"

He laughed, a real genuine laugh. "Cool? We're best friends, Matthew. It'll take more than a man to come between us."

"Even if it's Morgan Bentley? I know how much you hate him."

"I don't hate him. I never have. It was you who kept saying that. I was afraid of him because I knew from the start he wanted you, and I knew you wanted him back. You were just in denial. I was scared, but I didn't hate him. I never hated him, not really."

I gazed at him thoughtfully, remembered how he would always close up when I ranted about Morgan, how he was the one who always said Morgan was sad and lonely. He was perceptive, my friend, my best friend, Cory.

"Can you accept us?"

"Accept? I don't have much choice. It's weird. I won't deny that, really weird to see you together. It's going to be hard for me, but you're my best friend, so if you love him and he loves you . . . I just want you to be happy."

"I am. I will be . . . when . . . when it's all over . . . I hope."

"I'll always be here for you, Matthew, no matter what happens."

"I know."

Somehow, I didn't find the words comforting. Of course it was good to know Cory was there for me, but it made me face what was happening again—happening right now—to Morgan, and what the result might be. I didn't want to face it, couldn't handle it right then. Every time I paused, my mind strayed over to the barn. The pictures it was painting were uncomfortable, to say the least.

I wandered over to the window to stare out at the blank stone wall. It was dark as pitch, except for the little pool of light created by the window. Morgan's cigarettes and lighter were on the worktop by the sink, and I toyed with them for a while. Somehow, they became a link to him, a part of him that made me feel connected. After a while, I took out a cigarette and lit it.

"I thought you'd given up."

"You know I had. I just . . . I need something to keep my mind occupied."

"Try not to think about it."

"How can I think about anything else? I love him, Cory. I know that's probably not what you want to hear right now, but I fucking love him, and this is killing me."

"I know." I thought he was going to say something else, but there really wasn't anything else to say, so he shut his mouth again and sat down at the table, fiddling with the things that littered its surface.

I wandered around, picking things up and putting them down, smoking cigarettes until they made me feel sick, and never taking my eyes off the barn.

It felt like hours before I saw a figure slip, white as a ghost, from the shadows. I was at the door before he'd lifted a finger to the handle.

The boy took a step back, startled, but he recovered quickly. "The professor wants you."

"How did it go?"

"I . . . he wants you now."

Panicking, I ran from the house and skidded across the now icy yard. It was beginning to snow and was cold as hell, but I hardly noticed. The professor was sitting at his desk, bent over the microscope. I glanced at the cubicle where Morgan was, but the plastic sheet was closed, and there was no movement inside.

The professor didn't acknowledge me until I put a hand on his shoulder. "Calm down, Matthew," were his first words. I hadn't realised the panic was so evident. I made an effort. I really did, but my voice was still shaking and my heart racing when I begged him.

"Please. How is he? Tell me that . . . tell me he's okay."

"I won't lie to you, Matthew, it wasn't easy. I haven't practised as a doctor, not with humans, for many, many years. Such a delicate procedure should have had a specialist performing it. There were . . . problems, and I was very concerned for a while."

"Please . . ."

"Calm down, Matthew. Morgan is . . . he's okay . . . not good, but alive, and I intend to keep him that way."

Relief flooded me, and I collapsed into the chair Morgan had occupied earlier. The professor patted my arm awkwardly.

"So, what now?"

"I'm working on the cells right now, studying them. Shortly, I will start applying the formula, trying to find a way to suppress or reverse the mutation. I'm confident I can find something to help."

"But?" I heard it in his voice, the *but*.

"It's a matter of time, Matthew. This kind of thing takes time, a lot of time — too much time."

"Time he doesn't have?"

"Yes."

"Can't you give him more of that stuff you gave him before? It seemed to help for a while."

"The problem is that it's not so much different from the thing that caused this in the first place. It causes mutation, too, just of a different kind, and that's really not what we want. I can, I think, adapt the formula to act as a short-term suppressant, but it's all theory, all up in the air. I never meant for my research to be applied to humans, not yet. It's all at the early stages, too early. The truth is I don't know what to do, where to go from here.

"Oh, don't get me wrong," he said quickly. He must have noted my horrified expression. "I'm not giving up, no way. I'm going to keep working on this to the last possible moment, but I'm not confident, Matthew."

"But you told him —"

"I know, and maybe it was wrong to have misled him, but a lot of this depends on him. If he gives up, it's all over. He has to be strong in his mind to fight this thing, and he needs to believe."

"I understand, I think."

The professor smiled and squeezed my hand. "You're a good man, Matthew. Morgan is lucky to have found someone like you."

"Too bad it was too late," I said bitterly.

"It's never too late to find love, and who knows? Maybe that love will be the deciding factor, the thing that keeps him strong for long enough."

"Maybe."

"Do you want to sit with him?"

"Of course."

"I'm sorry I'm not able to make either of you more comfortable. We're just not set up for this, for humans."

"It's all right. Is he awake?"

The professor hesitated. "Because of the problems we experienced, and since he's likely to be in some discomfort, and possibly quite frightened, I decided to keep him lightly sedated. It's important he stays calm and still. He won't be completely out, but very sleepy . . . in and out, if you know what I mean."

I did, and it scared the hell out of me, but I just nodded, and the professor squeezed my hand again. "Good man."

I followed him across the floor and ducked under the plastic when he held it up for me. Apart from being covered with a multi-coloured and very tatty blanket, and having a drip in one arm, Morgan was exactly as he had been when I left. I was glad all the scary equipment had been moved back to the edge of the *room*. I could pretend there was only Morgan's *bed* and the chair that had been put at the side of it.

"I'm sorry I couldn't find you a more comfortable one. Maybe we can bring one out from the house in a while."

"This is fine, thanks."

I was desperate for him to leave now, and he must have picked up on it because he nodded and departed.

Morgan stirred as I approached, disturbed by the sound of our voices, perhaps.

"Matthew?"

"I'm here. It's okay."

"Is it . . . is it over?"

"Yeah, for now."

He sighed and forced his eyes open. "Feel like crap."

"Don't worry. The professor thinks you need to rest, so he's doping you up."

Morgan smiled—a faint, fleeting smile. "Good. For a minute, I thought I was dying."

"That's not going to happen, Morgan. No way. I won't let you get away that easily."

He smiled but didn't answer, drifting off to sleep again. I took his hand, and he squeezed my fingers weakly.

For a long, long time, I stood gazing down at him. He looked like an angel when he slept. The wicked glitter in his eyes made it impossible to think of him in that way when he was awake. My heart fluttered as emotion overwhelmed me and I had to close my eyes. His hand in mine felt delicate, even though I knew it wasn't. It was strong, like the rest of him . . . usually.

Eventually, I sat down and let myself cry, still holding his hand and resting my forehead on it. Morgan didn't stir, and I was glad. I really didn't want him to see me like this. I wanted to be strong for him.

Gradually, something began to break through my misery, ringing an alarm bell in the back of my mind. I sat up, instantly alert. At first, I couldn't make out what it was. But as it got louder, nearer, recognition broke over me like a cold sweat. It was sirens . . . the sound of sirens getting closer and closer.

CHAPTER SEVENTEEN

The sound of the sirens terrified me, and I unconsciously gripped Morgan's hand hard enough to make him start awake with a gasp.

"What . . . what's happening?"

"Shhh, it's all right . . . at least I think it is."

He blinked slowly, a frown creasing his brow. "I-I . . . what . . ."

I forced myself to smile. "It's all right, nothing to worry about. Go back to sleep."

The sirens were loud now, very close, and Morgan heard them. His eyes widened. "No." There was so much in that one word. Disbelief, horror, fear, and a terrible hopelessness that eclipsed all the rest.

"Hush. It's all right. The professor will sort things out. He won't let anything happen to you."

"My father."

"It's all right, Morgan. Please—"

He tried to get up, but he couldn't. He couldn't even raise his head without getting so dizzy he fell back.

"Stop him, Matthew, please. He won't . . . he won't . . ." Despite his panic, despite the fear in his eyes, he just didn't have the energy to fight the drugs, and as much as he railed against it, he couldn't stay awake. I held on to his hand, terrified.

I knew I ought to go out, to see what was happening. There were other sounds now—slamming doors, voices shouting, plastic being torn aside, glass smashing, more shouting. I was frozen, too scared to move. I knew if I went outside that I'd be torn away from him, and I didn't want that. I wanted to stay here, close to him, until the very last minute.

However, when I heard two familiar voices raised in anger when I heard Cory cry out as if in pain, I couldn't bear it any more.

I stood up, my legs trembling, and very carefully laid Morgan's hand on the blanket at his side. He muttered and turned his head but didn't wake. Slowly, my heart thudding in my chest, I pulled aside the plastic and peeped out.

The barn was full of people. All the staff were struggling in the grip of police officers dressed in blue assault suits. They seemed to be everywhere. The professor stood in the middle of the room, thankfully still unrestrained, toe to toe with a man who had his back to me. Even so, I knew who it was.

I caught snippets of their conversation. Betrayal . . . hypocrisy . . . thief . . . liar . . . monster. As I watched, Mr Bentley stepped back and said loudly, "Take him away. He's a thief and a liar. He stole my idea, my formula . . . and my son. Search the house, but be careful. Don't hurt my son."

Two police officers stepped forward and took hold of the professor by the arms. "You'll regret this, Paul. You know what's happening to Morgan, and I'm the only chance he has. You know I haven't stolen anything. This is *my* research, and it always was. It's very different from yours. Please think about this. If you let them take me, you're going to lose your son. Morgan is going to die."

"I can take care of my son." The coldness in that voice, the knowledge that behind it lay everything that had happened to Morgan, that had led him to this place, this desperate situation, chilled me to the bone. At the same time, it flared burning anger in me, and I wanted to throw myself at him, to hit him until there was nothing left but a puddle on the floor.

"Like you have been? Would you like me to tell the good

officers what you've done? I wonder who they'll lock up then."

"Tell them what you want." He sounded . . . odd, almost hopeless, defeated.

"Paul, please don't do this. Think of Morgan."

"That's what I am doing, Lionel. I was taking care of him, in my own way. I'm working on the serum, getting close. He would have been all right. He would have been safe. I was going to take him into the Institute. He would have been taken care of. Better than this."

"Is that what you want, Paul? To take him to the Institute? You don't have time. Without my research, my formula, my input, you have hours . . . if that. Let them take me, and you're dooming your son. In fact, we don't even have the time to have this conversation."

"I'm tired of you, Lionel, although I have to admit I'm impressed. You were always so cautious, so slow. To have set up something like this in such a short time — yes, I am impressed. Not impressed enough to let it pass, to let you get away with it, but — "

"Let me get away with it?" It was the first time I'd seen the professor really angry. "Get away with it? Get away with what? I stole nothing, Paul, nothing. This is all my own research. And I couldn't care less whether you're impressed or not. I have other things on my mind right now, and chief among them is the desire to save Morgan. You remember Morgan? He's your son. He's the boy you brought into work with you, the one I taught to be interested in what you do, the lessons you should have been teaching him yourself.

"He was the one who came to me in pieces when Elizabeth died, convinced her death was his fault, and you were punishing him for it, that you didn't love him anymore. He was the one I put together again as best I could. I was more of a father to that boy than you ever were and now — I can't believe what you've done. And I can't believe that, after what you've done, you can stand there and call me a thief and a liar, while your son's life is slipping away by the second."

The professor checked himself and the anger leaked from his voice. "Think about it. Can't we work on it together? Can't we find a way through? If you would only work with me. Please, Paul, please think about this before you do something you'll regret for the rest of your life."

For a long moment, there was silence. Then Paul Bentley drew himself up ramrod straight and said in a cold voice, "Take him away."

"No."

I couldn't help it—it slipped out. As soon as the word left my mouth, I regretted it. Until that moment, no one had noticed me, but suddenly every eye was on me, including Paul Bentley.

"Well, well. We meet again, Matthew. Why am I not surprised to see you here? Of course you would be, hand in hand with that thieving friend of yours. I hope you've been learning your lessons well because you're going to need a very good lawyer indeed to get out of this one."

Out of the corner of my eye, I saw two blue-clad figures moving toward me.

"I'm not here with Cory. I'm here with Morgan. It's his hand I've been holding for the last couple of hours. Would you like to see him, Mr Bentley? Would you like to see what you've done to him?" Surprising myself, my voice was soft and level, cold as ice.

Did I imagine, or did I see him flinch? "This isn't about Morgan. This is about theft, industrial espionage, and betrayal."

"Betrayal? Just exactly who betrayed who? It seems to me the only person who's been betrayed is Morgan. He was completely innocent. He didn't ask for what you did to him. He didn't deserve it. If your bloody formula is so important to you, then come and see the results of it. Come and see what you've done. I've been seeing it. I've seen nothing else for hours."

Someone took my arm and began to put pressure on it to move me away. I struggled, but it was no good. He had a grip of iron, and suddenly I was desperate. My voice was no longer calm and level. It was pleading and desperate.

"No. Please don't do this. Don't make me leave him. Please. He's so sick. He needs me. Please don't take me away from him. And don't take him away from me. He . . . he's dying, and I couldn't bear it if I wasn't there for him. Please . . . please don't do this to me . . . don't do it to him."

Paul Bentley's face could have been made of stone, and the panic rose in me. I started to sob, and the words just bubbled out. "Please . . . no . . . no, don't let them do this. Please. I love him. I love him, Mr Bentley. Don't take me away from him. Please . . . please don't."

My voice rose to a scream as I begged and pleaded with the stone man. Although his eyebrows rose when I said I loved Morgan, his mouth was compressed into a thin line, and he stood rigid as they dragged me away.

"Matthew? Matthew!"

Morgan's voice was weak, but the panic in it was clear. "Morgan!" I screamed, struggling harder than ever, throwing myself in every direction I could with only one thing clear in my mind—Morgan needed me, and I had to get to him.

"Matthew, what's happening? I'm scared, Matthew."

The sound of his fear raised strength in me I never knew I had. I broke free and ran for the cubicle, only to crash to the floor when I was tackled from behind. With the wind knocked out of me, I lay gasping and sobbing as Morgan continued to call me, his voice getting weaker. It was unbearable.

"Wait."

Paul Bentley loomed over me. "Is it true?"

"What?" I gasped.

"You and Morgan? Do you love him?"

"More than anything."

"And he loves you?"

"Yes."

His gaze flicked up to the cubicle where all was now silent. "Let him go."

"Are you sure, Mr Bentley? He's a feisty one. He could make a run for it."

"Don't worry. I know exactly where he's going to run. I think you'd better get your commanding officer in here. In the meantime, don't do anything. Keep everyone restrained, but in here."

The police officer looked as if he was going to say something. It seemed he didn't take kindly to receiving orders from a civilian. But in the end, he nodded, got to his feet, and disappeared. I didn't care where he went or what he did. I even dismissed Paul Bentley from my mind as I scrambled up and stumbled into Morgan's cubicle.

He was asleep but restless, breathing rapidly, turning his head from side to side, struggling.

I took his hand, and he gripped it hard. "Shhh. It's all right, Morgan, I'm here. It's okay, it's me, Matthew. I'm here now. Everything's going to be all right." I stroked his forehead, and slowly he calmed, his breathing slowing and evening out. With a sigh, he forced open his eyes and stared up at me.

"Was it . . . did I dream?"

"No, not exactly. It . . . it's all right now."

"I-I was afraid. You weren't here, and I heard you . . ."

"It's all right now. I'm here. No one and nothing's going to make me leave you again." I glanced up as I said it, my eyes hard. Morgan turned his head to follow my gaze and squeezed my hand even tighter when he saw who was standing in the doorway.

"Father," he breathed, his voice harsh.

"Morgan." Mr Bentley inclined his head, his face a study in cold inscrutability.

Morgan gazed at me, and his eyes looked confused. "Why? How?"

"It's all right, Morgan. It's going to be all right." I knew that wasn't what he was asking, but what could I say? I had no answers. I was just along for the ride.

"It was him. That's why . . . why you . . . he tried to . . ." He was fading but pulled himself together to grip my hand painfully. "Don't let him, Matthew. Please don't let him take you away from me. Don't . . . don't . . . don't . . . leave me. I don't . . . I don't want . . . to be . . . alone . . . again."

With his voice fading to less than a whisper, his eyes, sparkling with tears of fear and desperation, held me as firmly as his hand, until they lost focus completely and flickered closed. This time, I held on to his hand so it wouldn't slip out of my fingers. I hated that. Even when his eyes closed, tears ran from beneath the lids to wet his cheeks. I wiped them away and whispered, in a voice choked with emotion, "I won't. I swear. I won't leave you, not ever. You won't be alone ever again."

I deliberately blanked Morgan's father until he started to move into the room. I'll never forget the expression on his face at that moment. It was a mixture of fear, sadness, and fierce love. It was the most honest expression I'd ever seen there. At that moment, I saw him for what he was—a man who'd lost his wife, his anchor . . . and was now facing the reality he might well be about to lose his son. I was stunned.

Slowly, he crossed the floor as if every step cost him. His eyes remained fixed on Morgan, and that expression remained firmly planted on his face. After staring at Morgan for a time, he raised stunned eyes to me.

"I-I didn't realise. I never meant this to happen. I . . . you know Morgan? You know my son?"

"I know him as well as anyone. He doesn't show his true self very often."

Mr Bentley nodded. "I'm the same. Does he . . . what Lionel said . . . about him blaming himself for his mother's death and thinking I . . . thinking all this is some kind of punishment . . . is that true? Is that how he feels?"

"Yes. As far as I know, it's how he's always felt, even before . . . before . . . he told me you can't bear to be near him, that you hate him because of what happened."

"It's not true. It never was." He sounded lost and turned his face back to his son. Unbelievably, he was trembling. "That was never the way it was, never. It was me. I was the one I blamed. I was the one who should have been more understanding and less proud. It should have been me driving that car. That's why I couldn't face him."

"It's not me you should tell all this, you know."

He glanced up again, and I was even more shocked to see tears in his eyes. He didn't answer, just nodded.

At that moment, we were disturbed by the appearance of a strange man, who pulled aside the plastic, his cold eyes scanning the interior of the cubicle. I shivered when they passed over me.

"I see you found your son. I'll send the paramedics in."

"No . . . no, that won't be necessary. I was wrong, Inspector Blake. I thought these people were hurting him, but they weren't. They were helping him. I made a terrible mistake. I apologise for wasting your time, but there's been no crime here."

The inspector narrowed his eyes and glared at Morgan. "I wonder."

Mr Bentley pulled himself up straight and held those chilling eyes. "He has . . . he has a rare condition. I hadn't realised he'd fallen ill. I've not been there for him lately. When

I discovered he was here, I jumped to conclusions. The man who's running this facility used to work for me, and I assumed he'd stolen my research. I now know he's been conducting research of his own and has developed a medicine that can help my son. Again, I can only apologise."

The inspector narrowed his eyes again, suspiciously. "This doesn't look like a medical facility."

"It isn't. I've told you . . . it's a research facility."

"Wouldn't your son be better off in a hospital?"

"Possibly, but we don't have time, and they'll have neither the special facilities nor the medicine he needs."

"I see. You do realise you could be charged with wasting police time and resources?"

"I appreciate I've wasted your time, but I would remind you I was labouring under a misapprehension. I genuinely believed a crime had been committed here, and I acted accordingly, in good faith. I'm extremely grateful for your swift response and continuing goodwill. I'll make sure to commend you to your chief superintendent when I have dinner with her on Boxing Day."

The inspector glared at him, but he knew when he was beaten. "This isn't over. We'll be looking into this. Whatever's going on here had better be above board." With a curt bow of his head, he withdrew. Shortly afterwards, the sirens died, and I heard cars driving away.

"Boxing Day? Hell, so much has happened, I forgot." I gave a dry laugh. "It's Christmas."

Mr Bentley checked his watch. "In fact, it's about four hours into Christmas Eve."

"Merry Christmas."

"Ma . . . Matthew." Morgan's voice was weak, and he didn't open his eyes. He sounded as if he was only awake because he was trying hard to be. I was instantly disinterested in Christmas.

"I'm here."

"Matthew I . . . I had a dream. My father . . ."

"It wasn't a dream, Morgan. I'm here."

Morgan opened his eyes and shook his head. "No. Please, Father . . . please don't make him go away. I want . . . I need . . ."

Mr Bentley gazed at Morgan with the most . . . complex expression I'd ever seen. He reached out his hand, as if he was going to touch him, but drew it back at the last moment. "Morgan, I'm not going to take Matthew away from you. Not now, not ever. I'm sorry, Morgan, sorry for everything."

"I . . . but . . . but I . . ."

"Shhh. Just listen to me. Try . . . try to listen to me."

Morgan nodded once—his face was calm even though he must have been scared. I think it was the fear, the tension singing in the air between them, that kept him awake.

"There's something you need to know, something important. I don't blame you for your mother's death, Morgan. I never did. I blamed myself. I was arrogant, stubborn, and unreasonable that night. It should have been me driving the car. I should have taken you to that party. I broke a promise to you, and I've paid for it ever since.

"I wasn't there for you when you needed me. Not because I hated you, but because I hated myself. For a time, I fell apart, and I couldn't face anyone. Then I couldn't bear to look at you, to see her in your face, your eyes, and I couldn't live with the guilt. It was never your fault, Morgan, any of it. Never. I swear. I . . . Morgan . . ." His voice choked up as his face twisted in pain and tears scalded his cheeks.

I got the impression Paul Bentley rarely showed emotion to anyone, and weeping of any kind was painful to him. Nevertheless, he stood there with his head bowed and wept.

"I'm so sorry I let you down," he said, softly and simply. Morgan just stared at him, his mouth open, shocked. Even so,

I was surprised when, slowly and hesitantly, he reached out his hand and gently touched the sleeve of his father's coat. Mr Bentley jerked up his head and stared for a moment — they both did. Then suddenly something in him snapped, and he surged forward, pulling Morgan roughly into his arms. Taken by surprise, Morgan yelped as the hug tugged on the tube in his arm, but when his father would have pulled back, he hung on with surprising strength, clinging to him with his face buried in his neck, just like a child.

I felt almost uncomfortable intruding on this precious moment, but there was nowhere I could go without squeezing past, and that didn't feel right either. Unfortunately, for such a sweet moment, it didn't last long because Morgan just couldn't stay conscious, and after only a few moments, he relaxed, his arms falling away from the embrace, and his father gently lowered him back onto the pillow.

Again, I felt intensely uncomfortable when Mr Bentley, still with tears in his eyes, gently stroked Morgan's face and hair, just as one would a little one, and Morgan sighed, a slight smile playing on his lips.

Eventually, Mr Bentley turned to me and struggled to drop the mask back into place.

"Thank you for being here for him."

"I couldn't be anywhere else. I love him." Yeah, it was crass, but it was sincere, and it was all I could think of to say. There was nothing that could have expressed the intensity of what I was feeling right then.

"I didn't mean this to happen, you know. I was so sure . . . so absolutely sure my formula was safe. I would never have involved Morgan otherwise, would never have dreamed of putting him through this. And then, as soon . . . as soon as I realised there were . . . problems, I tried to correct them. I really tried to find a solution, and I thought I had. I thought I was neutralising the problem, but I was only making it worse.

When he started to get more and more ill, more and more quickly, I panicked. I tried everything, worked morning, noon, and night, and drove my research team into the ground. That's why it took me so long to notice your friend's escapades."

I blushed scarlet on Cory's behalf. "He ... he didn't mean —"

Mr Bentley held up his hand. "That's in the past, Matthew. He did me a favour. How much of a favour, no one will ever know. Even if things don't work out, at least I've been given a chance to say something I should have said a long time ago. I just wish there was more I could do."

"There is more you can do."

We both turned toward the door. The professor wasn't smiling, but his voice was kind. He pretended not to notice the tears.

"I ... I don't ..."

"We have a long way to go, Paul, and Morgan doesn't have the kind of time it will take. With you helping, it would shorten the time considerably, maybe even enough."

Mr Bentley hesitated, glancing down at Morgan, and I know what he was thinking. If Morgan's life was coming to an end, he wanted to spend every possible moment of it at his side. However, in the end, the possibility of saving that life, however small, was worth more, and he nodded. He was taking off his coat as he ducked through the doorway.

I heaved a sigh of relief. As wonderful as it was that Morgan's father hadn't had us arrested and had taken the first steps toward reconciliation, it had still been a ridiculously stressful half an hour, and too close a shave to make me comfortable in his company. I wondered if, when Morgan next woke, it would be me he asked for. The thought depressed me. At the same time, it made me feel guilty for my shallowness.

I was still musing and brooding when the curtain twitched aside. I felt almost angry with being disturbed in the middle of my self-pity, until I saw who it was.

"Cory."

"Shit, fuck, bollocks, Matthew . . . that was scary. When I heard the sirens, and then all those police bursting in, I thought if I was lucky enough not to get shot, I'd be spending the rest of my life in prison."

"I know. The same thoughts might have been going through my mind if I hadn't been so busy thinking of something else."

"Someone else." There was still a note of sadness in his voice, but the expression in his eyes was teasing.

"Yeah, well, you know how it is. Young love and all that bollocks. And, of course, there's the small fact that . . ." I glanced at Morgan, who looked as if he was fast asleep. However, I didn't really know if he was listening, so for once, I thought better of my words before they were out of my mouth. "Well, you know."

Cory glanced at Morgan, too, and nodded, frowning. "You were unbelievably brave when you fought with that policeman. You scared the shit out of me. The other one actually took out his stick. I thought they were going to beat the crap out of you."

"I didn't notice. I didn't care. It wasn't brave. I just reacted. I wasn't thinking."

"Well, I still think it was brave, so there."

I couldn't help but smile. Cory always did that for me, even when I was at my lowest. I guess by that stage we knew each other so well that we always knew the right buttons to press. I did the same for him, usually.

"Are you okay?" I asked, suddenly shy.

"Okay?"

"I mean . . . you know . . . with us."

"Of course I am. I told you that."

"Just checking."

"Do you need anything?"

"Need?" I shook my head. "There's only one thing I need." I glanced at the bed, and I was going to say *and he's right here*, but I bit my lip. Not only would that have been corny as hell, but it would have been cruel to Cory. He knew, though, of course he knew.

"I'll get you a coffee."

"Yeah . . . actually, I could really do with a coffee. See if you can't find some brandy. Now I come to think about it, with the adrenaline levels back to normal . . . that really was bloody scary."

Cory grinned. "I'll see what I can do."

CHAPTER EIGHTEEN

When Cory came back with the coffee, I was sitting in the chair, leaning on the edge of the bed, with my head on my arms. To be honest, I was almost asleep. I'd been affected more than I thought by the drama, and almost as soon as Cory had left the cubicle, reaction had set in, and I'd started to shake. Once the shaking had passed, exhaustion had hit me. I jumped, startled, when Cory touched my shoulder.

"Sorry, mate, I almost flaked out there."

He handed me the coffee. "Maybe you should lie down for a while. It's almost five AM, and you haven't had much sleep tonight."

I shook my head emphatically. "No. Thanks. I won't leave him."

Cory nodded stoically. "I didn't think you would, but I wouldn't have been much of a friend if I hadn't at least suggested it."

I nodded. "What's going on out there now?"

"It's weird. Considering what just happened, those two are thick as thieves, like old friends . . . sparring, nagging each other. They seem pretty upbeat."

"Good. That's good."

"I hope so."

"Me, too."

Our conversation petered out. There wasn't much else to say. Cory perched on the edge of a table, looking uncomfortable in so many ways.

"You don't have to stay here, Cory. I'll be all right on my

own."

He seemed surprised.

"You're an idiot, Matthew, you really are. You've just been telling me how you can't leave, how you need to be here with . . . with him . . . well . . . I need to be here . . . with you."

That really surprised me, and I didn't know what to say. I bit my lip and fiddled with my coffee cup.

"It's all right, I'm not going to make complications for you. That's not what I meant. But you've been my best friend for a lot longer than you've known Morgan. I've loved you forever, and I always will. You're closer than a brother to me. I won't leave you when you need me."

I was truly stunned. "Thank you."

"Drink your bloody coffee and get over it."

Now it was my turn to grin. "At least get a chair, then, and quit lounging around. You're making the place look untidy."

"Could we fit another chair in here?"

"Hmm, maybe a small one."

Cory disappeared. He returned a few minutes later with a small stool. To be honest, that was about as much as would fit. He set it down in front of one of the wooden posts onto which the plastic sheeting was attached, then leaned his back against it with a sigh. He looked tired. I realised he'd been through the mill, too. He must have been badly frightened when the police had burst in.

"You okay? You look beat."

"Yeah, I am a bit. That scared the shit out of me."

"So you said." He smiled tiredly.

"I went too far, didn't I?"

"You always go too far. I've been telling you that for years."

"Meh . . ."

We were silent for a while, and I cast about desperately for something to say. "Hey, did you realise it's Christmas Eve?"

"Shit, with everything that's been going on these last few days I completely forgot. Do you think Santa will find us here?"

I chuckled. "I hope so."

"So, what have you got for me, then?"

"Shit. I did get you something, but it's back at the flat."

"You did?"

"You know how OCD I am about Christmas. I had all my presents bought in July."

"Really?"

"No, but they've been wrapped and tucked in my case for a couple of weeks."

"Bugger." He pouted. "I didn't . . . think."

"It's okay. I'm used to your selfish ways."

"Selfish?" he exploded, outraged, and made me smile. The sound disturbed Morgan.

"Matthew?" I was ridiculously pleased, and instantly annoyed with myself for my continuing shallowness.

"I'm here."

Morgan opened his eyes and gazed at me, reaching for my hand, which I gave him instantly.

"Is . . ." He sighed, annoyed and frustrated by his weakness. "Is my father still here?"

"He's working with the professor."

Morgan's eyes widened. "Working *with* him?"

"Of course he is. They both want the same thing . . . for now."

"They do?"

"Of course they do, you idiot. They both want you to be okay."

"Oh." He sounded so dejected it shocked me.

"Doesn't that make you feel better?"

"I um . . . don't know."

"You don't know?"

He sighed and closed his eyes, and I thought he'd drifted off again, but after a few moments, he whispered, "It doesn't feel like I'm going to be okay."

"What do you mean?"

"It feels like . . . like I'm dying." Tears began to squeeze out from under his lids. When he opened his eyes, they were incredibly bright and vibrantly green. There was a strange expression in them. He wasn't pleading with me to convince him otherwise. He wasn't afraid anymore. He was resigned, at peace with his fate, and that scared me more than anything.

"Don't say that. It's just the drugs making you sleepy and muddled and—"

Morgan shook his head, slowly, his eyes heavy but alert. "It isn't that. It's something else."

"You don't know, Morgan. You can't *know*. Everyone's working so hard to find a way to help you. They're going to do it. I know they are."

Morgan grinned. "You can't *know*, Matthew," he parroted, with his usual sneer, and it made me smile despite myself. I sobered quickly.

"Seriously, Morgan, they're working hard, and they're going to find a way. I feel it. I know it. Besides, it's Christmas. Christmas Eve. Nothing bad happens at Christmas . . . only miracles."

Morgan's eyes widened. "Christmas?"

"Yeah, can you believe we forgot?"

He shook his head. "So what'd you get me, then?" His words slurred, and he was blinking a lot, but he still seemed pretty much with us, so I teased him.

"Is everyone just *me, me, me* today?"

Morgan frowned in confusion. I had to smile at him. "Everyone?"

"That's what Cory said when I reminded him. He's bloody selfish, too."

"I am not. I just know how mean you are."

Morgan looked startled and turned his head toward Cory's voice. He blinked but couldn't focus on him. He was too far away. "Cory?"

"Yeah, buddy, I'm here. I'm keeping Matthew company because, let's face it, you're not exactly the best entertainment tonight."

"Oh, I don't know. I actually find it very entertaining to watch you sleep. You snore very musically."

"I . . . do?"

He was beginning to drift, and the teasing was confusing him, so I snapped straight back to serious again.

"Don't worry about it, Morgan, just worry about keeping strong . . . hanging in there . . . yeah?"

His eyes fluttered and rolled, but he forced them to focus back on my face. Licking his lips, he managed to whisper, "So did you get me something?"

There was something in his voice that made me shiver and lean in very close to whisper, with my lips almost touching his, "Yeah, and because you're being such a good boy, I'll give it to you early." Then I kissed him, and for a moment, he kissed me back.

When I sat down, I was crying. Morgan's hand was limp and lifeless again, and after all the sweetness, the thought of losing him was unbearable. I laid Morgan's hand on the bed and buried my face in mine, sniffling, trying desperately to stop the flood because I knew if I let go now, I would fall apart completely, and I needed to be there for him . . . all the way.

It was a desperate struggle, but I finally managed to get my chaotic emotions under control, and I sat up, giving Cory a crooked smile. He didn't return it.

"It's the real deal, isn't it?"

"What?"

"You and him. You really do love each other."

"Yeah, it is."

"I think I was kind of hoping . . . ah well. I guess it makes it easier."

"Easier?"

"At least you didn't throw me over for a quick shag with a pretty face."

"Well, there was that." We both grinned but sobered quickly. "But it wasn't . . . it isn't . . . it never was just that."

"I know. It would have been easier for you, too, if it had been."

"Maybe."

Then there was really nothing to say. We sat in silence, but it was a companionable silence, like it used to be, and in other circumstances that would have made me so happy. At this point, however, there was only one thing that could possibly make me happy.

"What's that?" Cory asked suddenly.

"What's what?"

"That music."

I listened carefully and heard it, too. "I don't know."

Cory got up and raised the plastic. Then I could hear it, soft but clear. A Christmas carol, *Silent Night*. Someone must have brought in a radio or something. There was something about it that was strangely comforting.

"Ask them to turn it up, Cory, so we can hear properly."

Before Cory could do anything of the sort, Mr Bentley appeared, apparently having seen the plastic raised, his face anxious. I was shocked as he was so different. He'd shed his coat and jacket and was working in rolled-up shirt sleeves. His tie had gone, and his hair was rumpled as if he'd been running his hands through it, over and over. I smiled, thinking how very like Morgan that was.

"Is everything all right?"

"Yeah, I just heard the music, wanted to listen to the

carols."

He smiled tightly. "Of course. It's nice, isn't it? Calming somehow. I'll ask if they can turn it up, maybe move it nearer so you can hear more clearly. How . . . how is Morgan?"

"Sleeping mostly. He wakes up now and again, but not for long."

"I'll get Lionel to check on him in a while. He's better at that kind of thing than I am. I'm more the chemist . . . he's the people person." He nodded, then disappeared. A short while later, the source of the music was moved closer so we could listen to the carols.

We were on *God Rest Ye Merry Gentlemen* when the curtain twitched aside to admit the professor. He gave us a tired smile.

"How's it going?"

"We're making progress, but it's just so slow. I can't see anything coming of it for hours, at least."

"Hours is good. It's better than days."

He smiled again. "Better, yes." He left out the *but not good enough.*

Morgan stirred but didn't wake as the professor checked the drip and changed the bag. Not even when the professor took his pulse, then bent over him and lifted his eyelids, one at a time, to peer into his eyes. The stillness and lack of response scared the hell out of me. Panicking, I got to my feet.

"Is he . . . is everything all right?"

The professor glanced up. For a moment, there was something in his eyes, something I wouldn't care to name. Then the professional persona clicked back into place.

"He's all right. He's just . . . getting weaker. I'm going to lay off the drugs and see what happens. I think they may be overwhelming him at the moment. I don't think he needs them to be calm now."

"If you stop giving him drugs, he'll wake up, right? I can

talk to him?"

"Maybe."

"But . . ." Suddenly it was incredibly important that Morgan woke up. There was so much I wanted to tell him, so much I hadn't had a chance to say . . . or at least say enough. The last time he was awake, I'd wasted time teasing him. I hadn't thought . . . never thought it might *be* the last time. "But if . . ."

"I told you, Matthew, he's getting weaker."

"But—"

"Let's just wait and see. I'm not a doctor, not anymore. I can't predict. I'm sorry."

I hated to ask the question burning in my mind, but it wouldn't stay in there. It just burst out. "He doesn't have much time, does he?"

The professor gave me a look that initially was almost annoyance, but which softened. Sadly, he shook his head. "No, he doesn't."

"Not enough time."

He lowered his eyes, and when he raised them again, he wasn't smiling. "It's Christmas, Matthew. Pray for a miracle."

Now the question was out, it opened the floodgates, and my fear bubbled out of my mouth without me being able to do a thing about it.

"Pray? I have no one to pray to. A miracle? I don't believe in them. I believe in him, in Morgan, and I know . . . I know he believes in me, but . . ." I tore my eyes away from his beautiful face, so soft in sleep, and met the professor's baleful stare. "He's not going to see Christmas Day, is he?"

The professor gave me a searching look, then sighed. "We're going to keep trying, Matthew . . . right to the last moment. We won't stop trying, but without that miracle, no, I don't think he will."

I sat down so suddenly I missed the chair and found myself

on the floor with both the professor and Cory nudging each other out of the way to get to me. I stared up at them both, completely shocked, my mind a blank, numb.

"Come on, Matthew," the professor said in a voice that meant business. "Cory is going to take you back to the house, and you are not to leave there until you've drunk a cup of hot coffee, had a stiff drink, and taken time to calm down and settle yourself. You've been cooped up in here for too long."

"No. No, I can't. I can't leave him."

"Matthew, Morgan won't know you're here, and he won't know you're not. Nothing is going to happen one way or the other for a couple of hours. And if there's any change at all, I'll personally come and get you. You need to take an hour for yourself, or you'll collapse, and I can't cope with both of you."

"I don't want to leave him."

"I know you don't. But it'll only be for a little while. You can come back as soon as you're feeling better, and I promise I will fetch you if anything changes."

"You promise?"

"My personal guarantee."

If I'd been myself, I never would've gone. But I was still numb, my emotions battered into silence. Obediently, I got to my feet and let Cory steer me out of the cubicle, out of the barn, and into the warm kitchen. I headed straight to the packet of cigarettes as Cory put the kettle on. I wandered about, found a bottle of brandy in a cupboard and poured a large measure into my mug. Cory poured slightly less into his.

Cory insisted I take my coffee into the sitting room to relax while I was drinking it. I don't remember finishing the cup. I was asleep before it was half empty.

I woke with a start to Cory shaking me. He was grinning.

"They've done it . . . made a breakthrough. All hell's breaking loose over there. The professor told me not to disturb you yet, but I thought you'd want to know."

"Fuck. How long have I been asleep?" I asked, as I scrambled to my feet, fluctuating between anger — at myself for having fallen asleep and him for having let me — and wild hope.

"A couple of hours."

"Fuck, Cory, why the hell did you let me fall asleep?"

"Because you needed it. And because there wasn't anything you could have done anyway."

I stopped and turned to him. "You still don't understand, do you?"

He flinched but held my gaze. "Yes. I understand better than you think I do. I understand you would have worn yourself into the ground just to be there with him, that you were in shock and hurting, and I didn't want that. And I understand that if . . . that if you'd been there when . . . if he . . . I understand it would have destroyed you."

For a moment, it was as if time slowed and stopped, and I could see his feelings written all over his face. I allowed myself to wonder if, in different circumstances, there could have been something between us.

Then time speeded again, and guilt crashed in on me. How could I possibly have thought such a thing? Morgan needed me, now more than ever, and he deserved my unquestioning devotion. Besides, it was Cory, and I didn't look at Cory like that, I would never have looked at Cory like that no matter what happened . . . because if I did, it would spoil everything we had, and that was precious to me.

I was used to the barn being quiet. Everyone went about their business in silence, or speaking in hushed voices, partly because of the distortion the echoing barn gave to any sound louder than a low mumble . . . and partly because . . . well, just because. Now the place was a hive of activity, with the sound of excited voices audible even before we opened the door and threw back the plastic.

There was no sign of Mr Bentley, but as soon as the professor saw me, he hurried over.

"Matthew. It might be better if you stayed over at the house for now." He was very serious.

"Why? Cory said you've made a breakthrough. That's good . . . isn't it?" My voice petered off at the look in his eyes.

"It is good, Matthew, yes, but — "

"Morgan." I panicked and tried to push past him. He held on to my shoulders, surprisingly strong.

"Matthew, please."

"What's happening? What's happening to Morgan?"

"Matthew, he's too weak. If we tried to carry out the procedure now, it would undoubtedly kill him. It's not possible."

"You have to try. You can't just give up. You can't just let him die." I was almost beside myself, struggling in his grip, desperate to get to Morgan, to somehow make a difference. If only I could get to him, then I would . . . I would . . . it would be all right.

"Matthew, listen to me." The professor shook me gently, kindly. "We're not going to do that. We're not just giving up. You know I told you the serum Morgan's father was giving him had stripped the red cells from his blood." I nodded dumbly. I didn't really remember, but I was going along with it for now. "Well, we're going to give him a transfusion of healthy blood. We're hoping it will give him some strength . . . just enough to get him through, to let him survive the procedure."

"But where? You said you didn't have the right blood?"

"Paul is seeing to that right now."

"And me. I want to. It's not safe to take too much from one person. I want to give some of mine, too."

"Do you know what blood group you are?"

"I'm O negative. I've given blood for years, so I know the procedure, and I know I'm compatible with pretty much anyone. Please let me do this. I want to do this for Morgan. Please."

The professor nodded. "You're strong, fit, and well. I see no reason why not. Give me a few minutes to set everything up so we can start giving Morgan his father's blood while we're taking yours. Every minute could be vital."

I sat down on a chair at the edge of the barn and watched people running around, carrying things in and out of the cubicle, back and forth between the tables. Someone had their eyes glued to the electronic microscope, and someone else was working nonstop on something bubbling in a glass bottle over a Bunsen burner.

It seemed like a long time, but was probably less than fifteen or twenty minutes, before the curtain twitched open and Mr Bentley strode toward us. I stood up to meet him, and he completely shocked me by taking me into a rough hug.

"Thank you, Matthew. You've no idea how much this means to me."

"I . . . it's nothing. It's nothing more than I've done twice a year for most of my life."

"It isn't nothing, Matthew. It isn't nothing because this time it's for Morgan, for my son."

"How is he?"

Mr Bentley flinched. "Weak. He's gone down fast this last half hour. I thought we were going to lose him, but he's strong, stronger than I thought. He's holding on, but—" He sighed and dropped his gaze, looking old and weary. "He won't survive the procedure. We can only hope the transfusions will give him enough strength so we can perform it before it's too late."

"I-I want to see him. Please."

"I think Lionel wants you to give blood first."

"No, that will take too long. It might be . . . please. Is there any reason why I can't do it in there, with him?"

"There isn't much room."

"But—"

Mr Bentley put his hand on my shoulder. He opened his mouth to say something, but in the end, just nodded and motioned me to follow him across the floor.

The professor was with Morgan. He glanced up when Mr Bentley held the plastic sheet for me, to allow me to enter. Once more, he squeezed my shoulder. Then he let the plastic fall with him and Cory on the outside, shutting me away in this cold plastic world.

Morgan looked awful. He was so pale, almost grey. What frightened me most was that his lips had lost all their colour, and his whole face looked as if it were made out of clay. If it wasn't for the slight rise and fall of his chest, I'd have thought he was already dead. I couldn't believe he'd become so ill so quickly.

The professor had set up another IV in Morgan's other arm, and it made me queasy to watch the blood slowly dripping into him. There didn't seem anywhere I could safely touch him without hurting him. In the end, I braved the needle in his hand and slid my fingers into his. His hand was shockingly cold, and the fingers seemed stiff and lifeless.

"I didn't believe it, not really. I couldn't," I said through tears. "I knew it was a possibility, but I wouldn't let myself believe I was going to lose him. But now . . . I . . . now . . ."

"It's still not too late, Matthew. There is a chance."

"I know, but seeing him like this . . ."

The professor regarded me steadily. He looked as if he was going to say something, but he shook his head and said simply, "I know. Are you ready?"

"Yes, absolutely. If there is anything . . . anything I can do . . . I want to. I really want to."

I raised my head and stared full at him, and the professor smiled warmly. "Come on, then. I'll take you—"

"No, I want to do it here. I don't want to leave him."

"It would be better for you if you lie down."

"But I don't have to. I can do it here. As long as the bag is lower than my arm, we'll be okay. I won't pass out, I promise."

The professor smiled. "Stubborn kids," was all he said, rolling his eyes. I grinned at him and took off my jacket, hanging it on the back of the chair.

CHAPTER NINETEEN

It was strange, surreal, sitting in the chair next to Morgan's bed, watching my own blood trickle into the plastic bag at my feet. Every now and then, I tore my gaze away from it to look over at Morgan, searching for a sign, any sign, to tell me this was working and he was getting stronger, but there were none. Sometimes I touched his hand, and it was always cold, always lifeless. If I lifted the fingers, they were stiff and fell heavily when they slipped from my grasp.

When one bag was full, I insisted the professor take another—after all, I had enough to spare. He was reluctant. But after checking Morgan over, he agreed, and that scared me. Hell, everything scared me.

Despite my promise to the professor, I did start to feel light-headed and slightly nauseated as the second bag filled, but I hid it, at least until I dozed off and almost fell off the chair. Unfortunately, or maybe fortunately for me, the professor was in the room when it happened. He insisted I stop immediately. I tried to fight him on it, but the professor, in a determined mood, was more than a match for anyone. Luckily the bag was over half full, and I had to be satisfied with that.

He made me sit and drink water until I begged off on the basis that if he forced another mouthful down, he'd be getting it all back up. He then switched to making me eat cookies, which wasn't much of a chore, especially as I was starving by then. Finally, he allowed me to stand, clucking over me in case I fell down again. I didn't. In fact, I felt surprisingly good, and he finally left me with Morgan.

262

Standing next to him, I thought he seemed a little better. The greyness was fading, and he was a little pink again. He was still very pale, and his lips were more blue than red, but it was encouraging.

I was still grossed out watching the blood drip into his arm, but it had an additional weird dimension now the blood was mine. With my finger, I traced the vein in his forearm, swollen with the intrusion of blood that only a few hours ago had been in mine. *Shit, there's part of me in there now.* For some reason, the thought made me smile.

"We're blood brothers now, Morgan. Part of each other, together forever."

Did I imagine it, or did his lips twitch just the tiniest bit? I touched them, and they were so soft. I couldn't draw my hand away, and I stroked his face and hair. Again, I thought I may have imagined it when his lips trembled, almost as though he was trying to smile. I knew I didn't imagine it, though, a short while later, after the professor had been in, checked him over, and left again, when his eyes blinked and fluttered.

"Morgan? Morgan, can you hear me? I'm right here. You're okay. You're going to be okay." His eyes fluttered again, and I held my breath. "Morgan?"

I considered calling the professor, but I was both scared and hungry at the same time. Hungry for another moment just for us—just in case. Maybe I was foolish, maybe I was selfish, maybe I was suffering the effects of blood loss. Whatever it was, I didn't call, and there was still just the two of us when Morgan's eyes cracked open, and he sighed.

I took his hand and squeezed it. He didn't squeeze back, but his fingers definitely twitched in mine, and my heart soared, thudding almost painfully.

"Don't waste your strength, Morgan. You have to preserve your strength. Don't—" But of course he did.

I don't know if he understood what I was saying, but he

certainly heard me because he breathed, "Matthew."

"Don't speak, Morgan. You need — "

"Is it over?"

"No, not yet. You . . . you were too weak. They're giving you a blood transfusion to make you stronger, and it is. But you have to rest, to let it work."

The beautiful emerald eyes fluttered fully open and locked with mine. I could see so much, and I didn't want to, didn't want to see his doubt, his fear. I forced myself to smile and tried to put everything I felt for him, everything I dreamed for us, for a future together, into my eyes. He blinked and managed a weak smile.

"I love you."

Warmth flooded through me. I stroked his face and whispered, "I love you, too."

It was hot in the cubicle, with all the plastic, and it was sometimes hard to breathe. At that moment, I didn't think it was the plastic at all.

"Go back to sleep now, Morgan. It's important you conserve your strength. If you're not strong enough, they won't do the procedure, and then . . . well . . . you *have* to be strong enough, okay?"

Morgan nodded, just a little, then sighed and closed his eyes. I felt curiously alone as I watched him fall back into sleep. It was a small world, that little plastic cubicle, small and removed from everywhere, everything. I felt more alone here than I ever had before.

I didn't move from the side of the bed, not even to sit down. I held his hand and watched the colour flush his cheeks. It was slow, but it was hopeful, and it was all I wanted to see.

When the transfusion was finally complete, I stood in an agony of anticipation while the professor examined Morgan, with his father watching just as anxiously from the doorway.

At last, the professor straightened up and shook his head.

My heart dropped, but I was premature.

"I don't know how he's done it, but he's a strong one, this boy. Under ordinary circumstances, I wouldn't dream of doing this to someone in his condition, but I think he's pulled back from the edge far enough. I'm prepared to perform the procedure."

I suppressed a whoop of joy, and it was at me the professor directed his words when he said severely, "You all appreciate, of course, this is a desperate measure. It's still very possible the procedure itself will kill him. And even if it doesn't, the effects are likely to be severe and probably fatal. What I'm about to do is very likely to kill him, one way or another. The only reason I'm even considering it is because there's a chance—a small chance, but a chance nevertheless, that it won't kill him. And if it doesn't, then maybe . . . just maybe, it might reverse or at least contain the damage done. And that small chance is more than he'll have if I do nothing."

Considerably sobered, I nodded and dropped my gaze. The professor squeezed my shoulder. "I'll do my very best for him, Matthew, but you need to be fully aware this is a dangerous thing, and there are no guarantees. It's far more likely to go wrong than right. Don't raise your hopes. If I were you, I'd say goodbye now."

"Don't raise my hopes?" I shook my head. "Hope's all I have. If I don't have that . . . I won't say goodbye. I'll never say goodbye." I stared at him fiercely. "If I say goodbye, I'm admitting the possibility he might not come through this, and for me . . . there isn't that possibility. I have to have hope, to have complete faith in him. So I'm going to stay right here with him, and hold his hand and be here for him, and I *am* going to bring him through this. I am going to *make* him live."

"Matthew, I understand what you're saying. I commend your faith in Morgan and your devotion, but you can't stay here, at least while we're performing the procedure. Don't argue with me," he said as I opened my mouth to protest. "That's not negotiable. You have to leave, or I won't do it."

"That's not fair."

"Fair or not, it's the way it is."

I scowled at him, unaccountably angry, angrier than I'd ever been. "If I have to, I have to, but I won't like it, and I still won't say goodbye." My voice came out unintentionally petulant, but I didn't care. Let him think I was a pouty kid. I didn't care about anything.

"Fair enough. I can't let you stay. There just won't be room. But even if I could, I wouldn't. You've been a devoted friend. No one could ask for more. But there are limits to what even you can bear. I don't want to see you hurt."

"Hurt? It doesn't matter if I allow myself to hope or not, if I say goodbye or not. If anything happens to Morgan, I won't be hurt . . . I'll be destroyed, utterly destroyed. So . . . it's not going to happen. I'm not going to let it happen. I don't know how I can stop it, but I *will* find a way. I *will* make him come back to me."

"I'll leave you here for a minute. Then you'll have to go. It will take a while, but you can wait outside this time, if you want to."

"Thanks." I tried to make it sincere, but I suppose I'm just too good at sarcasm.

"I'll be back in a few minutes. Take your time to do whatever you need."

"I told you. I'm *not* going to say goodbye." Now I definitely sounded like a stubborn and petulant child.

"Whatever you need, Matthew."

I was angry with him. Why was he trying to force me into something I knew wasn't right? The anger remained even after the plastic fell . . . right up until Morgan squeezed my hand.

"Hush. No, don't. You need your strength now. Don't

waste it on me."

Nevertheless, he opened his eyes and gazed at me. "Thank you."

"Did you hear?"

He didn't answer, just smiled and closed his eyes again.

"I meant it, Morgan. I'm not going to say goodbye to you. I'm not going to let them convince me you won't make it through this. I know you will . . . we will. I'm going to make you strong. I believe in you."

He smiled again, and he was so beautiful I spent the next few minutes kissing him. He didn't respond, but I knew he was aware. I knew he was feeling it and that was enough.

When the professor came back, I reluctantly let go of Morgan's hand and ducked out of the room, leaving the professor and Mr Bentley with Morgan. I was blindingly and irrationally angry that Morgan's father got to be there when it was his fault this all happened in the first place. I knew he was there because he could help and I couldn't. He knew what he was doing, and I didn't . . . but still.

I couldn't stand still. I paced about, getting in everyone's way, and even managed to break some of the equipment when I picked it up listlessly, then dropped it when I thought I heard someone move aside the plastic. There was a lot of plastic, and it was moving all the time as people came and went.

Cory hovered, but he didn't know what to say to me, so he said nothing. After about ten unbearable minutes, he disappeared, and a few moments later reappeared with something in his hands. He grabbed me by the arm and towed me outside. It was snowing quite heavily. Cory thrust a coat into my hands. It wasn't mine, but I put it on gratefully and turned up the collar. He then pressed Morgan's cigarettes into my hand.

"I thought you didn't approve."

"I don't, but I figure you need one right now. And besides,

you've promised to give them up when it's all over, so it's fairly safe, I think. Once Morgan's on his feet again, I'm going to work on him, too."

I lit the cigarette and took a deep drag, staring up at the dark sky, blinking as snowflakes settled on my eyelashes.

"What if it goes wrong, Cory? What the hell will I do if he dies?"

I lowered my head to look straight at him for the first time. He seemed panicked. "It's all right. I don't expect you to answer that."

"It isn't that I can't answer it. I know exactly what you'll do. You'll fall apart completely. Then you'll get up, dust yourself down, put yourself back together, and then you'll go on. You always go on, Matthew, because you're strong. And I'll be here with you every step of the way. I'll help you in any and every way I can."

"I appreciate that, Cory, I really do, but I don't think I could . . . not this time. I've never opened myself like this to anyone before, except you. It's like . . . it's like he's part of me. If he was gone . . . it would be like if I ever lost you . . . as if part of me was ripped away, and I could never recover from that."

"Yes, you would."

"No, Cory, not completely. Oh, you're right, I'd get up and go on . . . or something would, but I'd never be the same again. I wouldn't be me."

Cory stared at me for a moment, then turned his head away. He was struggling almost as much as I was. In a way, it was worse for him, because, although I didn't see it at the time, I'm pretty sure that part of him, a part buried deep inside, was hoping it wouldn't work out with Morgan so he'd have me to himself again. I'm glad I didn't think about that at the time. It would have complicated things.

When I finished the cigarette, I lit another one. It was the last one and I held the empty packet in my hand, staring at it, thinking how Morgan had gone into a shop and bought it, then kept it in his pocket, close to him, how he'd opened it and taken out the first cigarette, which had touched his lips, those beautiful soft lips. Groaning, I crushed the packet, threw it viciously against the wall. In moments, it was covered with snow. Gone.

"Why don't we realise life's so fragile? Why do we waste it, throw it away for nothing? This was all so . . . unnecessary. It sucks."

"You're right. Life is very fragile and very precious. I'm not going to waste mine. I'm going to make a difference, a real difference. I'm not quite sure how right now, not since I screwed up the chance of working at ITM. But I know I will."

I smiled at him, believing. "I'm glad you screwed it up, Cory." I hastily continued, "Not that I'm glad you won't get to work with them, but I'm glad you did what you did. Otherwise Morgan wouldn't even have had this chance."

He smiled at me, tight-lipped. "I suppose it was worth it, then."

My grin widened, and I punched him in the shoulder.

"Ow. You don't know your own strength sometimes." He pouted.

The minutes ticked on, and I started to pace again. It was freezing cold, and the snow was getting thicker. It was only early afternoon, but it was already getting dark, with the sky feeling low and heavy.

Snow does a strange thing to sound. It doesn't only blanket the ground, but it blankets sound, too. It was deadly silent, in a closed-in kind of way. I felt cut off, even from Cory, who was only feet away, blowing on his hands and stamping his feet. I caught him gazing longingly at the kitchen window, where warm, liquid light spilled out to pool in the snow below.

"You can go inside, if you like."

"You're not, are you?"

"No. I want to stay as close as I can. It's unbearable in there. I feel suffocated inside."

"Then I'll stay here, too."

"Thanks, Cory. You're awesome."

He smiled, and for a minute, I really felt better . . . just for a minute.

"I wish I knew what was going on. It's the waiting that's worst. I hate it. I wish they'd at least tell me what they're doing."

"Are you sure?"

"What do you mean?"

"Are you sure you'd want to know? I know what you're like . . . the more information you have, the more vivid your imagination is. If you knew what they're doing, you'd permeate every possibility of things going wrong, and they all would—in your head. It's best for you that you don't know."

There was something in his voice that made me examine him more closely. "You know, don't you?"

He blinked at me like a deer caught in headlights, then stared down at his feet, scuffing at the snow.

"Cory?"

"Yeah, kind of."

"Tell me."

"No, and don't even bother with your usual persuasion techniques, because I'm not going to. I know you too well, and you'll destroy yourself."

"Believe me, Cory, there's nothing you could tell me that would screw me up more than the pictures going through my head right now."

"Hmm."

We were silent for a while until the pictures in my head got too unbearable.

"Have you seen it? Have you seen them do . . . what they're doing?"

"Matthew!"

"Please."

"Yes. Yes, I have, kind of."

"Kind of?"

"With a rat."

"Oh."

Again, that painful, snow-muffled silence.

"Did it die?"

"What?"

"The rat . . . did it die?"

"No, Matthew, the rat didn't die. As far as I know, the rat's still alive. And if you don't stop this, I'm going to go find it and get it to bite you, and hope it gives you rabies."

"Do rats even have rabies?"

"I don't know, but I can hope."

He smiled at me, but I didn't return it.

"Look, Matthew, it probably isn't as bad as you think it is. The real danger is in the effect of the serum. You saw for yourself, Morgan's stronger now. He'll be all right."

"If it's not as bad as I'm thinking, then why can't you tell me?"

"Oh, for gods' sake, Matthew, you have to keep pushing."

"I know. I'm sorry. I suppose it's the lawyer in me. You know I can't just leave things be. I need to know this, Cory. I need it."

"No, you don't. You don't need it, you just want it."

"Don't play semantics with me. I'm the lawyer, remember?"

"Do you ever let me forget?"

"Cory, I'm just scared. All that equipment . . . it's so scary, and . . . and I just have visions of them drilling into his head and—"

271

"Matthew, most of the equipment in there is scientific, not medical. It's microscopes, and viscometers, thermometers, rheometers—"

"Okay, I get the message. I don't understand much of that . . . but still."

Cory sighed. "They're not doing anything like that."

"Then . . ."

Cory turned to me and shook his head. "All right. They don't have to put the serum in with as much precision as they needed to get the cells out. They don't have to drill into his head, or anything as drastic as that." I sighed with relief, and Cory gave me an odd look. "They put a needle in the main artery at the side of his neck, the one that takes blood directly to the brain. Then they put a thin plastic tube through it and push it in as far as they can. They put a syringe on the end and inject the drug in very small doses over a period of time."

"Is that all?"

Cory narrowed his eyes, then shook his head with a tight little smile. "Yes, that's all."

"It doesn't sound very dangerous."

"No . . . it doesn't. So stop worrying."

I frowned, trying to process the information. "So why has everyone been making such a big thing about it?"

"Just leave it there, Matthew. You wanted to know, and I told you."

"I know, but—"

"Look, it *is* dangerous. They're injecting something straight into someone's brain. Of course it's dangerous. That's why they have to do it in tiny doses. If they overload the artery, or break a blood vessel, or breach one of the veins—game over. They don't have the facilities for major brain surgery here."

"Oh."

"So, are you happy now?" Cory was glaring at me, his voice unusually loud and harsh. "Are you happy now you know?"

"No."

"I told you."

"Yeah, yeah, you did."

Silence fell between us again, and we fell back into waiting.

It was a long time before anyone came, at least it seemed so. I've no idea how long it really was, but a lot of snow had fallen. Cory and I were sheltering against the side of the barn, watching the huge flakes falling, one by one adding to the thick blanket that changed the world in the space of a day. I smiled, thinking about it . . . that's what Morgan did, at least for me — he'd changed my life in just one day, less than that.

I didn't hear the door open and jumped when my name was called, muffled like everything else, by the snow.

"Here."

My heart started pounding, and my legs were weak. I was almost too weak to push off from the wall and take the half dozen steps to the door. The expression in the professor's eyes made me want to run . . . to run far and fast, and never look back.

"Don't tell me, just don't. I don't want to know."

I started backing away, and the professor reached for me, but I danced away, preparing to run.

"He's alive, Matthew."

I sat down. I didn't intend to — it just happened. My legs gave way, and I sat down in the snow. I didn't even feel the cold. I was numb.

The professor, also ignoring the cold, knelt in front of me. He reached for my hand and squeezed it.

"You have to be brave, Matthew. It was rough on him. He's holding on, but only just. It's not looking good, and he might . . . it could be any time, Matthew. I'm sorry."

For a moment, I just stared at him. Then, suddenly, surprising even myself, I was on my feet and running. Not away, as everyone, including me, had expected, but into the barn. I didn't stop running until I got to the cubicle. Then I froze. I couldn't move my hand to raise the plastic. I could see someone moving about inside, just a blurred shadow. I wished it were me, but I just couldn't make my body move.

There was a touch on my shoulder, but I didn't acknowledge it. Part of me felt it, but the bigger part of me was too focused on somewhere else to care.

"Matthew."

I couldn't respond, even though I could hear the pain in Cory's voice.

"Come on, Matthew. I know where you want to be. Take a deep breath. You can do this."

Again, only part of me heard. But when Cory reached past me and pulled back the plastic, I turned and saw him for the first time. I wanted to smile, but I just couldn't, so I squeezed his shoulder as I ducked under his arm. I expected him to come in with me, but he let the sheet drop between us, and to be honest, I didn't care . . . barely noticed.

Mr Bentley glanced up with sad eyes that had been crying.

"I'm sorry, Matthew. This . . . all of this . . . it was my fault. My pride, my arrogance . . . and now my son pays the price. I-I'm sorry . . . so truly sorry."

I stared at him and saw his pain. Part of me wanted to say something to make him feel better. As much as I'd hated him, I could see him for what he was now — a grieving father, truly remorseful for what he'd done, and I acknowledged that, but I couldn't bring myself to give him what he wanted. I didn't have the energy. I only cared about one thing.

Morgan looked like he was asleep, just asleep, gently, peacefully asleep. There was a dressing taped to his throat, just above the collarbone on one side. I saw it, but my mind didn't accept it, so I ignored it. All I cared about was that his lips were slightly parted, his chest rising and falling, and I wanted to kiss him so badly. I needed to touch him, to feel the life in him. I needed him to know I was here.

There was an instant when I felt uncomfortable Mr Bentley was there, when I was afraid to approach, to touch him, but it was brief because I simply dismissed Mr Bentley from my awareness and focused exclusively on Morgan.

I touched his hand, and it was warm. I slipped my fingers through his and leaned forward to kiss him. Again, there was no response, but again it felt as though he knew I was there, knew what I was doing, and was responding on some level beyond the physical, so I didn't stop.

At some point, I was aware of Mr Bentley getting up and leaving. Part of me acknowledged that perhaps this was too much for him to deal with, but I really didn't care. I kept on kissing Morgan, fantasising I was in some way breathing life into him. At some point, his mouth opened. I don't know if he did it consciously or if it was just the pressure of my lips.

I explored his mouth, crushing his lips beneath mine, closing my eyes and pretending everything was all right, and he was kissing me back. Then it hit me — the fact he might never kiss me back — and I couldn't do it anymore.

I raised my head, and hot tears splashed on his face. His lips were swollen and red from my kissing, and he looked better than he had for ages. This time, though, I wouldn't let myself hope. I was too numb for that, for hope.

I sat down heavily in the chair, then got up again and pulled it closer to the bed, so I could slide my hand into his and rest my forehead on them. I was suddenly very tired, too tired to hold it all in anymore. Allowing myself to relax a little, I began to cry, sobbing out my fear, my hopelessness, my desperation. No one came. I was alone. I sobbed for what could easily have been hours — hopelessly and utterly alone.

At first, I prayed desperately for someone to come, for someone to hold me and tell me it was going to be all right, but in the end, I was glad no one came, because I knew they wouldn't be able to tell me that, and I didn't want empty comfort and eyes full of pity.

I think I must have fallen asleep at some point because I jolted awake feeling hot, uncomfortable, and dead inside. My head ached, and the blanket under my cheek was wet and chafed my skin. I sat up, rubbing my eyes with one hand. They were dry and felt gritty and sore.

The emptiness inside had turned into a great chasm that was swallowing every attempt at feeling. I was so tired and so . . . dead. Even when Morgan's fingers twitched in mine, I couldn't bring myself to be happy or excited, although there was a tinge of fear. There was something not quite right about it.

I raised my head and noticed his lips were trembling, and then, by extension that his breathing had quickened considerably. In fact, he was practically panting, and his skin was covered with a fine sheen of perspiration. I had no idea if this was a good thing or a bad thing and I panicked.

I was going to go out to find someone, but as soon as I tried to slip my hand from Morgan's, he gripped it, and I really didn't want to tear myself away, so I did the only thing I could think of and shouted *Professor* as loudly as I could. I immediately regretted it because Morgan tensed, startled, and his hand jerked in mine.

"Shh. It's all right. I'm sorry. I didn't know . . . I didn't know you could hear me. It's okay, Morgan. I'm here with you, and it's okay."

Morgan took a shaky breath and moaned, "Matthew."

"I'm here. Just relax. It's going to be all right."

"Hurts, Matthew. It hurts."

"Does it? Where? Are you? Just hold on. It'll be all right." I was babbling, and I knew it. I prayed for someone to come, anyone. I didn't want to do this on my own. I didn't know how.

"Matthew." He sounded awful. He groaned and turned his head toward me, his face twisted, and all I could do was stroke his hair and talk nonsense.

When the plastic rose, and the professor appeared, I could have kissed him. I gazed up at him helplessly, and he took charge immediately. He turned Morgan's face toward him and spoke calmly.

"Morgan, it's Professor Burridge . . . Lionel. You have to tell me what's going on, Morgan. Are you in pain?"

"Yes," he hissed through his teeth.

"Where?"

Morgan groaned and tried to turn his head away. "Morgan, you need to tell me where it hurts."

"I don't know."

"Think about it. Concentrate now. Where does it hurt?"

Morgan murmured something I couldn't hear and tried to turn his head again, but the Professor still held him.

"Open your eyes, Morgan. Look at me." Again, Morgan muttered something that made no sense, but the professor was relentless. "Focus, Morgan. I know you can do it. Open your eyes."

Morgan's head jerked from side to side, and he gripped my hand so hard I yelped, but I didn't try to pull away.

"Morgan," the professor said sternly, but I don't think Morgan even heard him.

"Matthew." It was a cry of desperation, and I crumbled.

"Don't . . . don't do this, Morgan. You're going to be all right, but you have to listen to the professor. I can't help you, but he can. Please, Morgan, try . . . try to do what he says."

Panting, Morgan shuddered and grunted, but finally, his eyes flew open and oriented on the professor.

"Good boy, Morgan. That's the way. Just try to relax. I know it hurts . . . just take it easy now."

"Why? Why . . ."

"Shh, it's all right. Just calm down."

The professor peered into Morgan's eyes and laid a hand on his forehead. He was frowning so hard that I was certain this was it. Morgan was dying here and now, and I hated him for not letting Morgan's last moments be with me.

When the professor let him go and turned away, I stroked Morgan's face. He turned his head toward me and gave a hideous parody of a smile.

"Matthew."

"Hey, what you up to now? Scaring us all like this. Be calm, baby. Just chill out, and everything will be all right."

"I-I'm scared."

"Me, too. Just hold on. Please don't do anything silly, not now."

"Hurts, Matthew. I'm trying . . . I am . . . but . . . but . . . it . . . it hurts."

"It'll be all right. You're going to be all right."

His gaze locked with mine, and unbelievably, he did start to calm down, to relax, sinking into my eyes. I stroked his hair.

"I . . . love you, Matthew."

"I love you, too. That's why I've never stopped believing in you. You can do this. *We* can do this. Do you believe me?"

"I-I do."

"Good. Because it's Christmas Eve, and if you die tonight, you'll spoil Christmas for me forever, and I'll never forgive you . . . and every friend I ever have will never forgive you, because I'll be so awful at Christmas, so . . . for the sake of all those people you've never even met, you *have* to be okay."

He listened intently, then gave me a strange crooked smile and nodded slightly. We were interrupted at that point by the professor, who demanded Morgan's attention back on him.

"Morgan, I don't want you to worry about this. I don't

think it's anything to worry about. It just means the serum is working. Don't forget the cells we injected into your brain have a lot of work to do, and it's not surprising you're going to feel strange . . . or that it is going to hurt. But you need to rest. You need to let them do their job. Don't be scared, and don't be worried, because you're going to be all right. Do you understand?"

"I . . . yes . . . yes, I-I . . ."

"Conserve your strength. I'm going to give you something to help with the pain. It will make you sleepy, so don't fight it, just go with it. You need to sleep to get strong."

"Okay."

As he spoke, the professor injected something into the IV line. Within a matter of minutes, Morgan relaxed and drifted back to sleep.

"Was that the truth?"

"What?"

"What you told Morgan. That what's happening to him is a good thing."

"I didn't precisely say that."

"No, not precisely, but—"

The professor smiled at me. "I wouldn't go so far as to say it's a good thing, Matthew—an understandable thing, certainly, but not necessarily good. Not necessarily bad either. The truth is . . . we don't really know. This has never happened before. We're in the realms of the highly experimental, and we just don't know what's good or what's bad. We don't know what to look for, what to take as encouraging signs, and what to fear.

"The fact Morgan is able to raise enough energy to open his eyes and speak is a very promising sign. He's undoubtedly stronger than he was and that, at least, is a good thing."

I was badly shaken by the whole episode but managed to give the professor a shaky smile and sat down heavily again.

"Are you hungry? You haven't eaten since you've been here."

As soon as he mentioned food, my stomach rumbled. Although I wasn't really hungry, I nodded and the professor left, promising to find me something.

A short while later, Cory popped his head in. "There's food waiting in the kitchen. The professor said it's safe to leave Morgan because he'll sleep for a couple of hours at least." Seeing the expression on my face, he smiled, understanding. "He'll be all right for half an hour, Matthew. You're beat, and you must be starving. Come on, it's Christmas Eve. Come eat with us."

I was very reluctant, but in the end, he persuaded me to leave. The snow was really piling up outside, and it was still coming down thickly. The kitchen was warm and inviting, and as soon as I opened the door, I was met with the smell of cooking that made my mouth water.

Chapter Twenty

The kitchen seemed very crowded, although there were only four or five people in there. Mr Bentley was there, but he got up as I walked in.

"Is he . . . is Morgan okay?"

"He woke up in pain, but he's sleeping now. The professor says he's stronger, but he still doesn't know which way it'll go."

Mr Bentley nodded gravely. "I won't forget this is my fault. I don't expect . . . I'm not expecting any of you to forgive me, let alone Morgan, but I never meant this to happen. I never wanted . . . this is killing me, Matthew."

This time, I was able to give him something of what he wanted, what he needed. As he walked past me, I grabbed his arm, and he turned in surprise.

"I can't vouch for Morgan. I'm not in his shoes. But I'm grateful you managed to swallow your pride in the end, that you made up with the professor and worked with him to help Morgan. If . . . if he comes through this, it will be because of you."

"If it hadn't been for me, he wouldn't have—"

"No . . . but . . . you're still his father. There's still time."

He gave me an odd look, piercing and strangely open. Then he nodded and squeezed my shoulder. "You're a very special man, Matthew. I'm glad Morgan found you."

"Actually, it was me that found him . . . eventually."

Mr Bentley nodded. Then he left. I sat down at the table, feeling strange. Cory put a bowl of thick stew in front of me, and I devoured it. The three young people, who were also eating the stew, were in high spirits and were good company. When we'd finished, they insisted Cory, and I join them in the living room. I hadn't noticed before, but there was a Christmas tree in the corner. Perhaps it was because it was now all lit up with lights. There were a few presents under it, and crackers scattered through its branches.

I was forced into a riotous game of charades. At some point, I had a glass of brandy thrust into my hand, which was refilled before I'd even finished it. After that, the games became louder and more hilarious, and the time slipped away.

It wasn't until I looked up to see the professor smiling indulgently at us from the doorway that I remembered. I was shocked and disgusted with myself at having ever let myself forget.

"Come on, Professor, join us. I know you're a demon at charades. We need you on our team. We're getting creamed."

"Not tonight, Ben. I'm a little tired."

"But it's Christmas, Professor."

I'd frozen where I was, with the empty glass still in my hand. I was slightly dizzy and utterly horrified. Again, I had that debilitating feeling of being afraid to move. There was a crazy muddle of thoughts in my head, telling me that somehow, by abandoning him, I'd made Morgan worse. That by not being there for him, I'd doomed him. I was terrified of finding out I was right.

"It's good to see you letting your hair down a little, Matthew. You've been way too hard on yourself."

"No." I shook my head, my eyes boring into his, pleading, begging. "Morgan . . . I should . . . I should never have left him."

"It's all right, Matthew, Morgan's fine. He's . . . as he was."

"Do you know yet? Do you know if . . ."

The professor shook his head sadly. "He's stronger. He's

definitely stronger, but there's still a long way to go."

"But he is getting stronger?"

"Little by little, yes."

"When will we know? When will we know for sure?"

"I don't know. We'll have a better idea by the morning. He needs rest now more than anything, so I sedated him. If he . . . when he wakes in the morning, we'll have a fair idea of—"

"You said *if*. *If* he wakes. You mean he might not wake . . . but if he does, he'll probably live."

"Possibly."

I put my glass down and headed for the door.

"Oh, Matthew, don't go. We were having fun. Please stay."

"I'm sorry. I need to be with Morgan."

"But he won't know. Stay and have fun. It's Christmas Eve."

I stared at the girl who'd spoken, and from the expression on her face, it wasn't a nice stare. I blinked and turned away. "I'd know."

It had stopped snowing, and the sky was clear, the stars bright. I tilted my head back to gaze up at them. They were so far away, but they were still beautiful, twinkling like diamonds against the black velvet sky. I picked out one or two constellations I knew. Then I saw something I'd never seen before. One of the stars, not part of any constellation, seemed to be moving, and I noticed a streak behind it, like a tail. As I watched, it moved faster and faster, streaking through the sky toward the horizon. It was joined by another, then another until there were a dozen of them—falling stars.

I was awed, caught by the unexpected and breath-taking beauty of them. I'd never seen a falling star before, and now I was being blessed with a sky full of them.

"Make a wish."

I turned, startled, to find Cory in the doorway, his eyes turned skyward as mine had been.

"Huh?"

"They say, if you make a wish on a falling star, it'll come true."

"Really?"

"Can't hurt."

"No, I guess not."

Raising my eyes to the sky again, I watched the stars until they were all out of sight, wishing with all my heart and soul. It wasn't until they'd gone that I realised I was without my coat and bitterly cold.

"You're turning blue."

"So are you. Why don't you go in?"

"You need someone to take care of you. You don't do very well on your own."

I couldn't help smiling at that, because in a way he was right. "I won't be on my own."

"Yes, you will. You'll be more alone than ever. You'll be alone until he wakes up and you can be with him . . . properly with him."

I stared at him. This time he was completely right. "All right, then. If you really want to sit around for hours, doing absolutely nothing, instead of drinking and having fun . . . who am I to argue with you?"

Cory grinned and followed me inside. Mr Bentley was sitting in the chair at the side of the bed, bending over it and speaking softly to Morgan, stroking his hair. It was a very private moment, and I felt almost embarrassed at intruding. However, when he saw me, he got up.

"Come on in, Matthew. This is your place."

"No, I-I didn't want to intrude."

"Intrude? You didn't intrude, Matthew, how could you? If . . . when Morgan wakes up, it's you he'll want to see, not me. I'd be a fool to think otherwise, and a cold-hearted man not to act on it, and . . . much as I hate to admit, I have been cold-hearted where my son's concerned for a very long time, but those days are now in the past."

He smiled and walked past me, leaving me shocked. I sat down, and Cory perched on the stool as he had before.

"Did you make a wish?"

"What?" Cory started, as if he hadn't expected me to speak and had absolutely no idea what I was talking about.

"The stars . . . you told me to make a wish. Did you?"

"Yeah, I made a wish."

"What was it?"

"If I tell you, it won't come true."

"Yeah, right. Bullshit. Go on, tell me."

Cory regarded me, his face serious, and his eyes sparkling. "It was the same as yours."

To say I was surprised would have been an enormous understatement. I didn't know what to say. "Thanks."

"No need to sound so surprised. I don't hate Morgan. I wouldn't have wished this on anyone. I do understand, Matthew. I understand why this happened, why you fell in love with him. I'd be a fool and a liar if I didn't. I don't like it, and maybe I'll never fully accept it, but I would never want it to end this way."

"Thank you for being so honest."

"I always have been."

"Yes, I can't deny it."

Throughout the long, long night, Cory and I chatted as we always had. Whatever awkwardness there had been between us fell away, and we were as we'd been before. It was an enlightening time when I saw my friend with new eyes. I saw how he'd grown and matured in these last few months, how I didn't really know him anymore, and I set about changing that.

We talked about everything, from school, to friends, to life. We talked about the way we felt — about life, about us. I found out so much about him I didn't know because, for once, he was being completely honest, letting me peep behind the mask I'd never been aware he wore. I grew to like and admire him more than ever, and to realise that no matter what happened with Morgan, we'd never have been more than friends—we were too close for that.

A couple of times, someone brought us snacks and drinks, and sometimes they stayed for a while to talk. We learned a little about the bright young people who worked with the professor—their loyalty, their passion, how scared they'd been when the police came, and how much they hoped Morgan would be okay. My answer was always the same. "Not as much as I am."

That night truly was the longest of my life. It's so strange how time can slow and speed according to your perception, and that night my perception was that every second stretched to infinity and the darkness was never-ending.

After a couple of hours, Cory and I ran out of things to say and fell silent. I tried to doze a few times, but the chair was uncomfortable, and I was too tense.

It was impossible to tell the time by our surroundings. There was nothing to measure the hours with. The cubicle was outside time and space, lit by a single bare bulb that strained the eyes after only a short time and the dim light from the barn outside filtering in through the thick plastic sheets. I gave up checking the time on my phone after three AM because it took too much of the energy I was rapidly running out of.

Eventually, I did drop off, my head on the bed, and I must have slept pretty soundly because I woke up completely disoriented. I was still too weary to raise my head, and something was telling me not to. For a moment, I couldn't work out why I was sitting in such an awkward position, or why there was a rough, slightly smelly blanket under my cheek.

I became aware of something touching my hair, toying with it, and I thought *Cory*, but then I realised Cory's stool was too far away and it just wasn't something he'd do. Sleepily, I sat up and checked my phone. It was six-thirty. I'd slept for less than three hours. I yawned and eased my shoulders, cracking my neck.

Something felt strange. Something was nagging at the back of my mind. I was alone, so then who . . .

I glanced up at Morgan. He was smiling at me.

"Morgan. Are you . . . are you okay? Are you in pain? Do you need me to call someone?"

He just smiled and shook his head. I couldn't believe it. After all this time, all the fear and doubt, he was smiling at me, his green eyes sparkling in the harsh light.

Slowly, I stood up and moved closer. I stroked his face, suddenly speechless. Morgan half-closed his eyes and turned toward my touch, then opened them wide again, staring up at me with an unreadable expression.

"You kissed me."

"What?"

"I was . . . lost. I felt . . . I was afraid, and you kissed me."

"I did. I didn't know if you could feel me, if you even knew, but . . . it felt . . . it felt like you were aware . . . somewhere."

"Oh, yes, I was aware. I couldn't move, couldn't even open my eyes, but I could hear you, and I could feel you." He grinned. "It would have been better if you'd fucked me, but the kiss was nice."

For a moment, I was stunned. Then I started to laugh. Sure, there was a hysterical edge to it, but, oh gods, it released some tension.

"We'd have fallen off the bed. It's way too narrow for the both of us, especially if there was . . . um . . . activity."

Morgan didn't say anything, just raised his hand to cover my own, then turned his head to kiss my palm.

"You stayed with me."

"Mostly. They made me leave now and again, forced me to eat."

"Good. But still . . . you stayed."

"Where else would I be? I love you, Morgan. I thought . . . I thought that . . ."

"I know. But it's going to be okay now."

"How do you know?"

"I just do. Everything's different. I can't explain but . . . I knew I was dying . . . and now . . . now I know I'm not."

"I'm very glad about that."

"Me, too." He sighed. "I'm very tired, Matthew. I wish I could hold you, go to sleep in your arms."

"Maybe later. For now . . ." I carefully slid my arms under him and pulled him into an embrace. This time when I kissed him, the response was instant and eager. He was still too weak to put his arms around me, but he was able to grab a handful of hair and put the other hand on my face.

I never wanted the kiss to end, but like all good things, it had to. Morgan gazed up at me with bright eyes. "Maybe you should rest now. You look like crap."

"You don't look so hot yourself."

He grinned. "Give me a couple of days, a hot shower, and some decent food, and I'll look better than you."

"You always look better than me."

"Crazy man. You're beautiful." His hand was still on the side of my face, and his thumb stroked my lips, his eyes eating up my face, making me feel beautiful for the first time in my life.

"If I'm beautiful, I don't know what that makes you."

"Lucky," he whispered huskily. That made me grin. After everything that had happened, I was very emotional, and I couldn't stop the tears. Morgan wiped them away and noticed the second line in his arm. He frowned.

"What's this for? What have they been doing to me now?"

"You were too weak. They couldn't do the procedure because you wouldn't have survived it. So they gave you a blood transfusion to try and boost your strength."

Morgan's eyes widened. "They have done it, haven't they? It is over?"

"Yes, it's over."

He looked relieved, then puzzled. "Where did they get the blood? They didn't give me animal blood, did they?" He seemed queasy at the thought, and I had to laugh.

"Well, I have been called an animal now and again."

"You?"

"And your father." The smile faded from his face.

"Don't know how I feel about that." He brightened again. "But you . . . that's pretty awesome . . . to do that for me."

"Well, don't worry. You have more than twice as much of mine as his, so you shouldn't turn into too much of a bastard. Not that you weren't always a complete bastard, of course. I was always telling Cory what a bastard you are."

"Thanks, I think."

"Hey, it's Christmas."

"Christmas Day?"

"Yeah."

"So you won't have to hate Christmas forever, after all."

"Nope."

Morgan frowned, looking incredibly sad. I stroked his hair gently. "What's wrong?"

"Nothing. It's just . . . I've been making plans for ages, about Christmas, about you. I was going to make you see, make you . . . I even got you a gift. I was going to make this the best Christmas ever. Now all those plans . . ."

"You're an idiot sometimes. Those plans would never have

worked, not if you were intending to seduce me with *things.* I'd never have fallen for that, and we'd only have ended up quarrelling and hating each other . . . again. Don't you see? This is the best Christmas ever."

"But you've given me such a great gift, Matthew. So many. You're here, with me. You saved me. You gave me your blood, for gods' sake. I have nothing to give you."

"If that's all you're worried about . . ." I leaned forward and kissed him. "You've given me the best gift I've ever had. You're alive. You're here. You're going to be okay, and we're going to be together for a very long time. There *is* no better gift."

There were tears in both our eyes, and Morgan gripped my hand so hard it hurt, but I didn't care.

"Merry Christmas, Matthew," he whispered.

"Merry Christmas, Morgan," I whispered back, and he grinned.

We both jumped when someone threw back the plastic. We were lip to lip, and there was an amount of guilt in that jump.

The professor was delighted to see Morgan awake, and his hands were shaking when he examined him.

"You're looking good, Morgan."

"I feel like crap."

"I was speaking figuratively. You're stable. That is far better than dead, but nowhere near normal."

"I'm never going to be normal. I faced that fact a long time ago." Morgan chewed on his lip. "Not dead is a really good start. I'll take that for now."

The professor squeezed his shoulder. "You know you've got a long way to go before this is over . . . I mean completely over. What we've done here is put a patch on it. We're going to continue with the research until we find a more permanent solution, but I truly believe this will more than buy us the time we need."

Morgan licked his lips nervously. "How long?"

The professor smiled. "Don't look so worried, Morgan. Assuming you remain stable and the new mutation doesn't start degrading, which I don't think it will, then . . . depending on the precise effect the serum is having, I expect that, although we may have to perform the procedure again . . . maybe a few times . . . give or take a couple of months . . . and assuming we get access to the full lab . . . hmm, actually . . . if we do that, we'll have better facilities to perform the procedures as well, so the risk will be considerably reduced, and the accuracy increased. I shall have to ask Paul about that. It's been a while since I've been to the lab and — "

"Professor? Sir?"

"Hmm?" He blinked at Morgan, appearing surprised to have been interrupted.

"You didn't actually answer my question."

"What question?"

"How long do I have before the bomb in my head goes off again?"

"I can't say for sure, Morgan. Two . . . maybe three . . . with additional procedures, maybe more. And that's assuming we don't refine the serum, which we will. Now we have the basic key . . . the breakthrough we had last night . . . I'm confident we can fix this once and for all."

"But the bottom line, at the moment, is two or three months?"

"Months? No, Morgan, two or three years. As I said, we'll have to take some more cells in the next couple of days, to check their response to the serum, but the results so far are very promising. This wasn't like what your father was trying to do for you. This was a complete re-programming of the genetic changes inside your head. It won't give you the . . . um . . . benefits you had. It won't work like the other one did, but it's a lot safer. I can't say for sure until I examine the affected cells, but it looks promising that the serum is containing the mutation. It should remain stable for at least a couple of years. That should give us plenty of time to work on improving it."

Morgan turned to me, his eyes glowing, and squeezed my hand. "That's great. It's more than I expected." A huge smile spread slowly over his face, and it was mirrored on mine.

"Don't get too excited, Morgan. It's not going to all be easy sailing. The new formula is a lot more stable than the other, but it's not without side effects."

"If one of the side effects is being alive . . . the rest I can live with."

"We're going to have to take cell samples at least once a month at first, which means going through the procedure you had yesterday. It's not pleasant, or risk-free. You will have headaches, which at times will be crippling, and you may have seizures. Your balance may be affected. There's likely to be—"

"Okay, okay, I get the message. But it's still worth it." Again, he gazed up at me, and the warmth in his eyes blew the fear right out the window . . . at least it would have, if there had been a window.

The professor smiled. "Rest for a while. If you feel up to it, you can go over to the house later. It will be more comfortable for you there."

"You're not kidding. Lying on a bed of nails would be more comfortable than this thing I'm on right now."

"Well, it wasn't made to be a bed. It's not supposed to be lain on for as long as you have."

"Why can't I get up now? I'll be okay. I have numb bits, and my back is killing me."

"Let's give it an hour or two, Morgan."

Morgan frowned, then smiled. "Okay, you're the doctor . . . kind of. I'll bow to your greater knowledge. Or rather not, because my back's too stiff. Can you at least get rid of the needles? They hurt like hell, and I'd be a lot more comfortable without them. You don't need them in there now, do you?"

"Morgan, you're being very hasty. I appreciate you must be feeling a lot better than you were yesterday, but I'm not comfortable with letting down all our defences yet. We need to take it slowly. Another couple of hours . . . then we'll see."

"I'm not going to be able to make it another couple of hours. You have no idea how uncomfortable all this is. You have to give me *something*. If I can't get up, at least get me free from this crap so I can turn over and relieve my back."

"You're a terrible patient. I preferred you when you were unconscious."

"Lie on this bed for an hour, you'd prefer to *be* unconscious."

"Well, I could sedate you again." Morgan's eyes went wide, and the professor chuckled. "All right . . . okay, you win. Hold still. But you have to promise to take it easy, to just lie quietly for an hour or so until we're sure you're okay."

"You won't do that in an hour."

"No, but I'm going to take some blood, and we can get an idea from that. We won't know for sure until we get cells from the source, and there's no point doing that for at least forty-eight hours. I'm assuming you don't want to be lying on that couch for the next forty-eight hours."

Morgan shuddered. "You're right about that."

When the professor finished, Morgan rubbed his arms and grimaced. "Shit, this hurts."

"Be grateful you're here to feel it."

"I am. Trust me, I am." He frowned. "I am grateful. Grateful to all of you."

The professor nodded solemnly, his face grave but full of a fierce light. "I know you are, Morgan, and we're all grateful you're here to complain. Now lie quiet—for at least a couple of hours."

Morgan sighed and closed his eyes. "I will. I promise."

When we were alone, Morgan held his arms out, and I was able to give him a proper hug. It was wonderful to feel his embrace, so strong. He sighed deeply, and I pulled back.

"Maybe you should sleep. You look tired."

"I feel tired. I just wish I wasn't so bloody uncomfortable. I'm never going to sleep like this. It's hell."

"Try turning on your side, maybe that will help." It didn't, not much. In the end, he turned all the way over and lay on his stomach, the pillow bunched up under his head and shoulder.

"You still don't look very comfortable, I have to say."

"I'm not very comfortable . . . but more comfortable than I was the other way." He sighed again and closed his eyes. I stroked his hair and back until he fell asleep. Afterwards, I carried on because the touch was reassuring. I needed to be touching him, needed to feel his chest rise and fall, the steady beat of his heart. I needed to know.

"I heard the news."

I started. I hadn't heard Cory come in. I nodded and smiled, choked with emotion.

"I'm really glad, Matthew."

"Thanks. That means a lot to me."

"So is he okay?"

"He will be. The professor says it's looking good. He's got at least two years before things are likely to start going wrong again, and he thinks they'll be able to improve the serum by then, maybe sort out the problem permanently."

"That's fab . . . wonderful news." His voice was flat.

"It's not going to be easy, though. He has to keep going through the procedure. You know, where . . ." I shuddered and couldn't make myself speak the words. "He's probably going to be sick. Maybe quite sick for the whole time but . . .

but he . . . he'll be alive, Cory."

Cory smiled, tight-lipped, and nodded. "That's good. So . . . what . . . what are you going to do now?"

"What do you mean?"

"Will you come back to university?"

The question hit me like a slap. "I–I don't know. I hadn't thought about that, not that far ahead. I . . . hadn't thought past . . . I–I suppose so. Why not?"

"But . . ."

"Well . . . it depends on what Morgan wants . . . how . . . what he's up to."

"So, if he's not up to going back, you won't either?" There was a tone of accusation in his voice that unsettled me.

"I-I need to be with him."

"You need to have your own life, Matthew. You need to complete your education and qualify. You need —"

"Don't, Cory. I haven't decided what I'm going to do yet. I need time to think. When I do decide, I'll tell you . . . I promise."

"Matthew . . . don't . . . don't."

"I'm listening, Cory. I am listening, but I'm not ready to plan the future yet. I need to know Morgan's really all right first."

Cory ducked his head and shook it. "I'm just thinking of you, Matthew. I'm always thinking of you."

"I know. And I'm grateful. I am truly grateful. I won't just throw everything away. I'll sort something out."

"I'll be over in the house if you need me."

"The professor said Morgan can come over to the house later on."

"Oh, great. I look forward to it." The sarcasm completely took me by surprise.

"Cory?"

"I'm sorry. I'm really sorry, Matthew. I'm being a complete

jerk. I'm just . . . I miss you already."

"Miss me? You idiot, I'm right here."

"Yeah, sure you are. Right . . . here." He flicked his gaze to Morgan, and I knew what he meant.

"Cory . . . you knew the score. You said you were okay with it."

"I thought I was. But that was when—"

"When you thought he was going to die?" I was horrified. It was so fucked up. Cory was my best friend. He was the one who'd always been there for me. He was my strength, my anchor . . . and all along he'd been—had he actually been hoping Morgan would die?

"No! Matthew, that's a terrible thing to say."

"It's a terrible thing to think, but you're making it difficult not to. You said you were cool. You said you were all right with this . . . when . . . when you thought . . . when we all thought . . . and now . . . now he's better. Now he's going to be okay . . . suddenly you're not okay with it. You're behaving like . . . like a spoiled brat."

Cory hung his head. "I know. I know that's how it must seem to you, and maybe that's the way it was, but it was never the way I intended it to be. I really did think . . . I believed I'd come to terms with it. I believed I could be happy for you, that I could be okay with it. I really believed it. And I did wish— when we saw the shooting star—I did wish he'd be okay, but—" Impatiently, he dashed tears from his eyes and sniffed.

"We were close again. Yesterday, when I was sitting with you, and we talked, it was like it used to be. I started to . . . to . . . it felt like we were back to how we were, like we could stay that way. I thought no matter what happened, we'd go back, and we'd be the same. But then . . . then when I came in . . . just now . . . and I saw you . . . I saw you with him. I knew that no matter what happens, we won't go back. It'll never be the same, and I guess . . ." He sniffed again and rubbed at his eyes.

"I'll try, Matthew. I will try, I swear. I'm just . . . I don't want to be a jerk. I don't want to be anything but your friend, but this is hard for me."

"It's been pretty hard for me, too, Cory. I could do with a friend right now."

"You have Morgan."

"Yeah, I do, but it's not the same. It's not the same as having a friend, someone I know better than I know myself, someone who's always there to pick me up when I fall, who rings to remind me when it's my mother's birthday, who likes the same movies and hates the same boy bands. I need that. I need someone who can quote dialogue from films while we watch them.

"Morgan and I have to get to know each other. I will be . . . we'll be . . . I need someone I can slob with, be myself with— escape to. Do you understand? I need you, Cory. I really, really need you."

Cory stared at me. Then he was hugging me. I don't know who was most shocked, me or him, because almost immediately he pulled back, embarrassed.

"I'll always be there for you, Matthew," he said awkwardly as he ducked out.

CHAPTER TWENTY-ONE

"Nice save."

"You were listening?"

"You weren't exactly keeping your voices down."

Morgan raised himself on one elbow and grinned at me.

"I'm sorry. I didn't know what else to say. I guess I panicked."

"It's okay. I think you did a great job. I'd never want to come between you."

"It's not a matter of coming between us. No one could ever do that. No one could come between us, but he's my best friend, and you . . ." I leaned in to brush my lips gently against his. "You're my hot new lover, and it's important you get along."

Morgan turned over, pulling me down across him, and held me close. He was strong again, and I struggled, trying to get away, but he held me too tightly.

"Let me go, you idiot. Someone's going to catch us."

"You sound as if we're doing something we shouldn't."

"Well . . ."

"To hell with everyone else."

The curtain twitched aside, and Mr Bentley ducked in. Morgan ignored him and continued to pull me close and kiss me.

"Morgan." At the sound of his voice, Morgan went stiff and practically threw me off. I stumbled against the chair and sat down. Morgan turned to me with his eyes wide.

"Shit, Matthew. Shit, I'm sorry. I'm really sorry."

Ignoring his father, he swung his legs over the side of the couch, holding his hands out to me. He had his back to his father, who didn't see the pain that flashed across his face. He bit his lip and forced his back straight.

"Morgan, should you really be . . ."

"I don't see how what I do has anything to do with you."

Taking Morgan's hands, only because he was still holding them out, I got to my feet and moved closer to him. He put his arm around my waist and rested his head on me. He was shaking. I wondered if it was because of what was happening to him physically, or what the presence of his father was doing to him emotionally.

"Morgan, please —"

"I have nothing to say to you."

"I was hoping that . . . I was hoping we could talk."

"I have a really bad headache. I don't want to talk." Morgan's voice was completely closed down.

"Okay. Later, then?"

"Maybe."

"Morgan, I-I'm really sorry. I never meant this to happen. I need you to know that. I'd never, ever have deliberately hurt you. I was so convinced, so sure I was right. I wanted you to . . . I wanted you to share my triumph in a real way. I didn't know . . . I'd never —"

"Thank you, Father." His voice was tight, and he pulled me closer, against him.

"I just want you to give me a chance, Morgan. Give me a chance to explain, to make it up to you."

Morgan went stiff, and before I realised what he was intending, he slid off the table and stood rigidly at my side. Fury radiated from his body, and Mr Bentley shrank away from him.

"Make it up to me? How do you expect to do that? I almost died. I came so close, and it was all because of you."

"I-I helped you."

"Yeah, you helped to save me. Well, thank you very much. I'm very grateful you managed to undo a little of the harm you did. But it wasn't before I went through months of hell, weeks of torment. It wasn't before you let me believe I was going to die alone in that house. If it hadn't been for Cory and Matthew, I would have.

"You helped save me — after I had to endure blood transfusions, and needles in my brain. You saved me — for now, for a future of pain and uncertainty. You saved me from your own actions. Even if you do fix it, if you do find a way to permanently reverse what you've done, it doesn't wipe out what happened in between. It doesn't stop the pain, doesn't take away the fear . . . doesn't excuse what you did.

"I'm grateful for your help, but that doesn't mean I want anything more to do with you. It doesn't mean I can ever forgive you for what happened. It doesn't mean I want you in my life."

Morgan strode forward and pushed past him, holding my hand tightly and towing me in his wake. Mr Bentley was stunned, and he froze for a moment, then called after us, "Morgan. Where are you going? Shouldn't you be . . ."

Morgan stopped and turned around. His eyes were cold, and so was his smile. "Fuck off, Father. Honestly, I don't give a fuck about you, about what you think or about what you want. Go play with your toys and leave me to play with mine."

As soon as we were outside, Morgan slammed himself against the wall and threw back his head. He was breathing hard and still shaking. I didn't know what to say, didn't know if he was ill or just upset.

"So I'm a toy, then?"

"Huh?"

He opened his eyes and gave me such a glare I almost

laughed.

"You told your father you were going to play with your toys. Does that mean I'm a toy?" I spoke lightly, intending to distract him. It started as a joke, but the words filtered through to me, and suddenly they hurt. "Is that what I am to you? A toy? What happens when you get tired of playing with me? Are you going to throw me in the rubbish? You can't return me to the shop, can you? Not now you've taken me out of my packaging. I'm not—"

Morgan started off looking stunned. Then he grinned. Then he cut off my words by kissing me. I was angry and tried to pull away, but he held me close until the anger drained out of me.

"You're an idiot. After what we've been through, after having seen me at my lowest point . . . with your blood flowing in my veins . . . how can you ask that? I was rambling, talking shit. I was saying anything that came into my mind to piss him off. You are not a toy to me, Matthew, far from it. You're the most real thing in my world."

His gaze had been consuming my face, and he laced his fingers in my hair, cupping the side of my face with his hand and running his thumb over my lips. He licked his lips and pulled my face toward his, slipping his other arm around my waist and caressing my buttocks.

"Keep up with that . . ." I said breathlessly, "and you'll have to play with my toy, right here and now."

"That can be arranged."

He moved his hand round to stroke the front of my jeans, and I moaned. "Morgan. It's cold, it's public, and you're shaking so much you wouldn't even have to move your hand. I think we should get inside."

Morgan lifted his head. "Did you realise it snowed?"

"Yeah, it hadn't completely escaped my attention. I spent some time out here last night, watching the stars."

"You did? That's one of my favourite occupations—watching the sky in the snow."

"There were shooting stars."

"Wow. Did you make a wish?"

"Yeah." I stroked the hair back from his face and gazed into his eyes. "It came true."

He stroked my shoulder, then made a face. "I think it might have been a good idea to put shoes on before I came out in the snow. I think my feet are turning blue."

"Shit. Shit, I forgot. Come on, you idiot. I don't want to have gone through all that for you to catch pneumonia now."

Laughing, and shaking snow off our jeans, we tumbled into the kitchen. There was no one there, but the sound of laughter came from the living room. I started to walk toward the door, but Morgan caught me and spun me into an embrace, kissing me soundly before he let me go.

"You need to get warm." I took him by the hand and towed him through the door. He stumbled but caught himself on the door jamb.

"Steady on. I'm a bit wobbly."

I turned and waited, so he could put his arm around my shoulders and lean on me as we walked into the cosy warmth of the living room.

There were four people in there, including Cory, who was in the process of miming a charade. I had to laugh. "Have you been at this since I left yesterday?"

They all looked up, and suddenly they surged toward us, surrounding us with good wishes, questions, and good-hearted enthusiasm that completely caught Morgan off guard. He turned to me with dazed eyes. I smiled and steered him toward the sofa, which had been pulled round in front of the open fire.

Cory hadn't come over with the others, but had first frozen in his spot, then turned to pretend to poke the fire.

I moved to go to him, but Morgan put a hand on my arm and shook his head slightly. Leaving me, he preceded me to the fire and touched Cory's shoulder. Cory glanced up, expecting it to be me, and his eyes widened. Morgan bent and said something softly to Cory, and Cory nodded, his eyes widening. Morgan said something else, and Cory nodded and smiled, his attention flicking over to me.

I stayed back and allowed them to have a conversation, until they both stared expectantly toward me.

"Am I allowed to join the conversation now?"

"Of course you are."

"Are we cool?"

Cory grinned and nodded. Morgan looked smug, but that was okay, because I've always known he's a smug bastard, and now it just made me smile.

Morgan sank down gracefully onto the sofa and stretched out his hands and feet toward the fire with a sigh of pleasure.

"I love open fires," Morgan said, gazing into the flickering light.

"Me, too. The flames are hypnotic, don't you think?"

"They're not the only things that hypnotise me." I glanced at him, and he was staring at me with an expression in his eyes that made me blush. Cory laughed and straightened up.

"So who's for another round of charades, then? It is Christmas, you know."

Morgan fell asleep halfway through the game, his head heavy on my shoulder. I shifted my position a little, so I could put my arm around him, and he murmured softly in his sleep, snuggling into me. I couldn't have been happier. Not long afterwards, I started to drift myself, and as I fell asleep, breathing in the scent of Morgan's hair, it was as if the stresses of the past few days simply melted away.

We were awakened sometime later by Cory, who was

bouncing with excitement.

"What's up?"

"Come and see."

"See what?"

"Just come on."

Morgan stirred and sat up, rubbing his eyes. His hair was ruffled, and his eyes still sleepy.

"What's going on?"

"I have no idea. Cory's going insane, I think."

Cory grinned. "Just come on."

"Better humour the man or he might get violent."

The fire had died down, and the shadows lengthened, and I wondered how long we'd been asleep. Getting up wasn't easy as I was stiff and sore in places that I'd forgotten I had. Fortunately, a good stretch managed to iron out most of the kinks. When I turned to Morgan afterwards, the expression on his face left me in no doubt he'd appreciated it as much as I had. My t-shirt had ridden up, exposing an inch or so of flesh, which he was eyeing with a hungry expression. Blushing, I pulled my t-shirt down, and he pouted at me.

"Spoilsport."

"Later," I said in my sluttiest voice, completely forgetting we were not alone. Fortunately, Cory simply rolled his eyes and sighed exaggeratedly.

"I'd say get a room, but you haven't time right now. Will you please *come on*?"

"If you told us where we're going, maybe we would be in more of a hurry to get there."

"I'm quite happy right here."

Morgan sighed and smiled at me. Damn, I almost sat right back down and stayed there with him.

"Will you please—" Cory sighed in exasperation. "Okay, okay, take your time. Don't even bother . . . just stay here."

"Oh, all right, all right," Morgan grumbled, but climbed

clumsily to his feet. He groaned and rubbed his head.

"You okay?"

"Relatively."

"What's that supposed to mean?"

"I'm alive, but I have a bitch of a headache, and I'm stiff as hell. I feel a bit . . . a bit . . ."

"Can you manage to walk?"

It was like waving a red rag in front of a bull. Instantly he straightened, forcing his back rigid. "What kind of question is that? Of course I can."

"Don't forget what you've been through, Morgan. You're not dying anymore, but you're not well yet."

Morgan laughed shortly. "Yeah, I get that." He narrowed his eyes and grimaced.

"Want some help?"

Smiling gratefully, Morgan put his arm around my waist and pulled me close so he could rest his head on my shoulder.

"Being near you's all the help I need."

I got lost in his eyes. My lips were moving toward his when Cory's cough made me jump. Shit. I really had to stop forgetting his presence.

In the kitchen, Cory handed Morgan a pair of the white shoes people wore in the barn. They were a bit big but better than walking barefoot through the snow again.

Morgan leaned on me, lightly at first, but more and more heavily as we left the house and trudged through the snow to the barn. Cory bounced ahead of us.

"Are you okay?"

"I'm tired."

"Maybe we should've stayed over there."

"Cory's so excited." He sounded exhausted.

"Yeah, but—"

Morgan stood up straighter and turned to smile at me. "Just kiss me."

"Huh?"

"I need a shot of energy. I always get it from you."

We paused, just inside the barn door. Cory had already disappeared inside. The lights from the other side of the plastic seemed dimmer than usual. Here in the *porch*, it was dark and cosy. I looked into Morgan's eyes, and despite the pain, despite the weariness, they were shining.

Carefully, I ran my hand through his hair, and he turned to kiss it. Then, pulling me close, he kissed me. As always, it made my legs feel weak, and I melted against him. His lips were warm and soft, and his hand on my back, pressing me close, was strong. I don't know why, but for some reason, tears sprang to my eyes, and the more I tried to stop them, the faster they flowed. Surprised, Morgan pulled back and gazed at me with concern. He tried to brush away the tears, but more came at his touch.

"What's wrong?"

"I thought I was going to lose you."

He smiled. He didn't ask any more questions. He didn't have to. He just kissed me again.

"Will you two please put each other down for five minutes and get in here?"

We broke apart to see Cory's face peering at us around the plastic. This time he was annoyed, and we thought we'd better not piss him off any more, so we followed him.

The barn had been transformed. A lot of the equipment had been dismantled and stacked against the side, and the benches were pushed together in the middle to make a large table. The table was covered with white sheets, on which someone had painted sprigs of holly. Some of the decorations from the house had been transferred over and pinned to the plastic, and the table was laid with a feast.

I stared around, hardly able to believe the transformation. How long had we been asleep?

"Well, it is Christmas."

My eyes misted over again with new tears. Morgan was clearly stunned. Everyone was sitting around the table, with hastily constructed party hats on their heads. Even the professor had a paper cone with a wobbly Father Christmas drawn on it. Mr Bentley was the only one who was bare-headed. He stood up as we approached, and I felt Morgan stiffen.

"This is for you. A celebration if you like . . . so I'll understand if you don't want me here. I'm perfectly prepared to leave, go back to the house, or home . . . whatever you want, but I want you to listen to me first, just listen, and then, if you want, I'll leave."

For a moment, Morgan stared at him, still rigid, and I could feel him trembling. Then he nodded once, stiffly. "I'll listen."

"Come and sit down first." The professor came out from behind the table and guided Morgan to a seat. There was an empty one next to him, so I sat, too. All the while, Morgan never took his attention off his father.

"I know how you feel, Morgan." He stopped and shook his head. "No, that was a stupid thing to say. Of course I don't know how you feel, but I do understand you must feel terribly betrayed, and I don't blame you. I can't deny this was my fault."

He glanced at Morgan nervously, as if he was expecting some kind of explosion. Morgan just sat quietly with a blank expression on his face. Mr Bentley took a deep breath.

"I'm an arrogant, ambitious, and proud man. Throughout my life, those three things have caused nothing but pain for those I care for most, and never more so than now. They've stopped me being there for you, for my family. They've stopped me telling you how proud I am of you, of everything about you. I've watched you grow into a strong, confident, and beautiful person, and I've had no part in that. I should have told you every day how proud I am of you—your courage, your strength, your talent. You're a better man than I could ever hope to be.

"There are four things in my life I bitterly regret. That I didn't take you to that bloody party. That I wasn't there for you afterwards, and left you alone to struggle with the guilt that should have been mine. That I let my arrogance almost take you from me — from the world. But most of all I regret, and will regret until the day I die, that I didn't take the time to get to know you, that I wasn't part of the amazing person you've become, that I wasn't part of your life and didn't allow you to be part of mine.

"I wouldn't blame you, not even for a moment, if you could never forgive me, never want me to be a part of your life again. It would be wholly my loss. I completely understand if you hate me. But I-I need you to know that I love you. I always have, and I always will . . . no matter what. What happens now is entirely up to you."

Morgan stared at him, tears pouring unheeded down his face. He looked lost. I laid my hand over his and squeezed it. He glanced down as if it was someone else's hand, as if he wasn't here.

I squeezed again, and he gazed up at me, his eyes dazed, wincing as if the movement of his head hurt. I smiled at him and watched the emotions flow back into the blank eyes. He smiled back. Even though it was small and hesitant, it broke down a barrier for him. For a moment, he continued to gaze into my eyes. Then the smile became firmer, more grounded.

Morgan turned back to his father, still crying, but steadier. He gripped my hand.

"I don't know if I can ever forgive you." His voice was bleak, and Mr Bentley winced, then nodded, closing his eyes, his face crumpling in defeat. "But . . ." Mr Bentley's head snapped up, the hope burning in his eyes almost painful to see, "I'm prepared to try."

With a shaking hand, Morgan picked up the hastily constructed paper crown that sat beside his plate, stared at it for a moment, then held it out to his father. He swallowed heavily.

"Merry Christmas, Father."

As Mr Bentley's fingers closed around the paper, tears running down his cheeks, the whole table erupted. Suddenly everyone was talking at once, reaching for food, laughing, relaxing. Morgan was still frozen, his gaze locked with his father, his hand still extended, holding the crown, which neither had he released nor had his father tried to take.

Mr Bentley dropped the crown and began to move at the same time that Morgan released my hand and got to his feet. Then they were hugging, and Mr Bentley was sobbing into his shoulder.

"I'm sorry, Morgan. I'm so sorry . . . for everything. I love you. I love you so much. I always have. I'm so, so sorry."

Morgan said nothing, just rested his head on his father's shoulder and silently wept, his hands bunched in Mr Bentley's shirt, the knuckles white.

The party went on around them as the tears washed away years of pain and wiped the future clean.

YOU MAY ALSO ENJOY THE FOLLOWING FROM EXTASY BOOKS INC:

Lab Rat
Cheryl Headford

Excerpt

It's the lights. I hate the lights — they're so bright. I don't like bright. I want to go back to my room. It's not bright in my room. It's dim and cool and safe. I don't want to be here. I don't want to talk. I don't want to think. I don't want to . . .

"Good morning, Gabriel. Are you going to be a good boy today? You weren't yesterday, were you?"

"I want to go home."

"All in good time. We have work to do today, and the sooner we get it done, the sooner you can go back to your room. One more day. Just one more day."

"Can I go home then?"

"We'll see. Relax now, Gabriel. You know it's easier when you relax. I'm going to give you an injection, and I want you to relax and let your mind open. Relax now, Gabriel. I'm going to start now. Remember to relax."

The lights. I hate the lights. I hate the lights. I hate them. I hate . . . I hate . . .

It's the screaming that wakes me every time. This time,

though, it's different. The screaming is still there, the absolute panic. But this time I'm not alone. There's someone here with me. My housemates never come near when I'm screaming—they know better. It scares them. It scares me.

I prise open my eyes, and shock stops the screams. It almost stops my heart. I try to push him away, but he holds on. He's in my bed. He's . . . dressed, but I . . . I'm not. What the fuck happened last night? Was I that drunk?

"Get away from me."

"When you stop shaking."

"Fuck that. Get *away* from me."

I manage to push him back, and he stretches out like a cat, propping that head with its glorious hair on one hand.

"What the fuck are you doing here?"

"That's okay. I wasn't expecting thanks. Not from you."

"Thanks? What do I have to thank you for?"

"Well, I could have left you unconscious on your doorstep, but I thought you'd be more comfortable in bed."

"I . . . What? I . . . You undressed me?"

Laurie shrugs. "You threw up."

I groan. I'm not worried about passing out or throwing up—that's not unusual for me, especially after alcohol—but the thought someone saw it, saw me, and took off my clothes . . . I'm horrified. No one sees my body. No one.

"Get the fuck out of here."

"Just as well I wasn't expecting thanks, isn't it? Otherwise, I might be feeling crushed right now."

"I don't give a shit. Get the hell out of my room."

Laurie's face turns introspective. He reaches out and runs his finger over my arm. The touch sends shivers through me, and for a moment I freeze, staring at his hand. It's been a long time since anyone has touched me, especially there.

Stunned, I raise my eyes and gaze into the deep blue orbs. "Is it because of that?" he says softly. "It's all right. It doesn't bother me."

My heart is pounding. I'm overwhelmed. I can't cope with

this. I shake my head. "Get out of my room. Get out . . . get out!" I'm acting unreasonable, but I can't help it. I'm getting hysterical, but I can't help that either. By the end, I'm screaming at him.

Looking completely shocked, he does what I ask.

I collapse back on my pillow, shaking . . . and not because of the alcohol or the fits. What the hell just happened? No one, *no one*, sees me naked. No one sees. But Laurie . . . Laurie is . . . I turn onto my side and hug myself. I'm hardly aware of the tears until they overwhelm me, and I sob until I'm exhausted.

Eventually, the smells of coffee and bacon break through my self-inflicted misery coma and make me salivate. God, I'm hungry.

I get out of bed carefully. I have a pounding headache, and I think it's going to turn into one of those weird migraine-y things I've been having ever since . . . Ah well, I'll just get some coffee and maybe some toast. Then I'll come back to bed. I feel like I haven't slept in a week.

I glance at the clock. Seven-thirty. Shit. It's rare for one of the boys to be up at this time of the morning on a Sunday. To them, it's still the middle of the night. Unless . . . I smile. It'll be Andy then, coming home.

I pull on some pyjama bottoms and a long-sleeve t-shirt and stagger out onto the landing. Swaying, I lean against the wall for a moment to get my balance. Maybe Carrie's right, and I should stay away from the booze. Perhaps it would be better to go back to bed. My stomach rumbles and threatens to rebel. Maybe not.

After paying a visit to the bathroom to take care of business and swallow my meds, which lie like hot coals in my empty stomach, I carefully make my way down the stairs. God, my head hurts.

I open the kitchen door and have to grab the frame to stop myself from falling flat on my face in shock. It isn't Andy. Of course not. Why wasn't I expecting this? I should have expected this.

"I thought I told you to get out."

"Yeah, out of your room, not out of the house."

"Damn, I'll have to remember to be more explicit next time."

"So, there's going to be a next time?" Laurie turns and smiles at me while putting two plates of bacon sandwiches on the table.

"No, I didn't . . . I never . . ." I'm confused now. Confusing me isn't difficult when I'm like this.

"Sit down. How do you like your coffee?"

"Black with no . . . no . . . sugar." Numbly, I sit down. Everything has taken on a surreal quality. I'm sitting in my kitchen, in my PJs, with a stranger who slept in my bed last night making breakfast. This doesn't happen to me. This never happens to me.

About the Author

Cheryl was born and brought up in a very conservative, working class, Welsh mining valley. For generations, her family had been farmers and miners, and she was very much the black sheep. The first of her family to attend university she broke the mould, becoming a lawyer, an artist, and, of course, a writer.

When, at thirteen, her daughter became very open about the fact she was gay — and having known for years that her brother was — Cheryl became far more aware of the problems facing young gay people generally. Over the years, speaking to her daughter, who is an enthusiastic campaigner for gay rights, and her friends, Cheryl realised that there was very little out there in the world of literature for young gay people. It seemed that what gay literature there was, was highly erotic and sexual in content. She, therefore, set out to write m/m stories that were about romance and not sex, aimed at older teens and young adults.

Since that time, Cheryl has become totally addicted to writing gay romances, thrillers, adventures, fantasies, and all kinds of other genres, with little or no sex to get in the way of the story and the characters. She finds it extremely rewarding and has had a lot of positive feedback from young people who have read her works.

Cheryl continues to live in the Welsh valleys with her son and two cats. Her daughter has left her for the lure of her long-term girlfriend and the lights of the big city. She fills her days with the important things in life, such as writing and painting. She is a committed pagan, and unconventional mother, but, over and above it all, an obsessive writer.